Six-G

a-Laying

The sixth book in the
highly popular DI Murray series.

MICHAEL PATTERSON

Copyright © September 2020 Michael Patterson

Cover design and layout by JAG Designs

ISBN: 9798667034384

www.detectivestevemurray.co.uk

"Book six in the DI Murray series was written between March and August 2020. In what turned out to be a very strange time for everyone to say the least!

Co-Vid 19 and all its accompanying rules and regulations has taken over the world.

Six Geese was produced, rough copied and edited during that period. Like many others, my long list of upcoming music concerts and productions, along with travel plans were all instantly suspended and put on hold. Self-isolation seemed to be the in-thing and 'Zoom' meetings exploded and became the new working norm.

Let's hope that by the time...... Seven Deadly Inches is released, things are back to normal. Whatever that may look like!"

Happy reading.

Michael

Six

Geese - a - Laying

Prologue

"I do not gain from others' pain and then sell it back to them again. I'm not mad or insane, I'm not into early Miles Davis or John Coltrane. I am not a muse, I am not a muse, I am not a muse..."

- Paul Heaton

Thursday 1st December 2016

The diminishing sunlight also meant the fading of any remaining heat. The wintry air swirled like a magician's wand, taking every lick of warmth it could. The figure in the shadows wrapped their arms tightly around themselves. Pulling their heavy coat closed and tucking their chin downward, deep below their pullover. Their breath only visible under the sporadic streetlights, those few which still lit up the decaying wanton city.
"Very impressive," a voice bellowed. "Encore, encore."
The tone, angry and aggressive was matched with a firm focus. That had been their fourth determined, yet shameless throw. Like every previous misshapen rock or boulder, it had also successively struck its moving target. A slender hand was outstretched and previous projectiles were being regathered. With growing confidence a fifth missile was soon launched. Red, rectangular and made from clay, it was the size of a teenager's

balled fist. In actual fact, it was a half brick hurtling at great speed towards its intended mark.

"Bullseye!"

This time the announcement was smug and satisfied, even tinged with mild, theatrical excitement. Another voice, however, was also heard to scream out. Only this one came from the other end of the spectrum. Not of euphoric joy and bliss, but one of intense, agonising pain. It's anguish and brutal suffering clear for all to hear. The tortured cry belonged to a young, desperate, undernourished female. A teenager, whose once pretty face, had been for the last ten minutes continually used for target practice. Unsurprisingly, she was no longer a moving target. Her svelte features, now bloodied, lifeless and still.

A little known 'golden nugget,' that not many outside of his close circle of friends knew about Steven Murray, was the revealing fact that the Inspector still enjoyed writing poems, song lyrics and comedy sketches. At random times, like tonight, he even added the occasional journal entry. Those particular musings however, were for the eyes of no one else. Solely for the pained Detective Inspector. Maybe once he was dead and gone, they could ponder his words, pause briefly and more fully reflect upon and question his state of mind at the time. As a scribe his handwriting remained as elegant, skilled and precise as ever. His thoughts on the other hand, equally as dark and troubled.

His entry read......

Only as you grow older do you truly recognise the past seasons of your life. The simplicity of childhood. No worries, freedom and the unhindered creativity on offer. Adulthood brings responsibilities, relationships, family, and with it a whole new enthusiasm for each day and the things that you believe in. As one grows older still, perspective and experience come into play. Doing things the same way and getting the same results now seem futile, childish and unthinkable. Yet in many areas of our lives that is how it plays out. Wisdom seems to be overlooked. Others know best. Yet again, your passion and zest for life take another battering. During those turbulent and chal-

lenging times, you may choose to change course. To readjust your routine after decades of travelling the same path. Possibly the compass and direction of your life may change. Who knows? Or have you chosen the same destination, but just taken a more scenic route? One that involves different pastimes, new adventures and friends, coupled with ongoing educational opportunities. Where once the flames of your devotion and conviction burned brightly. Only flickering, faint embers remain. People - Individuals, can do that to you!

Over the past several years, I have travelled to many wonderful places. Been blessed with a multitude of beautiful experiences and memories. In recent times, I believe I have contributed in several meaningful ways at leaving a legacy that my friends and family may possibly even be proud of. And although not fully content with the thought of growing old, death does not hold the fear it once did. Unfortunately, trying desperately to accept the melancholy autumn of my life, may well be my most challenging journey of all!

Murray questioned and considered if his deep need for some journal writing tonight had been wholly cathartic? Had it been brought on by the stoning to death earlier in the day of the young female prostitute? Her body, the upper half at least, had been discovered positioned upright sticking through the sunroof of a burned out car. Eventually a nameless individual with some common courtesy had phoned up the Fire Service to report the smoke and flames. The vehicle had been set alight on some wasteland, in what was one of the most drug-riddled communities in Scotland - Niddrie.

'Drink, drug and poverty infested Niddrie...' to give it, its proper tourist tagline!

One

"Just to see you smile I'd do anything that you wanted me to. And when all is said and done, I'd never count the cost. It's worth all that's lost, just to see you smile."

- Tim McGraw

Nearly two weeks later...

Monday 12th December.

It appears that someone knew they were coming. The whole area seemed deserted. They must have been tipped off. The now familiar appearance of a dockside container, sat in the disused haulage yard. This particular one looked old and in need of attention and repair. A nine vehicle convoy of Police Scotland cars, vans and support vehicles had all pulled up outside the perimeter fencing. Night had fallen fast upon the land. No more than sixty minutes previous the heavens were aglow with flames of red, orange and pink. All that remained was a matt black canvas with no stars to be looked upon. It was to be a cold moonless night. The sky dark and low, the air so chilled that it hurt to breathe. As a surrogate father to him, in the force at least. DC Andrew Curry had a lot to be grateful to Steven Murray for. Tonight however, only fifteen minutes after arriving at the seemingly abandoned and disused transporter, haulage or so-called junk yard. Two more pieces of Murray magic made this young man question if he was ever going to be cut out to be a top notch detective. Both presentations had been simple in their execution and both should have been spotted by 'The Kid.'

In the dark of night, the sound of sirens and the neon nightclub lights of the squad cars, called out to all and sundry that something different and extra special was going down. This isolated location would soon be on everyone's radar. Within the next sixty seconds all the criminals in Lothian would be well aware of this particular police raid. Such was the modern-day beauty of smartphones with WhatsApp, social media, texting and the like. Tonight, as his trusted Detective Constable sat and watched him from the passenger seat, Andrew Curry knew that his Inspector was in a positive mood, with his 'black dog,' well out of harm's way and peacefully back at home. The clue that his regular partner, DC Joseph 'Sherlock,' Hanlon had to work with, was always the music. He could gauge his Inspector's mood by his willingness to sing and belt out relevant song lyrics. Words that would often relate to his current crazy circumstances. This evening was no exception and first up on Murray's karaoke playlist as he walked cautiously toward the firmly closed gates, was a Roy Orbison hit from the late 1960's. With a broad smile, cocky swagger and a gentle swaying of his shoulders, this DI began with... *'Step up and play each machine seemed to say, as I walked round and round the penny arcade.'*

The uniformed officers were well used to him also. In the cold chill of the evening as they greeted him, each breath rose in clouded visible puffs to join the darkened night sky.

"Evening, sir."

"Inspector."

"Sounding great,"

'Just ring the bell on the big bagatelle and you'll make all those coloured lights cascade.'

The trio of positive responses came from a group of suited and booted officers who were there on a suspected, mercy mission. Intel they'd received earlier in the day had informed Police Scotland that a recent shipment of illegals were being held in THE container in that yard. They knew nothing more. Were they seeking asylum? Unlikely. About to be sold into slavery or prostitution? More than likely. But who knows! Were they even there in the first place? Currently with the exception of a few old scrap cars, there was only the one steel corrugated box staring out at the specially selected group of officers. Two of which were from the Tactical Firearms Team.

"Looks like it's never been used for years and has just lain derelict." 'Kid' Curry proffered.

Murray pursed his lips and continued to look around in a more thorough and dedicated manner. He could quickly see obvious reasons why his young DC would come to that conclusion. The overgrown weeds at the entrance where they now stood were halfway up the fence. Fly-tipping rubbish, including two old refrigerators were piled up at the side. Plus a damaged and cracked plastic estate agents sign, which had obviously seen better days, now sat buckled and bent over, still desperately trying to advertise... Land For 'ale! Possibly a good deal for home brewers, one of the Constable's had thought to himself.

"Except that it is used regularly, DC Curry," Murray offered. "Or at the very least, it has been recently."

Curry's body twitched. His eyes peered quizzically at his DI. You know this how? They said.

"It's winter," Steven Murray reminded him. "The weather over the past two months has been awful, Andrew."

'Kid' Curry saw fit to nod this time. It was a nod that said - I hear you, sir. But I'm just not getting it. Sleet and snow had been delivered the week before and throughout the whole of November, it rained continually. Given the look and state of the yard, that it has been up for sale for years, that it is out in the middle of nowhere and has continually dealt with blustery and windswept seasons. With this all firmly in mind, The Inspector stepped over to the heavily padlocked area. 'Kid' Curry's gaze followed his every move.

"Looks can often be deceptive, 'Kid.' I mean take me for instance," Murray grinned. "People often assume that I'm mild-mannered and meek. That I hide away a caring, tender side, deep within."

Curry and a few of the others laughed at that last comment. Yet, no one corrected him or dared say anything different.

"How then, would you explain these?" Murray asked.

He left the question hanging in the air, as in his hands, he held up two of the six padlocks. None of which were currently being utilised. Each was brand new. So someone was definitely using the yard on a regular basis, they could be certain of that. Caution was required however, because this appeared too easy. With the outside gates unlocked, up to eighteen officers had steadily and carefully surrounded the large, twenty-foot long abandoned crate. Each side of its Combat Grey exterior was emblazoned with bright yellow warning triangles and blue information squares.

Container: PSLU 20122G1 was secured and ready for delivery. On closer inspection, bolt cutters and heavy grinding tools which had been brought along, were deemed surplus to requirements - it was securely closed over, but also remained unlocked. The Inspector had witnessed this once or twice in the past over the years. It had given him an idea of what to expect.

As Steven Murray's wingman for the evening, DC Curry was given the job of 'doing the honours.' Tentatively, 'The Kid,' pulled open the large swing door to the metal tomb. As he did so, at least half a dozen standard issue torches and mobile phone lights were shone deep into the unlit cavern. It took a few seconds for the reality of the situation to kick in. A multitude of blankets seemed to be scattered on the ground. Then slowly, gradually, they began to move. A scurrying could be heard. The bright lights were being gradually pulled back to reveal heads, shoulders, legs, feet and faces of people. Real people. The container's auto-release from the inside had been deliberately damaged. So although unlocked on the outside, those inside could not free themselves. The DI continued to nod knowingly.

"Listen up," Murray shouted to his team of officers, above the increasing noise and strains of grateful chattering. "Ensure that each and every one of these poor souls, stop at myself and DC Curry as they exit out. Understand?"

'Drew' Curry squinted at his boss. A puzzled look that clearly said... I don't understand! There was no familiar nod from his DI. No number seventeen, nor eighteen, thirty-three or eleven. Detective Inspector Steven Murray simply stated...

"Watch and learn, Andrew. Watch and learn."

'Kid' Curry (one of the two most notorious outlaws in the history of the west), had no idea what was going on or what he was on about. Granted, he could always 'watch and learn.' He did actually, a great deal of the time. But this was quite specific - 'WATCH and learn.' With the emphasis being placed firmly on that first word. Curry questioned and smirked disappointedly at himself. He couldn't even spot two brand new padlocks at the rusted gates!

Within seconds, the first degraded, filthy and half-clad female made her way toward the two men. Struggling to walk under her own steam and shivering intensely, she was ably assisted by a male police officer. The hours, which initially had promised to pass slowly, had stolen their body heat with indecent haste.

"Thank you, Constable." Murray offered.

He then turned toward the nameless woman and asked her to smile for him. His two Constables were stunned. Had he just asked this impoverished, fragile creature to smile for him? The two subordinates stared at each other in horror. One of them went to speak up. But their superior officer, as if reading their respective minds, immediately turned to address them with one question.

"Do I need to remind you both. Isn't a strong team all about trusting one another?" His voice was stern, but fair. Although its tone subtlety implied - 'because I really don't want to ask again!'

"Do you understand English?" Curry leaned forward instantly and asked slowly and politely. "We need you to smile for us, Ma'am." His request was quickly followed up by a facial demonstration on his part. Murray and the other Constable were then prompted to add cheesy grins of their own. To which the poor woman then set the ball rolling and by way of example to the queue of others that had now gathered behind her, she opened wide. It may have been hard, given her circumstances, experiencing the squalor and hardship that she'd just gone through and the quivering of her limbs with the cutting temperature. However, at the same time, there seemed to be a look of renewed gratitude, a sense of obligation and indebtedness. If all it took to repay these men was a forced smile - she could do that. Everybody in the line was female. Every one of them wore dirty clothing, some worse than others. A handful had several filthy layers, possibly taken from some of the younger less able and more vulnerable travelling companions. One woman in particular had just reached the officers. She was half-starved, skinny and shockingly black. Which was not a reference to the colour of her skin! The smell went with the territory. It was no one individual. The Inspector, 'Kid' Curry and PC Coull, whom Murray had asked to remain with them, all wanted to wretch up simultaneously. By now they all knew the score. So as the features around the woman's mouth began to change gradually upwards, Murray nodded and waved her past. As each desperate captive passed, they were being led away into a waiting police van. Four of these vehicles had been part of the original convoy, and a further two had now been requested. Alongside were three ambulances fully laden with sufficient blankets and medical supplies.

The original tip-off had stated several women. Murray had figured a dozen or so. Currently, it was definitely closer to thirty, than twenty. The chill in the air had quickly caressed their skin. Any remnants of feminine pink blush had been stolen and instantly replaced with a more concerning azure blue. At that, another two barefoot females beamed and walked past. The smiles were becoming easier and more genuine by the minute. Those that had been held in captivity, had gradually realised that these were official police officers. Murmurings and chatter between them had obviously concluded that these men and women had their best interests at heart and could be trusted. In terms of survival, it also meant food, water, warmth and ultimate safety.

What had previously been a strong and stout, middle-aged individual. Now limped past sick, aged, beaten and miserable. Holding tightly to her hand, was possibly her daughter or close friend? Both were dirty and wore shredded, ripped trousers. One pair trailed desperately across the cold ground. Over their shoulders was draped a wafer-thin blanket. Obviously the one piece of apparel that their captors had given out to each of them to survive. How generous and kind, DC Curry had sarcastically thought to himself. The younger woman's grip was firm and trembling. The biting temperature was impacting greatly on each of them. Initially, the container truck would have been like a sweltering oven. Especially with the body heat of thirty humans enclosed inside. But with, minus-two degrees forecast for the early hours, things would have changed dramatically throughout the night. Many casualties by morning would have been guaranteed. After the worn down, older lady's toothless grin. A forlorn, defeated smile was offered up by the younger of the two. Suddenly Andrew Curry could feel his Inspector's body tense slightly. You know that kind of feeling that you can't explain, but just immediately recognise when something is not right. He looked up at Murray and then glanced anxiously across at Constable Coull... Nothing. As polite and courteous as ever he continued. In fact, it was a line directly out of the Police Scotland training manual.

"Excuse me, Ma'am." Again use of that old-fashioned word that DCI Furlong hated being called and one that most young, teenage females in Scotland would not even know!

Regardless, Detective Constable Andrew 'The Kid' Curry felt comfortable with it.

"Ma'am, I wonder if you could please smile for me once again. Thank you."

His inner confidence was growing. He could see from Murray's body language that he had impressed. That he'd made the right move. Unfortunately for 'Drew,' he'd no idea why or what was amiss. A silent, nanosecond prayer of inspiration was offered up and a large sigh released as the woman eventually did as instructed. Witnessing her half-hearted attempted grin for the second time, Andrew Curry was now deciding which church to join and where to be baptised. Something was wrong and he saw it. Out of sorts and he got it. His Inspector extended to him 'the power and the glory.' Amen.

"Steven," the 'Kid' announced rather confidently. "Would you secure this young lady in a separate vehicle right away." He then added, "Please," as a courtesy, to his senior in rank.

Murray wasn't impressed. Referring to him in first name terms and asking him to secure the woman was just not...

"Constable Coull, Steve." Curry quickly and wisely amended his instruction. "Would you kindly put this woman in the Inspector's car and wait with her. Just until we tie things up here. Thanks"

That was better. Murray nodded at that immediate change of strategy. Recognising good leadership was all about being able to know when you've made a mistake and then being willing to rectify and repair it. It was now his turn to offer up a broad, beaming smile.

As PC Steve Coull went to oblige, the older lady deliberately jerked her hand free from the grip that she had found herself in. It soon became very apparent that the hold was one that she had not invited, nor participated in willingly. Because two seconds later she sent a mouthful of anger and contempt directly onto the younger woman's face. Her forehead and right earlobe took the bulk of the 'Recorded Delivery.' Her junior companion's eyes changed in an instant, as the frothy saliva began to travel down her face. Rage and fury erupted. From the timid mouse-like exterior they had previously known, emerged a ferocious, merciless and evil feline.

'A ruthless keeper of slaves and a bloodthirsty savage'...... at least that was what the tip-off note had said. And although found to be accurate, up until now, DI Murray had chosen to keep that part all to himself.

Steve Coull acted swiftly and the unnamed feral female was in handcuffs immediately. Before leading her away, curiosity got the better of DC Curry and he checked out the label on her blouse. A blouse that still looked in reasonably pristine condition under her disgusting, shabby blanket. And although it may have been discoloured, damp and came completely 'free of charge' with an unpleasant odour. It could still not disguise the distinct aroma of a high quality, expensively branded perfume.

"Her teeth were perfect, sir. She chose the wrong person to partner up with. The contrast could not have been greater. From mostly yellow, decaying stumps to pearly white veneers and fine white polishing. The botched attempt to wipe off her lipstick in the dark was also helpful. It was still all over her hands and cheek. You knew that though, right?"

Ignoring his question, he remarked. "Anything else, Detective? Although you got her and that was enough. You spotted plenty of clues and all on your own, well done. The blouse, I'm guessing not Primark?"

"Versace, sir. Probably worth more than all of the other women's clothes combined!"

Murray grimaced. He knew that it was a sadly accurate statement. A poor reminder of the greed obsessed and highly exploitative world that we currently reside.

"The routine visit to the container would always be high risk, sir. So I assume they would normally only send one person at a time? Also keeping less people out of the loop. So we won't have any need for any more smiles now and we can let these poor people get some food and warmth. And after they are all out, no doubt I would expect to find a pair of top quality high heels shoes discarded in one of the back corners."

His Inspector simply raised his eyebrows.

"Her fitted trousers were far too long without them."

Steven Murray was again impressed. It was the first time he had seen real potential in DC Curry. 'Drew' was always in Murray's eyes at least, the weak link in his team. And his conduct over the last eighteen months had never really changed that opinion. He had already been involved with Edinburgh gangster, 'Bunny' Reid. A position that his Inspector retrieved him from and had kept quiet about until this day. Although in fairness to his Constable, he did go out on a limb to get information for his boss to act upon, whilst flying with Reid's crows. However, under any other Inspector, Andrew Curry would have been kicked out of the force long ago. But today, his superior felt could be the real making of the lad. With that said, Murray's competitive nature wasn't going to let his Constable have the last word.

"Oh, by the way DC Curry. I wouldn't be surprised if next to those Jimmy Choo shoes, you found a rather expensive and exclusive, leather shoulder bag. Prada perhaps!"

Two more smiles were exchanged between the men. As well as a new level of mutual respect.

Two

Tuesday 13th December.

Their Queen Charlotte Street premises hosted its normal frenzy of activity the following morning and with her use of bad language decreasing, Furlong's imaginative outbursts were much less frequent. Which was a major disappointment to all those in her care who quite liked the occasional expletive being exchanged for something funnier. **'Jinglin' Jockstraps!'** and **'Sweaty Snuffsters!'** being two of her more recent additions.

 It would appear that DC Allan (with two l's) Boyd was keeping a written record. All of which had been correlated into book format. Copies were arriving next week and all proceeds would be sent to last month's Children In Need Appeal. Once Barbra Furlong finds out, it may well be that it will be the red-haired Boyd, who'll be in need of certain parts of his anatomy being renewed, Murray figured.

 The DI thoroughly enjoyed those early mornings when he arrived early and could people watch. He'd get there at dawn and literally sit back and monitor his colleagues. Each arrived one by one and bit by bit. Bit by bit was always a more enjoyable experience. It was where his valued workmates had ventured out on the town the night before and where a few drinks had been involved. It was his own personal preview of what he called their 'JIGSAW' arrival. It was where they would get to work and have no idea what the 'big picture' was! Making enquiries, they would twist and turn, enter and exit, venture up and travel down corridors. Taking a corner here and a corner there. In all, easily 'four corners' would be involved in their desperate recon-struction of trying to put together, piece by piece all their movements for the last twelve hours. It was a joy to behold and not recommended for those eighteen years and below! And regarding movement since last night...

"How are things with your missing person, Sandy?" He offered up. Detective Sergeant Sandra Kerr was striding at pace toward him. Her normally bright, flaming red hair was darker today. A deeper, richer auburn, Murray would have said.

"I was just coming to inform you, sir." Her stride slowed as she got closer. Her thunder was stolen. How does he manage that? She thought. He always seemed to have his finger on the pulse. His finger in every pie and with those same ten digits, keep eve-ry plate spinning! It was just one of many things that frustrated her about her, Inspector. Yet, unsurprisingly, it was also one that she quietly admired.

"We had been concerned, sir. That was the second night that he'd been missing. He was in his mid-seventies and had had no contact with any of his family."

"So where did they eventually locate him? His family will be relieved to have him..."

"No," DS Kerr hastily interrupted. "He's dead, sir. They found him at an abandoned building site, two hours ago. I've just had it confirmed. He'd been buried underneath what appeared to be a collapsed wall. Health and Safety and ourselves are already on the scene."

Murray looked apprehensive.

"Due to money problems, it would appear construction had been closed down six months ago. However a security firm still patrolled it twice a day. It was one of their guards that raised the alarm. The last two days he had only viewed the site from his vehicle, before eventually taking a proper look, earlier this morning. Good luck in keeping that job," she then added, cuttingly.

A dispirited and disappointed sigh was released from an emotional Steven Murray. No words were required. It never got any easier and both he and Sandra Kerr were time-served officers in death, disappointment and duty.

"Don't worry, I'll keep you up to speed, sir."

She then met up with the newly arrived DC Boyd and headed out together, toward the door to the car park. It was faint, but the Inspector grinned to himself, as he overheard Boyd's attempt at a whisper whilst walking away.

"Sarge, Sarge, how many copies of Furlong's book would you like?"

By lunchtime, it would only have been two hours since the latest, physical assault was reported. Officially, it had been over a week since Murray and his team had experienced an actual homicide in and around the capital city itself. With a near half a million population, that's a statistic for the general public to be very happy and contented with. But for an often radical and nonconformist DI from the west coast of Scotland - it was far too long. His feet were tapping, his thumbs drumming and a whole host of new lyrics were being learned to compete with the boredom.

Over the last ten years the actual number of homicide cases recorded by the police had decreased by nearly half. Forty-seven percent to be wholly accurate. Which worked out at just over five bodies per month. Of which, Glasgow and Edinburgh see the bulk of the dead. Perthshire, the Highlands, Islands and the friendly folk of the Borders, then get the occasional red-nosed farmer, cheeky crofter or vigilante bludgeoned tourist left on their respective bloodied doorsteps. During that rather lean decade, the most common method of killing had been with a sharp instrument. It was the main method of killing in exactly half of all victims. Only 2% of victims were killed by shooting! Stats, stats and more stats...

 DI Murray was never a big fan of these training days, refresher courses or whatever fancy titled terminology this year's facilitator would call it by. Today though, saw him survive and reach the half- way point of this annual three day session. **Homicide in Scotland - A Ten Year Review.** Okay, forget any originally titled header, Murray thought. This product did exactly what it said on the tin. And as 'a container sport,' Inspector Murray certainly felt like he was watching paint dry. Oh joy, and he still had one more day to go. His shoulders slumped forward heavily, as their smiley, fresh out of Uni, blue-eyed boy trainer for the day, once again bounced to his feet and announced...

 "So, irrespective of..."

 "Hell!" Murray was heard to cry."

 They had only just restarted after their official 'munch and mingle' lunch-break. The rest period had given every officer present the chance to pick up a paper plate, stuff it full of high cholesterol, artery clogging edibles and talk shop for a further 45 minutes. In the nearby Gents and more specifically, the second stall along from the left. The intrepid DI Murray was quietly catching up on all the latest Police Scotland gossip. It was truly eye-opening what one could learn hiding in a toilet cubicle for half an hour. Most of it made his greying hair stand on end. And plenty of his so-called upstanding colleagues, with the minds and morals of the proverbial 'alley cat,' should be pretty ashamed of themselves. Sadly, they weren't and never would be, and therein lies the problem. Unfortunately, the Inspector reminded himself, that is the sad reality of the world in which we currently reside. The no-strings-attached, one night stand quickie mentality, was not something for the future. It was and had been with us already for years. Some of the overheard frisky and risqué one liners from the sexy, saucy, Old Bill soap opera included...

 'She was with him all night, and he is half her age!'

'Seriously, DC Lennox has left his wife and moved in with that blonde haired Sergeant!'

'I'm still hungover. Has this guy told me anything today, that I really need to know?'

Or Murray's own particular favourite between two of his fellow attendees...

'She slept with two Constables, a Desk Sergeant and a Traffic Cop.'

'And they never found out about each other?' Another voice asked.

'What? What are you on about? The four of them were with her at the same time!!!!'

Oh, how they laughed at that shameful, sleazy, sordid true story.

Murray shook his head and once again thought about just how difficult it had become to tell the difference between the so-called good guys and the supposed baddies. The familiar mantra he often asked himself - Who is a god and who is a monster? Once again surfaced for air.

Five minutes after the restart was when he got the text notification from his DCI that stated: *The body of a Doctor Jeremy Crossland had been discovered at his home in Morningside in the early hours of this morning. We deliberately kept it quiet from you. So that you could attend and focus all your attention on your training course and review. You're welcome! Inquiries are in hand and ongoing.*

Murray was fuming on numerous counts. Two points mainly. One - that she was right about him happily abandoning this farce to have been in attendance at the crime scene. And secondly - that she was right! The text went on to say...

I am here presently. I want to let Sergeant Linn take the lead on it. Hayes and Curry are in support. Call me when you are done and I'll update you.

What seemed like an eternity later. He eventually heard the blue- eyed, boy trainer announce:

"Thanks everyone for participating today."

That was him. Immediately on speed dial to Furlong. An extra-long, exasperated sigh was given, as she answered. "Inspec..."

"No way I'm here again tomorrow, Barbra! I'd rather go for a hot night out on the town dressed as Gary Glitter and grind grubbily with Teresa May!'

"Have you ever seen her dance?" Furlong questioned, with a high- pitched air of amusement.

"Exactly! I rest my case." Murray laughed briefly. "Anyway, today?" He said. "You did the dirty on me."

Furlong could tell he was genuinely upset and that he had taken it way too personally. Noticeably, because he never normally called her, Barbra, during working hours. He hadn't at the beginning of their working relationship and still daily, did not do so. Unless that is, she had noticed on occasion, he was being playful and was looking for a favour or to get preferential treatment. He was only human after all. Although sometimes, even that had been known to be called into question.

"You promised me an update and I thought you would prefer to tell me on the phone, rather than..."

"Have you kept waiting?" she enquired.

Their voices had flatlined. A level of silence stayed in place for approximately two seconds.

"The update then?" Murray added, excitedly.

"Well it will be interesting to see what Sergeant Linn says. But, for me, it was definitely personal in some way shape or form, that's for sure. But the basics are - Dead Doctor. His name is Jeremy Crossland. Edinburgh man. Stayed in Morningside. Worked in Stenhouse. Killed in the early hours when a grandfather clock came down the stairs and decapitated him!"

"Oookkkaayy," Murray stretched it out to emphasise his confusion. "So not quite your run-of-the-mill, everyday murder then?"

"We certainly don't experience a murder every day, Inspector. So please don't start any of those rumours. But I get the gist."

"Sure," Murray smiled. "Your secret is safe with me."

"Funny thing though, Inspector. Don't know if this was planned or a coincidental double whammy? The clock that he was struck with had stopped at one o'clock and the call we received telling us of a disturbance at the property, was interestingly recorded and noted also, as one in the morning. What do you think?"

"You know fine what I think, Ma'am. I think I don't believe in coincidences."

"It was likely that he was unconscious at the time. His body had been carefully set up and positioned in place near the bottom of the stairwell. His head angled, slightly raised above the stairs. The clock was then put on its back, toboggan style and pushed down. The acute angle and its sheer weight gave it enough velocity to break the Doctor's neck and leave him partially decapitated."

"On that cheery note, Detective Chief Inspector, I will bid you, adieu."

"Thank you, Inspector." She said nervously. "Goodbye."

Three

"A bottle of red, a bottle of white. It all depends upon your appetite. I'll meet you any time you want - in our Italian Restaurant."

- Billy Joel

The T'inker, Doctor Thomas Patterson was on annual leave in Ireland throughout December. The criminal forensics team today would be watched over by his more than capable Assistant Pathologist, Dr Danni Poll. For the past two years, the American had done a great job and oversaw procedures using a great deal of professionalism and dignity. With continual talk of Patterson retiring, the rumour mill had closed all bets on his successor. Danielle Poll was regarded as an odds-on certainty.

"Late last night would be my estimated time of death, Sergeant Kerr. Although I can't really be one hundred percent, until we get the body back to the lab."

"Thanks, Doc." Sandy said. Giving off a rather mystified look at the circumstances.

"I know, I thought the exact same thing," the American confided. "That's another one for back at the lab. But it would certainly appear on first impressions, Sergeant, that he was killed by the back wall coming down on top of him."

"Wouldn't you have made a run for it?" Constable Boyd questioned. "I mean, in his seventies or not. If he was fit enough to get here and walk around, surely a quick three foot shuffle would have taken you out of harm's way. Wouldn't it."

Facial expressions were made, but no one cared to argue that point. It seemed sound. Press photographers and local news teams had gotten wind of the find and were loitering at the police tape looking for quotes and photographs. DS Sandra Kerr was happy to confirm that the body of an elderly man had been located. But no further comment could or would be forthcoming until his next of kin had been informed. She allowed pho-

25

tography from a distance. Collapsed brickwork, one remaining wall and a white tent not recommended for camping, were all that could possibly be captured on film.

Poll was departing the scene, her work done, when she spoke. "I might have him back in time and be able to give you an early indication of the cause of death tonight. More likely the morning though. So don't hold your breath." At that, she offered up a good- natured, quirky smile to both officers.

Maybe it just seemed strangely surreal, given a dead body sat buried below a mound of bricks less than ten feet away. But it certainly wasn't Doctor Patterson's way. Thomas Patterson was always very formal and disciplined. Generally he was serious faced and with his sharp Irish tone, he verged on being quite abrupt at times. Nonetheless, they were both great professional's, both lovely people. Yet, both very distinctly different people. Widowed in recent years, Tom Patterson had been previously married for decades. Whereas, quoting her very own words, Danni Poll was still to find - 'the right someone.' Allan Boyd's acknowledgement to Poll was made by way of a raised hand. Kerr simply returned the smile, plus a "Thank you," which was graciously added.

With the sweeping moonlight shining behind it, Barbra Furlong's cottage was being turned into a perfect silhouette. The DCI had left the Crossland scene fairly quickly. Part-timer, Dr Andy Gordon and the rest of the forensics team had that side of things all in hand. Plus, she really wanted to step back and hand it over entirely for Sergeant Linn to run with and see how he coped. Many people in and around their team, still mistakenly thought that Linn's nickname of 'Baldy," came about, because he had an overly generous allocation of blonde locks. When ironically, it was based on his actual birth name of Mitchell Linn. When run together, the words sounded like the tyre producer, 'Michelin!' It was then that some clever colleague came up with the kind hearted suggestion of, 'Baldy' and it stuck. Possibly slightly more appropriate for a traffic cop, but hey, it was a nickname. In the world of policing, that meant that he'd been accepted.

When Barbra Furlong returned to East Lothian slightly earlier than normal, she had a house to freshen up and an enticing meal to prepare. As experienced as she may have been, on her drive home it was near impossible to get the murder scene at Morningside out of her mind entirely. She'd turned up the radio fully, but to no avail. This was having a serious impact. In her mind's eye, she clearly saw the broken body of the mannequin as it lay limp and lifeless on the hallway floor. The carpeted staircase had acted like ice for the killer clock on its rapid downhill journey. Emptiness oozed out of his shattered posture. His chest crushed, the man lay dead with no beating heart and his neck hanging by the finest of shreds. The simple problem being, Jeremy Crossland wasn't a mannequin and these events every now and again get underneath the skin and impact deeply on you. She pulled over, turned off the car engine, sat in the quiet of the late afternoon and simply cried and cried and cried.

As the hours passed the sun gave way to the velvety dark of night and street lights sprung into action. In that soothing amber glow the Inspector, metaphorically speaking, was about to open his arms and welcome in the slower thoughts. It was a time for his brain to become a perfect empty horizon and it would allow the gentle energy of nature to wash in. Suddenly, interrupting the moment, his phone rang. Thank goodness he instantly thought to himself - All that claptrap was doing my head in!

"Hi, Sandy. What's up?" He asked with real energy. "How can I help?"

"And a very good evening to you also, sir"

"Give me peace, woman. You're not the one that had to spent your day in a room filled with egocentric, sex mad degenerates!"

"I thought you were at some training conference or other, with a group of fellow..." Her voice lowered and trailed off. "Okay, I get what you are saying. Sorry."

"That's alright, I'm just out having a lovely bite to eat."

Kerr made a curious facial gesture down the line. She could hear real positivity in his voice. Even picture him smiling.

"Somewhere nice?" His Sergeant eventually asked politely.

"What do you want, Sandy?" He offered, slightly less politely. Rather curtly in fact.

"I thought that you'd want an update, sir. Danni Poll has just told me that Jack Cannon was in fact killed by the brickwork."

"Well, that is good, Sandy, right?" Murray inquired. A tragic accident?"

"You would think, sir. But, not instantly though. He'd been left to die overnight."

"I'm still hearing accidental, Sandy. Why are you using the phrase, 'left to die?' What are you NOT telling me, Sergeant?"

"They found an old wooden chair crushed below him, sir. That plus the fact that Dr Poll found bruising around his wrists and ankles."

With reluctant alarm in his voice, he whispered. "Are you saying that he had been tied down and unable to move or get away?"

"Most definitely," Sandy replied.

Her voice was now the polar opposite of her DI's. It was filled with an eagerness, willingness and confidence to proceed. Those two words, 'most definitely,' told her boss that she was up for this. Sandra Kerr was still desperate for that full-time promotion to Inspector. She'd had a taste for it previously, when she'd filled in for Murray earlier in the year. DCI Furlong had taken her aside and told her that it wouldn't be long, to be patient and to be prepared and it would come soon enough. There was a brief silence on the line as Kerr remained quiet. She was determined that the next voice to speak would not be hers.

"Rope or some form of binding?" He eventually succumbed. His energy levels quelled.

"Don't know exactly with what yet, sir. But when you look at the crime scene photos you can clearly see where tunnels or clearings have been made by someone seeking access to arms and legs. Looking to remove whatever evidence was there. So I'm sorry to confirm it's a murder, sir. But don't you worry, I'll get onto it right away. Speak to you soon, Inspector. I've got another call to make."

She had said goodbye and hung up, before Steven Murray had taken it all onboard. His one lingering thought was that she didn't sound very 'sorry.' Indeed, it sounded very much as if DS Sandra 'Sandy" Kerr was in her element!

Several rings on her gas hob were now being switched off. A perfect pan of tiny boiled potatoes sat ready to be distributed. Steak, fried to perfection was sizzling in its own juices and a dish of mixed vegetables had been crowned with a lob of garlic butter oozing down every side. The time for relaxing had just begun. This woman got a lot of personal satisfaction from the work that she did and occasional evenings like this were medicine for her soul. A little alone time, was well deserved to refocus and recharge her batteries. Now it was the turn of Furlong's mobile to vibrate. With her hands generally engaged in culinary chores and busy, she immediately put it on speakerphone. She could clearly see it was from Sgt. Kerr.

"Sorry, to disturb you Chief Inspector," the emotion in her voice was hard to contain. "I tried calling Sgt. Linn first. Hoping he would pass a message on to you. But he told me that you had left early for the evening. Something special, Ma'am? Are you at home? Do you need me to call you back later?"

Barbra Furlong scoffed and quickly laughed all of that small talk off. "No, no, don't be silly, Sergeant. Yes, I'm at home. So what can I do for you, Sandy? What's with all the excitement I can hear in your voice?"

"Oh, it's a couple of things, Ma'am. But mainly I just wanted to let you know that Mr Cannon, the man that had gone missing, only to be discovered under a half ton of bricks..."

"Yes, I'm familiar with who you are so ably describing, DS Kerr."

"Well, he was murdered, Ma'am. I have spoken to Detective Inspector Murray..."

"Oh, you have?"

"Yes, I have, and he's happy for me to run with it initially tonight and take it from there."

"He is?"

"He is, Ma'am. But I just wanted to check in with you and update you also. So all being well, I'll see you in the morning."

Furlong could hear the big smiling grin in Sandy Kerr's tone. Which reminded her... "Oh, Sergeant, by the way. You said that there were a couple of things?"

Playfully, her mischievous subordinate decided to go for the personal approach. "Yes, well... Barbra," she whispered. Then she hesitated slightly before offering up. "It's that lovely, romantic music that you have playing in the background. It's beautiful."

Furlong pondered. "Well, thank you for that, Sandy." She lowered her voice to match Kerr's.

"Oh and what a coincidence, Ma'am."

"A coincidence! What do you mean?"

Kerr took a deep breath. She realised that a race car was a thing of beauty and precision engineering. But taking it to the track was what was required. The thing that was in everyone's best interests. Because it was like an animal that needed to run. Right now, Detective Sergeant Kerr's mouth was her race car and with her upcoming response, at speed she headed straight for the chequered flag with...

"Yes, because I would swear it was the exact same piece that was playing at Steven Murray's restaurant a minute ago. Funny that, Ma'am. Have a great night, Chief Inspector. Goodbye!"

Barbra Furlong was gobsmacked. Across the table from her, Steven Murray shook his head relentlessly. He knew that they had both just been stitched up good and proper. Their joint laughter did not build up softly, but exploded like two colliding sticks of dynamite. Billowing outwards and filling the whole room. His was like thunder, low and rumbling. Complemented by Barbra Furlong's high-pitched crystallised sound, cascading down upon the kitchen table like a gushing waterfall.

"Are you at home, Ma'am? Brilliant. She got you there, Barbra, without a doubt. She can be a slippery one, our Sandy."

The Chief Inspector shook her head in dismay. The couple then clinked glasses and held hands. Furlong proposed a toast in her own exceptionally unique way...

"Here's to Sexy Slippery Sausage Dogs, Malted Moroccan Muffins and Candy Crushed KERR'S!"

Steven Murray winked. "Oh, you smooth talker you..."

After they'd enjoyed some social chit chat and banter over their lovely blood-red steaks and Murray's favourite - new potatoes. The highly respected officers took their conversation through into Furlong's heated conservatory and back to business.

"I got a call just before you arrived tonight, Steven. It was from a female colleague."

Murray eyed his DCI dubiously, but said nothing.

"She had someone in her charge that had watched the evening news article about Sergeant Kerr's case. They certainly wasted no time getting it on the radio and television."

"It just so happened that the timings worked out well for them to make the early time slots, Ma'am. Sorry Barbra. They got lucky on this occasion. So your friend's underling, what did they have to say about 'unlucky' Jack Cannon?"

"Well, she certainly seemed convinced that he had a pretty credible theory, given his reputation."

"Cannon's reputation? What!"

"No, I think you'll find, she meant her associate's reputation, Inspector. He had seen the reports on TV like everyone else and came to her with his take on it."

"His take on it! What does that even mean?" Murray raised his voice slightly. "Is he a reporter as well?"

Furlong attempted to play it down. To make light of things. She was even about to change the subject, when...

"He is, isn't he? I can see it in your face." Murray began to toy with her also. "So you're telling me he is either a reporter, a mad axe murderer, a politician or a police officer maybe?"

It was the blush of roses. Champagne pink instantly adorned Barbra Furlong's pretty cheekbones.

"Initially, I had told her to leave it with me and I would consider it. I thanked her and left it at that."

Murray then shrugged, skeptically.

"However, with what 'Sandy' has just told us, Steven. It may well be worth arranging a meet.

Murray relented. He knew when he was beaten. He then gave a reassuring nod and offered. "Sure, okay, no problem. First thing in the morning I'll phone DC..."

"No, no, no, you misunderstand, Inspector. You'll take no one. I'll take YOU!"

Her colour infused cheeks, dimpled with a blossoming smile and her eyes shone in a way that only raw happiness could bring. It was eight o'clock. They made their way through to the bedroom for dessert and the door never reopened until the dawn.

Four

"Accidents will happen, we only hit and run. He used to be your victim, now you're not the only one. Accidents will happen, we only hit and run. I don't want to hear it, because I know what I've done."

- Elvis Costello

Wednesday 14 December

Every daily paper in Scotland had the elderly man's unfortunate demise on its front cover. What little physical editions were still churned out at their digitalised presses for distribution, had their cheaply inked pages turned over quickly. Every avid reader keen to finish off their lead article on the inside. Away from the printed newspaper brigade, the more computer literate of the lion rampant- infested nation, scrolled along curiously on their tablets and mobile phones. That favoured method was being carried out mainly at the country's assorted workstations, busy breakfast bars and upon scrambled egg-stained sofas and duvets. Standard headline fodder included - The Wall of Death. Tragic Accident Waiting to Happen. Missing Pensioner Found - Dead!

Accompanying pictures taken from a fair distance away, included the mound of bricks over the body. Although DI Murray suspected that in truth that was a photo of where the original collapsed bricks had actually then been moved to, so that access to the body could be made. Of the two further black and white snaps included in the article, one was of the only remaining wall still standing. Every inch of it had been spray painted. Obscure designs included names, signatures and tags. All different, yet individually they offered a potential clue or indication as to who each of the budding street artists might be. Possibly someone looking for notoriety, fame and fortune.

The most famous moniker in the UK that immediately popped into DI Murray's mind was Banksy, the English-based street artist. His satirical and subversive epigrams, combined dark humour with graffiti and were executed with a distinctive stencilling technique. The anonymous, social commentator had been active since the 1990's.

"Bollocking Baby Wipes," Furlong vented. "Wait until they hear that it's now officially a murder inquiry. They'll have a field day," she continued. Replacing her copy of The Daily Express back onto her kitchen table.

Her plus one, had already scanned the article an hour ago on his phone. He was always an early riser these days. After her feisty remarks though, Steven Murray, once again shook his head incredulously. He was now super impressed on two levels. Firstly, that Barbra Furlong was down to earth and grounded enough or at least appeared to be, that she read The Express, rather than The Guardian, Herald or Observer. Secondly, he was not just impressed, but absolutely astounded that she could still get her daily newspaper delivered to her whilst living in the back of beyond, in the middle of nowhere! This morning, that little speck on the map named Dirleton, had earned his new found respect and admiration.

It was late yesterday afternoon, after leaving the scene of the incident that Sandra Kerr and Allan Boyd had managed to break the sad news to Mr Cannon's family. Shortly afterwards, his son, Billy, formally identified the body of his father and was happy for the police to then release his name to the waiting media. As Murray had mentioned to his DCI the night before, on this particular occasion it was just good fortune that allowed all the examination and scheduling times to align nicely. Running so smoothly in fact, and perfectly, that TV journalists had everything they required for their 7pm evening bulletin.

Later today, Sergeant Kerr and her Detective Constable would be revisiting the deceased's home, yet again. The same location that they had first visited three days previous, when Jack Cannon had initially failed to return home from his regular Sunday evening walk.

There was no doubting that the Inspector and his Chief Inspector had certainly missed the rush hour traffic. Everyone was allowed a long lie occasionally. Plus, Steven Murray's vision of an early morning alarm call from DS Kerr (checking up on him), never actually materialised. Fair play to Sandy, he had called that one wrong.

It was ten past ten in the morning when they eventually set off from East Lothian, and there was never a quiet time on the M8 motorway, which connects Edinburgh with the second city of the Empire. However, after an hour or so had passed, they had made good time and were crossing the Kingston Bridge into Glasgow. Five minutes later and they were on the outskirts of the large Braehead Shopping Centre. Murray then asked for only the seventh time that morning...

"Are you ever going to tell me where we are going, Chief Inspector?"

"You'll know soon enough," had become her stock reply. "No matter. You're driving back."

The officers rapidly in quick succession by-passed Renfrew, bade farewell to Murray's home town of Paisley, ignored signs for the Erskine Bridge and ventured finally toward Port Glasgow, before graciously embracing a coastal hug from the town of their final destination. It had taken them just short of two full hours, and they had arrived for their twelve noon appointment with seven minutes to spare. Although, they still had to make their way to their final rendezvous.

The pairing had travelled a lot together in recent months, both professionally and privately. With the recent exception of Sandra Kerr, who Murray suspected had known for a while, or at least was suspicious of their close relationship. No one else knew. They had only started seeing each other, and officially began dating after the death of Murray's dear friend and colleague, 'Ally' Coulter. At that particularly low period in his life, Detective Chief Inspector Barbra Furlong had begun taking a very personal interest in the mental health and wellbeing of her favourite officer. By which point, DI Steven Murray had in turn been willing to openly reciprocate the gesture. At long last as they drove through town to meet up, DCI Furlong gave up the man's name. It was Maurice Orr.

"Maurice Orr, Maurice Orr," Murray repeated to himself. He whispered to the driver. "I genuinely feel like I should know that name. But you've got me. I give up," he said. Then automatically looking around him, the Inspector once again broke out into song. If it was between Barbra Furlong's habit of replacing expletives with utter nonsense or the Inspector's crazy musical renditions? - His impressive lyrics won hands down, every time. Sometimes links between the situation and the song were clearly evident. At other times like now, it took a little bit of extra brainpower and context to figure it out.

However, the impressive driveway to this man's property was well over two hundred yards long. By this point, the Inspector knew exactly where they were headed. He had the clues figured out long before they had pulled up and parked. Based on the fact that DI Murray was renowned for only knowing a song's chorus and the occasional brief snippet of a verse. His Detective Chief Inspector was then mightily impressed when she heard him alternate between speech and song for his rendition of what seemed like a cute little country number...

'There's no Michelin stars, no beer only bars. The paint is peeling in the rooms. No wi-fi for free or silver cutlery, there's no high tea in the afternoon. So many house rules, but no swimming pools and it's lights out every night at nine. Beds they're so hard, the concierge is a guard and there are sadder places to spend time."

"I like it," she said in an uncommitted, professional, yet non-judgemental manner. "And I know you'll have wanted me to listen to the lyrics. So rest assured, I did. And I get it."

But he hadn't finished...

"It's not an escape, the reviews aren't great and they don't recommend a long stay. With a large ball of keys and room service please, can you take all the heartache away. You keep coming back every year. Why, you can't tell. But your friends are all here. One more night in the Greenock Hotel."

Murray broke off. "You would love her Ma'am. Only thing is, she STILL swears like a trooper! But what a great sexy, raspy voice. She could be the love-child of 'Bunny' Reid. We should definitely go and see her together at some point."

Hesitantly, he then added - "Only if you'd like to of course?"

"Who? What? A love-child together?" His boss had been blown away. "Where and when? What are you actually going on about, Steven?"

Murray was equally panicked. The love-child part had seemed to backfire on him rather spectacularly.

"You recalled that song quick enough." Furlong blushed. She quickly looked around in case someone had magically appeared.

"What am I, on about? Have you just listened to yourself, woman?" Murray chirped up. He added a knowing smile. She was his superior after all and in so many ways, he quietly thought to himself. But it was funny to see her get so flustered. With his demeanour calmed, he politely informed her...

"Her name is Carly Connor, Chief Inspector. She's from the east end of Glasgow. Very much, the female equivalent of Gerry Cinnamon. So let me get this question just right. She uses rather blue, choice language, fiercely speaks her mind and is a little bit feisty. Who could that possibly remind you of, Ma'am?"

Again Murray struggled to bring himself to call her, Barbra. Even although she would always remind him and gently encourage it every now and then. He was happy and comfortable enough to call her Barbra when they were on their own or in the privacy of one or others, private residence. Either in his four-bedroomed, Barnton abode, or her more intimate, two bedroomed cottage in East Lothian. It had been three months now, since they started dating officially. However, that could be a sticking point in and of itself. Because when Steven Murray states officially, no one can actually know, officially!

Some like, 'Sandy,' Detective Sergeant Sandra Kerr, may well have had their suspicions, but that was all they were.

For now - Retirements do's, the odd work function and some overly boisterous meals with the rest of the team in public, had been balanced with some friendly drinks, quiet words and affectionate warm hugs and kisses in a more private setting between them both.

Today however, this particular high noon had them sitting like two starstruck teenagers at a drive-thru movie. Side by side, nervously waiting for the other to speak. They certainly would not be planning on staying behind afterward at this particular Greenock hotel for any secret liaison. Because during Steven Murray's earlier vocal performance, Barbra Furlong had indeed been listening carefully to the lyrics and had figured out exactly what the song was all about. She reminded herself that she wasn't a DCI for nothing!

Parked outside of an historic building, one which could host approximately 250 guests at any one time. In fact, it had been open for business since 1910 and was still known locally by its former name of Gateside. The impressive wall mounted sign in large cobalt blue was home to six foot tall lettering, which read: HMP GREENOCK. Before exiting the car, Steven Murray, gave one last five second rendering just to get them in the mood...

"There's no Michelin stars, no beer only bars. The paint is peeling in the rooms..." Two minutes later and they were inside.

Five

"It's a dirty story of a dirty man and his clinging wife doesn't understand. His son is working for the Daily Mail. It's a steady job, but he wants to be a paperback writer. A paperback writer."

- The Beatles

A further ten minutes later, after they'd gone through the relevant prison security checks and searches, visitor's lanyards were suitably distributed to each officer. Soon after that, they found themselves sitting alone in the Governor's office. Sat like two naughty, mischievous children in Primary School that had been sent directly to the Headmaster's room. Back then, that could only have meant one thing. Punishment! Corporal punishment, no less.

The Inspector's thoughts drifted toward just how lucky the inmates of today really had it. In the United Kingdom, Steven Murray remembered that generally speaking, Judicial Corporal Punishment had been abolished in 1948. It had persisted for prisoners committing serious assaults on prison staff, until it was finally stopped in 1967. However, the last ever prison flogging was in 1962. He had no idea where. But he did think that maybe, he had managed to retain some of the facts, figures and historical data and information from attending all those training conferences over the years, after all!

At that, female footsteps could be heard approaching along the corridor. Which made the three large rocks positioned erotically on the desk in front of them, seem an even more interesting choice of art in the workplace. The distinctive sound of high heeled shoes got closer by the second. Perfectly inscribed on the outside of the door and just below a carved image of a piece of fruit. A mouth watering red apple with a single bite taken from it. It said, Governor R. Loggenberg. Murray had noticed it clearly on the way in. It made him pause for thought because it was gender neutral. No Mr or Mrs, and different, very different from the norm. Sign-written professionally, with a distinctive Gothic font being used and layered with definite dark overtones. The personalised makeover and touches included: black lettering with minuscule scarlet teardrops dripping off the end of each one. It gave the regulated office a very modern and unexpectedly anti-establishment feel. Very liberal in fact.

So possibly - perverse or iconic?

Murray didn't quite know which. But he did consider briefly... was it to be here, with the UK's Head of State looking over at them from a framed picture behind the desk, that these two distinguished police officers were to be punished for their wild behaviour the night before? Or maybe, that was pangs of guilt and his vivid imagination, yet again running away with him.

Furlong though, was genuinely nervous for some reason. As the footsteps came to within a few feet of the room, tiny beads of sweat ran along her forehead. She felt it soak the clothes on her back and imagined it leaving an impression on her blouse, like the map of some foreign land. Gradually it trickled down her face into her eyes, and they were stung by a mixture of salty sweat and running mascara. Like schooldays of old however, no one spoke. They sat perfectly still and waited and waited and...

Suddenly the door swung open with one royally majestic sweep. Furlong could already see DI Murray begin to mouth along with... *'I've never seen you looking so lovely as you did tonight.'* And his DCI immediately jumped to her feet.

"Inspector Murray, let me introduce you to this beguiling lady in red, Governor Loggenberg."

Rising gently, slowly and certainly in a more composed, accomplished manner to his feet. He extended his hand and immediately spoke. "If you don't mind me..."

"Rebecca!" She said without hesitation. Having been asked the exact same question regularly over the six years she'd been in charge.

"So I am guessing, Ma'am," Murray turned his attention to Furlong. "That Maurice Orr is not actually an associate or colleague working under Rebecca? Not a journalist and certainly not a fellow police officer? Which is what you previously implied."

"Implied?" She laughed. Her tone clearly seemed to disagree. "To each of those, I think you'll find you quite possibly and probably made a few assumptions, Inspector?"

Did she just wink at me? Murray asked himself. He quickly looked across briefly at the Governor for confirmation. But she was already taking her seat and had witnessed nothing. Thank goodness for that, the Inspector thought. Flirting in full view and in public. Was she mad? No matter, even if she was, Steven Murray loved it.

A stern, crisp, business-like voice spoke next. It was direct, cutting, abrupt and assertive. This strong woman dressed in a vibrant scarlet red trouser-suit, had operated mainly in a man's world for the last six years. And not unlike Barbra Furlong, DI Murray suspected that Rebecca Loggenberg gave as good as she got, and then some.

"You would be one hundred percent correct, Inspector." She said. Sounding like a cross between Dolly Parton and a BBC weather reporter! "Maurice Orr is currently incarcerated here in Gateside Prison. He is inmate 2764," she sang sweetly. "He also happens to be the leading British expert on the history and background of nursery rhymes and children's fables. Everything that he told me yesterday seemed both logical and practical. He has been a model prisoner, Inspector. But I just thought it would be worth your while to sit down and chat with him face to face and see what you thought for yourself."

"So what exactly did he tell you?"

Five minutes later and both Police Scotland officers, Furlong and Steven Murray had been brought up to the prison library. It was bright and spacious, with lots of bells and shiny whistles. Murray guessed it had been given a makeover in recent years.

The DCI was mildly smitten with the floor to ceiling windows, running impressively down one whole side for about twenty feet or so. On the other, the dark side it could be argued - sat inmate 2764. The man was too perfect. He raised a hand and Furlong seemed to noticeably swoon. His smile was soft with a gentle hint of femininity, although his jawline and strong bone structure was most definitely masculine. Barbra let her eyes linger upon him for just a fraction longer than was customary. The man gazed back toward her. It was both unguarded and calm. Loggenberg had spotted the brief exchange between both parties, and as handsome, articulate and grounded as Orr certainly appeared on the outside. The prison Governor knew only too well, that on the inside, he was sinister, brutal, cruel and cold. Today, the man had passed his time waiting for them, by patiently and carefully constructing a house of cards. He was midway through the third row as they all approached.

With his unruly blonde hair thrown into a messy ponytail at the base of his head. He reminded Steven Murray of a younger, unkempt, 'Bunny' Reid from a few years back. The tiny hint of a scar slashed from his upper cheekbone to his lips on the right-hand side of his face, merely added to the macho mystique of the man. Here he had arrived first, got seated before the officers and was already in control. Dominantly taking charge of a situation that he had manipulated people into creating in the first place. Now comfortably ensconced behind a large functional desk covered with literature, his vibrant orchid eyes scorched deep in equal measure into the two females in the room. He was clearly and confidently ruler over this domain. He was ultimately the 'Headmaster' and his reading for the day included magazines and every early morning tabloid newspaper. Other prisoners had already been escorted out in advance, giving them the room to themselves. The standard issue, cheap plastic framed wall clock signalled 12.42. Those forty minutes since arrival had just flown in.

For himself, Barbra Furlong and others who visited in a professional capacity, were these people so productively engaged in matters, that each allocated segment of their day was over, before it had truly begun? Murray certainly suspected that was not the case for the inmates?

"Good afternoon, Detectives." His voice, more Harry Hill than Hannibal Lecter. Flighty and brisk.

Although the curt, "Afternoon," that he received from Barbra Furlong would have certainly seemed more encouraging to him, than DI Murray's response. Which was to basically say nothing at all.

The perky, cheery tone returned with, "And thank you also to our glamorous Governor, Miss Loggenberg, for the requested introduction.

Rebecca Loggenberg with her stunning good looks, red designer suit and black roll-neck jersey and shoes. Would not have appeared out of place as one of the Dragons, in an episode of Dragon's Den. Wrestling weekly with up and coming entrepreneurs, then striking lucrative deals and investing in their product or services. Instead however, this sallow skinned brunette with the wavy, shoulder length hair was investing her time and energy into rehabilitating drug dealers, murderers and businessmen of a very different breed entirely. Pointing with an open hand toward the seated man, the Governor offered a few words. Thorough and concise. Both direct and efficient. The Inspector quickly recognised why DCI Furlong and her would get along so well. But couldn't understand in the cool conditions of the modern library, why Barbra Furlong continued to sweat profusely.

"Thank you, Maurice," Loggenberg replied politely. Knowing full well, how to utilise and use her feminine charms effectively. "Let me introduce you..." She turned with the elegance of a catwalk model to her Police Scotland escorts and with a nod to the right, she said, "Detective Chief Inspector Barbra Furlong."

Furlong sat still and unfazed. The elegant Governor then turned to her left and nodded once again. This time, she was beaten to the punch. From nearby Paisley, his west coast accent was cutting and sceptical.

"I'm Detective Inspector Steven Murray, sir. And I am led to believe that you think you can help us mere mortals with our inquiries. Would that be correct?"

"Oh! What's with the early hostility, Inspector?" The man asked with an east coast bounce. "You don't even know me. You've not even heard what I have to say. Yet, you have already made your mind up. Now that's interesting."

'*Mm, mm, badger parade,*' Murray wanted to scream at the top of his voice. It was one of comedian Harry Hill's favourite routines from his early TV days. Along with - '*Norman St, John Stevas - a packet of Maltesers!*' You really had to see his act to believe it. It was surreal, pure Marmite. You either loved or hated him! DI Murray, unsurprisingly - was a definite fan.

Barbra Furlong was familiar with how good Steven Murray was at his job. She had also become acutely aware of the various personas and character roles that he took on to achieve favourable results. The bumbling, '*I know nothing Insp. Colombo,*' cop. The '*aggressive in your face, argumentative,*' officer. Or like today, the '*tired, slack and lazy,*' detective. The one that people may let their guard down with. All because they feel they have nothing to fear from him. The pouting red lips of Rebecca Loggenberg soon burst into life once again.

"I'll leave you three to it then, shall I? And don't give these officers any of your cock'n bull stories, Maurice."

Having never taken a seat, Steven Murray raised his fingers from his side. Barbra Furlong acknowledged with a blink of her eyes. A micro-gesture that Loggenberg recognised as, 'I'm happy for you to do so.' Underneath the flared trouser suit, expensive, black high-heels, began to turn toward the exit. Only two steps were taken before...

"I would like Rebecca to stay," Maurice Orr requested.

The accent definitely more Edinburgh's Morningside, than Glasgow's Maryhill! Although, *'Mm, mm, badger parade,'* was all the Inspector actually heard. DCI Furlong simply pulled out another chair and pointed. Steven Murray remained standing and bequeathed it to the long- legged lady on her return. Once seated and keeping her stern character profile in check. Rebecca Loggenberg requested...

"Inmate 2764 - please begin."

"I hear you rather like your music, Inspector Murray. How about...*Goodbye Papa, please pray for me. I was the black sheep of the family."* It was offered up in spoken word, rather than a musical melody.

The Inspector never flinched. Uncertain and unsure of the man's intentions, or what exactly he had hoped to gain by the quotation. Barbra Furlong glanced briefly toward the 'Scarlet Pimpernel' on her left.

"Ha Ha Ha," Orr laughed belatedly. "Your colleague was concerned, Inspector, about what the Governor here had told me. But Rebecca has told me nothing. That's because, I suspect she knows nothing about you, Mr Murray."

The Inspector flinched slightly at that last part.

"Whereas, I do. Look around you, officers," he said playfully.

He was still simmering with a toxic smile. Waiting to pounce at any given minute. As they both scanned the room. All around them was rows and rows of books. New, used, soft and hardback. Ring-bound, braille and traditional. Noticeably, though, behind the man sat a row of three computer screens. That was more than likely where Maurice Orr had spent some time and gleamed important background information on one, DI Steven Murray. Facebook, Google, et al, had already enabled - Inmate 2764 to get one rung ahead of them. He saw Murray's eyes register that same thought and immediately commented.

"Correct! I've read up on you Mr Murray."

This time the Inspector's knuckles turned white as he solidified his fists.

"I notice that you always like to say in interviews that you are a Paisley man, Inspector. Just as that was the very first piece of information that you felt inclined to share with me today also. But, between us," Orr looked menacingly around the room. "We know that you're not really, and that it's not true. So why would the first thing you say to me as an officer of the law, be a lie?"

It was Furlong, this time that winced, at that little revelation.

"Is it because it serves a purpose for you? Because, if so, I get that, Inspector. It's like saying you're from upmarket Gourock, when in actual fact, you're really from the rundown Port. Only for you, that actually works in reverse. Having been born nearby in the somewhat nondescript burgh of Johnstone. Paisley at least conjures up the famous working class mill town. The infamous Ferguslie Park, with its deprivation, squalor and in recent years, associated with numerous drug gangs and deaths. Helpful that, I would suggest for your macho, maverick, persona Mr Murray. In maintaining your friendly public profile and humble, down-to-earth image. Wouldn't you say?"

This man had graduated rather skilfully, yet another couple of steps on the oneupmanship ladder. He was now in full Hannibal Lecter mode, complete with his 'camp' Edinburgh lilt. Rebecca Loggenberg, on the other hand, had no idea what on earth was going on. Her eyes darted over to Barbra Furlong, then quickly flitted back up toward Steven Murray. The Inspector remained silent as Maurice Orr held court. DCI Furlong then realised that in, 'lazy, lack-lustre, couldn't care less mode,' it was only polite to give, inmate 2764 the stage.

Six

"There's a loud sudden bang as your heart ceases beating, as your ice-cream is flying as your divin' tae the grun. But you're helped to your feet by a dear old local lady, who will tell you you've been startled by the one o'clock gun!"

- Jim Malcolm

It was dry, with a chill to the air. In a few weeks time the promise of spring would once again blossom as flowers do, yet today as the two officers stand rubbing their hands outside the lovely Balerno property, the bitter wind blows cold. For the time of year, the weather was more than acceptable. But no matter what calendar month it was, the circumstances never were.

"So sorry for your loss," Sandra Kerr offered freely on the doorstep of Jack Cannon's home. "Would you mind if we come in for a few minutes?" She said, with DC Boyd in tow.

"Well, that was the reason why you called and asked me to meet you here. Was it not?" Came the caustic reply.

"Yes, absolutely. I'm sorry, Ma'am. It's just at moments like this, I appreciate it can be very tender and emotional and the last thing you want is police, social work or any other official body pestering you."

Suzanne Cannon was the deceased's youngest child. Although being in her mid-thirties, she could probably no longer be described as a child in the truest sense of the word. Unmarried, with one teenage daughter, she had readily agreed to meet the officers to allow them access to her dad's property. She was kitted out in a frumpy brown outfit that spoke to Allan Boyd. It said... 'I spend my money elsewhere and not on myself.' That was assuming she had disposable income in the first place, Boyd checked himself.

"Sergeant," the woman announced confidently. "I don't care how much you repeat yourself or stumble over your words because you feel awkward, embarrassed or that you may be over-stepping the mark and intruding. If it helps you find some clues that can bring justice for my father, that gets us a little closer to identifying his killer. Then you can recite the whole dictionary backwards to me, for all I care."

"I appreciate that vote of confidence, I think," Kerr nodded gratefully.

"Was that your brother that we met at the weekend, Suzanne? On Sunday evening? The one that reported your dad missing?"

As soon as the words left her mouth, Sandy knew she was about to get pelters, yet again...

"Did he say he was my brother? Did he meet you here? Do people often report stranger's missing and then turn up at their homes to meet the police and pretend to be related? Really! How am I supposed to have any confidence or faith in you two, if this is the level of competence that you show?"

Allan Boyd attempted to come to the rescue and ride out the storm.

"So could you point out Jack, Mr Cannon to me in these pho-tographs, Ma'am," Boyd asked assertively. But with a tender compassion and genuine interest. Each framed print had been angled to run up alongside the hall staircase. "They seem to be class photos ranging from Primary School to High School and over here on this wall unit, I'm guessing are some trophies that he won during that time? Was he a keen sportsman then?"

Kerr could see the woman's continued reluctance at what she perceived as a pointless charade.

"Miss Cannon, you can give us a great insight into your father here." He continued excitedly. "Trust me, Suzanne. Can I call you Suzanne?" He asked in soft tones that you would have nev-er associated with an ex-military man. "It will help us piece to-gether an accurate profile of the man and of his lifestyle, and that will be invaluable to us right now. In fact," he repeated. "You have no idea just how much we can glean from small, simple and seemingly insignificant information these days. Especially in the first few days of an investigation."

Allan Boyd paused for breath, Suzanne Cannon's lips seemed to move upward for the first time and Sergeant Sandra Kerr breathed a huge sigh of relief. The doorbell rang and everyone relaxed slightly. It then immediately swung open.

"Force of habit," Billy Cannon said. "Sorry, I forgot I now had a key."

Each of the four then went into the front sitting room, as Billy had referred to it on their last visit. Sandra Kerr gave an open hand gesture to Allan Boyd. The Detective Constable accepted the invisible baton and began to run with it.

"Sadly, folks, as we mentioned to you both on the telephone. It now looks as if your father was murdered."

"But I thought a wall on the building had collapsed on top of him?" The brother suggested, tears beginning to run down his face. His hurt and grieving for his father was still fresh and painful. His sister, already embracing and comforting him.

"And so did we, sir." Boyd replied.

"It would seem, however, that he had been restrained. Tied to a chair to be precise, I'm afraid," Sandy added.

The other female voice in the room began to emerge once again. The scorn and bitterness this time, had transferred over into anger and disgust.

"So my father was deliberately held down in other words. While he, she or others began to demolish the building and allow it to topple and reign down on him, a seventy-five year old, defenceless man?"

The silence said it all. But Billy Cannon's raised eyebrows were looking for confirmation.

"It would appear so, Suzanne." Allan Boyd confirmed. "But like I said earlier, Ma'am, that is why everything you can tell us now about your beloved dad, will help us immensely. It's not the pointless, futile exercise that you may think it is. We are good at our jobs, Ma'am. So if you don't mind, let's get started."

Boyd finished with that clear instruction and the talking began in earnest.

On their previous visit at the weekend. The officers were aware that Jack Cannon was a retired builder with four grandchildren and one recently delivered great-grandchild. William and his wife Shona were the parents to three of the grandchildren, plus the grandparents to three month old, Abbie. In a much quieter environment, Suzanne Cannon brought up fourteen year-old Stacey on her own. Intrigued, seeing them both together and without asking directly, Sergeant Sandra Kerr was able to ascertain that there was a fifteen year age gap between big brother and little sister.

Regular daily routines and diet schedules for the deceased were discussed. Jack Cannon had always been overweight they were informed. But in more recent times, he had loved going every night without fail, for his regular evening walk.

"So it was a routine that people would have been well aware of? That they could easily have figured out the times when he left and when he returned?" Boyd asked.

"I suppose so," Billy replied. "But he never went far and he certainly couldn't have managed a walk from here to the far side of Currie, where they found him. It was nine o'clock at night. Why would he go there, Sergeant? That would easily take a good hour or more at his pace and again I ask, for what? He would've collapsed well before that. A fifteen, twenty minute walk out and back again. That was his routine. That was his exercise."

Both officers nodded.

"He'd usually leave at about nine o'clock and be back in and on the phone to me or Suzy by nine forty-five. Fifty minutes, max."

Suzanne took over. "Dad had tried numerous programs over the years, officers. Weight Watchers and Slimming World more recently, but the Atkins diet was the one that he'd had most success with. But that was when he was still working and burning off plenty of calories every day though. Since he retired a decade ago, he had gradually put on a pound or two every year. He was happy, however," she added. "The grandkids and his evening stroll were more than enough for him."

"So you think it likely, that it was someone he knew or felt comfortable enough to accept a lift from?" Billy asked.

"Possible, Mr Cannon," Sergeant Kerr remarked. "But given his age and the fact that he was a heavy man. It's more likely he was abducted."

"By more than one person then, you are thinking, Sergeant?" Suzanne questioned.

"It's all speculation at the moment," Boyd added. "Let's not go there folks. Until we know for sure, exactly what happened."

The siblings once again exchanged glances. Both Boyd and Kerr noticed it that time.

"Did you know detectives..." Billy Cannon hesitated. "Where he was found..." Another pause. "It was..."

"We're listening, Mr Cannon," Kerr gently encouraged.

"Well you know," again the uncertainty. "It might be nothing, but..."

Boyd, again being supportive, added. "You know the sooner you tell us Mr Cannon, then the sooner we can decide if it is relevant or not. Please..."

"That location where he was found," the son said confidently. "Someone else died under a collapsed wall on that exact spot, thirty years ago!"

"What!" Allan Boyd exclaimed. Before quickly stuttering... "I think we may have our first real lead, Sarge."

"Wow. You decided on that relevance pretty quickly," Suzanne announced.

"Our boss really doesn't believe in coincidences, Miss Cannon." Kerr told her. "And to be honest, he has brought us up to generally go along with that belief."

"I understand," Suzanne said. "So I suspect you'll desperately want to hear the second part of the story."

Both officers stared at the woman as she stood and anxiously rubbed her hands up and down her thighs. Her actions portrayed how important or vital that she felt this new information may be. Instantly she turned to her elder brother and rasped.

"Go on tell them," Suzanne pleaded with him. "Painful or not, tell them everything Billy."

Encouraged by his sister, William Cannon was about to get everything off his chest. Whilst in a prison facility on the west coast, someone else was also just about to begin.

"I was awarded a PhD for my in-depth research into: Jack and Jill - Creating Monsters at Bedtime. My paper was published, you know."

Maurice Orr stated these facts succinctly, with authority and genuine pride. On the other side of the desk he received two nods out of a possible three. The Governor, Loggenberg, had heard his background on numerous occasions before. Even last night, Orr regaled her one more time with the story of his education and the reason why he was more than an interested amateur in this particular field. This potentially bloody minefield.

"Including my bachelor's degree and postgraduate qualification, I was just over a decade in the higher education system. I loved every minute of it, officers. Just as I am relishing my experience within the judicial system here in Inverclyde."

"The nation's foremost expert on Nursery Rhymes?" Murray exclaimed.

"Would you like the shortened version of how I came to be here, Inspector?"

Again he appeared to ignore the more senior DCI and concentrate and speak directly to Steven Murray.

"I think it would help you understand me a little bit better." He once again sang the words. "But more importantly, it'll let you see why I feel qualified to offer up an opinion in the first place."

"Agreed," Loggenberg chirped in. "Now get on with it Maurice or I will start putting feelers out for a new librarian."

"Ah, Rebecca, dear. I do love it when you tease me so. I suppose sooner or later in the life of everyone comes a moment of trial."

For the second time within their interview with Maurice Orr, DCI Furlong winced and this time Murray spotted it. She knew those words, she recognised that statement, because it was out of context and didn't make sense otherwise. He was showing off his literary prowess. He was teasing them. Barbra Furlong certainly enjoyed her books and reading in general. But the fact that he used it in such a throwaway manner, it was going to bug her for the next few minutes during their meeting with this man.

Murray's train of thought meanwhile, had travelled down a rather unsurprisingly surreal route. He was thinking how Harry Hill, Hannibal Lecter and Maurice Orr had all in fact been Doctors. With only the comedian, an actual medical doctor. Inmate 2764 was a doctor in the academic sense and then there was a certain Mister Lecter, probably the scariest of the three, yet he didn't even exist.

"Like I sang to you earlier Inspector, I was definitely the black sheep of the family. I raped and murdered someone. That is the minimalist, clinical version."

The prison Governor knew he would go for the short, shock announcement and it worked. Both detectives, one a DCI and the other a Detective Inspector who has been 'around the block' several times, both sat stunned. Rebecca Loggenberg pursed her pretty lips and ironically, slowly encouraged her bona fide librarian to speed things up once again.

"The proper brief version Maurice, please. Seriously, get a move on. The officers have a busy schedule and a meeting at four o'clock."

Steven Murray and Barbra Furlong's eyes met up. First they knew of any meeting. That telepathy was something they could check out later. But even in that simple facial gesture that was exchanged between them, you could tell that they both thought it more likely that Rebecca Loggenberg was the one with a hair-dressing appointment at four o'clock more like.

Orr, gently chastised and rebuked, was happy to elaborate... "From an early age at my Braid Hills home..."

Knew it, Murray thought. I'm taking that. It's a two minute drive to Morningside.

"... no different from most youngsters, I was introduced, or indoctrinated more like, Inspector (again he ignored the DCI) into the cult of nursery rhymes. Their easy language and catchy hooks get lodged in your brain instantly. But for the most part, the evil songs lie dormant in some neurone storage facility toward the back of your hippocampus until you have a child of your own."

"Really?" Murray snorted with derision.

"My parents, Inspector, dutifully sang those songs to me to uphold one of the many tenets in the parent-child contract. As I got older, I started to notice that some of the song lyrics were really, really strange. Subversive, even. At the very least, they were creepy as..."

"We get the idea, Mr Orr," Furlong said.

The DCI was also now noticeably growing impatient. It was beginning to feel like the man just wanted an audience, to be listened to, to be out on parade strutting his stuff. He was no doubt engaging and possessed plenty of charm and natural charisma. However, so did many individuals who were currently detained at Her Majesty's pleasure, Murray recognised. Orr though, was exceptionally eloquent. Easily a class above the others and obviously knowledgeable to boot, which most inmates positively were not. In addition to this, he had also methodically done his homework on DI Murray. However ultimately, so far, he had given them nothing.

"Your theory, Maurice. Just tell them your bizarre, but plausible theory, man." The scarlet woman once again scolded him.

His look toward her this time lacked its previous warmth, Murray noticed. Was that to be a slight chink in the man's armour.

It was ego related, so no real surprise there then. But he was being interrupted during his performance, his speech, his possibly rehearsed presentation, and he didn't like or take too kindly to that by all accounts. As Murray nodded, it was a point duly noted and tucked away for future use.

"It was all about his name, Inspector." Maurice Orr stated boldly. His voice had dropped an octave or two. As if trying to be taken more seriously. Whilst DCI Furlong's isolation from the man's remarks, was beginning to seriously infuriate her.

"His name?" The Inspector questioned.

"Absolutely, Mr Murray. Humour me firstly. Allow me two more minutes to paint the scene."

Murray hated being referred to as Mister, especially as a derogatory put down. That was at least the third time now that he had let it go. But his resistance was on the wane.

"During my historical studies at University," Orr continued. "I discovered how in more repressed times, people were not always allowed to express themselves freely, for fear of persecution. Gossiping, criticising the government or even talking about current events was often punishable by death. So in order to communicate at will, clever rhymes were then constructed and passed around to parody public figures and major events of the time."

Murray, Furlong and even the time pressured Loggenberg, all signalled their awareness of such deeds.

"But nowadays," the man said eagerly. Carefully scanning the three faces of his captive audience. "We have public news, twenty-four hours a day. There is no hiding place for royalty, cabinet ministers and their ilk. Everything and everybody is held to account." His excitement grew and couldn't be contained. "You know the very first nursery rhymes can be traced back to the fourteenth century." Then glibly, Orr informed them... "So while the Bubonic Plague ravaged England, peasants used a nifty couplet to spread the word about equality. *When Adam delved and Eve span. Who was then a gentleman.* The little known rhyme made peasants realise that they were important to the economy and contributed greatly to the Peasants Revolt of 1381. It highlighted the fact that there was 'no class distinction,' when there was only Adam and Eve."

Admittedly, Murray was absolutely blown away by some of the man's details and observations. His Chief Inspector on the other hand, looked suspiciously at Rebecca Loggenberg. As if to question - 'you brought us here for this?'

Finally with menace to his voice, Orr concluded his opening chapter...

"So there you have it DCI Furlong and DI Murray. Under the guise of children's entertainment, many rhymes that were encoded with secret messages throughout history, have endured the test of time and are still with us today."

Seven

"Oh, I don't know why she's leaving or where she's gonna go. I guess she's got her reasons but I just don't want to know. 'Cos for twenty-four years I've been living next door to Alice."

- Smokie

The Detective Chief Inspector was first to speak.

"That was genuinely fascinating," Barbra Furlong said. "But you stated earlier, that it was all about his name. So help us out here. We have literally come so far, Mr Orr. What is the theory that you shared with Governor Loggenberg yesterday? A belief that a woman of her stature and standing, felt worthy of inviting us all this way to hear."

The room fell silent. After about half an hour of introductions, back stories and marking his territory, it seemed that inmate 2764, Maurice Orr, was finally about ready to share.

"Is this all about your 'Jack and Jill bedtime story?" Murray asked.

"Ah, there speaks the voice of an unbeliever," Orr laughed. "But the reality is Inspector, you are not a million miles away from the truth."

The DI was about ready to turn and go. He'd had enough of this man's own self-importance.

"Inspector Murray, stay right there."

Barbra Furlong's voice was steady and calm. But more than that. It was authoritative. Orr had chosen deliberately to ignore her for the majority of their meeting, even although she was the senior officer. The one with the power to make or break any deal with the man. But she had let all of that go and was now using that rank to keep Steven Murray in check.

"Sit down, Inspector," she requested mildly.

That was just before her demeanour changed somewhat dramatically. Maurice Orr sat back with a look of satisfaction. He was just about to smi...

"And as for you, Squat Thrust Man," she added. "Don't even think about grinning. Simply get talking before I crack your spine wide open. And trust me when I say, that is in no way a reference to any of your books!"

As Orr's face went deadly serious and even paler than normal. It was a certain Steven Murray who beamed from ear to ear. Wasn't she just a sight to behold when she got going, he reminded himself. In so doing, the decision to stay put was easy. Loggenberg anxiously looked at the clock on the wall and thrust the curls of her lengthy hair over one shoulder.

With the merriment gone from his voice, Orr asked, "Your man was called Jack Cannon, correct?"

A tired shrug and a liberal nod were offered by Murray and Furlong, respectively.

"It was on the early evening news coverage footage that I first saw the connection. That was where all the dots joined up. If I had heard it on the radio, I wouldn't even have given it a second thought. I mean, 'wall collapses on missing elderly man trespassing on a building site!' Just some mundane news piece like any other. Seemed perfectly feasible and plausible. But the live pictures, told a different story entirely."

"Is your spine tingling, yet, sir?" Furlong encouraged him. "Because, my patience is..."

"I'm getting there, Chief Inspector," he snapped.

Again, he wasn't happy at being interrupted. Ideally, right now, Inspector Murray would quite like a game of poker with this scholarly misfit.

"Maurice..." Rebecca Loggenberg reminded him. "The TV coverage. Continue..."

"It's all about Humpty Dumpty," the man exclaimed. His small scar seemed to glow in frustration.

"What the..." Murray matched Orr's voice level and instantly stopped himself.

Furlong's head hung forward and only the best of listeners would have heard... "Shooglenifty" whispered from her parched lips. It was painful for her to look at the man. Only in truth it wasn't. At that moment a silver lining once again sprung forth in the shape of Rebecca Loggenberg. Murray wasn't sure that the whole of Greenock had two better looking people than her and the librarian. What was that all about?

"It was his name, coupled with the graffiti on the lone wall, left standing," the Governor declared to Furlong and Murray. "Do you want to take up the story, Maurice?"

The jaunty lilt to his voice returned. "Pray continue, Rebecca. I'll add or subtract as I see fit," Orr informed her confidently.

With Loggenberg's abrupt and direct management style, we'll have all the details in five minutes. Why, oh why, did we even bother meeting the man? Murray questioned silently.

"So from what I recall from my conversation with Mr Orr last night. He believes someone is sending you a message or clue of some sort. A warning maybe, perhaps?"

"How so?" Furlong asked her directly.

Maurice Orr was intrigued to see if she would remember the finer details. He raised an eyebrow and a rainbow of freckles danced on his cheek.

"Well, that's interesting Barbra, because after telling me his theory last night, I became fascinated by what he had said. So I came here, into the library for a further hour or so, to simply clarify, confirm and acquaint myself better with all the facts.

"And!!!" Steven Murray exclaimed sharply. "This is the west of Scotland. Someone for Pete's sake spit it out. Who or what holds the crucial key to the theory or connection?"

Chris de Burgh's favourite lady, spoke up once again. The lady in red repeated...

"Humpty Dumpty! And before you poo poo the notion, Inspector, let me actually explain."

"Please do!" Echoed Murray and Furlong in unison, whilst Maurice Orr gently saluted her.

"Some other nursery rhymes don't always seem to carry a particular message at all," Rebecca Loggenberg said. "But they convey a grisly, macabre sense of humour. It's amazing Inspectors, but these words have been so ingrained in us since childhood that we hardly notice that babies are falling from trees, women are held captive and that live animals are being cooked alive."

You could see a slow dawning, perhaps even a look of recognition come across both faces.

"It's only when you stop and absorb the actual words of these catchy, sing-song rhymes," Loggenberg continued. "That the darkness and absurdity is realised. A handful of them do not even reference historical events at all. But instead, they seem to convey warnings or common sense wisdom. In this case it is Humpty Dumpty and to my untrained eye, it is a warning!"

Maurice Orr was mightily impressed. As were both Murray and Furlong, he believed. If not impressed, they were certainly now at least, far more intrigued.

"You see, Officers," Orr took up the reins again. "The rhyme became famous due to Lewis Carroll's book, 'Alice Through the Looking Glass.' Where Humpty Dumpty was shown as a round egg."

"Really?" Barbra Furlong questioned. "I never knew that," she added.

Murray was surprised slightly. He was delighted to have stumbled across an origin story that his DCI was unfamiliar with. He then pursed his lips and continued to listen intently. For he knew that there would be more reveals to come. This man liked to play things close to his chest, but also he played the game to impress. That was why they were there, was it not? Because inmate 2764 needed an audience, a captive, attentive audience.

"It was a common nickname as far back as the 15th century," Orr continued. "It was used to describe large people and this led to many ideas as to who, or what, the Humpty Dumpty in the nursery rhyme really was."

"The deceased was a bit overweight," Murray replied, "but not like..."

"It wasn't necessarily his weight, Inspector." Again the DCI was ignored. "It's the fact that a wall came tumbling down and killed a man by the name of... Cannon."

"Unsurprisingly, you have lost me yet again," Murray freely announced.

The man's smiling countenance and mirthful singing voice continued. "One of the ideas taken most seriously during the English Civil War was that Humpty Dumpty was a powerful cannon used back then."

"Not an outlandish idea, by any stretch of the imagination," Furlong said, with a very reasoned attitude. She looked across at Steven Murray. Her persuasive eyes encouraged further contribution. He was having none of it and remained silent.

"Was there any glass fragments in or around the body?" The librarian enquired politely. "Obviously excluding any normal shards or pieces from window panes, bathrooms or interior doors, etc."

Both officers were cautious. The man was now asking 'Joe Hanlon' type, exploratory questions.

"Think about the Lewis Carroll novel, detectives. I would be surprised if you didn't find something from the modern-day, 'looking glass' equivalent. So possibly, it may be reading glasses, a monocle, or I suspect more likely a magnifying glass. Possibly even a broken one."

"The Cannon connection I will give you, Mr Orr. Sounding every day at one o'clock in Edinburgh Castle, as you'll no doubt be aware, we have Meg's Cannon. Humpty's Cannon doesn't quite have the same ring to it," Furlong said with a smile. "But ultimately, on its own it's a very tenuous link. However, like listening to the radio, why did you even think that there was anything suspicious just based on a spoken clue? You are the very one that told us, that you would have thought nothing of a wall falling on a man named Cannon."

Having sat quiet for long enough, with only fleeting glances at the clock to save her sanity. The *lady in red* was definitely *waiting to dance cheek to cheek* with someone. At least, so Murray thought. Maybe not a hairdresser. Then again, maybe he was the one and the same. The Inspector's distracting thoughts were quickly dismissed as the Governor spoke softly.

"You'll like this," she said.

Maurice Orr had some photographic stills of the previous night's TV coverage in front of him. Rebecca Loggenberg chose one and slid it carefully across the table, turning it around in the process.

"Do you mind if I continue to run with this one, Maurice?"

"By all means, Rebecca. You take it away."

"Okay," she said. Still low key. Desperately trying to restrain her excitement. "Look carefully at that graffiti tag in red. Ignore the actual word, but focus on what has been spray-painted around the name. Or had that been sprayed first and then the name added later and inserted perfectly in place within the framework of a..."

"...A looking glass," Furlong sighed. "Chinese Melon Pluckers," she exclaimed.

Maurice Orr was becoming more and more curious at some of the strange, bizarre mutterings being delivered from this woman's mouth. "Ever thought about writing children's nursery rhymes, Chief Inspector?" He added. "You just seem to have a natural way with words and I think they would love your choice language."

"It's a magnifying glass," Murray added, in a calmer more sedate manner. "But I get your point, Mr Orr," he agreed.

"Thank you, Detective Inspector. Still too tenuous, Barbra? What do you think?"

"What I think inmate 2764, is that you have something else in store for us," she said. "I think that you have another major announcement to make. I don't believe for a minute that you would let anyone else steal your thunder and allow them to finish off this production for you, and most certainly not a woman. So what do you have for us, Maurice? What is your big finish? Your afternoon clincher to seal the deal?"

"Rebecca Loggenberg stared at Maurice Orr with serious disappointment. Had he really held back from her. Convinced her to invite down two Police Scotland officers and yet all this time had something else up his metaphorical sleeve. Given the fact that he wore an attractive bronze T-shirt!

The man with the golden top, blonde locks and pearly white teeth, eventually held his hands up and let out a piercing, yet arrogant and imperious laugh. It was an outward expression of an inner superiority. Murray though, confidently believed the librarian was on to something and that was before getting his final offering. But he didn't like the man.

"You actually, don't want to ignore the moniker or the tag that was written inside the looking glass, Miss Loggenberg. In actual fact that is the confirmation required. The key signature being underlined for you. That is warning you of more to come. That a Genie has been unleashed from the bottle."

"What Genie? What bottle? And what warning Maurice?" His Governor asked in a very theatrical, over-the-top manner.

Loggenberg was a noticeably unhappy bunny at being kept in the dark. Her voice was sharp and cutting. Inmate 2764 had obviously been expecting repercussions for his deceit of omission, but simply shrugged them off.

"So tell us then, Mr Orr," Barbra encouraged. "What is the final piece of today's jigsaw?" Although, even Furlong was drained by the experience. She drew the photo close once again. Re-examined it and continued...

"It says, 'Tracie.' Inside the artist's impression of a magnifying glass. It clearly states the name Tracie."

Maurice Orr smiled once again at Steven Murray. "It's over to you Mr Music Man. What have you got for us?"

"I was already sold on your theory, Maurice, when the Governor here showed us the photo earlier. I knew you must have seen it also and that it was probably your number to bow out with. Sure, I remember it. Sung by Tracie, it was a hit in or around 1982 or 83," DI Murray announced confidently.

Both ladies shook their heads and looked at him none the wiser. Orr graciously nodded and conceded the point. But he was still keen to nip in and hopefully have the final say. He stared once more at the two female figures of authority and stated....

"March 1983 to be exact, Inspector. Well done. You were correct and needless to say with the singer also. The relevance of all this to our female friends, Inspector, and to the case in general? Would you like to tell them?

Steven Murray licked his lips, breathed in and sighed deeply, before declaring: "That hit single by Tracie over 30 years ago was entitled... Who Owns the House that Jack Built?"

The ladies were stunned. It was as if the impact on hearing that piece of information had knocked every last wisp of air from their lungs. Murray, not so much.

This time, in a more Hannibal Lecter than Harry Hill mode, the Doctor of letters, Maurice Orr, slowly proffered...

"I think you'll find that the killer has only just started.

On that alarming note and persuaded that they would probably be revisiting Maurice Orr once again in the coming days, the two officers began to take their leave and head back toward Edinburgh. Barbra Furlong had been so hoping that her faith in Steven Murray had not been misplaced. As they exited the library doors, the Detective Inspector turned back toward the still seated Maurice Orr and Rebecca Loggenberg.

"Oh, and on behalf of my Chief Inspector and myself, thank you to both of you for today. No doubt we will be in touch."

Go on Steven, Furlong willed him. Go on. I don't know what with, but you always have something. Go on, go on, go on she willed, sounding like an actress on 'Father Ted.' But sadly, it was to no avail.

DI Murray simply went to close the door.

"Good-bye," Orr said. Trumpeting with a definite sound of triumph in his voice.

Murray responded tunefully... *"Goodbye Papa, please pray for me. I was the black sheep of the family."*

Orr swallowed hard. The trumpet had just become lodged in his throat. A look of dismay and defeat was about to wash over him big style. Even the lady with the appointment was happy to see the smug smile disappear from view and thanked the Detective Inspector. As the door closed behind them, the words from the next line of the song filled the lengthy corridor... *"You tried to teach me right from wrong, too much wine and too much song."*

Barbra Furlong leaned over and kissed him on the cheek.

"Humpty Dumpty - who would have thought it!" Murray laughed, exiting the prison gates.

"So what you're saying, Mr Cannon and let me get this straight here," Sandra Kerr said. "You are telling us that Jack Cannon & Son, Builders Limited. Which your father ran and as the son, you worked for. They were responsible for the construction of a wall on that particular site, thirty years ago? An extension to part of a council building?"

Billy Cannon sat perspiring in his father's living room, chest heaving and nodding in agreement.

"We built a small entrance way to the front of the building," he said. "Dad had been trading for a good fifteen years by that point and he'd established a good reputation."

"He must have. Because even back then you always had to jump through hoops to get awarded a council contract. I'm guessing that it wasn't his first either?" Allan Boyd pried.

"That's right," Billy said proudly. "Dad and I had done a few local authority jobs before that one, and we'd never encountered any problems or hiccups, whatsoever."

"You would have been just a boy, a young man back then, sir. If you don't mind me saying."

Amongst the sadness and melancholy, William Cannon, junior, smiled at Sandra Kerr's remark.

"It's amazing how the time has flown by, but you are right, Sergeant. I was just an innocent young, rosy cheeked, twenty-year old apprentice builder. One that was happy to have served his time with his father. Dad did it for over forty years."

There was a short silence before DC Boyd this time, looked for clarification on what he had just previously told them.

"So when this wall collapsed, a man was killed you say and a young boy injured. With eventually a Fatal Accident Inquiry being held?"

Again, Billy Cannon nodded.

"FAI's don't do guilty or not guilty," Kerr added. But I'm assuming no further action or prosecution was taken against your father, his company or both. Is that correct?" Kerr asked.

"Absolutely." Suzanne said. "That event happened over thirty years ago. But what about what happened to our father two nights ago?"

"We'll not discount anything else that comes to light, Miss Cannon. But we'll explore this further firstly. Like Sergeant Kerr said earlier, our team is not big on coincidence and this is the mothership of all coincidences. Don't you think? Miss Cannon?"

You could see the poor woman fight against the fact that it made sense to at least check out what had happened and any unresolved connections to the present day. She was grieving. She was angry and on edge. Feeling down, lost and totally unable to help her deceased parent in any constructive or practical way. Both Kerr and Boyd were well used to it.

Sandra Kerr went for a philosophical, comforting approach...

"You know Suzanne, often at times like this we have feelings that are not visible, we do things to prevent ourselves from being miserable. However being honest is what makes us believable, for our feelings may not always be reachable."

"Sergeant, I do believe that you are good at your job."

"Thank you, Ma'am. That means a ..."

Before she could finish, Miss Cannon had jumped in to add... "And I have no idea what that load of claptrap even meant!"

Her brother was embarrassed. Kerr frustrated and Allan Boyd desperately tried not to laugh out. His approach was more keeping with the honesty that Kerr mentioned in her 'claptrap.' He said...

"Okay, Suzanne, so they're thirty years apart. That in itself, may not be significant. But in the same location, two people are killed in the exact same manner? That is freaking suspicious." Allan Boyd accompanied that summation with an all-singing, all-dancing, facial expression of the highest order.

"What is an even more believable coincidence, however," Sandy mentioned. Getting the attention of both brother and sister. "Is the fact that only earlier this year at the request of the Scottish Government, Lord Cullen of Whitekirk, undertook a major review of the whole process surrounding Fatal Accident Inquiries."

"What will that look like to every Tom, Dick and Harry in the street?" The younger sister asked in her now familiar, robust manner.

"In time, Ma'am, I really don't know," Kerr replied. "Currently it has just resulted in the passing of the Inquiries into Fatal Accidents and Sudden Deaths (Scotland) Act."

"I just remember learning at the time and it has stuck with me for thirty years," Billy Cannon said. "That they take place before a Sheriff in a Sheriff court and that there was no jury. Kind of like what you mentioned earlier, Sergeant. Although the terminology that was bandied about back then was that - Proceedings are inquisitorial, as opposed to adversarial. And for a twenty-year old builder's mate, that was a real mouthful."

"Aye, and that's still the same Mr Cannon," Boyd confirmed. He then added, "But I think flaws have been highlighted in recent years. So the Government has felt duty bound to review procedures. High profile examples have included Lockerbie in

1988. The helicopter crash that killed rally driver, Colin McRae in 2007, and then in even more recent times, the tragedy of the 2014 Glasgow bin lorry crash."

The two officers stayed for a further twenty to thirty minutes. Both colleagues knew that they were simply going through the motions and did not wish to give the impression of totally lacking in compassion. But they also now knew the road that they were most likely to travel down. For whilst Allan Boyd played his hand at being the understanding, relatable one in the partnership, his Sergeant discovered that Birkhill Library and Community Centre was the council building that had previously stood on that site. It was there, that in the summer of 1986 that the tragic accident happened. A seventy-year old was killed and his six-year old, great-grandson seriously injured. She had also requested a copy of the FAI findings be sent to their Leith station. All in all a very productive time had been had. Boyd shrugged his shoulders in a - 'I'm pleased for you,' kind of a way. They both then, graciously thanked Billy and Suzanne Cannon, commiserated with them once again on the loss of their father and told them that they would keep them informed. The Police Scotland officials offered up a generous farewell wave and Allan Boyd closed the garden gate securely behind them.

Eight

"The path was deep and wide from footsteps leading to our cabin, above the door there burned a scarlet lamp. And late at night a hand would knock and there would stand a stranger - Yes, I'm the son of Hickory Holler's tramp."

- O. C. Smith

It went unsaid as both officers clicked in their respective seat belts and prepared for their lengthy rush hour drive back east. Furlong observed the rugged outline of her current beau. A slightly old- fashioned, unconventional description perhaps. But then, Barbra Furlong wasn't exactly a modern conventional woman.

"We roomed together at University," she offered. "We were close." Murray's eyes began to...

"No, not that close." Furlong snapped. Nipping any potential misunderstanding in the bud straightaway.

"I joined the police force and Rebecca the prison service. We hadn't been in contact for a while. Her postings were mainly down south and we just failed to keep in touch. Our paths crossed at a conference on Prisoner Reform last year in Glasgow. That was the first that I knew she was back in Scotland and based down here, in the back of beyond."

"She had been back all that time and never got in touch? She's been there for six years!"

"That works both ways, Steven. I mean, I knew through the grapevine that she was possibly back in Scotland, yet I chose to do nothing about it also." She promptly shrugged her shoulders and sat up straight. "Friendship takes time and commitment these days, Inspector. You, more than most, should be well aware of that."

Steven Murray wasn't quite sure how to take that last remark. As he was driving, he opted to firstly lick his lips in preparation, adjust the car seat and mirrors, gently reverse the car from its parking spot and head smoothly for the exit. Obviously by now, he was also a few extra lines into... *"It's not an escape, the reviews aren't great and they don't recommend a long stay."*

It took DI Murray all of five minutes to get back onto the A8 coastal road. In the summer months, heading out of Port Glasgow you could look west across the River Clyde and catch the historic summit of Dumbarton Castle. Today at four o'clock in the afternoon, a chilly Caledonia offered no such scenic view, no sultry blue waters and definitely, no rolling hills cascading on the opposite side. The Detective Inspector had generously bade farewell to the Greenock Hotel. Having twice serenaded Barbra Furlong with it in its entirety, since leaving the prison. No sooner had he pressed the fancy Touch Screen Infotainment System as instructed and the Radio Scotland drive-time news programme came at them loud and clear from every hidden speaker.

Unbeknown to DI Murray, the assistant Chief Constable had sent Furlong a message just after they had arrived in Greenock at lunchtime. She had no idea what to expect. She was only told that a news piece relevant to her investigation would be airing later on the radio news. So after the most recent national news headlines and the normal break for the local sports update, their ears pricked up when they heard the announcer say...

'The recent spate of murders in the heart of Edinburgh has left many members of the general public on their guard. Alice Jones, gives us this report..."

"Two weeks ago, a young, as yet unnamed homeless girl was stoned to death in Niddrie. Her callous, cold-hearted attacker, rather than take her pulse to ensure that she was no longer breathing. Instead, took no chances and set the poor woman alight. Then three days ago, an elderly pensioner had gone missing whilst out on an evening stroll from his home. Yesterday morning, he too was found dead in highly suspicious circumstances. It was

later confirmed that he'd also been murdered. Sadly, in a world that often talks about things happening in threes, we were not to be disappointed. Only a short time after the discovery of the missing senior citizen, the body of a local GP was found at his home in the upmarket suburb of Morningside. However..." her condescending voice continued. *"Not even a photo-finish could decide currently between the retired builder, Mr Jack Cannon or Doctor Jeremy Crossland, as to who was actually murdered first. Are the deaths connected? She asked. Do Police Scotland even know? Need we be worried? Should we be in fear for our lives?"*

After visiting with Maurice Orr, complete with all his failings as a decent human being, Murray and Furlong had both bought into his deranged theory. Because too many of the dots, sadly, DID join up. So as they jointly tuned in to the reporter's take on things. They both listened with a very different perspective and that was about to soon prove vital.

Alice Jones went on to speak frequently about the drug culture in the city. She was without doubt, the up and coming reporter on the Scottish scene. Both Furlong and Murray had spoken to her at various news conferences in recent months. Furlong was patient and even-tempered with her. Neither for or against. DI Murray on the other hand, how would he put it? Well, he had no time for her whatsoever. He thought that she was a dreadful journalist. Everything that was wrong with modern reporting, she typified for him. His experience also told him that ultimately at some point within the two years - she'd be sitting cosily ensconced behind the main news anchors desk, presenting national broadcasts. That was her focus, first and foremost. Today, she mentioned the gangs and the everyday problems people faced in some of those deprived, run down, low level areas. Both Steven Murray and Barbra Furlong thought she was way off base. She had no actual theory or substance to what she was saying. It was just sensationalist journalism, sound bites that they had seen and heard a thousand times before. But alarming words that the majority of the public continually lapped up. Her two-minute broadcast, with the exception of people's names and locations, contained no helpful information. Just plenty of speculation, accusatory remarks and blame.

"Couldn't the police have done this? Hasn't the Scottish Parliament failed in its duties? Is it safe to open the toilet door?"

That last one, admittedly, Steven Murray added himself. Simply to highlight the nonsense that he had to accept as responsible journalism these days. However, her quirky take on the Crossland murder, did by default, seem to reap dividends for the DI and his Chief Inspector respectively.

Jones had said...

"At the upmarket Morningside home of Doctor Crossland, we are led to believe that at one o'clock this morning he was struck by a heavy blow. We have also been told that inquiries are currently ongoing," she reported. *"Although, it is believed that an ornamental, heavyweight grandfather clock was responsible. It was deliberately aimed down at the poor man. A man known personally to his neighbours as Jeremy!"*

Steven Murray immediately switched on his police lights and instantly pulled up onto the darkened hard shoulder of the dual carriageway at Langbank. They were literally only minutes away from his hometown of Paisley. An honourable fact that had been brought into question earlier by Maurice Orr.

"Are you okay, Steven?" His Chief Inspector asked. "What's wrong? Why so dramatic?"

"Didn't you hear it Ma'am? I'm sure you did. Would you like a recap?"

"Absolutely," Barbra Furlong asserted. "Fire away, Inspector."

"Well I never thought I would ever be grateful to Alice Jones for her quirky, pathetic and downbeat narrative."

"So what did I miss, Steven? Help me out here."

"Take a breath, Barbra. Try to remain calm. Relax and then think Doc and not Doctor." He continued to pose her some teaser questions. "What did Jones say killed him? And at what time? Think Tom's pal Jerry and not Jeremy."

Out loud, Furlong began to play along. "So he's a Doc, okay. A clock... and supposedly at one o'clock."

"And Tom's pal?" Murray encouraged.

Furlong began to speak slowly and try and put everything in place. In an order that made sense. That is, if everything had a place? Which sounded like a trite Alice Jones by-line right there. As Steven Murray sighed, Barbra Furlong cautiously tried again...

"So if Tom's the cat... Jerry was the mouse. A mouse... that encountered a clock at one o'clock... and rhymes with Doc!"

Steven Murray appreciated that often, like a stunning portrait you can be too close to something and it can actually blind you from seeing the bigger, fuller picture. And that it's only when you take a step back and remove yourself slightly, that it all comes into focus and becomes crystal clear. This was one of those moments.

"I will not sing it for you, Barbra. But feel free to join along when you recognise it. Hickory..." Was all the man needed to say.

Furlong's mouth swung open. The next two words leaped out automatically, such was their familiarity.

"Dickory Dock."

Murray nodded and watched as the DCI continued.

"The mouse ran up the clock."

Her hands clawed through her glowing hair with sweeping anxiety, as Murray spoke next.

"The clock struck one. The mouse ran down." He looked at his Chief Inspector.

Her red lips painfully spat out the remaining trio of words... "Hickory, Dickory, Dock!"

"Surely just a coincidence Ma'am!" Murray smiled. "One best kept strictly between you and I at the moment, I'd suggest."

"And Sergeant Linn's team?" Furlong reminded him.

"Sure, absolutely, Ma'am. I was really just meaning, we don't want the Alice Jones' of the world spinning out of control with tall tales of a Nursery Rhyme serial killer - just yet!"

The Inspector then greatly exaggerated a reporter's voice and with careful nasal overtones announced…

"Extreme caution is advised whilst out and about folks. There appears to be a Jack or maybe a Jill on the loose. They are rampaging and terrorising tourists on the streets of Scotland's capital city. So take care and keep safe people. For any Mary's out there. Please don't be contrary and ensure that your pretty maids are all in a row! Thank you. Steven Murray, reporting live for Police Scotland, Greenock!"

How he was ever able to laugh and joke in moments like this, she never knew. Although, she got that it was a coping mechanism more than anything else. But it still often sat uncomfortably with his Detective Chief Inspector. However, given all the relevant circumstances and what Maurice Orr had given them, including the fact that he thought the man, or woman would strike again. DCI Furlong had no immediate need to disagree with Murray's overall assumption. Even although she knew his normal thoughts regarding coincidence. She regained both her sanity and composure before offering up a smile and encouraging him to get them back to the station as quickly as possible. The newly appointed amateur reporter took that as a green light for some blue lights, and they made it all the way back to Leith in record time. Which was gratefully appreciated, as his DCI had plans for later that evening.

Nine

"You must have heard of Little Bo Peep, she was the gal with all the sheep. I'm sure you know about Jack and Jill, they're the ones that went up the hill. Humpty Dumpty was his name. I guess you've heard the same."

- Cliff Richard & the Shadows

Steven Murray went to pull up outside the unconventional East Lothian cottage. The parking spot directly behind Barbra Furlong's recently acquired Audi TT sports car, which the Inspector normally parked in, was taken. He recognised the vehicle, but couldn't quite think who it belonged to. After finding another place nearby, ambling slowly up the path and looking at her garden, which was still in pristine condition for the month of December. Murray gently lifted the letterbox and let it drop. After twice more repeating that action, his curiosity regarding the car was satisfied. For the door pulled back to reveal...

"Oh, hi." Murray said warily. Taken aback by the red-haired woman answering the door. "What brings you here, Sergeant Kerr?" he then asked.

"I was invited, SIR. And I'm quite sure we are all officially off-duty, STEVEN. So I am more than happy for you to call me..."

"Apologies, Sandy," her Inspector said. "It was just that you took me by surprise. I wasn't expecting anyone else. Wait! Did you just say, WE? WE are all off-duty?"

"Evening, sir." The dulcet tones of Joseph Hanlon sang out. "Are you okay to drop me back later?"

"What? Me! I'm taking you..."

"Let the man in, why don't you?" This time, thankfully, it was the voice of the homeowner that cried out. "I told him that I was sure you'd be more than delighted to swing past his flat on your way home, DI Murray. Was I not right in thinking that?"

"Ah, it's the hostess herself. Take 'Sherlock' home later? Delighted! How could I refuse, Ma'am? Although, I never knew it was a 'Party Night. I wish you had told me, I'd have stayed at..."

"Now don't be like that, Steven."

"Steven," Sandra Kerr quickly whispered to Joe Hanlon. "See! That's a fresh twenty you owe me," she smiled knowingly.

"But she calls us all by our first names a lot," he said. "You just stitched me up," he added. Upon opening his wallet.

The DCI certainly knew how to command a room. She was dressed comfortably and casually and in the eyes of her Inspector, very attractively. She never wore earrings at work. Tonight however, even with all that was going in, she was literally letting her hair down. With a slight 'Woodstock' vibe to them, her earrings were bright feathers. They wafted in the delicate breeze of her movement. Vibrant against her skin tone. They somehow accentuated her smile and the slight ripple in her hair. With a loose fitting mohair jersey and skin tight blue denims, she looked great. It was her home environment, but even so, she held court effortlessly. Normally this was the domain of Steven Murray. Actually, based on Sandra Kerr's entrepreneurial flair and private theory, this may well become the domain of Inspector Steven Murray on a more personal basis in the coming months anyway. Kerr smiled a satisfying smile to herself.

"When Inspector Murray and I visited Maurice Orr earlier today, the man fascinated me," she said positively. "Now as you know, DC Hanlon here and myself, love our Marvel comic books. We also like to learn, to understand others through various means. 'Sherlock' likes to put on a 'Mr Benn' hat and explore more thoroughly relationships, backgrounds and connectivity. Which he does most admirably and to a very high standard."

Joe Hanlon blushed slightly, but would happily take praise like that from a Chief Inspector any day. Especially one, who a short while back promised to '*delicately roast his chestnuts on an open fire,'* if he ever took her for granted again. He has successfully avoided doing so ever since.

"Sandy, I suspect you've never even heard of 'Mr Benn.' Would I be right?"

The mother of two-year old twin girls, gave a giddy nod of agreement and offered...

"You know me too well, Ma'am."

"Yes, you are probably too busy writing restaurant reviews in your spare time!" Murray offered cheekily, with a silvery glint in his eye.

His DCI flinched slightly at the playful remark. Kerr smiled broadly, tilting her head at 'Sherlock.' Who in turn appeared to be handing over yet another freshly printed twenty pound note!

"Do some research into him, Sergeant Kerr," a blushing Barbra Furlong encouraged. Before adding with a touch of intrigue. "Because that is what tonight is all about."

Murray tried his best. But never one to hide or suppress his feelings, his face suddenly had disappointment written all over it. Barbra Furlong, seeing his discouraged look held his gaze momentarily and winked at him. His heart instantly missed a beat, Murray's magical, musical mind jumped straight to - It Must Be Love, Love, Love and the line that said... *'How can it be that we can say so much without words?'*

Because that is exactly what she did with that one seductive eye movement. Caught off guard, Murray then heard his DCI laugh and extend an invitation for everyone to follow her into her intimate and cosy dining room, by way of stating...

"Are we going to get this 'Research and Development' party started, or what?"

More corny, than cool. More nerdy, than with it, but encouraged by large 'whoops' of support from the increasingly wealthy Sandra Kerr, each of Furlong's minions obediently followed. The cottage was naturally dark inside with its narrow corridors, short windows and low timber beams. Their hostess had at least four lights switched on in the room. Two table lamps, one standard floor lamp and her main light. Which consisted of three smaller powerful spots. The Chief Inspector was unsurprisingly well prepared. Without fail that had been a strong character trait she'd possessed ever since day one. She had charged up her laptop and it was raring to go. Her home computer sat poised, ready to assist in the corner of the room. Her compact, circular dining table was filled with at least twenty or so books. Most of which she told her assembled audience, "had been borrowed from her local community library."

"That must have been half their stock!" Murray typically and sarcastically volunteered.

"It's actually an old bus, Inspector. It's a mobile library. It comes and visits us once every fortnight."

"Interesting, I thought they had done away with all of those travelling libraries except for possibly up in the more rural Highlands and Islands and suchlike, Ma'am?"

"Possibly, Sandy. But my friend, Shirley, voluntarily operates this one in and around East Lothian. So I pulled in a few favours for tonight. She picked us up a few extra books, including one or two new releases from Musselburgh and Dalkeith this afternoon."

"Will they fine us if we don't return them back on time?"

"You may laugh, Inspector Murray, but welcome to tonight's book club."

Hanlon on the other hand, was in his element. A massive grin upon his face. A cheery countenance that spoke volumes to the others. It excitedly announced - Exploration here I come! And everyone soon got what exploratory road this 'topical party' was headed down when they discovered some of the book titles that were involved...

Nursery Rhymes and What You Really Need to Know.
Little Red Who?
The Secret Life of Jack Sprat and his Killer Friends.
And of course, the surprisingly not Pulitzer nominated - *The Simple Satanic Truth about Jack and Jill.*

Other, blander, more civilised titles also on the hit list included - *Britain's Favourite Bedtime Tales. The UK's most loved Nursery Rhymes* and *Sweet Dreams My Child,* which sounds as if it could easily fit in with the first lot of sinister reads!

Barbra Furlong again explained passionately to each of them, just how much the death and crime scene at Doctor Crossland's had impacted on her. Conscious of the fact that Maurice Orr was also a Doctor, although not medical. She mentioned how the detailed information shared by him from his *Greenock Hotel* room, had made her more curious than ever to re-examine and research some of the so-called folklore and legend. The myths, truths and untruths surrounding those innocent stories. She had been blown away by the bedtime tales that should have offered comfort to small children back in the day, but more than likely gave them nightmares. Bad dreams that at the time, neither a parent nor a Doctor could explain away. Tonight as the quartet sat huddled together, the Detective Chief Inspector continued to dispense even more of her recent findings with the others.

"Firstly, let me just say that it's no surprise that the country's foremost expert on children's nursery rhymes and fables is locked up in prison. Because anyone who gets so much pleasure and satisfaction from these sick, sordid and morally atrocious tabloids of their day, has to be seriously deranged and capable of anything."

"I'd do anything, for you dear, anything," Murray typically began to sing under his breath.

"From Oliver, sir." Kerr said. "I do recognise that. Me and Richard watched it recently with the girls."

An appreciative smile was exchanged between the two colleagues. DCI Furlong's furtive glance on the other hand, was less appreciative.

"In my defence, M'Lord," was how he then addressed Barbra Furlong. "There is a line or two in it that song which would suit Mr Maurice Orr to perfection." He then continued. As if he was ever going to do anything else. *"Would you rob a shop? Anything! Would you risk the drop?"*

"ANYTHING!" Constable Hanlon and Sergeant Kerr joined the chorus for that final word.

"Thank you, Inspector. Now as I was saying, before being so rudely interrupted by Fagin and his fellow waifs and strays."

The trio of colleagues accepted that slap on the wrist gracefully, pouted their respective lips and continued to listen with genuine interest to their tutor for the evening. She had obviously been busy, doing lots of her own personal research in preparation.

"Nursery rhymes aren't all pudding and pie," she told them. "Look closely and you'll start to notice the starving dogs, nose-severing blackbirds, the women being held captive in pumpkin shells and numerous tails being lopped off with dangerous carving knives. Those horrific images however, are just tiny fabrics. Small remnants of what was a sicker, larger, failing in that society though. Mother Goose rhymes have been continually sanitised over the years," Furlong informed them. She then lifted up a hardback from the table. It was entitled: *Once Upon a Time - The Mother of all Evil.* "It's right here, all the early versions and every one chock-full of atrocities."

Steven Murray could see that this had genuinely gotten to her and that was no easy thing. It had taken him long enough to break through Barbra Furlong's stoic facade. But she was feeling passionate about it and was on a roll. So he was happy enough to go along with things. The DCI then gave out four or five books to each person sitting around the table and encouraged them literally, to get tore in!

"I thought we could brainstorm together. Gather some ideas, throw them around and take it from there. Even fact check items on our phones or as you can see my PC is fired up and ready to go." She then announced in a serious tone to everyone. "If we only get one idea that takes us a little closer to finding our killer or killers, then tonight has been a success. Agreed?"

"Agreed, Ma'am." Was offered back in unrehearsed harmony from Hanlon and Kerr.

As Murray raised his glass of Coke or Pepsi, to be more accurate. He tipped his head toward his DCI in acknowledgment, but smiled without conviction.

"Before we begin in earnest, here's a little ice-breaker." 'Sherlock' said. For the next twenty seconds, each of his colleagues' jaws all gradually lowered until they could go no further. It was an impressive feat and so was his tongue twister.

"The sick sixth sheik's, sick sixth sheep, shed seven shiny short sheared sweaters. Since seven sick shepherds, sheared six sick sheep, silence spread sounding oh so sweet. When sound asleep swiftly shearing sick sheep, six sheiks so to speak, spoke softly. So surprise, surprise, seven sheik's should arise, wearing silly shiny short sheared sweaters."

Everyone laughed thoroughly and then got down to work. As the night wore on, they continued to read independently and jump from chapter to chapter and book to book. Sleeve notes were recorded. Details of the illustrations were photographed, cropped and saved. However, by way of an edited version of what she had learned over the last couple of days, their DCI continued with her intermittent commentary.

"The farther back one looks, the more gruesome the rhymes become. Some even believe that the seemingly harmless, *'Eeny, meeny, miny, mo,'* counting rhymes were derived from ancient methods of choosing human sacrifices."

"Conjecture, surely?" Sandra Kerr opined.

"Quite possibly Sandy," DCI Furlong agreed. "But that's exactly the problem with all of this stuff though. It's probably enshrined in a basic element of truth, but sadly, accompanied by an even bigger element of doubt. Domestic violence meanwhile, has endured the test of time. It was one of the more common themes in the old principle-orientated nursery rhymes especially. With wives and daughters bearing the brunt of the abuse. From beatings with a stick to flat-out murder."

Lifting his eyes from his own book, 'Sherlock,' added... "Yes, but be mindful. Even although the early Victorians no doubt thought these rhymes were instructive to their daughters, who would learn to be obedient, dutiful wives. I've just been reading how women weren't the only ones to suffer in verse."

He continued to educate the others with a few prime examples from his book. They included plenty of men burnt, hacked or otherwise disposed of. As well as the same fate dished out to an array of children of any gender and a bevy of pets and wildlife. It was eye opening and appalling in equal measure. As each of the group continued to read, the red hair of DS Kerr seemed to come up for air more often and more rapidly.

"Something up, Sandy?" Furlong asked her by name.

Hanlon gave his Sergeant a small grin and a telling nod. It was a number fifteen. It accompanied a look that said, 'You'll be giving me back my twenty then!'

As if reading his mind. "Forget it," Kerr declared loudly. Then reacting to her DCI, announced...

"It's just when you told us earlier about where you and DI Murray had been today, Ma'am."

"Yes, what about it?"

"Not quite the romantic drive I'd expected." Murray laughed.

"Behave yourself, Inspector. Please." Barbra Furlong offered in a professional manner.

Hanlon then stared at his Sergeant in mock desperation with a pleading face. It was a comical look that said - 'I've no more money. You win!' Unfortunately, Kerr at this point was oblivious to the light-hearted camaraderie going on around her.

"It all started to come back to me, Ma'am," she said.

"What do you mean, Sandy? Come back to you?" Steven Murray asked in a deeply concerned manner.

Coldly, she stated. "I am actually very familiar with that man in your Greenock Hotel."

Ten

"And he works in a library, standing there behind the counter. Willing to help with all the problems I encounter. Helps me find Hemingway. Helps me find Genet. Helps me find James Joyce. He always makes the right choice."

- The Go-Betweens

"It would have been about 5 or 6 years ago," Sandra Kerr continued nervously. "Not long before I joined your team, sir. It was an arduous, horrendous experience. One I never wish to repeat. That I have tried desperately to forget ever since."

Kerr cringed at the mere thought of Jeremy Crossland's demise. DCI Furlong could relate entirely to her Sergeant's current mindset, when Murray coughed politely.

"Sir," Sandra said.

"It didn't feel right earlier today," DI Murray expressed. "I simply didn't want to hand any power whatsoever over to the grinning, all- singing Maurice Orr on his home turf."

Furlong nodded. Whilst Kerr and Hanlon shrugged in understanding.

"But what didn't feel right, Inspector?" Sandy asked him bluntly. Murray remained coy for a second. Before returning equally candidly, to offer up...

"The question of who he attacked that day, Sandy. For some reason I held back. I never broached the subject. I didn't ask the name of the woman that he raped and murdered?"

Hanlon, Furlong and DI Murray all watched with alarm, as the contorted look on Kerr's face intensified. Each person in the room was taken by surprise at her anxious, rapid response.

"He never raped any woman, sir. I thought you knew that?"

"What! But, he said... Geez... more lies, fabrication and deceit no doubt. I should have known. I knew there was something off when he said it."

"But I checked his notes," DCI Furlong insisted. "I never read them all carefully, but they clearly stated that he had been incarcerated for rape and murder."

As Sandy went to speak, her bottom lip quivered, the same as a baby pushed past endurance. The Sergeant's eyes became glacier blue under the sheen of water, constant, yet allowing the tears to flow without pause. In that moment, as she gently wiped at the steady stream and witnessed her own reflection on Furlong's wall mounted mirror. She understood the depth of pain that had been sitting for all these years just below the surface of her skin.

"And you would be correct, Ma'am," she stammered. "It was for the murder of Mrs Angela McMinn."

Hanlon, Furlong and Murray all hung on to her next word, because each of them knew from experience that there was a but coming. So as not to disappoint them, DS Kerr continued.

"But......" she slowly offered up. "The rape was of Angela's fifteen year-old son, Anthony."

This time, tears instantly welled up in the eyes of the other three present. Steven Murray often mentioned to others that his team was made up of people. Real people. Sensitive people. People with everyday emotions. Individuals that understood and felt the pain and suffering of those that they collectively served, and that made them what they are. Not only good, but great at their job. Right here, right now, was a perfect manifestation of such hurt. They were a clan, a family, a mini tribal unit with a sense of anger at injustice. A determined rabble not to be messed with. Once again her colleagues continued to sit perfectly still, as their Sergeant enlightened them further.

"He had been extra keen to drop off a library book that Angela McMinn had requested. It was all part of the service, he told them in court. Mainly because he had flirted with her and she sadly had reciprocated."

"Sorry to interrupt, Sandy, but I am guessing from what you are saying that our latently depraved Mr Orr was a librarian. Is that right?"

"I assumed you knew that already, sir"

"No, I didn't. His file simply stated that he was a District Council employee, nothing else. Also in fairness, we were only going to meet him to get some information pertaining to our case. But events at Greenock today are beginning to make more sense now and I didn't necessarily remember his name, because that is not how most of the newspapers referred to him, was it?"

Kerr shook her head, but before she could respond to her Inspector fully, her DCI threw in an obligatory... "Highland Hillbilly Humpers," she let fly. Not one of her more appropriate sayings, Joe Hanlon reckoned. On this occasion, even Murray thought that his Chief Inspector would have been better off letting loose with a whole host of familiar expletives and fiery swear words.

Furlong instantly reflected on Maurice Orr's impish throwaway lines and his playful charming interactions with both herself and Rebecca Loggenberg earlier in the day. A bit of a player, she questioned. Oh yes, indeed, she thought. Confirmation of his job had also made DS Kerr recall key elements of her afternoon conversation also.

"Sorry, apologies again, Steven Murray said. "Please continue, Sandy."

Finishing her story, Kerr took another deep breath... "After a few days, the book finally arrived. Orr, decided that he would deliver it in person that lunchtime. It was only a brief eight to ten minute drive away. He told those in the courtroom that day, that his plan was to simply get there, drop it off, have a chat, maybe arrange a date and then return again. All within his scheduled one hour break. Sorted, or so he had thought."

She paused again. Wiping another tender tear from her eye. Gathering thoughts and recollecting harrowing memories like those from your past, can be a fairly traumatic and often overwhelming experience. DI Murray was your expert in that department. He knew full well how a strange alignment of situations and circumstances could lead you to make poor and often devastating decisions. Joseph Hanlon who sat by his side tonight, could also testify to that. Having on at least two previous occasions, he provided 'mercy missions' in respect to his Inspector's physical well being. In layman's terms: He had saved him from taking his own life!

"And finally, Sergeant?" Her Chief Inspector encouraged, by taking her hand.

Sandra Kerr once again looked up through her flaming red tousled main. She swept it confidently to one side, maintained eye contact with Barbra Furlong and focused on her words.

"Two hours later, when Maurice Orr still hadn't returned. His work colleagues called ourselves. Twenty-five minutes after that, the woman's tenement flat was being sealed off and your beloved murderous psychopath taken away in handcuffs."

Kerr could hear in the silence that prevailed that her fellow book club members were not keen on her finishing there. That she was still a few pages away from... The End!

However, like many of the disturbing nursery rhymes that they had been trawling through that evening, there was to be...... no happy ever after.

"Whilst there," Sandra Kerr added. "Angela McMinn had unfortunately told her unexpected visitor that her teenage son was having a shower. If she had just never mentioned that fact, things may have been so, so different. Unknowingly and for whatever reason, it flicked a switch in their seemingly kindhearted delivery man. According to his testimony, he strangled the mother in all of ten seconds flat. Then as the well-toned, muscular teenager, Anthony, emerged from the shower wearing only the skimpiest of towels around himself. A self-satisfied, smirking Maurice Orr, subjected him to the most disgusting, prolonged rape and assault. I can't even bring myself to repeat his description of his final acts with that young lad. It was sickening. He then viciously hacked up Angela McMinn's torso and split it equally between the - top, middle and bottom into three large white bin liners. He wrote on each bag and left them in plain sight on the kitchen floor. He never made any attempt to get away. He never tried to clean up or hide any evidence. In fact, he never moved. He just sat still in his chair and waited patiently for us to arrive."

Again quiet prevailed. It appeared to be an unofficial minute's silence, offered up in memory of Angela McMinn and her son. Briefly, the Inspector thought about his own quiet moments and how for him they often lingered in the air, thick and heavy, like a blanket. Wherever he moved that silence followed. Always watching, never fading. It was his own, personal shadow. How blessed was he? He thought. Before coming back to the present.

"He toyed with you and I today," Murray said. Pointing across at DCI Furlong. "He was doing his own inquiry into us. To see if we knew what he was locked up for. It had nothing to do with knowing about my musical knowledge. It was about him bragging to us, Barbra."

"He told us that he was the black sheep of the family, Steven. That was something, surely." Furlong argued.

Murray's face raged. "Yes, sure, Ma'am. But it had nothing to do with Terry Jacks', Seasons in the Sun." He then sang aggressively - *"Goodbye Papa please pray for me, I was the friggin' Baa Baa Black Sheep of the family,"* he stuttered. "He literally pulled the wool over our eyes, Chief Inspector. And we, like a couple of idiots, were none the wiser." Murray shook his head in sheer frustration. "That had been the start of his nursery rhyme obsession. Something else may have inspired it, but that was when he decided to become the number one expert in its field."

"Each of the bags?" Furlong reluctantly asked. Hanlon was glad she did, because he had been desperate to do so.

"Sandy, will confirm that for you, Barbra," Murray said. Breaking his normal habit of refraining to address her as such. But I would be mighty surprised if they weren't labelled..."

He turned to Kerr for corroboration.

She nodded firmly and proffered. "Master, Dame and Boy, sir. Three bags full!"

This had no fairy-tale ending, Murray was certain of that. It was coming back to him slowly. He was fearful that afterwards the circumstances and situation, the mental and physical state that the fifteen year-old would have found himself in, could have easily led to poor decision making. As was just witnessed, Sandra Kerr knew Steven Murray well. Certainly well enough to know exactly what he was currently thinking.

"It was six weeks later, sir. That was when Anthony McMinn took his own life."

The papers had called him, 'The Black Sheep killer.' Murray realised that was why the name Maurice Orr never struck a chord with him. But he was still gutted. He firmly believed that he should have recalled the case. Especially given that he was supposedly Scotland's literary expert on nursery rhymes and based upon the song lyric that he chose deliberately to test the Detective Inspector. The man from Johnstone, not Paisley. One of them hadn't done their homework and it wasn't Maurice Orr. In fact, he was reluctantly due a gold star and a happy face. Which was more than DI Murray currently displayed.

Holding back angry, anguished tears and with his stomach convulsing, Steven Murray swallowed hard and nodded. He knew it was coming and it was the stark reality of life as a police officer. Shielding the vast majority of citizens from heartbreaking scenarios, time after time, after time. Who knew? Not the public, that was for sure!

Another hour passed and Joseph Hanlon quietly slipped on his jacket in the corridor, as DI Murray went to say goodbye to the ladies.

"Sandra is going to stay in the spare bedroom tonight, Inspector," Furlong informed him. "For the best I suspect."

"Absolutely, Ma'am." Murray agreed. "Where is she?"

"She's just this minute nipped to the loo."

"That was worthwhile and productive tonight, Barbra. I just wanted you to know that."

"But? Inspector. Because like earlier, I know there is one. I could see all night that you were not quite yourself. That you were holding back slightly, Steven. For some reason, a little reluctant to fully participate."

Joe Hanlon was now perched, listening by the doorway. He had decided privacy was the best bet currently for his two superior officers.

"I know you have always supported us being a strong team, Ma'am. That you continually strive for the level of transparency that allows us all to be aware, for the most part, of what is going on. And I know how much you wanted to be and feel a part of, and let's be honest, what was my team."

Furlong baulked somewhat at his vain arrogance. Whilst recognising that he was right.

"That is okay though. Because after DCI Browne, we desperately wanted our next Chief Inspector to be an HONEST and well liked team player, and you are certainly that, Ma'am. Know that we are genuinely delighted and honoured to have you. None more so than myself."

The DCI breathed a sigh of relief on hearing those words at least, along with a hidden tear or two. She then also realised that...

"There is still a but..."

"Of course there is, Barbra. For you cannot be part of a team, make decisions on behalf of that team and ultimately lead that team, BUT then choose deliberately to exclude half of that team from those discussions and interactions."

She appeared puzzled. For such a clever lady, Murray couldn't believe her naivety at times.

"You, me, Sherlock and Sandy - Really?" He said. "That was very badly thought out, Barbra, and extremely ill-judged in my humble opinion. For what that's worth," he added.

Murray pulled up the collar of his jacket. "Good-night, Chief Inspector."

Unsurprisingly, at the other side of the small cottage, Sandra Kerr had also stalled in the bathroom. Waiting patiently for the cease fire and all-clear. It was an intimate interior and there was no real hiding place from Murray's heartfelt tones. Both Hanlon and Kerr were much more than acquaintances to him these days. They had both worked closely with the man. Hanlon currently, and Kerr previously. They KNEW him and he would be well aware that wherever they were right now in the home, that they would hear him. That was his point to Furlong. If she really wanted honesty and transparency, then don't be afraid to show it. There can be no favourites, no exclusive dinner parties or brainstorming sessions for a select, elite group. Especially an invite that would later cause a divide. When those excluded, discover other members of the team had taken part in some unofficial briefing! Both Kerr and Hanlon nodded to themselves in their respective hiding spots. He was some man. Often maligned and misunderstood, they weren't sure if either of them had come across a more sensitive, yet so-called, hard man. The latter of which, Detective Inspector Steven Murray most certainly wasn't.

Eleven

"You better watch out, you better beware. Albert said that E equals M C squared. Einstein a go go. God does not play dice with the world, but things aren't right in the outside world. Einstein a go go. Einstein a go go."

- Landscape

Thursday 15 December

That morning with inquiries into the 'Nursery Rhyme' deaths ongoing. Barbra Furlong thought it rather apt that as she walked the length of her short hallway, according to another such tale - *Thursday's child has far to go*. Which was so true. Because investigations into all three murders were at a very early stage and a substantial amount of long man hours and behind the scenes police work was going to be required moving forward.

Hearing her DCI knock politely on the guest bedroom, Sandra Kerr stirred slightly.

"Some bacon and eggs are ready, Sandy. Come and get them while they're still warm."

One too many glasses of wine after Joe Hanlon and Murray departed, certainly hadn't helped matters. She felt weary, her head popping and fizzing like a sherbet fountain. Had she embarrassed herself in front of her Chief Inspector? Had she said anything out of order or disrespectful? Had she ultimately harmed her longer term career prospects? With a multitude of questions and uncertainty surrounding her behaviour hanging over her. She did the sensible thing. She thought about what her mentor and friend Steven Murray would have done and decided that she would be happy to copy that. In truth, she already knew what her rebellious Inspector's action would have been. So happily, she followed his example exactly to the letter. In five seconds flat, Police Scotland Officer, Detective Sergeant

Sandra 'Sandy' Kerr had dived for cover, drilled hard back under a soft welcoming pink pillow and sought further refuge. Another ten minutes, she told herself. However, two minutes later and any polite knocking was long gone. DCI Furlong burst into the room and communicated clearly...

"Forget a shower and forget my wonderful cooked breakfast, Sergeant. There's been another body found!"

Kerr swung around rapidly from beneath the covers and impressively within three seconds, she was standing directly in front of a well groomed DCI, who was complete with make-up and hair done. Kerr, for her part, looked like the dishevelled bellows on a worn out accordion. She had obviously never got undressed the previous night. Drink, tiredness or both playing a significant part in proceedings. Furlong looked her up and down disappointedly. But soon remembered what Sandy had re-lived and shared with them all last night. Thus her look changed quickly to one of a supportive leader.

"Thankfully on this wet and blustery Thursday, we don't actually *'have far to go.'* It's just along the coast at Port Seton. Twenty minutes will do it. I've arranged for Boyd to meet us there and you two can head out and get on with looking into the 'Humpty Dumpty' case."

"Do we know if this one is connected, Ma'am?"

"No deaths for long enough," the Chief Inspector said dismissively.

"Then along come three in a couple of days, Sandy. I'll just assume that that was a rhetorical question, shall I? Now give that face of yours a quick wash young lady and I'll drive."

Rushing toward the toilet all Barbra Furlong heard as her flustered Sergeant rushed past her, was a slightly sarcastic groan, which sounded very much like, "Okay, mum!" Followed by a bathroom door being firmly locked.

Standing at the sink and looking through the window, Sandy soon realised that she could have just as easily have washed her face on the go. Outside, the harsh early morning rain obliterated the crystal reflection of the sky and had turned it into disorientated chaos. Even when both female officers left the cottage, the icy grey heavens restlessly grumbled. Or could that have been Sandra's groaning stomach?

For the start of their twenty minute, twelve mile drive, DS Kerr felt compelled to keep a close eye on her feet. Whilst her right hand gently massaged her forehead and temple. As the DCI monitored her plight, Furlong felt inspired to offer up...

"Did you know Sergeant Kerr, that the temple is a juncture where four skull bones fuse together. The frontal, parietal, temporal and..." The fourth bone would remain a mystery for now. Kerr had thrust an open palm into the air, accompanied with a, "Now! Really? Ma'am?"

As they sat in silence, their destination this morning was interesting. The unification of Cockenzie and Port Seton grew from what were initially two small fishing villages. The older parts of the town, between the two harbours retained a more traditional look and feel. Similar to many other small fishing villages on the east coast of Scotland. And although the fishing industry had certainly declined in recent years, the harbour at Port Seton still retained a small, impressive fleet of vessels. To the east, there was Seton Sands Holiday Park and also nearby there was the creation of a coastal walk. A part of The John Muir Way, which Barbra Furlong has hiked along often in the past.

"I'm sorry, Ma'am." Sandy offered. Daring to lift her head above the imaginary parapet. "Too much to drink midweek and I throw your kind hospitality back at you and snap your face off into the bargain. Not a very good house guest, I'm afraid. My sincere apologies about that."

"To be fair, some question marks could be raised about your host! Giving you two minutes to depart and no breakfast. I'm not sure your review on TripAdvisor will be too favourable given those shortcomings."

"Well if it's any consolation, Ma'am. I did know that the occipital was the fourth bone!"

They both laughed and the mood lightened somewhat.

Apologetically her DCI began with, "None of us knew, neither myself nor Steven, about the fact that you were involved in the Maurice Orr case and I'm sorry for bringing it all back to the surface last night."

"At least, hopefully with him onboard, psychopath or not. It might give us a little extra helpful insight into these deaths." Kerr then continued. "The so-called children's nursery rhymes are fascinating though, aren't they? And interesting that the Inspector spoke fervently last night about you both literally having the wool pulled over your eyes."

"And he was right, Sandy. We'll be paying Orr another visit soon I suspect. We'll see what we have waiting for us in Port Seton first. Then I'll maybe arrange a time for tomorrow. Would you like to..."

"No, no. No thanks, Ma'am." Kerr interrupted. Before swiftly changing the topic ever so slightly. "DI Murray said that Orr mentioned that he was the black sheep of his family?"

Furlong nodded suitably, as she manoeuvred a small mini roundabout outside Gullane.

"I know you like your trivia origins and the like, Ma'am. But did you know that Baa Baa Black Sheep was actually all about a tax increase on wool?"

Her Chief Inspector's eyes raised at that information. "I did not." Furlong informed her.

It may well have been early morning in East Lothian, but windscreen wipers and lights were a must. High above the twisting coastal road, the thick blackened clouds seemed to be desperately weighed down by the heavy rain which it held in its delicate frame. As the quality of darkness shifted in the sky, the rain kept pouring. Although momentarily distracted, as DCI Furlong carefully and cautiously dealt with the adverse weather, DS Kerr soon got her conversation back on track.

"It was while I was on the Maurice Orr case that I first learned all about it. It was from way back in the late 13th century. Unusually, compared to many of the others, it wasn't creepy so much as vocal. Complaining deeply about King Edward's wool tax. The fact that the punishing tariff he applied, gave a third of the cost to himself, the King ("the Master"), another third to the church ("the Dame") and the rest to the farmer. The very man who could barely cover his expenses. The original version, Ma'am, had actually said, *'but none for the little boy who cries in the lane.'* Compared to most of the others, it was basically the happiest nursery rhyme of all time."

Once again both colleagues laughed refreshingly. It was nice to see Sandra Kerr's spirits lift. Last night had definitely taken an awful lot out of her. Making her recollect many upsetting moments and memories. This morning, Barbra Furlong also seemed to be doing extraordinarily well in keeping the balance steady between being, the *'Head Heed Yin'* and a 'trusted colleague.'

Her in-car telephone rang. Steven Murray's name displayed proudly and Furlong duly answered.

"Good morning, Inspector. How are things? Are you still on your way there? Is DC Hanlon travelling with you?" Reception was a bit weak, but Murray responded in kind...

"Fine. No and Yes," the Inspector coldly replied.

"What do you mean, you are not on your way there?"

He desperately wanted to mess with her some more, but quickly figured that maybe today was not the ideal time.

"I'm already here, Ma'am! I'm staring at the body as we speak." Assuming that she was on speaker, Murray then declared...

"Morning, Sandy. How's the head?" He added wisely.

"How does he do that?" She whispered. Glancing across at the driver's seat. "Ma'am?"

"Don't look at me, Sergeant. Half the time, I wonder the exact same thing."

Murray laughed heartily at the other end of the line, before filling the female detectives in with some details.

"I think you may know the man, Ma'am?"

The Chief Inspector's heart sank.

"At least in a professional capacity," Murray added. "He was Sheriff Andrew King. Not long retired, I believe."

Furlong appeared to be rotating the photographic Filofax in her mind. Suddenly her eyes flickered with recognition. A visual connection had her gaze briefly at Sandra Kerr.

"Was he made from girders, Inspector?"

Kerr bit her lip and rolled her eyes. She more than most was familiar with that phrase. Even a slight distorted crackle on the line could not hide DI Murray's excited response.

"I knew you would remember him, Ma'am. 'The Bru' some of us old-timers called him. Based on the colourful bushy mop of energetic orange hair that he possessed. We swore it had a life of its own. He was Albert Einstein personified, only in vibrant technicolour."

Both Furlong and Kerr laughed gently at that crazy image. But the only sound you could hear clearly was the windscreen wipers hammering away effectively... left, right, left, right, left. The heavy rain showed no sign of easing.

"His whole appearance..." Murray continued. "Often looked so badly tousled, you would assume that he had just swivelled straight out of bed."

Barbra stifled her laughter this time, as she looked knowingly at the lady in her passenger seat. The spawn of a red-headed Einstein, who was currently trying desperately to rearrange her trousers, blouse, jacket AND hair!

The Chief Inspector spoke to deliberately distract herself from her Sergeant's current dilemma.

"What do we know, Inspector? What happened? Do we have a cause of death? Do we think it's connected to the others?"

"Whoa, whoa, slow down, Ma'am," Murray interrupted. "All will be revealed when you get here."

Taking him literally, DCI Furlong applied pressure to the brakes and eased her speed. Anxiety, pressure, stress or whatever you want to call it, Furlong's lengthy experience knew that each of those were all instantly connected to an accelerator pedal when driving. She smiled at Sandra Kerr. The rain had receded and behind the waning clouds, small appealing glints of azure could be seen. She had switched off her headlights and streaks of bright yellow rays were breaking through and hastily dismissing all clouds. Barbra Furlong then recognised the deep positive impact a certain Detective Inspector was having on her, when she randomly declared...

"Mr Blue Sky please tell us why, you had to hide away for so long, so long. Where did we go wrong?"

Kerr's broad grin from ear to ear, told her boss immediately that she got it. As the two female officers arrived at the cordoned off house. The driveway instantly rocked to the highly inappropriate strains of a powerful duet... *"Hey there Mr Blue. We're so pleased to be with you. Look around see what you do. Everybody smiles at you..."*

Murray stood at the front door and watched them approach. He grew concerned when he witnessed each of them wipe away what looked like tears. Based on Kerr's appearance, she had been through the wars. He quickly hopped off the front step of the impressive Georgian built mansion.

"Are you both okay?" He asked quietly. "Sandy, you look a mess," he whispered. "What's happened?"

Furlong could see his genuine concern and struggled not to grin. A sombre, more official downbeat tone would normally have been called for. But that morning this new side to Barbra Furlong, one that Sandra Kerr had gotten to know and like quite well in the car ventured to be a little different. She responded, speaking slowly...

"Inspector, the sun is shining in the sky. There ain't a cloud in sight."

"I can see that, Chief Inspector, Ma'am." He hesitated. "Seriously, are you BOTH okay?"

"Steven, its stopped raining," Sandra Kerr added. *"Everybody's in the play and don't you know..."*

Both females now pressed their faces up close to Murray. This was girl power at its worst and most powerful. In a low sultry whisper they both sang... "It's a beautiful new day, hey hey."

No more was said and minus The Electric Light Orchestra, DCI Furlong and Detective Sergeant Kerr entered the premises.

Had I just been given a taste of my own medicine? DI Murray wondered. Because if so, WOW! That was strong stuff indeed, he thought and smiled.

Twelve

"Right away Mary Anne flew in from Atlanta on a red-eye midnight flight. She held Wanda's hand as they worked out a plan and it didn't take them long to decide - that Earl had to die."

- The Dixie Chicks

As the Chief Inspector and her Sergeant were shown through to the back of the large impressive home. People in white SO-CO suits seemed to be everywhere. Once again it was Danielle Poll at the helm. Currently the pathologist was working with the dead man's head and neck area. Lifting, stretching, tugging and probing. Andrew King was sat slumped over at the head of the eight seater kitchen table. His red hair had been hacked at and cut unevenly. A smattering of seed or grain had been spilled across the table. Not a large amount, but if you looked closely it became very apparent. The hair loss was a clear symbolic gesture or message being sent. Two expansive skylight windows overhead, ensured plenty of daylight. In front of the deceased sat a fancy ceramic pie dish. It was still filled to the brim with contents. Golden pastry sat wilting and weeping into the dark gravy below. His cutlery knife looked untouched at its place setting, whilst the fork was still firmly grasped within the man's hand, although his pinky was bent outward.

Furlong and Kerr entered the room, blue bootees were all that they required to put on to finish off their attractive makeover. Certainly in Sandra Kerr's case, it was a vast improvement. Her concertinaed trousers and blouse magically gone. Her hair could now also be blamed on the hood of the protective suit when it comes time to remove it. Furlong was fairly certain that behind Sandy's white face mask, lay the biggest, cheesiest and most grateful grin ever. What female in the history of the world, apart from Detective Sergeant Kerr, ever thought that she looked stunning in a SOCO suit?

Andrew E. King was seventy-five years of age and had been in the legal profession for over forty of them. He retired as a Sheriff about six years ago. Having sold his humble, two bedroomed Edinburgh penthouse city centre flat for £2.1 million. A self-confirmed bachelor, living on his own, he then purchased this incredible, seven bedroom Georgian villa. Complete with 3 acres of land and a small stable block. It was a bargain at only £1.75 million. Leaving the very shrewd Sheriff with a handsome quarter of a million pound, safely banked away for a rainy day. Not that he'd have much need for it now.

"What did the E. stand for Steven?"

"He had a regular housekeeper, Ma'am. A Mrs Needham. That's her over there talking to that young WPC."

Furlong took a sharp intake of breath.

"I know, I know, she's just a PC you're going to tell me. Apologies, force of habit. Anyway according to Mrs Needham, she had asked the exact same thing when she first started here over 5 years ago. Seemingly the bold Mrs King, senior, his mother, was a massive music fan and he got the E. as a way of paying tribute to Ben E. King of The Drifters. Although it actually doesn't stand for anything."

Furlong was dumbstruck.

"You know... *Stand by me, ooh ooh stand by me.*"

" I know who Ben E. King and the Drifters are, Inspector."

"And you probably know what his E. stands for too, right?"

Barbra Furlong. Chief Inspector Furlong to give her due respect, smiled suggestively, straightened her skirt and walked over to Dr. Danielle Poll.

"How goes it, Danni? Anything at all you can tell us?"

"Not really, Chief Inspector. Like I told DI Murray earlier, this is a definite return to the lab and check him out job. There are no external signs of foul play. No noticeable contusions or lacerations."

She then paused at that. Her west coast American accent was reluctant as always to speculate, but she immediately saw the look of disappointment on the Chief Inspector's face.

"Everything would appear to point toward poisoning of some sort, Barbra. So that is where I would be leaning. But I'll let you know as soon as I find anything. I promise."

The Chief Inspector took a step back. She was then joined by Steven Murray and Sandra Kerr at her side.

"I feel as if I know this man, Ma'am." Sandy offered up.

"Like we said, Sandy. He was a Sheriff in the Lothians for decades."

"That may be, Ma'am. But I never knew him then and I don't actually recognise him today, either. Yet, he still seems vaguely familiar."

"He could be your father?" Furlong joked. "It's the Bru connection," she grinned.

Inspector Murray then added to the conversation. "I could easily take a guess at the nursery rhyme."

Both his female colleagues were slightly taken aback at that. Last night's drinks and their indoor car ride filled with distracting frivolity had somehow steered their collective focus well away from the recent deaths and to how knowing today's link, may well help them join up the dots. Murray on the other hand, was making up for it.

"As soon as I saw the scene. It seemed like the most obvious one yet. As if he or she was making it really easy for us. Why would that be? Why would they feel the need to do that? I personally don't know. But it does seem rather too straightforward. Although to be fair, I am basing my choice all on one very blatant line in the rhyme."

"One line, Steven. That would be impressive, Inspector. Are you going to share it with us then?" Furlong teased him.

"Well, let me ask you both if you get any clues from this lot first?"

Murray posed the question whilst pointing out three items at the other end of the elegant, dark wood table. Each of the three things had been found in the man's jacket pocket. The unsurprisingly, expensively tailored and well stitched tweed blazer, hung over the back of one of the kitchen chairs.

"A child's toy car?" Sgt. Kerr remarked.

"It's an ice-cream van to be precise, Sandy," Murray countered.

"But it's relevance, Steven?" Barbra Furlong inquired.

"No idea, Ma'am."

Sandra Kerr had quickly moved on to items two and three. With her blue nitrile gloves, she edged them carefully around the table. One was an ice-lolly wrapper, the other a picture postcard of Derry in Northern Ireland. A handy toothpick from a container on the man's display cabinet also helped Kerr rotate, grip and inspect the random clues. The display of crockery on the nearby cabinet was noticeably missing one specific piece. A gap lay vacant. Its normal occupant : A pie dish. The exact same one no doubt, that currently sat below the ex-trial judge.

For whatever reason, Furlong suddenly felt the inclination to call Lizzie, their IT specialist. Radical Lizzie had been her earlier nickname, but that had been before she committed to work privately alongside Police Scotland. Now her radical actions were being put to good use to eradicate the bad guys on a regular daily basis. As an ethical hacker, she was already working around the clock trying desperately to track down worthy leads in regards to the deaths of Jack Cannon and Doctor Crossland. Barbra Furlong apologised for the extra workload, but nevertheless gave Lizzie all the background information she had on the man and then left the girl to do 'her thing,' and work her magic. A bit like the Constable that had just arrived alongside DC Boyd.

Joe Hanlon maybe didn't have the modern day IT skills of Radical Lizzie, but he knew forensically how to explore, delve, route around and persevere. Then he could enlist Lizzie to cross the t's and dot the i's. Between them, they made a fairly impressive team. One that Furlong thankfully remembered she was in charge of. One that she had to make amends with several of its individuals. Twenty seconds later her text was sent. A further thirty seconds after that and an email followed. Her invitation was delivered on all fronts.

"Ma'am, are you still with us?" Murray questioned, his voice maybe slightly louder than he intended. "You seemed to be having a moment, Chief Inspector."

"Yes, yes, I think I was, Inspector," she said softly. "Thank you."

A series of morning greets were exchanged between all. It was then agreed that Kerr would head off with Allan Boyd and explore further the background to the death of Jack Cannon. That Sergeant Linn, 'Baldy,' could keep 'Hanna' Hayes whilst they proceeded with Jeremy Crossland's checks and information gathering. Which would then free up 'Kid' Curry to partner Steven Murray back at the Greenock Hotel. Meanwhile Barbra Furlong would spend her day mentoring also. This time she decided that she would have the newly arrived Joseph 'Sherlock' Hanlon by her side. Let the partnership and adventure begin.

"DC Hanlon," she said. "Often it is easier to unearth and discover things when you have no preconceived ideas, wouldn't you agree?"

"It can be Ma'am," he said warily. He knew a pitfall of sorts lay ahead. Intuitively, he then added. "Chief Inspector, what can I help you with?"

He was becoming distinctly more confident and assertive. Furlong liked that, and she couldn't help but admire just how well Steven Murray had influenced and guided him.

"Ma'am, how may I help?" He repeated.

"Ok, so with no advance knowledge or notification Constable Hanlon, I want you to take your time and look at the three items behind us on the table and see if you can spot what unites them? What is the link that we are missing? What does our friendly, prearranged and totally deranged killer want us to learn from them?"

Murray, Kerr and Furlong stood aside and let the tall, gangly officer have a closer look. He could have charged just for his facial expressions alone. His blue eyes narrowed, peered and blinked. His nose twitched, snorted and was rubbed continually. Then his mouth burst into action. Lips were licked, sucked and pursed, whilst his tongue seemed to travel and journey upon every contour inside his mouth. 15 seconds, turned to 20. 35 to 40. A grin and a nod at the minute mark allowed him to say...

"I'm satisfied. Do you wish me to reveal my conclusion?"

"Seriously? You honestly have a solution for us, Joe?" Furlong questioned, not meaning to sound so surprised. Each of the others looked on in excited anticipation.

"Well, I have an educated suggestion for you, Ma'am and we can certainly see where it takes us."

"Go on," Murray encouraged. "Impress us. This is your thing, son. Don't be so modest."

"Trust me, I'm not being modest. It's just that based on the recent murders, you will all see it immediately. I guarantee you, as soon as I point out the first one."

"Go on then super-sleuth," was the first contribution of the day from Allan Boyd.

With the steady use of the tooth-pick, Hanlon drew each of the items to the edge of the table. The first one, the old Corgi toy ice- cream van, he gently rotated and gestured toward it with a hand. His body language saying - Really you don't see it? He smiled and with his gloved hand carefully picked up the corner of the 'Twister' wrapper. Again his eyes said - Seriously?

"Okay," Hanlon said. "I am going to ask you one question about this last item and I guarantee you will have the clue to them all."

"Mind your chestnuts lad. Now you are just showing off," his Chief Inspector grinned.

Hanlon needed the reassuring grin, because when it came to DCI Furlong and her moods, he still wasn't quite clever enough to figure them out. As he held item number three in one hand, he suddenly pierced the postcard with his trusty tooth-pick. Low gasps from the others, indicated that he maybe shouldn't have done that. Furlong's grin had instantly vanished. That was possibly material evidence, vital to their case. However, he had learned from the hands of a man that continually would utter - 'Go with your gut!' So today, he did. Straight through the heart of the sturdy card.

"It's fine. They are just clues to confirm that this murder scene is part of one large compendium of nursery rhymes. Each specifically linked. For what reason, we are still desperately trying to figure out."

"And your question?" Sandy asked.

"Sure," Hanlon said. "Take a careful look." He raised it up and slowly guided it into clear view for everyone. "So you can all see that the postcard represents Derry in the north of Ireland."

Shrugs and nods seemed to be in agreement. They got that part.

"So my question to you is... What is Derry famous for? Or at least known for?"

After a few seconds of apprehension, one or two responses were forthcoming.

"The Peace Bridge is in Derry, I think," offered Kerr.

"Yes, the Peace Bridge is what I would have said," Boyd agreed. They could see by Hanlon's face, that this was not the answer he was looking for. Murray's eyes then caught Hanlon's. They were ablaze with certainty.

"I've got it."

"Kindly hold that answer for a second then, sir," 'Sherlock' said.

"Ma'am, any final thoughts?"

His Chief Inspector spoke. She often found it helped her to talk things through aloud.

"The River Foyle flows through Derry and is synonymous with the city," she offered. "It is one of Northern Ireland's six counties. It's in the province of Ulster and none of this is helping," she shrugged. "Aaagh, I've also been there," she added. "I've seen the row of cannon's that..."

"Cannon's," Kerr interrupted. "It's to do with Jack Cannon, our Humpty Dumpty man," she excitedly announced.

"That may well be true," Hanlon agreed. "But how does that include an ice-lolly wrapper and a toy car?"

Kerr was stumped on that one. Furlong then jumped back into the conversation.

"They have loads of cannons all located on their city walls, as you walk around...... Their WALLS!!!" Furlong screamed.

Hanlon retreated in genuine fear. The Inspector smiled and with Boyd and Kerr it slowly dawned. Murray, wanting to ensure Hanlon that he had guessed correctly, spoke up.

"Indeed it was Wall's. Wall's made the 'Twister' ice lolly and the toy was a replica, pale blue and yellow Wall's ice-cream van. They were a popular sight throughout the country in the 70's. Plus, like you said, Ma'am. Derry is most famous for its old, historic city walls."

"The Jack Cannon link was just thrown in for good measure then!" Allan Boyd stated.

"Much more than that," Kerr announced, with deep satisfaction in her voice. "I think I may have just remembered where I know this man from." She instantly sent off a text. "It's a definite confirmation that he is part of the collection," Kerr added. "But let's just hope I am right. We'll soon see later today."

"Before I say," Murray gestured to the head of the table. "Doctor Poll, Danni. Could you do me a favour and check the contents of that pie?"

She could see by the Inspector's smile, that he was deadly serious. "Just check under the pastry, please. I think you will solve this one for us, young lady"

Her look would have skewered a lesser man. Whereas Murray continued to extend an expression of sincere gratitude. It was all part of the man's charm. A character trait that Barbra Furlong had already found so alluring. Whatever shiny instrument Poll was now using, she tapped and scraped at the crust and burrowed neatly into sections with it. Suddenly from the bright clink, clink, clink of metal on pottery, a dull clunking sound was heard. To the east... clink, clink, clink! And back west... clunk! North... clink! Back south... clunk! Only then did Murray notice that the good Doctor had been using her own personal pen on this 'home made' mission. Using her gloved hand the female pathologist dredged the mystery item up from below the cold pieces of diced steak. To the group of gathered officers she presented...... a penny!

"Not what you expected, Inspector?" Kerr felt his disappointment and puzzlement.

"Not really," he said. "I was hoping that..."

Clunk! Clunk! Clunk! They all heard again. Poll moved her pen and again... Clunk! Clunk! Clunk! This time her hand produced another penny and then another and then another. In total by the time the skipper of the pen had trawled throughout the waters of the murky pie, a stack of six one pence pieces had been found.

"No mystery treasure that's for sure," Murray told them. "But one mystery solved!" He smirked. "Slightly different, but it still works," the Inspector concluded.

"And your one line?" Furlong queried. With a look of intrigue upon her face.

"Oh, that's easy," he declared. Then he suddenly stopped himself. "Sorry, Danni. One last thing. In his shirt pocket, does that contain the same seed as what's scattered on the table?"

Filled with curiosity herself now, Dr Poll gently tugged at his pocket with her gloved hand and looked inside. The firm nod that Murray received was enough for him to go on and openly declare...

"Wasn't that a dainty dish to set before the King?"

Again, similar to Hanlon, a quartet of stunned faces. Every one of them said - It was so obvious! Eyes closed, some looked heavenward and others simply shook their heads.

"Sing a song of sixpence." DC Boyd began. "A pocketful of rye," Kerr added.

'Sherlock,' gave a brief review. "The walls collapsed in on Jack Cannon for Humpty Dumpty. Jeremy Crossland was the subject for Hickory Dickory Dock and now today in the presence of a King, we are re-enacting Six a Song of Sixpence. Three bodies and we know that they are definitely connected. But we just have no idea how or why or by what."

Silence.

The Chief Inspector turned her attention to Murray and mentioned.

"By way of a consolation prize, Steven. Do I get anything for Ben EARL KING?" The couple smiled and all parties went their separate ways.

Thirteen

"I read in the Sunday papers what lovers' tokens are. There's amulets and there's talismans, like a ring or a lucky star. It says that half a sovereign is a thing they use a lot, but sixpence is the only thing I've got."

- Tommy Steele

From *four and twenty blackbirds baked in a pie.* 'Baldy' - Sergeant Mitchell Linn was continually reciting *Hickory Dickory Dock.* The man with the thick mop of unruly blonde hair had checked out several versions and variations on the nursery rhyme. He had even found one with six verses. The other animals caught making their way up the clock included: a snake, a squirrel, a cat, a monkey and an elephant. That final verse ended, one surmised with the clock breaking. It simply read: *Hickory Dickory Dock. The elephant went up the clock - Oh no!*

Detective Constable Susan 'Hanna' Hayes, working alongside Mitch Linn for the first time, was more than happy to check out the Doctor's computer and laptop to see what she could discover. She had learned a fair bit from Joe Hanlon in the last couple of months. Once a week, 'Sherlock' had been tutoring her on some of the finer skills he had picked up in recent years, and by all accounts she was an excellent pupil. Learning quickly how to continually scrape back layer after layer of metrics, to hopefully unearth something of substance. Unfortunately, her Sergeant, somewhat unfamiliar with Hanna's new skillset, coupled with her natural abilities, made her hand it all over to Radical Lizzie.

"But..." Hayes went to complain. Then quickly thinking better of it, added, "Straight away, Sarge."

Jeremy Crossland's flat had not thrown up anything new. The forensics team had scoured it thoroughly and found nothing of any significance. He had no alarm on the premises or any security devices or cameras. A straightforward knock at the door earlier in the evening would easily have allowed his assailant access and currently that was their theory.

The Inspector drove back down to Greenock, with 'Kid' Curry given the task of driving home, mainly because Murray anticipated and hoped that his duties travelling back may involve several interesting phone calls. Those being received, those newly made and those missed voicemails from earlier. Busy, busy, busy. But first, having arrived ten minutes ahead of schedule, he had time to teach Drew a few lines of a song...

"So many house rules, but no swimming pools and it's lights out every night at nine. Beds they're so hard, the concierge is a guard. There's sadder places to spend time. But you keep coming back every year and why you can't tell. All your friends - they are here. Yes, one more night in the Greenock Hotel."

It was very much the same scenario as before. Everyone was excluded from the library. Maurice Orr sat impressively behind a large desk surrounded by a vast range of reading materials. Only the bottom row of pointed playing cards had been attempted this time. About eight peaks in all. A large pile of cards were centred directly in front of him, possibly two or three decks added together. This time the prison librarian even had a laptop with him. It was positioned just within reach to his left. Rebecca Loggenberg informed Inspector Murray that the whole library was being reindexed and that Mr Orr was going to be an extremely busy man for the foreseeable future.

The Governor, today wearing shimmering black nail polish, obviously had a preference for trouser suits. Because matching her fingertips this afternoon she wore a figure hugging jet black outfit, complete with fitted waistcoat. This lady certainly liked her expensive designer clothes, that was becoming very clear. To complete the look this time, her partners-in-crime were a charcoal blouse, which only began halfway down her chest and a pair of classy, low lying court shoes that shyly kept away from all publicity, choosing instead to hide discreetly under her fashionably flared trouser legs. Murray was not sure if that particular pair possessed a back pocket? But he was certain that if he asked Andrew Curry he would know. Because his Constable's eyes had never drifted from that spot since he had been introduced to the woman.

Sadly, the Inspector could see it for nothing more than a statement of intent. He had come across female's like Rebecca before, reporter Alice Jones for one. Probably okay at their job. Mediocre at best, but they appeared brilliant. Fawned over and promoted way beyond their means and abilities. Their body language and speech was assertive and proactive. Their positive contributions, their willingness to engage on public forums and to keenly attend meetings certainly didn't go unnoticed. Everyone knew someone like that!

With Rebecca Loggenberg, all of those meaningless attributes were greatly enhanced and underlined by her sensual and compelling wardrobe. Over the last couple of decades, not unlike Furlong's desperate need to address her foul language in the workplace. Power dressing was a fashion statement that enabled women to establish their authority in a professional and political environment. One traditionally dominated by men. Murray feared however, that the confident Miss Loggenberg had missed the point of power dressing completely. Especially as she worked in a male dominated environment alongside hundreds of sexually frustrated men and females for that matter. Individuals that are currently incarcerated behind bars for years with only the bare minimum of jump-suits or t- shirts to get by on. Ideally, power dressing attempts to counterbalance a woman's natural femininity and inherent sexuality with the goal of preventing sexual misinterpretation through her clothes that might otherwise allow. Curry's magnetic eyes, spoke volumes and said it all.

With those thoughts in mind, Murray was convinced that was exactly this particular Governor's thing. That was her power. She lorded this power over the inmates and her fellow staff on a daily basis, the Inspector was certain of that. Certain that she ruled her fully monitored Kingdom from a distance.

He could hear her say, '*Here I am and here I sit. I am delicate to the touch and delicious to the taste. Both of which, you will never sample!*' Thus the story behind the tempting red apple with the bite taken out resurfaced. The image carved painstakingly onto her office door made complete sense to him now. She was that forbidden fruit to everyone that dared enter. Set in a rehabilitation institute, it was a clear homage to Adam and Eve, to the Garden of Eden and ultimately to the continuing pull of - Good versus Evil.

Some colleagues had travelled nearby, with a quick drive across to Morningside. Others had journeyed considerably further. Like motoring down the west coast to the land of the Green Oak tree.

Whilst back at Leith along with Allan Boyd and following up on several aspects of the Jack Cannon case, DS Kerr was feeling unsettled and at least a little ashamed. So having locked herself in a two hundred year old toilet cubicle in the Ladies and trying to address the anxiety that had been with her all day, she dialled through to Furlong. Her DCI, funnily enough only five minutes earlier had used a slightly more modern convenience at Sheriff Andrew King's home. She and Hanlon had been there all day, carefully scrutinising all areas of the property and searching for valuable clues of some sort. The bathroom facility there, included every mod con you could think of and could only have been revamped about a year or two ago. With nearly two centuries of plumbing separating the fraternity sisters, Sandra Kerr spoke up. A quiet whisper was all that was required and a beautiful echo reverberated around the ceramic walls and floors.

In a light waspish voice, she enquired. "Ma'am, I'm sorry to disturb you. Are you and Sherlock finished up at Port Seton, yet?"

"Not quite, but soon Sandy. We've come across a wall safe and now we're just waiting for a locksmith. We're certainly curious to find out what Mr King kept inside."

Then quickly remembering that it was her Sergeant that had called her, she backtracked and apologised.

"Sorry, Sandy, you phoned me. What can I do for you?"

"It's just, I..." Kerr hesitated. She couldn't bring herself to speak. She was choking up."It's about last night," she managed. "And this morning," she later added.

"You're fine, Sergeant Kerr." DCI Furlong professionalised the conversation simply by addressing Sandy by her rank.

With her years of experience she could hear the gentle quivering in Kerr's voice. She was emotional and on edge, Barbra guessed. As were each of the team currently. A number of deaths, no clear leads and a handful of links connecting two of the bodies. Plus a series of nursery rhymes connecting them all. It wasn't an easy time.

"I just wanted to apologise, Ma'am. I let you down, I let the team down and most importantly, I let myself down."

Again remaining professional, DCI Furlong responded with...

"I don't know about any of that, Sergeant Kerr. But can I thoughtfully remind you, that up until the others left and only two more individuals remained, both of whom you know well. That up until then, you hadn't even had a drink, you were great company and you actively and positively contributed all night long." She then paused. A trick that she learned from her new sleeping partner.

"It was only when you had to relive and relate to us all about Maurice Orr's past, that things got to you. We sat and we talked. We had a few drinks by the fireplace and thirty minutes later you dragged yourself off to the spare bedroom. No harm done whatsoever. My biggest disappointment in you, was that you never even spilled the beans on any juicy gossip about your workmates. Although you did keep going on about a certain Steven Murray's recent restaurant visit and his favourite choice of music!"

Kerr could feel the heat glowing in her cheeks. By now they must be well beyond an attractive rosiness. They must be marking her out as a social incompetent. Thank goodness she was locked away in the basement vaults of the old Leith Town Hall. She had previously felt that all her insecurities were writ large across her face and there was nowhere to hide. But listening to Furlong's generous and kind words, Sandy's anxieties had mellowed and she had been reassured.

"Thank you, Ma'am, I needed that. Can I just add and it's probably no surprise to you, that both 'Sherlock' and myself overheard the Inspector's words to you last night."

"Sadly, no surprise, you're right. Go on..."

"I just want you to know that ALL the team loves working with you. That they are so grateful for the support that you continually offer them, tonight being the perfect example. And that each of us feel privileged to have YOU lead our team. Thank you, Ma'am. I'll see you later."

The call ended with a tear being shed in both sets of eyes.

Whilst back on the shores of the River Clyde...

"There will be no need for you to sit in with us today Miss Loggenberg. The guard at the door will suffice. You can go. Thank you once again for arranging the meeting though."

Short, sharp and to the point. Whatever way you wanted to look at it, Murray was not up for the long drawn out meeting of last time. One with Maurice Orr in control and calling all the shots. Especially now that they were fully aware of the nursery rhyme connection. Admittedly, they still had no idea why. But they were working on plenty of leads and every 24 hours would get them a little closer. At least that is what Steven Murray remembered DCI Furlong telling the media. He smiled across the well used beechwood desk at Maurice Orr and began to hum...

'Me and the farmer get on fine, through stormy weather and bottles of wine. If I pull my weight he'll treat me well, if I'm late he'll give me hell.'

Cavalier laughter echoed back at him. Not tinged with ridicule or dismissive in any way, but in recognition. DC Curry, aware that he'd missed the first leg of this important and highly competitive game, cautiously watched it play out.

"I guess, based on the farmer reference, you are now fully aware of my crimes, Inspector." Orr merrily announced. "Lacking that knowledge last time was a tad disrespectful. Don't you think?"

Murray remained silent and unimpressed.

"Would you like another agricultural reference in regard to your most recent find?"

The man spoke with a smug arrogance. Without delay his facade of charm and courteous deference changed instantly. It was immediately replaced with a self-righteous pride. The smarmy smile that accompanied both looks, unfortunately remained.

"On many levels you will get this, Inspector. Unfortunately you had left before we got to hear about 'Hickory Dickory Dock.' But like 'Humpty Dumpty,' someone had gone to a great deal of effort to make it work. So I would ask you. Who or what type of misguided individual are you looking for?"

'Misguided individual.' Murray abruptly paused and simply played around with those two words for a second. Two innocent words that had been uttered by a perverse human being. An evil man with no regard for life. A shameless specimen of man. A deviant that callously raped a teenage boy after having brutally slaughtered his mother only minute's earlier. The Detective Inspector had to quickly dispatch those particular thoughts from his mind or he would quickly lose this particular game, and it was far too important to lose at this point. He had done well these past few weeks surviving on his own steam and without any trace or shadow of his 'black dog' whatsoever. Every type of emotion is okay. He knew that. Each one helpful in the right situation. However, his dark emotions were like salt. Just a tiny pinch adds flavour, yet too much ruins the whole dish. So he remained silent and offered up his own insincere look of contentment and satisfaction as Orr spoke.

"This is the farmer sowing his corn - That kept the rooster that crowed in the morn - That woke the judge all shaven and shorn - That married the

man all tattered and torn - That kissed the maiden all forlorn - That milked the cow with the crumpled horn - That tossed the dog that worried the cat - That killed the rat that ate the malt - That lay in the house that Jack built."

"Sir? The house that..."

"I heard the man. Thank you Constable," Murray interrupted.

"A third body, I hear, Mr Murray. I told you there'd be more. So did any of the things I mentioned apply? The body found with a cow, a rat, a cat or a dog perchance?"

"None of the above," Murray replied.

But the Inspector knew that he didn't believe him. His denial had fooled no one. For when Orr had uttered the line about, *'that woke the judge all shaven and shorn.'* 'Kid' Curry flinched and froze like a rabbit in headlights.

"So a new recruit with you today, Mr Murray?"

Inmate 2764, was determined to scratch away at the things that most irritated the Inspector. He had obviously spotted being referred to as Mister was something that bugged Murray. The exact same way Steven Murray noticed that Maurice Orr never liked to be interrupted.

"Detective Constable Curry," the 'Kid' piped up. Keen to respond and be recognised as part of the investigation.

Possibly, too keen, going by his Inspector's gruff expression.

"So it was a prominent Lord or judge or..."

"Sandra Kerr was asking after you," Murray broke in.

2764's knuckles began slowly to visibly turn white from clenching his fists too hard. In contrast, gritting his teeth firmly in an effort to remain silent, gave Maurice Orr's face a rather intense glow. Not the popular scarlet or crimson. This was one of the very latest trending shades of red. It was known as... 'Suppressed Rage.'

Fourteen

"Some boys try and some boys lie, but I don't let them play. Only boys who save their pennies make my rainy day. 'Cause we're living in a material world and I'm a material girl. You know that we are living in a material world and I am a material girl."

- Madonna

A few tense moments passed in silence. With the exception of swelling chests and exhaled breaths on both sides. With his eyes closed and a rotation of his neck muscles complete, Maurice Orr looked poised, as if preparing to speak. Murray, on the other hand with a large satisfactory smirk hiding behind his present countenance, was anticipating just that. Would he counter or let him talk? He was undecided. The librarian then relaxed and stretched his fingers several times before he recommenced verbally.

"Ah, Sandy! Yes, I remember her, Inspector. Good looking woman with red hair."

He obviously did remember her, Curry thought to himself on hearing those remarks.

"So tell me. How is Detective Constable Kerr these days?"

"As I am sure you are well aware, Mr Orr. Sandy, is Detective Sergeant Kerr these days."

Not a flicker from Orr. Though Murray suspected he knew fine well her current rank.

"So I suggest a truce, Inspector. I'll address you correctly and you let me complete my remarks?"

Steven Murray went to interrupt, but decided against it.

"How does that sound, Mister Murray?" Orr smiled. Getting one last derogatory name check in.

The engaging, rather camp, singsong hybrid of emotions had returned to the voice of the over confident librarian. A man by all accounts that was now the most knowledgeable in Scotland with regard to nursery rhymes.

"Let's see," the DI uttered. "Agreed." He stated, before adding, "He was a Sheriff and a King. Andrew King. The rhyme was Six a Song of Sixpence. So today, I don't really know why I'm here Mr Orr. Because you certainly figured it out for us early on and although not a trained profiler or psychologist, you confidently hinted that they would strike again. Little did we know, that as we spoke, Doctor Crossland's death had been confirmed as another one for our 'Nursery Rhyme' killer."

"One thing that I omitted to mention last time, DI Murray and I think it may be of real significance for you. Is the fact that later lines and narrative in the rhymes are often much more sinister and gory. It's just that we don't always know those parts of the story. It's like being very familiar with the chorus of a song, but none the wiser with any of its verses. So I hope that is useful. But listening to you today, I'm hearing that you don't think I can help you further, Inspector. Would that be right?"

"Well unless you have some way of predicting the killer's next movements and where they will strike precisely? Then no, I can't possibly see how you can assist us further, Mr Orr. I mean now that we know he or she is killing based on old children's songs and tales. We are more than capable of joining those dots. Dots that as I see it are currently of no worth or value to us. We already have victims, they are already dead. What we have to do now is join up the dots between those murdered. That is how we stop the next potential threat Mr Orr. Working backwards I'm afraid and I don't believe a convicted murderer and rapist can be of any help to us on that score. Do you?"

Wow, Andrew Curry thought. That certainly told the man. His DI seemed to cover all bases. He thanked him. He appreciated his limited knowledge in a specific field. Then he questioned his ability in general to contribute. He reminded him of his deviant past and his limited access to assist moving forward. His Inspector seemed to run his hand over a keyboard in an attempt to push all the buttons and see if he could get any reaction. At present that response looked like...

Maurice Orr's brain had stuttered momentarily. His eyes took in more light than expected and every part of him had paused while he caught up with the Inspector's rapid statement of thoughts and opinions.

"Thank you once again for your initial help. But we'll leave you to get back to your important indexing, Mr Orr."

Murray hoped that he had struck the right balance. That his tone was a dismissive acknowledgment, a less than courteous expression of gratitude. In fact, in his actions, he had hoped that he had cut the man off in mid sentence. And they both knew he didn't like that.

Inspector Murray turned to his young colleague, put a finger to his lips to indicate silence and then gestured for 'Kid' Curry to get up and follow him from the room. Both men departed and left the lone figure to sit and contemplate with only his silent guard for company.

Outside in the corridor, Murray took a large breath before exhaling mightily. A few other deep breaths followed. Curry recognised that his Inspector had obviously found that far more intense and exhausting than he had made it appear. He then slumped over double.

"Are you okay, sir?" A concerned Curry asked.

A distant rumble echoed up from between his knees. "I'm getting no younger for those situations, son."

Another large sigh followed. A few seconds later and his full six foot one frame resurfaced, ready to continue.

"Are we going back in, sir?" Curry inquired.

"Absolutely NOT," came the firm reply. By this point Murray was walking at pace down the corridor. "We have to follow protocol now DC Curry and go and say thank you and goodbye to Governor Loggenberg. I know that you'll be disappointed to hear that."

The slight hint of a grin on the Inspector's innocent face was nothing compared to 'the cat that had just gotten the cream,' dawdling ten feet behind him.

Steven Murray stifled another smile, as Loggenberg's efficient looking secretary showed both officers through into Rebecca's office. The woman's age and appearance gave you the distinct impression that she had been at the prison since the ribbons were cut on its opening day. A thought that Murray shared as part of his mentorship with young Drew.

"When was that, sir?"

"A hundred and six years ago!"

'Kid' Curry spluttered, choked and laughed just as Rebecca Loggenberg came into sight. That was not the impression this unattached professional police officer had wished to portray. Murray on the other hand was about to change tact rather quickly. Something unexpected had come to his attention. Something that would definitely require further investigation.

"That was an exceptionally brief visit with our *'black sheep'* to-day, Inspector." The woman stated candidly.

She was now comfortably sitting behind her desk working on paperwork, and by the looks of things, plenty of it. Her waist-coat buttons had been undone and she was in real practical, 'roll up your sleeves and get tore in' mode. Which was quite ironic, as she had removed her jacket, revealing her charcoal blouse to be sleeveless.

"Governor, can I just say that is quite a stunningly attractive blouse you're wearing."

Andrew Curry was taken aback by what seemed a rather overtly personal and over the top statement. Especially one made in public. He could feel his cheeks burn and turn a rather interesting colour. A shade, he guessed, that lay positioned somewhere between cranberry juice and a fine red vintage.

Not a hint of embarrassment on the face of the recipient though. Rebecca Loggenberg loved adoration. She was a big follower of celebrities and stylists on Instagram. In fact, she herself had over twenty thousand followers. Fashion and beauty were most definitely her thing. Trailing in a distant third on that list was law and the prison service. Although, Murray had a feeling that even they may be edged out by... Health, Fitness, Personal Development, Massages, Makeovers, Gossip Pages, Nail Bars, Spas and numerous other prideful pursuits.

"I'm so glad that you like it, Inspector. I always dress to impress. So thank you. Most men, or should I say boys would not have the confidence to speak their mind. They would give you some cock'n bull story, rather than be honest with you."

Murray began to allow his head to sway from side to side. In a rather shy, nervous school boy kind of way. Appearing momentarily vulnerable and weak.

"My apologies, Inspector. I didn't mean to make you feel uncomfortable."

"No, no, indeed you didn't, Ma'am. It's just I have a friend, a lady friend that I think that style and design would look pretty good on..."

Loggenberg laughed gently and smiled. "...and you'd like to know where to buy it?"

"Well, that for sure," he said. Sticking with the hesitant, uncertain, little boy lost approach. "But you know what men are like Miss Loggenberg, sure to mess things up. So I was wondering, to be on the safe side. Would you mind if I got a picture of it. Just to ensure I end up getting exactly the right one. Or I may even send her the picture and double check she would be happy with it, rather than surprise her. What do you think?"

Again playing to her ego, Murray was confident of her response.

"Absolutely!" She announced. More than happy to have her picture taken and be the elite influencer that she believed she was. "Although I would purchase and surprise. That's the best way. But that may be a challenge for you. For you'll not get the exact same one, Inspector."

Murray's puzzled expression required more.

"It's because they're exclusive to the individual, Inspector. You'd need to arrange a personal fitting, Steven."

"Then I'll do just that," he replied. Adding, "Thank you, Rebecca."

All this while Detective Constable 'Kid' Curry stood by his Inspector's side and cringed. Initially he had wished he'd adopted his Western persona five minutes earlier and ridden off into the sunset. Intimate flirting, first names being used and seamstress addresses required. That was all good and well, but as soon as the embarrassed schoolboy came out to play, that gave the game away. That was when the Curry knew that his Inspector was up to something. The DI he knew, didn't do flustered, adolescent teenager. So Murray had clearly spotted a flaw, a chink in her armour, a weakness that he was prepared to exploit. One that required him to appear timid and mild to breach her defences. But for the life of him, the 'Kid' had no idea what it was. Which was exactly what Murray had hoped.

"Drew. DC Curry, would you mind doing the honours with your camera? I have no memory left on my phone."

"Aye, right," he said sarcastically. But in a low whisper.

"Sorry?"

"Aye, right away, sir." Came the louder, positive response.

What was this wily old fox up to? What or how did the Governor of Greenock Prison factor into all of this? Or was he genuinely wanting some fashion tips? The 'Kid' had heard rumours that Murray was actually dating. I'm not going there, he thought, before retrieving his mobile from his jacket pocket.

"Right. Where would you like me to start, sir?"

"Don't ask me Constable. Our star model here will keep you right." Rebecca Loggenberg rose from her desk. Her long flowing locks teasingly hung curled over one shoulder. She was in full sexy Rapunzel mode. More fairy tale than nursery rhyme.

"Take a couple of close-up shots from the side," Murray stressed. "Anywhere else, sir" Curry asked. Now happy to play along.

A selection of shots were approved and recommended. And a name, address and phone number, one that would get a blouse or two made for his special lady friend was handed over.

"Thank you again for everything, Governor Loggenberg," Murray offered sincerely.

As the two policemen stood at the open door and expressed their goodbyes. This rather unconventional prison Governor asked one final playful question and in a rather suggestive tone.

"This female friend of yours. Does she have a name?"

Time stood still. Loggenberg pierced the Inspector's blue eyes with hers. She ran a seductive finger across her lips, sat on the corner of her desk and provocatively crossed her legs. Her expensive court shoes had nowhere to hide. Curry held his breath. Would he be the first to hear about this mystery lady? Steven Murray cleared his throat and began to gesture his Constable toward the corridor. As he placed his palm on the large round, aged door knob, an experienced Steven Murray proffered...

"Oh, indeed she does Ma'am. Thank you for asking."

The heavy oak door swung closed behind him. It was straight out through the parking area and back safely inside the car, before either man resumed speaking.

"Right DC Curry, I'll drive us toward the town centre. In the meantime, you get that jack-of-all-trades phone back out and use it to locate for us a tattoo studio here in Greenock."

"Sir?"

"You heard right. So search. I want to be there in 5 minutes."

It occurred to the teenager that she'd never truly been thirsty before. A refreshment was generally always on hand. At home they were sparkling, cool and flavoured, the ice jangled and enticed her to drink. Never once had she drank to quench her discomfort. But right now, just plain water would be a God-send. The urge to drink dominated her every thought.

Fifteen

"Oh what fun we had. But, did it really turn out bad? All I learnt at school was how to bend not break the rules. Oh what fun we had, but at the time it seemed so bad. Trying different ways to make a difference to..."

- Madness

Whilst beguiling, come-hither eyes and other sexy enticing signals were being displayed in the Inverclyde area of Scotland. In the bleak rain swept community of Balerno, Jack Cannon's impressive home was once again deemed the ideal rendezvous for his son and daughter to meet up with Detectives Kerr and Boyd. On arrival the first thing Billy Cannon did was inform the officers that Suzanne was running late, possibly up to an hour.

"Not a problem," Sandy said and Boyd nodded in agreement. Kerr then immediately sniffed and smelled the pungent air. With the fiery temperament of Suzanne not present, the Detective Sergeant felt that it was probably safe enough to offer up some hygiene advice.

"You may want to open a window or two Mr Cannon. It feels rather stuffy in here today."

"I've got a bit of a cold, Sergeant. But, yes, I thought it was a bit off. We'll look to give the place a good airing in the next week or two. Not looking forward to that though."

The puzzled look on both faces gave it away.

"Packing everything up, I mean. Getting rid of all of dad's personal belongings and such."

"Ah, yes. That can't be easy," Allan Boyd added. "Then putting it on the market?" He inquired. A typical police follow-up question.

"That's still to be decided. You see, Dad told Suzanne and I a couple of years ago, that he had left everything to his grandchildren. Each one of them were to be given an equal share. So possibly we may keep the house and rent it out."

All three individuals were now sitting in the same front room as before.

"Sir," Kerr announced. "The thing is, unfortunately we discovered another dead body this morning. A man by the name of Andrew King. Ring any bells at all?" She asked.

"The one over at Port Seton?" Billy Cannon asked immediately. "I heard bulletins on BBC news throughout the day about it."

"Indeed," said DC Boyd. "But that doesn't answer my Sergeant's question, sir. Does it?"

Rather flushed now, the hard working father asked Sandy to repeat the deceased's name.

"Sheriff Andrew King. He was unmarried and had no childr..."

"No, no, I don't know the man," Cannon said. Feeling the urgent need to interrupt Sandra Kerr in mid sentence.

"Really, sir? You didn't even give me the chance to tell you a little bit about the man."

"Sorry, that was rude of me. But there's really no need to Sergeant. I've never heard of him, so that would be a waste of everyone's time."

Allan Boyd gently pushed himself further back onto the leather sofa. He was just getting comfortable for the next part of their conversation. They were working well together as a team these days and the five foot, five inch Glaswegian had been paired with Sandra Kerr for just one month short of a year. She had been well trained and Steven Murray's influence was clear to see.

"You've opened a window or two now Mr Cannon. So hopefully that may help with not only the smell, but as you seem to be a little flushed and red in the face, possibly with yourself also. Any particular reason that you should be feeling the heat to that degree?"

"Sergeant, why are we back here again?"

The man's tone for the first time in all their interactions with him, was noticeably different. It was cold, not welcoming or apologetic like before. Previously, he had always come across as the peacemaker. The friendly, genial and certainly more amiable and easy going of the two siblings. So what had changed? Had he just experienced a lightbulb moment, such as the one that Kerr received that morning?

"The walls, the walls, the walls," she sang. Her voice at mid-level and sounding kind of like a husky female Hunchback of Notre Dame. "This morning we got left a clue, sir"

Boyd grinned and continued to enjoy the show, whilst Cannon was less than convinced.

"You see for everyone else, it just cemented the fact that Andrew King was part of our attacker's group. Our current select group of bodies. Each one belonging to..."

"The Nursery Rhyme killer!" Billy Cannon finished off for her.

"You certainly seem to enjoy listening to those radio and TV reporters," Allan Boyd remarked.

"For me though, the clue meant more than that, sir," Kerr emphasised. "My eureka moment only led me back here and to the walls, the walls, those covered walls. On my way out the other day, I made myself familiar with all of those photographs that your sister and Constable Boyd here, were so busy scouring at the beginning of our visit. Would you mind, Mr Cannon?"

Sergeant Kerr then gestured to Billy Cannon to lead them back through to the stairwell. It was there that Jack Cannon's range of framed Primary and High School prints ran up sideways upon the wall.

"I noticed it clear as day, last time. But I was heading out and it wasn't your dad. So it was of no importance to me. Apart from the fact that he is one of our team, he's in our weird group."

When she made that last remark, she focused solely on DC Boyd. But even he was lost at that point. Because like her trusted mentor, Kerr loved to keep those mystery endings close to her chest and private, right up until the last second. Mainly because copying DI Murray, she liked to do her Miss Marple thing and slowly roll out all the clues one by one.

"Constable, look carefully, he is the only one in each picture that looks anything like you or I."

"You or I, Sarge?" It then twigged. "You mean the red-haired guy."

Allan Boyd now appeared to press his nose right up to the frame.

"I think you are right, Sandy. Sure enough, that young ginger was the spitting image of Andrew King."

"Now correct me if I am wrong here, Mr Cannon. But he has managed to be seated on the front row in every picture and has his hands positioned firmly on his knees."

William Cannon had not heard anything untoward in that comment, so was happy to nod and speak. "But that wasn't a question, Sergeant."

"Ah, well spotted, sir. But this is. Isn't he sitting next to your father in all four of those pictures?"

"So he may have been a friend of my dad's during their schooldays, Sergeant Kerr. But that was over half a century ago. That doesn't mean that I know or knew of the man."

Again no one spoke. Silence. Sandra Kerr did not like playing this particular card and it was not often that she ever felt the need to play it. In fact, it was so little used, she was fairly certain that in their eleven months together, DC Boyd had never actually witnessed her play it previously. Grim-faced and sullen, Kerr then broke the harsh truth to William Cannon.

"Sir, did you know that your kind hearted and generous, loving father was a life-long paedophile?"

Boyd stood rooted to the spot. He had certainly not seen that one coming.

Billy Cannon erupted. "What! Where did you get that from? Who told you that pack of lies?"

Fires of fury and hatred were smouldering in his small narrowed eyes as he weighed the pros and cons of the various and creative means available to him to respond.

"What evidence do you have? What's going on here, Sergeant? Why would you say such a cruel, hurtful thing?"

Allan Boyd had a good idea why, but decided to let Sandy play it out, and she stuck with it.

"Sir, Mr Cannon, I think we need to go back through to the sitting room and have me explain."

"Explain! Explain what? How you fabricate evidence? How you lie to the media?"

"Mr Cannon," Boyd interrupted. "Why don't we head back through... " The Constable made a move to touch his shoulder.

"Get your hands off of me." Cannon screamed. "Are you in on this?"

Kerr then raised her voice substantially.

"Mr Cannon, you have told us several times about hearing things on the radio, seeing TV coverage or press bulletins during our last couple of visits. Now let me tell you that everything you see and hear is not always true. But let me also tell you that it often leaves a lasting impression. As the old saying goes: Mud sticks! So let me lay this out for you. I am about to give you one last chance to help us catch whoever is doing this. The warped individual who is tearing families like yours apart. Remember we have others like you and your sister who are grieving also and they want answers. In fact, again like you, they seek justice."

Cannon's chest was still frantically rising and falling. His anger only slightly receded. Boyd sat with an arm around the man's shoulders. Half to calm him down and half to prevent a possible lunge forward toward his daring, yet foolish Sergeant.

"So," Sandra Kerr continued. "Either we let it be known to the press that we believe the murdered man, Jack Cannon, had certain predilections and tendencies and besmirch his good name. Or you can come clean with us and tell us whatever the hell it is that you've been covering up." Raising her voice, considerably upped the ante. "We don't care about other misdemeanours or petty family issues, Mr Cannon." She powerfully prodded the man's chest, to which even Allan Boyd flinched. "We are desperately trying to catch a murderer here," she strained. "Your father's killer no less! Do you even remember that?"

After everyone took a few seconds out and tensions gradually eased. A full minute or two of quiet reflection passed. It was then that Billy Cannon spoke up. He began with a low murmur.

"I get it, Sergeant. I do. Although that seemed a pretty cheap shot to take."

Kerr simply shrugged and replied. "But did it work? What can you tell us?"

The son nodded his head slowly. "He was the Sheriff in the Fatal Accident Inquiry."

"What!" Allan Boyd exclaimed. "Ah geez! Now there's a right turn up for the books."

Kerr was silenced for the first time in five minutes.

"We'll need to let Murray and Furlong know straight away," Boyd encouraged.

Only just getting her head around this turn of events, Sandy declared... "Okay, sure, fine. Just send them a text. We'll update them in person later."

Within 30 seconds, that was exactly what Allan Boyd did. He could only imagine DCI Furlong's face when she read his text. It was thirty years ago, but that just made him wonder how corrupt or bent the system had been all this time. Even in hindsight, Boyd assumed favours must have been required.

"You had told us that your father's business had been cleared of any wrongdoings, wasn't that correct?"

"Absolutely, Sergeant." Cannon replied. Though his response was far from convincing.

"Spit it out. All of it," Kerr insisted.

"He'd always had regrets and remorse about THAT man's death. That was how he would refer to it. He never personalised it by calling him by name."

"And what name should he have personalised it with? Because I bet you never forgot it?" Boyd asked.

William Cannon was beginning to crumble now.

"Text your sister and tell her not to bother meeting us. She doesn't need to see or hear any of this. Because I now know for a fact that we will be needing to speak to you again. Only next time it will be well away from the foul smell of corruption and death that lurks within these walls and it will be down at our friendly, local police station in Leith."

As Kerr spoke, Billy Cannon texted Suzanne and responded with...

"I didn't even know that there was a station in Leith."

"Easy to miss it," Allan Boyd said, tongue in cheek. "The building has only been there for nearly two hundred years."

Cannon's eyes rolled at that fact.

"Now fill us in with some details, sir," Sandy encouraged him.

"Because some of us are working late into the night."

"We are?" Boyd questioned.

"Oh, make no mistake Constable, that invite for us all to go to the DCI's home tonight will be long and gruelling."

That was based on her memory of the night before and still wearing the same clothes. DS Sandra Kerr allowed herself a small, self-satisfactory smirk at that. Then got back to the business in hand.

"You were saying Mr Cannon..."

Going back thirty years, the son told them how he had noticed his father taking shortcuts over the previous few months leading up to the accident. How Jack Cannon had started to buy inferior concrete and cheap poorly produced bricks. Other products, that previously his father had said were hopeless and no good, they started to use.

"I know that it's no excuse, but I was only 19 or 20 at the time. I was still a kid myself. Naive and wet behind the ears. I had no actual idea what was really going on, although I assumed things were obviously tight financially. I never ever found out if it was just good fortune or by design that 'Andy' King headed up the inquiry. Andy was what dad called him."

"And when was this?" Boyd asked.

"Sheriff King declared his findings that afternoon and by midnight, dad was putting the world to rights and sharing all sorts of things with me that I wish he hadn't."

"And your sister?" asked Kerr.

"Suzy was sound asleep. Remember she would've only been about five or so."

Boyd was taking a few notes. Whilst Sandy pondered on the accuracy, truthfulness, and or maybe the completeness of his recollections. She couldn't help but feel he was still holding something back.

Billy Cannon went to continue. "So yes, that night, after the Sheriff's Ruling..."

"Determination," Kerr interrupted.

"Sorry?"

"It's a Determination, not a Ruling, Mr Cannon," she reminded him.

"Ah, yes, I'm remembering that now. Thank you, Sergeant."

Kerr nodded.

"Anyway," Billy Cannon continued. "It was that night when he first pointed Andrew King out to me in those photos. Up until then I never knew that they were even schoolboy pals. Suzanne still doesn't know, Sergeant Kerr."

"So throughout the whole of the proceedings and everything running up to it. He had never hinted at anything? You never saw them together? Throughout the years, nothing?"

"Exactly that. I mean maybe when I was still in school, he was in touch with him or met for drinks, I don't know. But since I was old enough to accompany dad into the pub after work, I had never seen or heard of that man until that inquiry."

"And in the last thirty years?" Boyd contributed. "Nothing?"

Cannon shook his head.

"Really?" Kerr stated sarcastically. "And with your father a paedophile, as well!"

"Nothing, I'm telling you. Obviously I've seen his name occasionally in the papers, but that is it. That is all."

He was lying, Kerr concluded. But that would do for this afternoon. All those years ago Andrew King had sold his soul to help save a schoolboy friend from ruin. But why? And had that been his only corrupt deed? It may well have been. But who can be sure? Who else had been aware of it? A whole messy can of worms was about to open up here. Thirty years ago the dutiful Sheriff had ridden into town to rescue Jack Cannon, a man he hadn't even kept in touch with since school. It didn't make sense, nor hold true.

Kerr whispered a historic thought to Allan Boyd. "Surely, 'Hanna' Hayes and 'Kid' Curry, the two most notorious outlaws in the history of the west, should be dealing with this 'dodgy' Sheriff."

They both offered up a much needed smile of light relief.

"I suspect this is going to have some serious repercussions, Mr Cannon. For you and ourselves. What about the name of the man that was killed. I am assuming that is something you've never forgotten."

"You would think Sergeant Kerr. Yet, the irony of that is that every day for the past thirty years, I have desperately tried to forget it and had succeeded quite nicely up until now."

He paused, as if recalling a name from well over a quarter of a century ago. What are the chances?

"It was Frost, I think. A Mister Liam or Ian Frost."

"And what about..."

"They never ever told you his great grandson's name," he interjected. "Just that he was six years of age and at that point, still in hospital with serious injuries."

"Allan," Kerr addressed her Constable. "Given what we unfortunately now know about our 'Sing a Song of Sixpence' man, please send a brief summation by text over to Lizzie and see if she can chase up some background for us. Especially on an Ian or Liam Frost and his great grandson."

"Will do, Sarge." Boyd responded. "Straightaway, I'm on it!"

Suddenly - Bang... Bang... Bang... What was a steady pounding on the front door, was quickly followed up with a quick-fire successive sound of knuckles... chap, chap, chap.

"It's me, it's me, it's Suzanne," the voice yelled out. "Hurry up, let me in."

Allan Boyd was first to react. "Miss Cannon, what's wrong? You didn't have to come. Didn't you..."

"It's Stacey," she managed to blurt out. "She has disappeared!"

By which point, Sandra Kerr had literally dragged the poor mother through to the front room. Her brother began comforting her. Late afternoon rain had drenched the shaking woman. Trying to speak, adrenalin had kicked in and she was stuttering and stammering.

"Relax," Boyd encouraged her. "Relax and take those deep breaths. In through your nose and out through your mouth." He repeated that mantra several times. "Well done, we've got this, and again."

It took nearly five minutes to fully settle and relax her. To get her breathing back to something resembling normality.

"Suzanne, what are you desperately trying to tell us?" Kerr eventually asked again.

"On Sunday evening, the night dad went missing. We got into an argument. We didn't normally ever row. I guess I was uptight and anxious. Things got heated and she stormed out. That's why it was only Billy that was here when you came by that night. I stayed at home waiting for her to return. She sent me a text about ten minutes after she had left." Suzanne Cannon then handed her phone over to Sergeant Kerr.

"I take it you have called her since?" Sandy asked.

"Every quarter of an hour, if not more."

"The fact that she texted you only minutes after storming off is a good thing. You know that she left of her own volition and it wasn't pre-planned. It's not like your father's nightly walks, which were taken at the same time every evening."

"I suppose you're right, Sergeant," Suzanne mulled over. "But this is day five and still nothing. She has never answered or called. Probably most worrying is that she hasn't even text. She would have wanted to let me know that she was okay. But I think also, more than that, she would have wanted to know that I was okay."

"I notice she never said which friend."

"She only has two or three and I have tried all of them."

"Teenage girls," Kerr exclaimed. "I don't think the species has changed much over the years, Miss Cannon. Which means every one of them could be lying. They know all the excuses and are not going to inform on a mate."

"However, five days, Sarge," Boyd added. "That's not the norm for a mother and child fallout. Not by any means."

"Food? Money? A change of clothes? Did she take anything with her at all?" Kerr checked. "Her phone charger?"

"Nothing," the mother reaffirmed. "We argued. She left and I've not seen her since."

Suzy once again broke down and was consoled by her brother. Sandra Kerr then immediately phoned DI Murray with the news about Stacey. It went unanswered and she left a message for him to let DCI Furlong know also, but that she would update them both later, regardless.

The girl's head rose and fell at regular intervals. Her brain thought it was being stretched and let go like an elastic band. Her lips and mouth parched. Her eyes dry and puffy, becoming more and more desirous to close. She seemed to be fighting a losing battle on that score. Naked and locked away. No food, no drink, no hope is what she'd told herself. She had wanted to cry. But couldn't produce any tears. She had been sitting in a car about to head somewhere. Now she had no idea of her destination. Again her head slumped forward, only this time it never rose.

Sixteen

"Some may be from showing up, others are from growing up. Sometimes I was so messed up and didn't have a clue. I ain't winning no one over, I wear it just for you. I've got your name written here in a rose tattoo, in a rose tattoo."

- The Dropkick Murphys

'In the **BLINK** of an Eye,' was a seven minute drive away by the time Murray double parked directly outside. It was the most popular tattoo studio in the area and had been open for nearly eighteen years. That length of tenure clearly enhanced its credentials. Nowhere stays open nearly two decades in any industry these days, unless they are doing something right.

"They'll never let you park like this, sir, while you go inside."

"So glad to hear that 'Drew, because I'm not going in. You are. That way, I'll be free to drive away or sweet talk a friendly traffic warden should one come along. Though to be fair, I am far more likely to simply whip out my badge and encourage THEM to move along in that 'friendly, old Uncle' persona of mine."

"Why are we here?" Curry asked. With both voice and face exhibiting serious contorted tendencies.

"Look at those photos you took of..."

"I knew it, I knew you were up to something or that she was up to..."

"Keep quiet for one minute man. This goes no further and is between you and I only. Whatever you discover inside there is for no one else's ear's, with the exception of mine - Are we understood Constable?"

He soon got the severity of the operation and nodded. Although he still never knew what was required.

"Look at each of those photos that you have just taken 'Drew. That tattoo at the top of her forearm. It will have significance, I know it will. Find out all you can about it. What it signifies or represents? They all mean something or stand for something. I might not have any, but I at least know that all tattoos are special or symbolic to the individual in some way, shape or form. Then, let's get back up the road pronto and remember, you're driving."

In the short distance from the car to the shop doorway, the heavens in their thoughtfulness and generosity had opened once again. A mild damp coating sat upon the officer's head and shoulders as he entered. It was quiet inside. Not even any mind-numbing muzak being played in the background, to create an appropriate ambience. The bearded gentleman behind the desk rose to greet Andrew Curry. 'Drew thought it all very stereotypical so far. Lots of graphic designs on every wall. Many depicting weird abstract figures. Including diamanté clad Princesses, multi-coloured dragon slayers and each of course, with their ferocious animated beasts in tow. The man approaching him was in his late 40's or early 50's. Easily about 6' 2' and built to impress the ladies. However, as soon as he spoke... Wham! It was high pitched and camp. Very, very, very camp. Raymond, who wore a name badge, confirmed that he was not gay! It was a point he made to Andrew Curry in fast succession several times. In fact Raymond and his girlfriend owned the 'gallery' as he called it, and he was now equally as excited and keen to help assist the police in the inquiries.

"So what do you require? Tell me, tell me. Just tell me what do you require from me?"

"How did you know I was a Police Officer?" The 'Kid' asked at a normal pace.

"Oh, really!" And off he went again. "Really, really. You get a nose for it you know. A nose I tell you. It was so obvious. You are so obviously a policeman. Is it okay to be gay and in the police these days? So anyway, what do you require?" He asked once again.

Feeling rather intimidated in the voice department and thinking that was rather unusual phrasing with, 'what do you require?' And where did he get the 'Is it okay to be gay?' question. What was the towering man trying to say? Flustered and frustrated, DC Curry quickly opted to show him a couple of photographs.

"What can you tell me about that tattoo?"

"Mmm, not very good camera work, is it? The lighting, the way it has..."

"The tattoo, sir! Focus on the tattoo. Apologies for the cinematography not being up to speed for you."

"Well I was just saying, I mean..."

A temperamental sigh and a dismissive twist and wave of his hand had the Constable once again question the man's own sexuality. Although some of the incredibly intimate tattoos that adorned the man's bare arms certainly seemed to back up a heterosexual lifestyle. Having inadvertently viewed a few of them, 'Kid' Curry once again blushed profusely. The gallery owner must have the whole 'Kama Sutra' displayed on his biceps, he thought. On even further reflection he questioned - Maybe I'm just not cut out for this job?

"There are so many ways to show your eternal love for your partner, I mean just so many," Raymond started off by saying. "And getting matching tattoos is seen as a great option these days. This one used to be very popular back in the day... The Tumbling Panda! It's so cute. Don't you think it's cute, officer?"

"So this is part of a pair? Her... or his partner," he quickly added. "Would have one also."

His new best pal, Raymond - Nodded.

"And not as common, any more?" Curry followed up with.

"Occasionally," the man said. "But they really had their day about a decade or two ago. They were easily the most popular couple's tat for about five, six, maybe even seven years in a row. But the market was very different back then. They would have had them done separately. Went into small back street studios independently, if you know what I'm getting at officer? Are you sure you're a policeman?" Raymond playfully pinched Curry's glowing red cheek.

'The Kid' hesitated.

"I'm just teasing you. Having a laugh. You know, laughter? Or maybe not! But yes, 'The Tumbling Pandas,' are very much a symbol that you are in a relationship with another. These days for male and females, it is 'The Leprechaun,' with its little pot of gold and rainbow backdrop!"

Drew looked totally bamboozled at that.

"Me too! I don't get it either. It's all to do with good fortune and having the luck of the Irish with you at all times. Whatever floats your boat, I guess."

"I guess," the poor Constable managed to stutter. But his pal hadn't finished yet.

"Getting inked together is a great bonding experience," he added. "Ever thought about getting one, Constable? I would give you one you know! But like I said previously, I'm not that way inclined!"

Again the man let out a hearty, playful laugh. This time pushing Curry gently on the chest with his fingertips.

"Just having a laugh. I get it." Curry repeated. "Anything else you can tell me?"

"Well, you're cute looking," Raymond grinned.

Curry sighed and the light drizzle that had greeted him on entry was about to absolute drench him on exit.

"Seriously though," The giant, fun-filled fellow added. "When you choose a design to have done together you are sending out a clear statement about your relationship and you are intent on showing the world exactly what your other half means to you. Getting a matching tattoo is a beautiful way to celebrate your connection with your partner. Having the same tattoo links you together for life."

"So in essence, it represents being soulmates?"

"Absolutely," Raymond said.

"Couldn't you just have said that at the start?"

The large gregarious man's face fell flat.

"Just teasing. Just having a laugh!" The 'Kid' informed him. Getting his own back, before making for the door.

"Oh, by the way, officer. Can I ask you one question?"

"Of course you can, sir. And thanks for your help by the way."

"You're more than welcome, but answer me this. I do a little sign-writing for some local stores and businesses around the town and I was just wondering......" The man paused.

"Wondering what?" Curry encouraged.

For the first time that day the owner slowed his speech pattern down to one word per second.

"I was just wondering if you, yourself, had managed to get a taste of...... Miss Loggenberg's forbidden fruit?"

Gallery owner Raymond immediately smiled, licked his lips, winked and nodded all in one suggestive movement.

Andrew Curry closed the door sharply and hastily headed back toward the car. He accurately repeated the gist of all that was said to Inspector Murray. Remembering, deliberately, to forget that last part!

Seventeen

"Oh, Grace just hold me in your arms and let this moment linger. There won't be time to share our love for we must say goodbye."

- The Dubliners

"So 'Tumbling Pandas' - Everlasting love?"

"That's what he said, Inspector. Soulmates! It's a bonding thing... For life seemingly. Wow! There is never a dull moment when I travel with you, sir, that's for sure."

Curry instantly began to reflect on the tumultuous list of events that he'd been involved in that afternoon alone. It started by playing footsie with a murdering rapist; seductive sweet talking with a power dressing high priestess and finally, getting chatted up by a six foot plus, straight man! Geez, roll on tomorrow, he started thinking. Then he suddenly remembered, he still had tonight. At that - Murray's phone buzzed.

"What in the name of the wee man are you going on about, Constable. Sure, nothing exciting ever happens in my life."

Curry's facial expression was straight out of a Marx Brothers movie or maybe a low budget Abbott and Costello flick. Whichever one it was, they were both made in black and white, and Steven Murray recognised yet again that he was getting no younger. He eventually lifted his vibrating mobile from his pocket. The caller's name was clearly visible.

"Hi Lizzie. We've certainly kept you busy these past few days. What have you got for us this time, young lady?"

"I wouldn't want it any other way, Inspector." She began.

Andrew Curry liked Lizzie. But since his engagement ended a year or so ago, he 'liked' most people. Except for tall, bearded, forty-plus, tattooed white males it would appear! The I.T savvy, social media guru had enjoyed working more closely with Murray and his team of late. The past few workloads and this case in particular were proving to be no different.

"So, what's up?"

"It's about the girl stoned to death in Niddrie, sir. The one from just over a week ago..."

"Yes, yes, I know the one, Lizzie. What about her? No harm, but we have kind of put her death on the back-burner just now."

Curry looked across sharply, as he listened to his DI's language. Lizzie, on the other end of the phone also guessed that the Inspector was oblivious to the phrase involving 'back-burner,' that he'd just used.

"It's simply that we've got plenty going on trying to catch our Nursery Rhyme killer," he said.

"I am well aware of that, sir," she reminded him. Feeling rather slighted. "That is why after Humpty Dumpty, Hickory Dickory Dock and this morning's..."

"Six a Song of Sixpence," he reminded her. Perfectly sure she didn't need any coaxing.

"Quite," she said sternly.

She didn't go by Radical Lizzie for nothing. She may be young, but she was no pushover. Not someone to be taken for granted or disrespected and Detective Inspector Murray should have known better.

"Maybe I was mistaken," she said mockingly. "It's just that I thought, given all those nursery rhyme characters, you might have been interested when the words, Lucy Locket, make an appearance on my screen. Was I wrong?"

"What! What do you mean?"

The line went silent. Neither party willing to concede an inch. The old hand and the young pretender. Another second or two passed. Curry monitored it all, because Murray had put her on speakerphone to drown out all the traffic sounds from outside. The 'Kid's' puppy dog eye movements may have swayed him, for it was Murray that caved in first.

"Okay, okay, I'm sorry for being so snippy, Lizzie. But what are you telling me here?"

"She must have been the first victim, sir. Flew in under the radar as we had nothing to connect it with. Another junkie waster? A low-priority life that no one cared about. Just like you said, sir."

"I didn't quite put it like..." Murray stopped himself.

Sadly, that was exactly what he had said. Even if not in his actual spoken words. It was certainly what he'd implied. It was definitely the way he had treated her in his actions. But Lizzie had touched on it. They had to prioritise. They simply didn't always have the manpower and resources, especially the funding to follow up as thoroughly and as dedicatedly with every single case. So sometimes assumptions were made. Terribly misjudged assumptions, that allowed real people to suffer and fall through the gaps. This was one such occasion.

"It was actually a member of the forensics team that had put me onto it, sir. They had discovered what they'd thought may have been an old bank or Visa card. Seemingly whatever way her body had been bent over and angled during the fire, it had remained fairly intact. It had been in the tiny extra pocket within the main right-hand one of her jeans. Why does that even exist?" Lizzie questioned and then answered herself. "I suppose I should ask DCI Furlong?"

Murray laughed aloud. Andrew Curry smiled, but concentrated on the road.

"Anyway, sir. Turns out it wasn't a credit or debit card, but an old Cineworld card. One that I was able to work my magic with and track down her identity from."

"Seriously? From a numbered cinema card?"

"And her address," she announced proudly. "Which I have just sent you." She then added... "Although."

"I don't do well with - Although's! What does that mean?"

"As long as it wasn't a stolen card!" She commented hesitantly.

Murray sighed. Sarcasm at the ready. "Yes, well let's assume that she wasn't travelling around with some random strangers cinema card. That being the case, what can you tell me, Lizzie?"

"If it is her, sir. Then she is or was, only nineteen and has been on our missing persons list for the past six years."

"Oh, crap," Murray exclaimed. Both Inspector and Constable frowned.

A resigned knowledge in his voice knew that someone was going to have to break this news to someone else. That someone else being either a lone parent or parents. One that couldn't care less and had never treated her well in the first place and were actually glad to see the back of their child, or possibly a decent individual or partnership, a married couple even, that had literally been dreading this day coming for years!

"She was only 13 when she left home or at least was reported missing, sir."

"This is all good and well, Lizzie. But pray tell, where did you make the 'Lucy Locket' nursery rhyme connection from that information?"

Lizzie spoke as both her colleagues listened intently. As darkness fell, Detective Constable Andrew Curry drove carefully along the M8 motorway. At that moment, passing Glasgow International Airport on their left hand side.

"The girl's real name was Grace Adam, Inspector," Lizzie announced. "And I made some inquiries into that particular rhyme's origins because when I thought about the life she seemed to be leading, the circumstances in which we found her and the fact that the words... 'Lucy Locket' had been scrawled onto the Cineworld card (Murray knew she'd be grinning at that point). I just put two and two together and thought to contact you and let you do what you do best. You're the one that gets paid the big bucks to investigate it further."

Murray considered. Was she flirting with me? Big bucks! The young ones these days had a way of making everything seem flirtatious. The thought that she, Lizzie, could have been his very own Grace Adam, sobered him up quick enough though.

"Let me know how you get on, sir. Please."

"Don't you worry, I will." He confirmed courteously. "Oh and Lizzie, by the way. Two things..."

The young technical recruit froze at her end of the line, at those words.

"Sir?" She once again politely addressed him, as she always did.

Without missing a beat Murray declared. "It's a real pleasure to have you as part of our team. We genuinely would have been at a loss without you involved in this case. Modern police work is more and more about forensics, both digital and physical, I get that. And although I may not always fully understand how it works, I do fully appreciate its importance and the importance of those who do get it, and who carry it out for us mere mortals. Thank you for that invaluable contribution, young lady."

Unseen, Radical Lizzie was happy to blush and take on-board all the compliments generously offered up. However, she was also fully aware that...

"You said two things, sir?"

"Oh, yes. Here to finish off with is a twenty second blast of old-style police work. Knowledge accrued through living a somewhat humdrum, non-achieving life."

"I don't believe that you could have ever lived a humdrum, non- achieving life, sir"

Lizzie had assumed he was being somewhat self-deprecating. When suddenly he began...

"Some people called it a ticket pocket. In more recent years a condom pocket. Generally these days it is now known as a coin pocket. And this is all without the help of DCI Barbra Furlong remember."

Smiles would be in place at both ends of their respective phones with that particular observation. Then the humble DI continued...

"It came about in the 1800's and it was designed to be a fob pocket. Levi's introduced that specific area to keep your watch in!" he stated succinctly. Before adding, "Good-bye Lizzie and thanks again."

Murray hung up and quickly decided to call the aforementioned DCI Furlong. He had an idea and it involved inviting her out for a drink. However, he immediately cancelled the call. Forgetting - One, that Curry was with him, and - Two, that he would see his DCI in about three hours time at her home once again. Where Lucy Locket and all the others would doubtless be the number one topic of discussion. He then listened to a voicemail that had come through as he spoke with Lizzie. It was Sandra Kerr informing him about Stacey Cannon and would he let the DCI know. He immediately called Barbra Furlong's number once again. This time making her aware of the young girl's plight and holding back on the drinks invitation until later.

What a day! With age taking its toll, the Inspector sat back and thought about Rebecca Loggenberg's tattoo. With age also taking its toll on his young Constable. 'Kid' Curry sat back, rested his hands carefully on the steering wheel and thought lovingly about Rebecca Loggenberg's back pocket!

Eighteen

"Wish me love, a wishing well to kiss and tell. A wishing well of butterfly tears. Wish me love, a wishing well to kiss and tell. A wishing well of crocodile cheers."

- Terence Trent D'Arby

The narrow, normally deserted streets in and around Dirleton village were exceptionally busy that evening. The team of officers had travelled the twenty miles east of Edinburgh and gathered. Some for the second night in a row. Their DCI's text and email invitation that had been sent earlier that morning had stated clearly... 7.30 for 8.00pm

The Chief Inspector knew that they would all be coming from various parts of the city. Plus, she was well aware that 'Kid' Curry and Steven Murray were travelling back from Greenock. Joe Hanlon who had accompanied his DCI all day, came straight back with his Chief Inspector to her cottage at slightly after 6pm. 'Sherlock' had made himself busy, as you would expect. Based on the fact that he knew Barbra Furlong was a neat freak and always liked everything spick and span and in its place. He helped to spruce up the small front room and tidy up the kitchen from the night before. He had easily surmised that Sandy and her had stayed up late and chatted the previous evening. He too, was also well aware of the emotional turmoil that the memories had caused to his Sergeant. Now at 7.40pm he was about to return back from a special assignment. One that he had felt honoured to have been given at short notice an hour ago. Especially as his Chief Inspector said it was a responsible task that she would not entrust to everyone. Detective Constable Joseph Hanlon was out walking three miles. '3 Miles,' of course, being the trusted name of DCI Furlong's beloved pet dog!

Even in the pitch black, Joe Hanlon and 'three miles' had probably ventured half a mile from his boss's lovely two-bedroomed cottage. A ten to twelve minute walk away was Dirleton Castle. The well preserved medieval fortress which now belonged to Historic Scotland, was adjudged by 'Sherlock' to be the ideal turning point. It had been a gentle shower that caught out both man and dog.

As 'three miles' barked, leaped and happily rolled on the wet grass verge outside the castle walls. Hanlon seemed to have been caught in a rather surreal daze. He stretched out his hand and temporarily imagined that each individual raindrop was a kaleidoscope. He wondered as he walked, how it would be to stop time, to suspend this watery gift and peek through each solitary one. Perhaps it would be fun to sit inside those raindrops and take that gravity propelled ride to earth. As he imagined it, he felt his inner-self laughing a little, both at the crazy daydream and also at his own silliness. He saw the rain beating upon the cars, upon each leaf and washing down his outstretched fingers. Soon the individual droplets would pull together, forming puddles and opening up a whole new avenue of rain-related fun. One that 'three miles' could fully immerse himself in. Hanlon had just assumed that the dog was a HE! Perhaps it isn't normal to love a rainy evening quite so much, he smiled. But ultimately, who cares about normal anyway? I'm pretty sure 'normal' is a made up thing. Maybe I should ask Steven Murray about that, he thought. Before heading back.

On his return, he was surprised to see that with a quarter of an hour still to go everyone that had been invited had turned up. With the exception of two. Those being - 'The T'inker,' Doctor Thomas Patterson, who Furlong knew full well was in Ireland visiting his grandchildren for the best part of December and certainly over Christmas. But as she had been gently reminded the previous night by Murray, they are all part of the team. So the invitation was extended. It meant he was included and kept in the loop, holiday or not. He was also more than capable of giving an opinion or sharing his expertise via social media. He had grandchildren, so they would set it up for him and keep him right, if he cared to join. The other one still missing, but simply delayed in a taxi was Danielle Poll. Patterson's, Assistant Pathologist.

The Inspector and 'Kid' Curry had arrived, having picked up Sergeant Linn and 'Hanna' at Queen Charlotte Street en-route. Allan Boyd and Sandy had agreed to travel in separate cars. As DS Kerr had made it clear that she would only be staying for an hour or so. 'Things to do, people to see, was her exact quote.' She was also aware that given the so-called disappearance of Stacey, her team, Furlong's for that matter, were on standby if anything further developed with regard to that situation. She had informed Suzanne Cannon that DI Murray had already put extra people on to the case and that from first thing tomorrow, half his team would concentrate fully on finding the teenager. Hopefully, she would come to her senses and return home tonight and that would make her mother a very happy woman.

Since Suzanne had arrived at her late father's home in the afternoon at her wit's end. Sandra Kerr had done nothing all day but think as a mother. At what she would do if her twins were taken or went missing. It's not a pleasant mindset and she hoped that their second brainstorming session in a row would take her mind off of those terrifying thoughts.

When Joe Hanlon arrived back, caught short by the weather. Barbra Furlong insisted that he removed his soaked jersey and shirt. She gave him a couple of replacements that fitted quite snugly, while she dried his clothes by the open fire. The exact same routine worked well for 'three miles,' also. Wow! Her home was full. By now, Danni Poll had also joined the party and more than doubled the number from last night. Eat your heart out Murrayfield - filled to capacity!

Elsewhere, the sparsely furnished two bedroomed flat in the south west of Edinburgh was quiet. It appeared clean and tidy and well maintained. You wouldn't really expect anything else from a builder's daughter. Lots of her father's handiwork could be seen in each of the rooms. Shelving, bespoke skirting, TV cabinets and a range of new wall sockets. Each would prove to be a constant reminder to her. Always bringing back a mixture of combined emotions.

All evening Suzanne Cannon had wept until her fount of tears had dried up. Her brother, William, said he would stay with her until Sergeant Kerr rejoined them later. They both had eventually encouraged Sandy that afternoon to go and be part of her team's strategy meeting. A description that Allan Boyd had given to it. So as not to make it sound too light-hearted. Given all the circumstances currently surrounding this poor family, including the fact that Billy Cannon may well face prosecution for lying at the Fatal Accident Inquiry all those years ago. You couldn't help but feel that life could be harsh. However, both officers recognised the other side of that particular coin. The fact that a 70 year-old's family back then, wanted justice also.

From her fourth floor flat she could hear the wind howling, trying desperately to scatter the clouds, yet they were stuck together like soldiers. Like a 'Band of Brothers.' As one dramatically fell away, another took its place in the ranks. The drums of war resonated as the skies declared the battle had begun. Thunder and lightning were the first to strike. Seconds later the rain launched regiments upon every roof, pounding down, battering the panes of each rattling window.

Outside in the overgrown Wester Hailles backyard, Suzanne could see that under the glare of the streetlight, a set of small pools had formed quickly. In her desperate state she imagined each one as her own personal wishing well. Filled with hundreds of pennies. Some green with age and others still shiny brown. Suzy glanced down at them through the clear water. Each one stood for a heartfelt wish or prayer. Each one offered renewed hope. The frantic mother then made a hand gesture at the window. It was a clear representation of her throwing a penny into one of the impressive outside wells and joining the host of other assorted coins.

It was then that Suzanne noticed the worried, concerned look on her brother's face.

"What? This is how I am, Billy," she mused. "All of us need hope, even if it's just from pennies in an imaginary well."

Billy Cannon, offered up an understanding smile. He then threw in his own humble offering.

She inhaled a trembling breath, sweat accumulating on her icy cold skin. Death wasn't as beautiful or peaceful as she had previously imagined, with her stomach turning in on itself. Hope appeared to be dwindling. Faint breaths could only occasionally be felt. Oxygen was slowly being ripped and snatched from her lungs, leaving scars of regret on the weak tissue. Every waking minute was painful, every movement sent screaming agonies dancing across her nakedness.

Prayers, pain and hope were also in abundance at a small Dirleton abode. It was two minutes past eight and Barbra Furlong had just begun her welcome speech. Tonight she was in much more formal attire. It genuinely felt more like a work briefing and in honesty, that was exactly what most were expecting. No one was dressed in jeans and t-shirts. No one even in smart casual. It was very much skirts, trousers, blouses and shirts. Each, relaxed enough to work comfortably in and yet, each disciplined enough to be back on shift in minutes. As she went to begin, her doorbell rang.

"Got it," Steven Murray announced. He'd deliberately been on hand, waiting nearby for this person's arrival.

"Firstly, the elephant in the room has to be addressed," Barbra Furlong announced brusquely. "For those of you that know I had a meeting last night and weren't invited to it, I apologise fully. It was a basic error and a massive oversight on my part. I'm genuinely sorry and moving forward I hope to make it up to each of you personally, and show you all just how much I value you."

Most people were fully accepting of that and happy to move on. But surprisingly, it was Detective Inspector Steven Murray who chose to contribute a little something extra.

"Apologies, Ma'am. But maybe you could just repeat that for our last minute arrival."

All the heads soon turned around, as the feisty, youthful sounding voice from the doorway spoke up.

"Apologies, Chief Inspector. Sorry I'm late. I went to your neighbours house by mistake. I must have misread the number that Inspector Murray texted me."

The DCI felt a little warmer than normal. Was her guest having a slight dig? She was uncertain, but growing flushed, she nodded an appreciative thanks to Steven Murray and offered up...

"No problem, Lizzie. I'm glad you could make it."

Furlong then graciously repeated her apology and after which, she opened the occasion up to DC Hanlon for a review on some of his 'Nursery Rhyme' findings.

"The floor is all yours, Sherlock!"

Standing two deep around Furlong's table, the intimacy resembled an All Blacks Haka performance. The Maori war dance was aimed at intimidating the enemy, so no pressure then on Joseph Hanlon, who was now given centre stage. The DCI had managed to find time since she returned home to print off some small A5 agenda sheets. She even entitled them 'Brainstorming Session!' Herself, Hanlon and Murray were all down as named speakers! A brief overview of the deceased, their nursery rhyme name and background were also listed. A summary section at the bottom, added some poser questions. They'd always thought Barbra a bit quirky - think replacing her bad language with new! But they were only now witnessing other slightly unconventional character traits also. Not really surprising, Murray thought. This is a woman who remembers to take a 'three mile' walk at the start and finish of each day!

"I found some really weird and alarming stuff," Joseph Hanlon told his overly warm and packed audience. "Back in the day, nursery rhyme reform was the rallying call of a few upstanding gentlemen. A certain Mr Geoffrey Handley-Taylor, back in 1952 to be exact, surveyed 200 popular rhymes and listed in detail what sorts of unsavouriness they each contained. He was a literary scholar and actually only died about 12 years ago folks, at the grand old age of 85."

"So much like parents groups today, who decry animated films or video game content," Barbra Furlong contributed.

"Quite so, Ma'am." Joe agreed. Adding, "Handley-Taylor's list of unsavoury elements in the rhymes he read, was a whole page long and included bothersome incidents such as: Eight allusions to murder. Two cases of choking to death. One case of cutting a person in half. One case of death by devouring. Fifteen allusions to maimed human beings or animals and twenty-three cases of physical violence."

Some exceptionally puzzled looks around the room led 'Sherlock' to confirm and state...

"Either as a crazed group or a seriously warped individual, there is no mistaking that a tremendous amount of work has been put in behind the scenes to correlate and carry out each of our three deaths. Not to mention the effort gone in to leaving suitable and smart clues at each of the murder locations. However, my question would be this. Are these not the actions of someone desperate to be caught? Someone playing with us? Someone that sees us all as small children, each needing to be held by the hand and then have the next scene carefully explained to us. Don't you think? I mean the clues are reasonably straightforward. But why bother with them? Are we in some sort of nursery rhyme production for adults? I mean, what is its real purpose and what will be its legacy? Will we be singing about our killer in a few years time? Will an innocent, trendy Instagram or Facebook post be set to music about them and then go viral with millions of hits and followers? And that being the case, through the years will their actual heinous crimes be forgotten? Let us just be aware of how much our past may or may not, be a key indicator to our future."

Murray nodded at Joe. It was a number 31 questionable head movement. It asked, 'Was that you finished?'

"Sir, do you mind if I take up one more minute? It's just a brief illustration of my point."

Murray's two-handed gesture, said the floor is still yours, Joe, carry on. And so he did...

"Did you know that a creepy rhyme, still sung by children today, is based on one of the most sensational unsolved killings in history?"

No one did. But to a man, they knew that they were about to find out. Ahhh, exploration and 'Sherlock' were simply made for each other.

"It was a murder made for nightmares, news and nursery rhymes. When a wealthy businessman and his second wife were axed to death inside their home in broad daylight, their murders turned into one of the most sensational unsolved killings in criminal history. The death of Andrew and Abby Borden made international headlines when their 32-year-old daughter, Lizzie, herself a churchgoing Sunday School teacher, was arrested for hacking her father and stepmother to death on the morning of August 4, 1892 in Fall River, Massachusetts."

Murmurings and chattering by the fireplace, now told Joseph Hanlon that several of his work colleagues did in fact recognise the tale.

"It took 19 hatchet blows to crush Abby's skull, leaving her lying face down on the floor in a guest room at the family's home. Andrew, her father, was found sprawled across the sitting room couch. His face and skull shattered by 11 intensifying blows," Hanlon added.

"Horrific," 'Hanna' Hayes commented.

"It would have been devastating for the local area and community," Boyd remarked. Personalising it. Likening it to the fear and gossip that was already circulating around the frightened streets, paths and walkways of Scotland's capital. If these people are not all connected and are simply being randomly chosen then that was worrying and would lead to real panic in the city.

"There is however, Joe continued, "a historical society in Fall River. It is the central repository for information, photos and exhibits from the crime. It includes a blood spattered bedspread and the hatchet introduced into evidence during her murder trial. Today, the Borden case remains one of the most perplexing, unsolved mysteries in the annals of crime," Hanlon told everyone.

"You see," he informed them. "Lizzie Borden was never convicted of the murders, even though there was certainly enough circumstantial evidence against her. Instead, after just 90 minutes of jury deliberations, she was acquitted of the crime and freed. Returning home briefly to live in the house where her father and stepmother were killed. No one else was ever charged in relation to their deaths."

"Fascinating, as always," 'Kid' Curry exclaimed.

Radical Lizzie simply shrugged. Eerily acknowledging that her namesake was not the nicest of individuals. However, she did actually remind her of a Sunday School teacher that she once had!

"My point, people," Hanlon concluded. "Is that today, more than 120 years after the bloody slayings. A disturbing, although not quite historically accurate children's rhyme keeps the memory of Lizzie Borden and her parents alive. The rhyme, that many of us will be familiar with, was used in school days with jumping and skipping games and it's actually making a comeback again now. It goes like this: *Lizzie Borden took an axe and gave her mother 40 whacks. When she saw what she had done, she gave her father 41.*"

"Thank you, Constable Hanlon," Furlong announced. Drawing the curtains on Joe's rather macabre performance. "He can talk for Scotland," she whispered to Steven Murray.

"Yes, I believe I taught him well, Ma'am."

Standing up close, shoulder to shoulder, his DCI whispered.

"Oh, and Steven, thank you for inviting Lizzie. She completely slipped my mind."

Murray gave her a knowing look and nodded. It was a very indignant, number 18 nod that she was the recipient of. One that clearly questioned - 'But she won't slip your mind next time. Will she, Ma'am?'

Point taken. DCI Furlong offered an accepting smile, wiped some crumbs from her Inspector's forearm and left him to do his thing.

Nineteen

"Picture yourself in a boat on a river, with tangerine trees and marmalade skies. Somebody calls you, you answer quite slowly. A girl with kaleidoscope eyes. Oh yes, Lucy in the sky with diamonds."

- The Beatles

Their Detective Inspector took over... "Thanks to 'Sherlock' first and foremost for reminding us not to create 'an iconic personality,' out of this ruthless killer. A callous relentless individual that I hasten to add has now killed four people and not just three, as Joe stated. On our way back from Greenock an hour or so ago, Lizzie called me to inform us of some links with our homeless, teenage prostitute from a couple of weeks ago."

"Why are we only hearing about this now?" DCI Furlong asked, rather disappointed in Murray.

"Lizzie had to do further checks, Ma'am, and literally just confirmed things to me as I answered the door to her.

"Lucky, I was invited then, Ma'am. Don't you think?"

The cheeky, little, straight talking minx had been having a go earlier, Furlong concluded. Now she was a partner-in-crime with Steven Murray and that can't be a good thing, she thought. But they were both exceptionally talented and excellent in their respective roles. So Furlong remained quiet.

"The link being her online name...... Lucy Locket," Lizzie confirmed. "Sadly, she was also on the National Register of missing schoolchildren. She'd disappeared six years ago when she was only thirteen. Inspector Murray has kindly volunteered to visit with her parents tomorrow morning. I've brought you a file on her, sir. There you go," she said. Handing over a bright green cardboard wallet.

At which point, Danielle Poll questioned, "Online name?" Intrigued by the reference.

"I'm guessing that would be her 'official' escort name. Would that be right?" Sergeant Linn asked. Before smiling and giving the Doc a gentle wave of his hand.

"Absolutely, Mitch," Murray confirmed. "And now there were four!"

"The thing is, sir. Often as you know, during any series of murders or killings the assailants take a keepsake or a trophy."

"Yes, I would agree with that, Lizzie," Murray said. "Often that is the case."

"For the others we will just have to wait and see what might turn up, but for Grace, sir. Given, not only what she did for a living, but to simply survive on the street, I would be very surprised if her phone was not the trophy. There was no sign of it near or on her body. No melted plastic on her clothes or skin came back from the lab. And it would have been her lifeline to the world. It would have gone everywhere with her."

"Noted. Thank you for that Lizzie," Murray said appreciatively. "And the thing is, both Grace Adam and Jeremy Crossland have no current connection to anything else that we have found. The poor girl herself was surely random. From what Lizzie told me earlier, she had been calling herself Lucy Locket since starting on the game at age 13, six years ago. So someone involved must have known her working name. Possibly been a client? Who knows? But she was chosen specifically to audition and unfortunately, chances are she would still be alive if she'd just chosen a different street name.

For Grace Adam, folks, it would appear that evening was a dress rehearsal. To check how smoothly things went. To see if they could get away with it undetected, and they would have. For Lucy, it was the opening night of what she had hoped to be a busy, productive winter schedule. But remember everyone, 'The Premiere' is when the cast may be prone to nerves and make the odd mistake. Errors that could be rectified in all the future upcoming performances moving forward. However, having lasted five or six years, Lucy had proved herself to be at the very least, a 'streetwise' adult performer. Yet her only aid to communicate with the outside world, her means of support, help, back-up - her mobile phone, was not by her side and has never been recovered."

For the next twenty minutes, DI Murray did actually have everyone brainstorming. Wild ideas, random theories and crackpot suggestions were all forwarded, mainly slated and then disregarded. With all the larger than life insane proposals, generally kicked into touch. The team had narrowly drilled down deep and hopefully the foundation leftover was more solid and reliable to move forward on.

"Each death had been staged to coincide with a nursery rhyme. Making them personal and relevant," Murray stated. "Definitely not random."

"So nothing that the general public should be scared of then!" Barbra smiled. "We need to make them aware of that first thing tomorrow," she further announced. "Sergeant Linn, speak to our Press Liaison Officer in the morning and get that news circulated quickly."

"Ma'am, should I correlate with Dr. Poll to verify the boundaries of what we want to share with the public at this moment in time, and what we wish to keep under wraps?"

"Good idea, Mitch," his DCI said. "Get that done this evening, if you can."

Linn nodded in the affirmative across the room to the curly haired American. A gentle wink from the pathologist confirmed the exchange and Murray carried on.

"We now know that King and Cannon were schoolboy friends."

"Again, even more than that," Lizzie interjected.

She immediately stepped forward and handed over another bright green folder. This time the recipient was one DS Sandra Kerr.

"Very Celtic," the I.T girl stated. "I like it!"

Admiring verbally, just how Sandra Kerr's striking orange roots contrasted and complemented the Emerald green wallet.

Kerr, never fully knowing how to react to Lizzie, quickly opened the document holder and peeked inside. She began scanning and reading aloud various bits and pieces of the information that Lizzie had gleaned for her and DC Boyd.

"A payment from a now defunct Building Society was made by Sheriff King the day after the FAI. It was for £20,000 and paid into Jack Cannon's personal account."

"Surely the payments should have been going in the opposite direction?" Allan Boyd questioned.

"You would have thought so," Sandy warily agreed. "So, what? Favours called in or simply guilt on the good Sheriff's part?"

"Any ideas, Lizzie?" Boyd asked.

"Sorry, that would be your part of the arrangement I'm afraid, M'Lord." Lizzie said. Having a dig at the judiciary's salutation of each other. "Although I can tell you," she added. "That for the four or five years leading up to that Fatal Accident Inquiry, Sheriff Andrew King had already been paying £100 per month into the same account via a lawyer's office. All the dates and times are included."

The exchange between Kerr and Boyd was a picture to behold.

"Happy reading you two. Definitely something shady going on there," laughed the computer specialist.

Kerr expressed her thanks by way of a playful shoulder rub. Boyd, by means of a bright smile and a cheery thumbs up.

"Last night, Ma'am." Murray smiled playfully. "We came across a local author. Some guy off the TV by all accounts."

"Johnston Webster," Hanlon remarked. "He's a theatre critic actually. But appears regularly on TV as a panellist. He's very funny."

"I don't know about funny, but he's most certainly..."

"So what about him?" Furlong interjected, before Allan Boyd said something wholly inappropriate.

"He had a few interesting things to say. I had a quick flick through his hardback copy last night," Murray said. "He's got quite an unusual take on things, I thought."

"I'm sure he has," Allan Boyd muttered under his breath.

"Is this it here, Inspector?" Lizzie held up the orange and black cover in her hand. "Life Inside: Thespians, Lesbians and Plays," she read aloud.

"That's the very one, Lizzie."

The room went quiet. The verbal tennis ball was back on the DI's side of the net. What was his point?

"He's local, Ma'am. I just have a gut feeling that I think we should speak to him and get a different perspective on things. We are already speaking to one man on the inside who is credited with being an expert on nursery rhymes, all because he was able to tie up what he saw on the TV with one. A little bit of the old 'self- professed' psychic!"

"Really, DI Murray?"

"He's here on our patch and he'll cost you nothing. He'll be happy to do his civic duty I'm sure. What do we have to lose?"

Barbra Furlong was never going to be able to refuse. As soon as he played his 'gut feeling' card, she was always going to have to go along with the idea. Furlong agreed to look into contacting Mr Webster and Murray handed out a host of tasks and assignments for people to get busy with, first thing in the morning.

They then went on to discuss how straightforward access to each individual had been. Crossland and King had the financial means, yet chose to have no CCTV. Which surprised most in attendance. So both could have easily answered their door and then ultimately invited their murderer inside. They wouldn't even have had to have known them. Just opening up the door would have allowed their attacker to have forced them back inside. Jack looked to have been abducted whilst out on his walk, although again possibly a knock on his front door, would have allowed him to have been taken straight from there. No witnesses had yet come forward to verify any of what had just said mind you. And sadly, Grace Adam advertised her services all over the place and would have happily have gone with anyone for a bit of drugs money by all accounts. Again, she would have been easy to get hold off and meet up with. Murray wasn't looking forward to meeting up with her parents. The Inspector then spotted 'Hanna,' making a mad dash for the loo, whilst more importantly, he had noticed Sandra Kerr making to get her jacket. Which suddenly reminded him...

"And don't forget, hopefully Stacey Cannon will return home tonight."

Sandy, stopped immediately on hearing those words.

"But if not," he continued. "Remember, two groups plus a handful of uniforms will be out looking for her, first thing tomorrow morning."

"Thank you, sir," Kerr was heard to offer up, just before her phone pinged.

"Are you okay?" Joe Hanlon asked. He was standing next to her as her face drained of any semblance of colour.

"What has happened?" Murray said persuasively. "Quickly, Sergeant Kerr, spit it out."

"It's a text, sir. But it appears to be from Stacey Cannon's phone."

"That's good surely," Danielle Poll commented. "Hopefully it's her mother making her apologise to you for everything."

"I wish it was, Doc." But Kerr's pale complexion said it all. "I need to get over to her mother's flat at once, sir. Thank you for tonight, Ma'am."

"Sarge, you still haven't told us what the text says," her red haired, Glaswegian partner reminded her.

"That's the worrying part, Allan. In block capital letters it states: OLD MOTHER HUBBARD WENT TO THE CUPBOARD - WHEN SHE GOT THERE, IT WAS BARE."

"Phone Suzy Cannon right now, Sandy," Murray encouraged. Furlong nodded in agreement. Followed by several of the others.

"What did I miss?" Hayes whispered to Curry on her return.

"Just listen up," he said, and the voice answered on the second ring.

"Suzanne. Miss Cannon. It's Sergeant Kerr. What, no, no, I'm still coming over. No, nothing yet. Although I just wanted to check if you had heard from her at all? Not a thing. Nothing. Okay. What! Yes, it's just that I got a message sent to me from her phone. Did you ever give her my number at all? No! That's strange, yeh. Anyway, the thing is her message says..."

As Sandra Kerr repeated the text, she could clearly hear the girl's mother getting upset. Billy Cannon took over.

"Sergeant, should we be taking that as a clue or an instruction to search somewhere for her?"

Kerr's colleagues seemed to offer a range of differing opinions, but no defining option was put forward. Sandy had composed herself well, though.

"I think searching would be a good idea Mr Cannon. Is Suzy, okay?"

"She will be," he said. "We are just making our way through to Stacey's bedroom."

"Understood," Sandy said. Choked with emotion and on speakerphone.

The whole room fell silent. Some shuffling could be heard. Muffled voices and a door or two appeared to be opened and closed. The next thing that they collectively heard was a harrowing scream from Suzanne Cannon.

"Noooo-oooooo-oooo."

"Please don't be, please don't, please don't be," Kerr stuttered in low tones to herself.

The robust, level headed stoic voice of Billy Cannon returned.

"Her cupboard is bare. Stacey's cupboard. Someone has been inside the house and emptied it. All her clothes and belongings are gone."

"Mr Cannon, Billy, you never know, but that may be a good thing." Colour was beginning to flow back through Sandra Kerr's face. "Possibly she is being stubborn, rebellious even. Maybe some angst and teenage steam being let off. What do you think?"

Billy Cannon remained silent. Which conveyed unconvinced.

"I mean if she's contacted me and cleared everything out, could it be a bad joke gone wrong? An attempt to get back at her mum? And that she just simply needed fresh stuff?"

Neither Kerr, any of the others or Billy Cannon for that matter, believed that. DS Kerr however, was trying to offer up some glimmer of hope in a desperate situation. The next voice they heard was Suzanne Cannon again.

"That may have been a possibility, Sergeant. But she would have taken toiletries as well then, wouldn't she? Possibly sanitary products? And she didn't!"

"I'll be right there," Kerr said and hung up.

"I'm coming with you," Allan Boyd told her.

"No, indeed you are not Constable," Kerr said. Before adding, "Ma'am,' and facing both her senior officers. "Inspector, Chief Inspector, let me head over there on my own and check things out first. It will allow everyone here to also head home and get a good sleep. We are going to have to come at this fully charged in the morning. Please," she pleaded.

Murray being outranked, cautiously turned to Barbra Furlong. It would be her call.

"I hear you, Sandy, and I understand where you are coming from. But I think you have become a little too close to this one."

Kerr's face fell toward the ground, as a growl of annoyance drifted out from within.

"Now, you hear me Sergeant. We are not going to have some poor child disappear and be left on her own during our investigation. Sure, WE do need to get some sleep, but I am also going to call in the night shift and get another special crew working on it right now for the next eight hours, then we'll take over. How does that sound, Sergeant Kerr?"

"A heck of a lot better than my stupid, amateur hour cock-up suggestion." Sandy exclaimed with a smile. "Thank you. Thank you so much, Ma'am."

Murray knew full well that she'd be supportive. She had been nothing less in the eight or nine months that she'd been in charge.

"But you're tired, Sergeant. So right now go and sit with the Cannon's. DC Boyd you drop off your passengers and then head straight back over to join your partner and take it in turns between you to get some sleep."

Allan Boyd nodded and Kerr once again smiled. That order also got her seal of approval.

Death wasn't kind. It snatched where it could, taking people who were far too young and far too good. It didn't pretend to care, it didn't pretend to distinguish. The hooded vale of death had hung over the world for a long time with its sinister threats and bullying tactics. The female's face was sunken and haunted, her mind empty. The warmth of her body began to rapidly diminish.

Twenty

"Auld Nick - Patron Saint o' merchants, pawn men and the judges. Who barters with the lives o' men, the battlers and the bludgers. Go haunt the dogs a- while they sleep and thrash 'em round to sense. For there's far too many good boys on this side of the fence."

- The Rumjacks

It was now 10.15pm and one by one all the foot soldiers began to make their way home. Sandra Kerr was having no embarrassing repeat of the night before and had left only minutes after chatting with Suzanne Cannon. She'd been the first to leave, approximately twenty minutes before the others. If she had been driving home then ultimately she would have had the furthest to go, heading back across the bridge to the Kingdom of Fife.

Earlier in the evening, Sandy had told 'Hanna' Hayes that she had to drop in and check on somebody on her way home. It was now clear who she had meant. At which point, she had also briefly called her husband, Richard. He was to deliver each of her adorable girl's a goodnight hug and kiss from their mum. She had last seen them at breakfast the day before. The instructions given were clear and he was not to wait up. Richard Kerr continued to be her super dependable rock.

As the clock neared the half hour mark, Doctor Danielle Poll and Sergeant Linn departed in a cab. Which their Inspector found interesting. Granted, Danni lived in nearby North Berwick. But 'Baldy,' the bold Mitch-Linn man, stayed back in Leith. Every flamin' morning you would hear him bleat on about how energised he felt after his 15 minute walk to work, Murray reminded himself. So that was an intriguing delivery route for that particular Uber driver. However, he had also noticed numerous glances be exchanged between the couple all night. So he was pretty sure that they would be 'correlating' pretty substantially, possibly into the early hours about that 'Press Release!'

Finally, a full car load driven by Allan Boyd pulled away. Accompanying him for various drops were Hayes and Curry, along with Joseph Hanlon. The very man who would no doubt go home and then sit up into the early hours and continue his research. However, giving him a run for his money on that score would be the young lady currently following the quartet out of Dirleton on her bright yellow, ten year old, Vespa scooter.

Radical Lizzie had been a revelation of late. With the rain gone from earlier, a fair chill now existed in the air. Lizzie pulled on a pair of trendy, slim fitting, brown leather gloves and a 'How to get spotted from a mile away,' pink helmet. She was a definite character. Before she headed off and as night fell, the youngest member of the team watched as the blue haze of day lifted to reveal the stars. As an energetic teenager, Lizzie always felt that this was closer to the truth of who we are. She regularly wondered if we were nocturnal, would we feel more connected to those far away stars? Perhaps sensing the fragility of earth all the more. To her the night is when the curtain is pulled back and we get to see out of the window we call 'the sky' to the universe beyond. As her spluttering moped disappeared off into the distance, Murray immediately realised that she was the 'Miss Marple' to Hanlon's 'Sherlock.' Only much better looking and with far better taste!

As the Detective Inspector stood at the cottage doorway to bid farewell and wave to his current 'Magnificent Seven,' plus Doctor's Patterson, Poll and Gordon. It made him reflect as he often did, on departed team members. Barbra Furlong secretly held his other hand behind his back as he continued to gesture fervently and allow a small trickle of tears to venture south.

He thought tenderly and with fondness about 'Taz' Taylor, 'Mac' Rasul and 'Ally' Coulter. He reflected on his relationship, or lack of one, with his late wife Isobel. Of how his addictive behaviour had driven a wedge between both parties. He recalled childhood memories with his oldest son, Thomas, and with his only daughter, Hannah. Both of whom now reside permanently in the United States. Tom was still single, whilst his sister was married and Murray now the proud Grandfather to the beautiful two-year old, Maisy.

"Can we chat?" Steven asked politely. "What a day. What a night."

In the heaven above, stars shone as sugar spilt over black marble, glistening in the sun. The night sky was such a welcome sight. One could clearly understand Lizzie's instant love affair with it. Appearing like magic at each sunset, promising to return after fading in dawn's first light. There were times in the daytime, under skies of blue, where Murray himself, would think of those faraway stars and how they'd return after the shadows blended into the dark. It was then that his 'black dog' would bark and all the mystery and wonderment would disappear in an instant.

Barbra Furlong simply pointed back toward the deserted sitting room. They soon positioned themselves on the Chief Inspector's new fabric sofa. The embers of the fire faded and a stilled silence engulfed them.

"I thought that was productive," Barbra said softly. "Although, I suspect we are about to find another body."

Murray nodded. No number accompanied his nod. It was like the double zero on a roulette wheel. It was always there, surrounded by the others and only very occasionally did it make an appearance all on its own. This evening he looked tired. Twice today, she had heard him refer to his age. 'I'm getting no younger' and 'Maybe a few years ago,' were just two expressions she remembered him saying within the past couple of hours. But also the old-fashioned way he referred to people gave him the air and presence of an 'older' man. Things seemed to be taking a toll. His 'Good morning, young lady, how was your weekend?' Or 'Tell me, young man, how are you doing this weather?' Expressions from the 70's. Which she appreciated wasn't always a bad thing and the DCI knew that he used it all as part of his act, his persona, his 'Who should I be today?' routine.

"I agree. It was a success," Murray eventually said. "Definite lines of inquiry, plenty of assignments given out, homework to check out from Lizzie, certain connection between two and an absolute link regarding all four being nursery rhyme related. Yep, very positive on all fronts. By the way Barbra," he then sneaked in. "Would you like to go out for a drink tomorrow night?"

Furlong chose to ignore that last part deliberately. She was well aware of Murray's ongoing battle with depression and mental health. There had never been any official recognition of his illness and that was the way Murray preferred it to stay. Although, Barbra continually encouraged him to seek professional help and support. Her brother had committed suicide in recent years and being in this relationship, often worried her sick of what news may await her every day. In the past few months as their relationship became even closer, she had opened up to Steven Murray and shared some personal thoughts and reflections with him. Tonight she recognised the signs. He simply wanted to talk, to vent, to put it out there and unwind.

"I know I get a lot of stick and good natured ribbing about my fascination with origins," she announced quietly.

Steven Murray's eyes flickered heavenward at the remark.

"But this one is appropriate and relevant. In fact I think I may even have shared it with you when I first came to Leith. Anyway... Jolly Old Saint Nicholas. Do you know the story of Saint Nick?" she asked. Without expecting or giving Murray a chance to respond.

"He was the Patron Saint of...... Thieves!!! Although not just repentant thieves, but also of: Sailors; Merchants; Archers; Children; Brewers; Pawnbrokers and Students in various cities and countries around Europe."

Murray in childlike innocence stretched out on the settee and placed his head on Furlong's lap. It was his turn to whisper out into the ether. DCI Furlong listened intently, looking down on him, grateful for this period in her life and gently caressing his cheek.

"It was Christmas time, Barbra. Maisy was spending the festive season with her grandfather in Scotland. We walked the capital's bustling streets, holding tightly to each other's hands. Carol singers constantly enchanted us, as I gave her wings and carried her high upon my shoulders. Colourful hats, billowing scarves and a multitude of smiling shoppers. Markets, landmarks and delicate snowflakes. With seats on the Edinburgh Eye Ferris Wheel, we experienced breathtaking, spectacular views from our 'Winter Wonderland' location in Princes Street Gardens. Taking our lives in our hands, we soon managed a few exhilarating laps around the 'skating rink' and followed that up with sticky 'hot donuts.' Our sugar laden faces laughed and frolicked all day long."

The winter's tale would not have been complete without Murray breaking into song. With what little energy, the 'old man' had left. A line or two sufficed...

"Snow is falling, all around me. Children playing, having fun. It's the season, love and understanding - Merry Christmas everyone."

Barbra Furlong continued to stroke at his hair, arm and cheek for a further few minutes, until she was certain that her Detective Inspector was sound asleep. His Christmas wanderlust had given her an idea. Everything was available online these days. So without disturbing 'Sleeping Beauty,' she carefully picked up her iPad and got clicking. Ten minutes later and she was all done.

In the coming weeks ahead she hoped that she would feel confident and comfortable enough to share the following with him in person. After all the challenges and heartache that he had gone through in recent years. It was her own private psalm. A message of transformation and optimism that she dearly wanted for him also. But one that she knew, he would have to want for himself.

"Steven," she breathed softly. "Are you listening?"

With Murray seemingly out for the count, she began to gently whisper from memory...

"I hope those days return when your favourite drink tastes magical. When your playlist makes you feel desirous to get up and dance. For when random strangers once again make you smile and the beautiful night sky reaches down and touches your soul. I pray for those days to return - when you fall in love with being alive again."

In Wester Hailles DS Kerr exchanged places with Billy Cannon and encouraged the man to get home and give each of his own family a tight hug and kiss. Especially three month old Abbie. Situations and circumstances like this made everyone feel a little bit more vulnerable and precious, each in equal measure. As a mother of twin girls, Detective Sergeant Sandra Kerr was delighted to be a comfort and support to Suzanne Cannon at this time. Holding hands together, both women sat in silence. The adverse weather conditions had not relented and the non-stop rain had continued to constantly replenish the wishing wells in Suzy's back garden. Every last drop of 'prayerful hope' would be required. With the definite intuition of a future Inspector, Sandy sat clasping hands and interlocking fingers with the worried mother of missing Stacey. As she looked at the firm grip they had made, she knew then that there was an even closer link between the Cannon's and Andrew King - But she would address that, after Stacey was found.

The internal clock counted down and her time left was limited. She was slowly nearing her departure from earth. Only one question remained to taunt her... Heaven or Hell?

Twenty One

"Some take the attitude that life is a drag. They say and I quote, 'Man that just ain't our bag.' But if that's where it's at, then why the hell don't they just go. Houdini said that to get out of bed was the hardest thing he could do. Yet when he's tied and strait-jacket plied, he's out at the count of two."

- Gilbert O'Sullivan

That Friday morning, Steven Murray woke early. Not sure that he had ever really slept. Cautiously the Inspector looked under the bed clothes - He was naked. That certainly got his full attention and made him sit upright in bed. Two pillows by his back and a further one either side supported his arms. Onlookers would have thought him paralysed. With the relatively constructive discussions of last night, including the last minute news surrounding Stacey Cannon and a late night caressing chat with an attractive police woman, he woke up lethargic and hosting an overwhelming feeling of guilt. What had he or the rest of the team missed?

This man had never smoked or drank in his life. However, his exercise and eating healthily regime could certainly have been improved upon. In the past, football had been his sport, right up until his mid-twenties. That was when his family life and busy job prohibited it more and more. On and off over the years he still enjoyed the occasional weekly game of badminton. More off than on, in recent times sadly.

Given the right motivation, 90% of the time he could rise no problem. Today, he had no desire to engage with the events of the world. As he lay his head back and closed his often tear filled eyes, his chest burned like a deep fire from within. Pain pulsed and surged across his temple. Passing the baton from eyelid to eyelid with flickering images and recollections. Painful memories of the past and present did not help his feelings of hopelessness and low self-esteem. He didn't want Barbra to witness this and his head shook and twisted violently. He had to focus outside, to stare at the bigger picture away from the tiny cottage he currently found himself in.

The modern, double glazed square window sat ajar at the top. That one inch opening could allow all the sounds of life to filter his thoughts. On the inside, the cloth blind swung gentle like a soothing hammock. Outside, trees surged wildly before relaxing for another breath. Occasionally, gentle birdsong contributed to Murray's rich tapestry of life. The Detective Inspector coughed slowly and tenderly. He continued to relax and pick at the stitches of his illustrious career. To continually question his worth and undo much of the good he had quietly helped with in the world.

The fact that he didn't drink was one for which he was grateful. Because if he had done so, those lone survivors that he presently called friends, the small number of individuals that stuck by his side. They too, would surely have been targeted, verbally abused and possibly even physically attacked from time to time - who knows? What he did know, however, was that he would have no doubt drunk himself into oblivion a long, long time ago.

These days, even his black canine pal had grown tired and weary of his self-loathing and melancholy. 'Put me down,' he could hear it begging from time to time. 'Give us all peace, Steven and get on with your life for goodness sake, or at the very least, JUST GO JUMP!' And that was coming from an imaginary dog.

Another ten minutes of unleashing his woes of his life had come and gone. Gradually, his breathing returned to normal and another twenty-four hours was at the door asking him to come out and play nicely. A faint smile seemed to return to his unshaven face as he thought about life as a twelve-year old. An innocent, naive boy, growing up on a community driven council estate in the west of Scotland. The happiness that having a football in his arms and jumpers for goalposts could bring. Tears yet again instantly fell from his cheeks as Edward Sharpe and his Magnetic Zeros began whistling. His favourites playlist had been found and by the time the drum beat had entered the fray, Murray had made his way into his host's bathroom and turned on the electric shower. As the powerful jet of warm water streamed across his scarred torso, his zest for life returned... *"Alabama, Arkansas, I do love my Ma and Paw........."*

Next time the chorus came around his 'black dog' was scurrying away down the narrow hallway. Choosing to go stay with friends for the day, for the afternoon or maybe only for the next ten minutes. Who knew? Whatever that freedom looked like, Steven Murray was about to make the most of it. He was now in full flow... *"Ah, home, let me come home. Home is wherever I'm with you. Ah, home, let me come home. Home is wherever I'm with you. I'll follow you into the park, through the jungle, through the dark. Girl, I never loved one like you......"*

Indeed it was a small, compact cottage and DCI Barbra Furlong, who had already been for her 'three mile' walk that morning. Couldn't help but hear him sing along to those lyrics...... and wonder.

Seven minutes later. Shaved (as he kept a razor there now), showered, dried and dressed, he perched precariously on the edge of his immaculately made bed. A fresh set of clothes also helped and he had one drawer full of those in situ also.

Murray didn't normally do stress. So he was now pleasantly relaxed, certainly felt refreshed and was ready and prepared for his busy day ahead. An unconventional day for most. One which started off with him telling a middle aged couple that Police Scotland had found their missing daughter of six years. He instantly pictured their relief and smiles. Oh, excuse me he would then add - Can I just kick your feet from under you, because we have a slight snag. Which is? They ask. Oh, she died two weeks ago, literally stoned to death. But hey, you don't happen to be Hindu do you? Because she had her very own, personalised funeral pyre Mr and Mrs Adam! His wild surreal thoughts then continued with - Mind mapping, domino style. Every image connecting to the next: 'Three miles' became his own 'black dog,' which in turn became 'a sheep' - 'a black sheep' - 'Maurice Orr' - 'last meeting' - 'only advice' - 'further in, more sinister!'

He was remembering last night's shock and disappointment for the Cannon's, when another crazy, but quite possibly relevant thought based on Orr's advice, struck him. He grabbed his phone and checked out a couple of versions of Old Mother Hubbard. One in particular concerned him. Sandra Kerr was called urgently. As if sleeping with her phone attached to her ear, it was answered without Murray having even heard it ring.

"Boss, sir. What do you have for me?"

"Gut feelings of dread, I'm afraid, Sandy. Where are you? What time did you get home?"

"You know me too well, Steven." She was scared and wary. She never called her DI, by his Christian name on duty. Never.

"I do. So is Suzanne within earshot?"

A low whisper responded. "No, I'm on her sofa, sir." Formality returned to proceedings. "I also told, or should I say ordered DC Boyd not to bother coming over last night. He would have felt uncomfortable, sir. It was a mother/bonding thing."

"I get that. Plus I already knew. Allan texted me late on just to okay it, and let me know he'd be at home if required for anything."

"I thought he might, fair enough. Then what's bothering you? Gut feeling, you said, and yours is normally pretty accurate. So what is it telling you, sir?"

He reminded her firstly, about what he had said last night, about Orr's advice on his last visit. That everything else seemed a waste of time, but that one throwaway comment about the deeper you delved, often the more sinister they became.

Even more fearful to ask, especially as Suzanne Cannon had just entered the room, having heard Sandy speaking.

"Do they have any news?"

"Two seconds, Suzy. Inspector Murray is just about to tell me something."

"Your Inspector is about to tell you to try and remain calm for everyone's sake. Especially if anything I say triggers alarm bells - Understood?"

"Yes, thanks, sir. I understand. I will certainly try to do that."

Stacey's mother was frantically making gestures. Hoping beyond hope. 'Anything, anything,' she was mouthing.

Whilst listening to Steven Murray, Sandra Kerr was trying desperately with lowered hand signals to get Suzy Cannon to remain calm and take a seat. But that wasn't about to happen any time soon, and Murray continued to share his concerns...

"So one of the less familiar Old Mother Hubbard verses says that - She went to the cupboard to get her poor daughter a dress. But when she got there, the cupboard was bare and so was her daughter, I guess!"

"But that was last night, sir. The empty cupboard, nothing there."

"Yes, but Maurice Orr said the acts portrayed were normally even more sinister and depraved, Sandy. Because they were generally later, further back in obscure verses, that was why we never became familiar with them or got to recognise them. That, plus hopefully some morally educated people having the power and wherewithal to edit them out of the versions that still get distributed to our playgroups and schools."

"What am I missing, sir?"

"That the child won't be, Sandy. Stacey Cannon will be there also. It read - *and when she got there the cupboard was bare and so was her daughter!*"

"Naked, sir?" His Detective Sergeant questioned.

Those particular words amazingly made Suzy sit down with fear and worry, after treading the floorboards continually for the last few minutes.

"Sandy, who did this all begin with? A man that some warped individual felt still needed to be punished? Someone that had been hiding and covering up a secret for years."

"Sir?"

"Someone, who I suspect links all the others?"

"Go and get our coats please, Suzanne." Kerr asked politely but firmly.

"Sandy, are you listening to me?"

"Sir. Are you listening to me?"

"Detective Sergeant."

"Your gut was right, once again, sir."

Her voice was distant and resigned. Feeling nauseous, she stood to open the small window in the sitting room, but knew full well that she had to inform Steven Murray before Suzanne returned. She had heard her nip into the bathroom, so a few more precious minutes were gained.

"Sandy, what is it? What do you know? Don't you agree with me?"

"Oh, how I wish I didn't, sir. But unfortunately I do. You are right, Inspector. It all revolves around getting vengeance on Jack Cannon and his family."

Kerr then heard the toilet flush and a door unlock. Suddenly to Murray, she added...

"Get yourself, Furlong and forensics along to his home straight away, sir. Stacey is upstairs and she's dead!"

Twenty Two

"Dark clouds roll their way over town. Heartache and pain came pouring down. Like hail, sleet and rain, yeah, they're handing it out. And we're caught up in the crossfire of heaven and hell and we're searching for shelter. Lay your body down, lay your body down. Lay your body down."

- Brandon Flowers

Boyd was already parked as his Sergeant and Suzanne Cannon pulled up outside about 8.25am. According to Kerr's radio, the extra bodies, two vans worth and forensics would be there in about five minutes or less. DI Murray would be twenty minutes behind that. With blues and twos from his own home, he'd have made it in around six minutes door to door. From his 'favourite restaurant' in East Lothian, it was taking him slightly longer.

Forced or at least gently encouraged to stay in the car, Suzanne handed over the house key. No early morning airs or graces were exchanged with Boyd. Sergeant Sandra Kerr, as a mother and a police officer determinedly turned the key and rushed in.

There was something once again unsettling about the smell. But this time Sandy knew exactly what. Billy Cannon had obviously tried after they had left the other day to disguise the putrid, rancid odour with a heavily scented lemon furniture polish. It had failed miserably.

"I should have realised. We should have known. Why did we not figure it?" She gasped.

It only just dawned on Allan Boyd why Sandy had called him and insisted he meet her here. Nothing else had been shared and that was less than fifteen minutes ago. Today, the foul reek had certainly turned into the stomach churning stench of death.

Upstairs, the nauseating trail led them directly to one bedroom. Cream coloured bedroom units sat neatly along two walls, with a neat chest of drawers and shelving on another. The remaining wall with the outside window had a headboard below it. Continuing to follow the rotting decay, at this point with matching handkerchiefs over their respective mouths. They stood at the bottom of the bed and what appeared to be seen initially as a normal laundry or linen basket was beginning to look more and more like a miniature coffin. It was in the shape of a hand-made treasure chest. No doubt made by the master craftsman, Jack Cannon, himself. It certainly looked about twenty or thirty years old and was made from quality hard wearing timber. It was completed with a large, sturdy padlock. Of course, it had to be, Kerr thought. In fairness to the late JC, who had the same initials as the most famous carpenter in the world. He had left an old toolbox sat in the corner of the room. Spotted immediately by Boyd, he fetched out a sturdy hammer and a thick, capable although rusty looking chisel.

Wham! Wham! Wham! Three thumps and it was off and the lid thrown back toward the bed at pace. The smell of decay neither lessened or worsened. Detective Sergeant Sandra Kerr and Detective Constable Allan Boyd froze at the sight of the naked, rotting, decaying corpse that lay before them.

In life they had been told on numerous occasions that Stacey Cannon had a ready smile and knowing eyes. In death she was ghostly pale, her lips already blue. Scrunched downward into a tomb only half her length. Her eyes were closed, yet she didn't have the appearance of sleep. DC Boyd had seen this up close and personal many times whilst serving his country. He was fully aware that even in a deep slumber, there were tiny movements and a healthy glow to the skin. Sandra Kerr turned away as her stomach heaved and her nostrils filled with the smell of rotting meat. The young, innocent teenager on the floor was lifeless and although her emerald green eyes were hidden to the world, her twisted face held a sudden sadness. Her body was bent over. Half-sitting, half-laying on the floor of the solid casket. It was blatant her bowels had been released, and all too soon. Sandra Kerr slumped to her knees. Her heart pounded as one question continued to race through her mind:

Who did this?

"Hello, hello," a frantic, frenzied voice cried from the front door. Beginning to gag, Suzanne Cannon sought out Sandra Kerr. "What's that smell? What's happened? Is Stacey here? Sergeant, Sergeant," she cried in despair, gasping for a breath.

As she saw Allan Boyd's blanched face descend the stairwell two steps at a time and head directly toward her. Any remaining hope vanished instantly. It all began to make sense and sink in. She automatically began to drop to the floor, but with one final desperate lunge the ex-Royal Scot gathered her safely in his arms. DI Murray strode in through the busy doorway, arriving sooner than expected. He helped Boyd get Suzanne Cannon back outside, before deliberately and cautiously making his way upstairs. From the landing hallway, he could see his friend and colleague hunched over on the floor. In a kneeling V position, Kerr's ankles pointed wide behind and her head buried deep in front. Murray's depression and his isolated moments of low self-esteem were never present during these times. The detective's mind was always far too busy wading through facts, information and context. Then filtering accordingly what was relevant and what was not. Preserving the crime scene, respecting the body and looking after the welfare of his previous partner also came into play. This was the job description part about... 'spinning the plates!'

"Sandy, it's me," he whispered. Not wishing to startle her.

Without turning around, a raised hand acknowledged his presence. Murray took another step closer to where X marked the spot of the treasure chest. Experienced as he may be, it didn't make this part any less squeamish. With a protective hand over his nose, the Detective Inspector shook his head. In a considered manner, he then stood still and gave a longing look at what was once someone's precious child. He could hear Suzanne Cannon sob loudly still. In a low, heartbroken tone, he gently whispered... *"and when she got there the cupboard was bare* and so was her daughter."

Outside, plain clothed, uniformed and SOCO officers had all piled into the residential cul-de-sac. Every curtain in every house in the area was on high alert. Two further ambulances were on their way. The December morning was overcast but dry, as DC Boyd sat emotionally on the pavement comforting Suzanne Cannon. Holding his jacket around her shoulders with one hand, he dialled a preset number with the other. His message was courteous, but curt.

"Mr Cannon, Billy. It's DC Boyd here, sir. You need to get to your father's home immediately."

Having served for eight years in what was once the oldest and most senior infantry regiment of the British Army, Allan Boyd saw sights that he never wished to see repeated. He very seldom spoke about his time in the service of his country for that very reason. In many respects, today was worse. This was no enemy fully equipped and intent on doing you harm. This was a faultless fourteen year old child, not involved in any war of her own, but sadly caught up in someone else's. An innocent victim in the crossfire. Stripped naked, starved of food and drink and then bent over double to die a truly horrific and torturous death. On such a cold, crisp, soul destroying start to his day, the small sturdy Glaswegian reflected on The Royal Scots motto: 'Nemo me impune lacessit' - 'Nobody harms me with impunity.' Or as Allan and most of his fellow hardened soldiers translated it literally to mean: *No one can harm me and go unpunished.* That was certainly this man's opinion on this ugly sad day. Commotion, chatter and vehicle distractions continued to surround him as Suzanne Cannon visibly shook in silence and cowered deeper and deeper into his side. Boyd was mindful of the supposed origin of the motto and how his current Detective Chief Inspector would have loved it. He managed the faintest of smiles as those thoughts took over for a spell...

According to ancient legend, the 'guardian thistle' (Scotch thistle) played a vital part in Alexander III, King of Scots' defence of the ancient realm of Scotland against a night-time raiding party of Norwegian Vikings, prior to the Battle of Largs in 1263. One or more raiders let out a yell of pain when stepping on a prickly thistle, thus alerting the Scots. In the motto: 'No one hurts me with impunity.' ME was therefore originally the thistle itself, but by extension now referred to all the regiments that had adopted it.

Yes, Barbra Furlong would have thoroughly enjoyed that piece of irrelevant origin trivia, Boyd concluded.

Now even more determined than ever, Steven Murray headed off to visit with the parents of 'Lucy Locket.' Sandra Kerr was gradually coming to terms with events as they unfolded and Boyd was in deep discussion with the newly arrived Billy Cannon. They appeared to be somewhat heated, but no doubt the ex-soldier was breaking the upsetting news to him about Stacey, because the older brother immediately headed over to console his distressed sister. It was the experienced, although semi-retired, Andrew Gordon who was the pathologist on call today. A jovial and larger than life character, the DI quickly pondered on just how difficult it must be for him in particular when he is working. Gordon's natural persona consisted of good natured banter and raucous laughter. Now there goes a disciplined man, Murray thought, as generous waves were exchanged between both men. The troubled Inspector then slipped into his car and prepared to drive off. The mood had been one of sombre contemplation, but that was before this surprisingly unconventional officer found a further playlist. One that he had entitled: Folk/Punk. He then excitedly chose a song probably more suited to Allan Boyd than any other member of his team. He knew however that its energetic lyrics would both scramble his brain and recharge his batteries on the fifteen minute drive ahead. Promptly, after he had calmly arranged with 'Kid' Curry to meet him there, Murray ramped up the volume. Which then left only one outstanding thing to be done...... Belt it out!

"I was sent over the mountains and over the sea. By the Hercules transporter to fight the Afghani. With a rifle in my hand to set the country free. It's your picture in my pocket that means everything to me. Your picture in my pocket means everything to me..."

Twenty Three

"Photographs and memories, all the love you gave to me. Somehow it just can't be true, that's all I've left of you."

- Jim Croce

Leaving behind a busy congested murder scene, it was fast approaching ten minutes after nine when Steven Murray walked up the path of a house that had obviously once been a local authority property. A new roof, fresh rough casting and a range of fancy triple- glazed uPVC windows and doors were all telltale signs that it was now in private ownership. 'Kid' Curry was on the phone with his back toward his Inspector as he advanced.

"So seriously, Sandy, anything I can do to help, just let me know," 'Drew said.

Curry swung around, spotted DI Murray and immediately said his farewells. His Inspector nodded, chapped firmly on the letterbox and followed that up with two more substantial rings on the doorbell. The education of DC Andrew Curry was continuing, whilst Joe Hanlon in his spare time was off delving deeper and deeper into the abyss. Currently that abyss was a serial killer's MO. His Modus Operandi; his way of doing things. Alongside that, 'Sherlock" was also assisting Sgt. Linn with the Jeremy Crossland murder.

The silver haired man that opened up the door to the two men could easily have passed for 65 years plus. Murray, basing it on Grace Adam's age, had been expecting a man in his early to mid 40's. Fashionable, rimless framed glasses looked slightly out of place perched on his nose. Nervously he pulled the door back fully. Both officers began to take out their warrant cards, but Mr Adam had already begun to usher them through into the sitting room, front room, lounge or whatever this particular couple had chosen to call it.

Growing up in the Foxbar district of Paisley, a young, youthful and adventurous Steven Murray never knew anything but a living room!

"Go on through into the lounge," the wiry man said. There it was... a lounge! Murray had his answer.

"Officers, this is my wife Gillian."

Steven Murray had to be extra careful not to overreact. He had been expecting an older, dull, plain looking woman. But no, this slim built woman must have been easily twenty years younger than her hubby. Her dark highlighted hair ran down to the arch of her back. Plus no frumpy, unfashionable gear for her. A classy, floral, halter neck dress ran from shoulder to ankle, complete with flat red pumps. Charming, sweet and very much a real 'girl next door.' Why did she marry her Uncle? Murray and sympathy were such awkward bedfellows most of the time.

"Come in and sit down, please," she requested.

"And your first name, sir?" the Inspector, encouraged.

"Sorry, so sorry. I am Gordon. Gordon and Gillian Adam." The man appeared extra nervous when he spoke. "We had only been married a year when Gracie was born. We were young. On our wedding day we were both still only 19. My apologies, I walked away when you had gone to introduce yourselves, I missed your names," he said.

Murray was so taken aback that he was not even 40 years of age yet, that he failed to respond. But not to worry, his ever eager sidekick broke in with...

"It's good to meet you Mr and Mrs Adam. I am Detective Constable Curry and this is Detective Inspector Steven Murray."

Handshakes were then half-heartedly exchanged all round. With Murray reflecting on 'Kid' Curry's opening gambit. 'It's good to meet you!' Really? Not the ideal opening before you tell a family that their missing daughter has turned up dead after six years.

The Inspector chose not to comment. He simply recalled a lesson taught to him by a female Police psychologist at an enforced counselling session once. Whilst no words were being exchanged between them, he chose to remark...

"Ah, you are going for the silent treatment I see."

"The silent treatment. What do you mean, Steven?" she asked. "Because whatever silence may be. Is there not always the sound of your own heart? Just as with whiteness there's light, and blackness is a canvass for dreams; Surely if there is a soul present, there is always something."

That rather profound and surreal statement was one, if not, the only thing he ever learned from that series of sessions with the woman.

So today as the quietness in the room grew, he could hear his own steady rhythm from within. There WAS no true silence he had decided, and hoped that both parents were now ready for the news.

"Mr and Mrs Adam, there is no easy way to tell you this..."

Gillian Adam squeezed tightly on her husband's hand. They were clasped firmly together on adjoining laps. An emotional embrace followed. Suzanne Cannon had only gone through this for a few short days before her hope was sadly diminished. What must it have been like for this couple for six years? Over two thousand continuous days of torture and sheer hell. Desperately keeping some form of hope alive, believing that it just needed time to surface and that everything would work out all right. Today that was about to be snuffed out forever, their lives as they knew them, gone in a puff of smoke. All this, and the Inspector had not even officially broken the news to them yet.

"We have discovered the remains of a body that we believe to be that of your missing daughter, Grace. Gracie," he stated in a quiet, respectful manner.

He then allowed them time to express their grief. Over the years he had seen it all. There was definitely no one size fits all when it came to grief. Ranting, screaming, quiet acceptance. Tears, tears and more tears. It would appear on the surface that Gordon and Gillian Adam were in the middle category. A dignified, reserved acknowledgment of what they had just heard. News that was most definitely unwelcome, but also unsurprising.

Photographs and certificates with their daughter's face and name adorned the walls of their lovely lounge. In the corridor walking through, DI Murray had spotted an impressive row of medals and trophies on several of the shelves at the end of the hallway. Not unlike hundreds of thousands of parental homes throughout the country, mums and dads were proud of their child's achievements and wanted to recognise and display that fact. This property in many respects was entirely like that. It was a faith-promoting shrine to their daughter. Over all of these years Inspector Murray had no doubt that it had remained a house of hope and possibility, and on so many levels.

"What can you tell us, Inspector?" A quivering female voice asked. "We were always expecting it..." She cut off at that and her husband's hand was reached for and gripped even tighter.

"Before I do so, Mr and Mrs Adam, would you be kind enough to just give me a brief overview of how or why she went missing all those years back? I wanted to let you know as soon as we had identified her, but I didn't have time to familiarise myself fully with the case, so myself and my young Constable here are flying blind. My sincere apologies for that."

The parents both nodded in a grateful and yet understanding way. "It was so simple, yet avoidable," Gillian Adam began with real regret. "She, Gracie, had argued with us both over being allowed to watch a TV programme. Two minutes later, she stormed out the house..."

Emotion cracked the mother's voice box.

"And we never saw her again," Gordon Adam finished off.

"Hindsight is a wonderful thing," Murray replied. "Take it from someone that truly knows, Mr and Mrs Adam."

The woman could instantly recognise the deep pain scorched into the man's eyes. She had endured that anguish for over half a decade. It was obvious to her. She could see that DI Murray had been, if not still is, a fellow sufferer. She should've remained quiet, but the mothering instinct within her could not be contained.

"Inspector?" She quizzed. He knew precisely what she meant and he was certainly under no obligation to reply.

"It was with my youngest son, Ma'am," he said.

Curry was shocked. He never normally spoke about David or 'the incident,' and people never broached the subject. Often deliberately steering well clear of it understandably.

"He chose not to see me for 5 years. So not unlike your daughter Mrs Adam. But honestly, you're in shock and I'm supposed to be here for you. Please, this isn't about me. Let DC Curry and myself help both you and your husband at this time. I suppose though, what I was really trying to convey to you and very badly I hasten to add. Was that it was no one's fault. You mustn't and can't continue to blame yourself."

Detective Constable Curry was impressed at what he did there, deliberate or not.

"Come up stairs a second, both of you." Gordon Adam encouraged. The lilac door directly opposite them as they reached the top step was probably the giveaway. Although DI Murray also immediately wondered if it was also part of the problem. The girl was thirteen. Would inside the room change his opinion? Mr Adam opened the door and the Inspector's worst fears were confirmed. A set of colour coordinated, glossy Ikea wall cabinets faced them. Murray would have called them light purple. Andrew Curry had knowledgeably informed him that they were lavender. Gordon Adam had agreed with the latter description. A pile of teenage magazines sat neatly on her bedside cabinet. A neat selection of CD's took up two or three rows on a nearby shelf. Her library of books included many classics for young children: The Secret Garden; Black Beauty and The Water Babies to name but a few. One of the Harry Potter novels seemed to be about the latest or most recent addition to her collection. The purple light shade hanging from the ceiling (or was it violet, Murray smiled), was kitted out with children's animated cartoon characters.

Steven Murray had experienced all this before. It was the day when time stood still. Parents of missing children keep everything the same. Waiting and clinging to some wanton hope that their child would return. And that's okay if their son or daughter is found safe and well within the week or so. After that, they are probably dead. Or at the very least, not coming home. If they do, if Gracie or Grace to give her a 19 year-old adult name, had returned, well...

She would have been a fully grown woman. For whatever reason her childhood had passed her by. She had been fending for herself on the streets for the last six years. By any social worker's standards, she had done exceptionally well to have lasted 12 months, never mind six years. However, her High School years were - gone. Further dance presentations and award nights - gone. Teenage pals and boyfriends - gone. Today, if she had been brought home alive to Gordon and Gillian Adam. That much loved and well remembered little girl with the never-ending twinkle in her eye... was gone. This room, beautiful as it was, was a child's room. Gracie Adam had already outgrown it by about six or seven years, even when she was here. She was a teenager, she had been suffocating, she'd had a desire to grow and develop, to explore new avenues and opportunities in life. The amateur children's counsellor in Steven Murray recognised that within five minutes. What a shame, he'd thought to himself. Why couldn't her parents have seen it also? With that specific thought burning in his mind, the Inspector asked the father if he could kindly use their toilet. He had already taken a step toward it across the hallway, before a positive response had been given by Mr Adam.

DC Curry gazed around the girl's room. It was immaculate. 13 year- old Gracie's bedroom had remained untouched.

"Cleaned regularly," the dad stated proudly. "Her mother polished and hoovered it at least twice a week. So that it would have always been ready for her return at any time."

Could the man not hear what he was saying? The young officer questioned in his mind. Steven Murray meanwhile in the nearby bathroom, questioned something very similar in his mind.

Firstly he tried to compose himself. Having stood-by and watched as the onlooker today, he had only just realised that this was his life also. Every day grieving for his wife and son. Not accepting that they were not coming back. Rejecting the fact that Isobel and Davie were gone. Understanding that their respective deaths had not been his fault. That he had not been responsible for them. That he hadn't been the one driving the car that struck his wife. That he most certainly never pulled the trigger that killed his middle child, and that standing still and not moving forward with his daily life was no longer an option. Wiping his eyes one final time, he pushed on the cistern lid and literally flushed his burdens and feelings of guilt away. What he had been putting off for long enough, would now be put in place as soon as he resolved this case. He opened up the door and by way of an apology offered up...

"Bit of an upset stomach," he said.

The homeowner nodded.

Andrew Curry however, never believed a word of it. He was getting used to this man and his idiosyncratic ways and tendencies. The 'Kid' loved to watch how his colleague empathised with people. How he won them over to his side. How he had the uncanny knack of getting them to root for him and be part of the team that was trying to uncover and seek out justice. Plus, how his DI always liked to be prepared and for others to be equally prepared. So both Detectives had indeed been well versed with the background to this particular case. The duo knew full well the reason recorded for Grace's disappearance.

But there was certainly no harm in double checking things after six years.

"Shall we head back down, gentlemen?" "After you, sir," Murray said.

Deference, Andrew Curry nodded and took a mental note of that character trait also. Yet another for the 'likes' column.

As they sat back down with Mrs Adam, Gillian spoke up.

"I was just thinking how we are equally grateful to you, Inspector. For coming to us as soon as you could."

Murray shrugged modestly and uncomfortably. He knew from experience that in the midst of this heartache the sun would not shine and that birdsong would pass. The melody unable to glide through the air, as it once did before. Those were some sickly saccharin sweet words that he'd always remembered from a sympathy card sent to him after his wife's death. Sheer insincerity up close and personal. Words that he never repeated. Wise move, he counselled himself!

"Can you tell us how she died?"

Wow, that came from nowhere. Both policemen rocked slightly on their respective heels.. It had not been unexpected and certainly seemed to open up the floodgates. Because, before any response could be made by the 'Kid' or Murray to Gillian Adam's request, a barrage of questions was thrown at them by both parents.

"Where had she been? Was she living and working nearby?" Her dad asked.

"Did she finish school?" Gillian remarked. Before continuing with. "Why now, Inspector? What changed? After all this time we finally get her back... and she's dead."

The emotional couple had been bottling it all up. DC Curry recognised that fact. But Murray needed to set course and steer this ship accordingly. So he decided to listen not only to his heart this time, but give each of them the time to calm down, to settle back into their previous state. He needed to answer some of their assorted questions and to allay their fears, and no better time than the present, he thought. So he looked at a rather ash-en faced man opposite and said...

"Andrew, Constable Curry could you please fill Mr and Mrs Adam in with a few details."

The Inspector's phone buzzed, indicating a text message. He quickly read it and sent a thumbs up in reply, before returning to the conversation.

"We are good to go, Constable. But just before you do 'Drew, can I just say to Mr and Mrs Adam firstly, that you may read a few things in the coming days and weeks ahead in the press. Please, please, please pay them no heed." Steven Murray tried his best to fully emphasise that point. "They will make up headlines, they will create sensation and dig up dirt that is unsubstantiated, but it will help shift papers and capture viewers."

"Inspector, what are you saying about our Gracie?" Mrs Adam sobbed.

With passion, Steven Murray told them clearly. "What I am saying to you both right now is that your daughter was the victim here. Don't allow others to change the conversation."

A brief nod was then exchanged toward his young colleague. Nervously and warily Andrew Curry began.

"Grace or Gracie, as you knew her Mr and Mrs Adam had made her way in the world in recent years in tele-sales we believe."

While a little economical with the truth, his DI liked what Curry was trying to do.

"We are still actively trying to find a permanent address for her. However, unfortunately she was trapped in a car fire a few weeks ago and was only traced via access to a cinema chain's computer records."

"We would be happy to formally identify her body," Mrs Adam jumped in keenly. "Would that help? I feel I could manage that."

Murray butted in at that point. "Trust me, Mr and Mrs Adam when I say, that won't be required and you wouldn't want to."

Both sets of the parents' eyes were sent heavenward.

"When you say a car fire, Constable?" It was the same way she captured Murray earlier.

"Sadly, Ma'am, your daughter was trapped in a car that was deliberately set on fire."

"You mean, she was murdered?" Gordon Adam yelped. While Gillian held her head in her hands.

"Like I said earlier, keep focused on the fact that she was most definitely an innocent victim in all of this. Once the media get fully involved, it will be nasty," Murray reminded them.

Trying to remain unflustered, Curry's response to her parent's was...

"It's okay, she was already dead."

On that rather insensitive note it was time to leave.

Back out on the street his Detective Inspector asked him... "Did you enjoy that experience Constable?"

Murray looked down at his watch: Which read 10.45am. "Not really, sir. How sad, and on so many levels was that?"

"Well, hold that thought. Because the text I got in there, was informing us of another murder. I was to call the DCI as soon as we finished. So let's see what she has for us."

"Steven," Barbra Furlong said. "I just wanted you to know that we will be taking on the jumper that came in this morning in the early hours. At around 4am, I believe."

"We?"

"Well, yes, more accurately, you Detective Inspector Murray."

"Why would WE do that, Ma'am? I thought it was definitely a suicide?"

"The body belonged to a Mr Barry Cadogan, Inspector. It was one hundred percent, a suicide. But it's the reason for his jump that makes it special to us and to you in particular. It would seem to be that he could no longer live with himself..."

"Is this the part where I say - Why?"

Silence at the other end. After a few more seconds in a stand-off, he eventually gave in and played along.

"Why?"

"Because he claims to have been responsible for all the nursery rhyme deaths."

"What?"

"Exactly. He also kindly left us a note to say so!"

"Any credence to it though, Ma'am?"

"I would say, yes, Steven. He is even aware of us visiting with Maurice Orr."

"But how on earth could he know that? Surely not someone else on the..."

Furlong wouldn't even let him finish that sentence.

"No way, Inspector Murray and don't you dare suggest it. DNA comparison will help eliminate him one way or the other. Based on his diligence with everything else, I suspect it's more likely he was watching us."

"I get that, Ma'am. But once we entered that prison, no one knew who we were there to visit."

"Except for all the staff, privy to the visitor login book. A record will probably be stored, backed up on the computer also I suspect."

"Which brings me back to an inside job. I didn't necessarily say it had to be the police. Prison service staff would also happily suffice."

"That's for later, Inspector. For now, let's take on the case and see where it goes."

"I am good with that, Chief Inspector Furlong. Send me over all that we have currently, and then give me a further 10 minutes to decide how I'll divide things up."

"I'd already asked forensics at 6am this morning to rush through a DNA comparison with the other scenes."

"At 6am, but I was..."

"Still sound asleep. Yes, I know. I could hear you snoring."

"Well, I was actually thinking I was still naked," he laughed. Forgetting that Andrew Curry was standing right next to him and growing redder by the minute. Even he must have cottoned on by now. Sgt. Kerr could make a fortune from him!

The DCI ignored him. "It would take a few hours at the earliest, they told me."

"Okay," this time it was Murray's turn to hesitate. "So I'm guessing they've now been in touch, Ma'am?"

"They have indeed Inspector Murray, and Barry Cadogan's DNA is a match for samples taken at each of the murder scenes, including Jack Cannon's, Jeremy Crossland's, Andrew King's and Grace Adam's. So is it any wonder that he felt the need to top himself?" DCI Furlong yelled passionately.

"Right, well thanks, Ma'am."

"Yes, eh, well there is just one more thing though, Steven," Furlong hesitated.

Offering a brief clearance of her throat, she launched straight in with. "It might just be your lucky day, Inspector. I sent it over to Sergeant Kerr initially. But when she read the file, she genuinely thought that you, yourself would be best suited to the task. So maybe not much to divide up, Steven."

"Oh, great," Murray sighed. "Wait until I get hold of her."

"In fairness to Sandy, Steven. She has already had the news of his death broken to his wife. The couple had recently separated and she is living in a home specifically set aside for vulnerable females. There seems to have been gambling and abuse issues in the home, and like I said, Sandy, thought that you were best placed to......"

"She did, did she? Well she'll be owing me big time for this."

"I somehow suspect, you'll get that back tenfold, Inspector Murray." Each individual smiled and hung up.

Inspector Murray then offered. "So, 'Kid' Curry, let's get you straight back on the horse and go visit another grieving widow. Although reading between the lines, Drew, I suspect that she isn't!"

Twenty Four

"It's a long road out to recovery from here. A long way back to the light. A long road out to recovery from here. A long way to makin' it right."

\- Frank Turner

Suzanne Cannon had been checked over by paramedics and then been driven back to her 4th floor flat at Wester Hailles by Sergeant Kerr. The grieving mother had refused the invitation from her brother to return with him to his home. In fairness, that was now a property that DCI Furlong had put a couple of officer's on guard outside. Based on the killing of Jack Cannon and his granddaughter Stacey's abduction and murder, Barbra Furlong feared reprisals for Billy Cannon and his family may well follow. If truth be told, looking back, she can't believe that neither she nor Murray had chosen to do so sooner. Certainly they had no clear idea what this deranged executioner's specific grievance was, but even so, possible protection of the extended family should have been on their radar.

Meanwhile Lizzie was working non-stop on various bits and pieces, but none more so than trying to track down details in relation to the seventy year old Ian or Liam Frost, who died thirty years ago. Surely the obvious suggestion would be someone wanting payback and justice for that man's death. The initial clues seemed to allude to that. But paper trails just seemed to have disappeared, a FAI report could not be tracked down, seemingly paper copies were shredded after 25 years. But why would it be deleted from any computer records? Purely coincidence? Lizzie began to wonder if it had ever been entered in the first place. Had it possibly disappeared on paper, before it could even be backed up electronically? That at least made sense. Plus, that being the case, then it was NO coincidence. Although according to DI Murray... nothing ever was. His most recent quote on the subject was -

"Coincidences mean you're on the right path!"

Lizzie certainly hoped so. Again if it was to do solely with the death of that great-grandfather, then of what significance or role did Jeremy Crossland and Grace Adam play? As things stood, they seemed to have no link with either Cannon or King and no connection to each other either. Oh, that famous 'riddle wrapped up in an enigma,' had an awful lot to answer for Lizzie thought.

With William Cannon and his family being placed on protective lockdown for the foreseeable future, DC Boyd was determined to have one final chat with 'Bill' the builder. After the brutal murder of his niece, the possible imminent threat to his own family and the latest information that DCI Furlong had passed on to Sergeant Kerr and himself whilst at Stacey's crime scene. He felt certain that the man would eventually come clean. That whatever he had been holding back previously, he would now unburden himself and share.

Through his diligent and disciplined approach, the ex-army man was proved correct and it certainly gave him a better historical understanding of things. However, it didn't really shed any light on a potential or possible suspect. The hard working, Allan Boyd, then drove over to join his Sergeant and together they would break even more alarming news to Suzanne Cannon.

Having just arrived back at the station to do a Press Conference at 11.00am, Sergeant Linn had fifteen minutes to freshen up. All of five minutes later and he was ready.

"It's a man thing! Isn't it?" 'Hanna' Hayes quizzed him. He didn't seem to understand the question.

"What did you do? Turn on a tap, soak your hands and run it through that super blonde scalp of yours?"

The tint getting redder and redder on his cheeks answered for him. "What's wrong with that?" He genuinely exclaimed.

Hayes let out an exasperated groan and stepped forward to do up his tie. At least he had made the effort to put one on in front of the media circus that was waiting in the wings to grab hold of it and hang him out to dry. Just then, Linn's phone rang...

"Hi Lizzie," he said. "Sorry I missed your call a minute ago. I was just getting ready for the eleven o'clock media conference."

'Hanna' shook her head in disbelief. "How can I help? What's up?"

"I have eventually unlocked Doctor Crossland's diary on his computer," she revealed. "It doesn't make much sense to me, but maybe you guys have other information that would allow the clouds to clear."

"Okay, great. What do you have?"

"Well it would seem to be entitled: *Summer Job From Hell* and it had only recently been added. So something must have happened to bring that to mind, wouldn't you think?"

"Agreed, you would think that there had to be a catalyst."

"It was at a town centre supermarket," Lizzie told Sgt. Linn. "But he doesn't say where. Although I'm guessing it was somewhere on the west coast, based on other references that he makes. He was just looking to earn some extra cash before studying full-time after the holidays. So he would only have been about 16 or 17, certainly no older than 18."

"Yes, but I'm guessing there was something in particular that made you call us."

"Is 'Hanna' listening in?"

"I'm here, Lizzie. So what's got your juices flowing?"

"Several things, my dear," she said mockingly and with such an accurate West Country accent, that you could clearly picture a large stereotypical piece of straw between her gleaming teeth. "But they're all about one person," she continued. "Someone that he refers to as R. It's all in my report. I'll email it through to you both straight away. Although before you go off to do your Press Conference, Sarge. I'll give you some headlines of my own. He mentions how R. forced him into having sex with her and how R. made him take her along to his regular lunch-time haunt. But like I say, you can read about that for yourselves.

More recently however, he mentioned how he had bumped into that 'nut job' R. again and how she asked for a right, good 'hug!' Only she didn't use that innocent terminology. The Doctor quickly encouraged her into a taxi and sent her on her way. That's it, sorry."

"We'll check it out," 'Hanna' confirmed. "If there's something in it, we'll find it."

Lizzie was still fired up by the discovery. She got like that with her work. It was her passionate approach that people loved and had attracted Steven Murray to pursue and seek her out in the first place.

"I just figured maybe R. felt spurned, possibly envious or jealous of Doctor Crossland's successful career," she said vigorously. "A young Jeremy wrote about how he eventually made excuses not to go out at lunchtimes. How she would physically threaten him. How she had become hooked on him. After what he called the longest four months of his life ever, he started University and never saw her again. Up until now at least. Anyway good luck, Mitch." Lizzie added teasingly. "They'll only be about half a million listening!"

They both thanked her. 'Hanna' laughed heartily, while Mitch Linn's face fell and he headed back off in the general direction of the toilets.

Currently every memory played like a song in Suzy Cannon's head. Each one repeating itself for what seemed like forever. Grief was the price we had to pay for loving someone, she understood that. But all the pretence of quiet coping was lost, as the heartbroken mother's trembling fingers clasped tightly to a framed photograph of Stacey singing in the school choir. The girl was smiling, and why wouldn't she be? She still, at that moment in time had the whole of her life to look forward to.

Inside, as the hands on the hallway clock indicated 11.35am, DC Boyd arrived at the Wester Hailles apartment at the same time as another police colleague - Constable Alexandra Cloy. The female had been assigned as Suzanne's FLO, her Family

Liaison Officer. Sandy had interacted with the blonde haired officer on numerous occasions and like DS Kerr, she was a reliable, experienced individual. One that could be trusted to do her job and do it well. The Sergeant was grateful to see that a dependable, familiar face had been assigned to Suzy, and suspected that Steven Murray may well have had a slight hand in ensuring her placement. It was strange that after their initial skirmish at Jack Cannon's home, a mutual trust and respect had gradually formed between the two women. With introductions and greetings toward PC Cloy done and dusted, Allan Boyd spoke up...

"One of our other Sergeant's, Miss Cannon. A Sergeant Linn, has just recently finished giving a Press briefing. No doubt a sound bite will be on the 12 o'clock news at mid-day. I know, before that however, that myself and Sergeant Kerr have something urgent to talk to you about. But I just wondered initially, if you would like to listen to that bulletin or would prefer not to."

"This will be about all the deaths and your search for whoever is responsible?"

"That's correct, Ma'am." Boyd answered, rather officially.

"I believe that there is an extended piece by Inspector Murray's favourite reporter also," Kerr added. "DCI Furlong texted me, to let me know."

"That woman, Jones?" Boyd asked in a truly derogatory manner.

"She's not a fan of ours, that's for sure," he added. DS Kerr nodded. "Agreed."

Another nod was forwarded from Suzanne Cannon.

"Yes, I think I would like to listen and get an update. A balanced take on things would be good to hear," she said.

"Remember that is also part of what I do for you, Ma'am." Alex Cloy said. "Any questions, at any time and possibly, I would like to think, a far more balanced view than you'll ever hear on the radio or see on TV. Especially if Alice Jones is covering the story."

"Sure, sure. Thank you Officer Cloy."

She then looked briefly at Allan Boyd, before returning and focusing her attention on Sandra Kerr. She then asked...

"He said you both have something urgent to tell me. What would that be?" "I'll go make some tea and leave you to it," Cloy smiled. Well used to these situations.

"Would you care to sit down Suzanne," Kerr asked politely.

"I'm fine, thanks."

She was standing in the exact same spot as last night. At that time she still had a sprinkling of hope, as she watched individual wishing wells pop up and form in her garden. This afternoon, a broken non- believer stood before them. Broken in spirit, in heart and in life. It was going to be a long road back to recovery. People shouldn't forget that she had only just lost her father and was already feeling an increased level of pain, hurt, grief and suffering.

"Clinodactyly," Kerr said in a kind of matter-of-fact manner. "How long did Stacey have it, Ma'am?"

You could see by Suzanne Cannon's expression that she was surprised that DS Kerr was even able to call it by its medical name, rather than, 'bent pinkies!' Which is what most people called it.

"It's a congenital condition Sergeant Kerr," Suzy said, with a resigned look. "That means a child's born with it, as opposed to developing it later on. It is pretty rare amongst the general population, officers. Approximately only three percent."

Allan Boyd nodded.

"I see!" Echoed, Sandy.

"My own condition," Suzy said, holding up her hands. "Went unnoticed until I was in my mid-twenties. Stacey wasn't so lucky. Since she started High School a couple of years ago, it had been getting increasingly worse. It's hereditary. So it came as no real surprise to me that she had it."

"Did it come as a surprise to your own mum?"

"Well, like I said, it went unnoticed throughout my childhood years, so it was never an issue. Plus my mother died shortly after I was born, so she would not even have known that she had passed it on to me."

"She didn't though, Suzy." Sgt Kerr said sombrely. "That is what we are here to tell you."

"Take a seat, Miss Cannon. Please," Boyd once again invited.

As she relented, bent her knee and sat opposite Sandra Kerr on her settee. She then gave both officer's alternate stares.

"Let's be honest. No matter what you tell me today. It all pales into insignificance against this past week's events."

Two understanding nods of acceptance, quickly acknowledged that statement. However, something else flashed beneath the surface of Suzanne Cannon's hardened expression. Something which Sandy hurried to investigate. But it was too late. The sudden shift of emotion had disappeared before Kerr could identify it. It was like reaching desperately for an escaped balloon; the string had dangled tantalisingly close, but the wind blew to push it away and it was lost forever.

She was spot on about it all paling into insignificance and that was partly why Kerr and Boyd wanted to break the news to her. Sandy had also had time to think about other potential financial implications that may well benefit Suzy Cannon's cause.

"What do you mean, she didn't? What are you trying to say? Help me out here."

Allan Boyd stepped forward in real military fashion. He was happy to be the bad guy on this occasion. The scapegoat, buffer or whatever was required to keep Kerr's relationship good with Suzy Cannon at this point.

"Honesty and forthrightness was what was required at this moment in time Miss Cannon. Are you happy with that, Suzanne?" he asked. His voice was authoritative, yet trusting.

She licked her lips and nodded. She then took a sharp intake of breath and clasped her hands together upon her lap. DS Sandra Kerr then placed her gentle palms reassuringly on top.

Boyd began and never held back.

"Sheriff Andrew King was your real father, Ma'am. He'd had an affair with your mother, resulting in her being pregnant with yourself. Then 30 years ago, when you were aged 5, he helped your father's business escape prosecution by heading up that Fatal Accident Inquiry. Whatever stirred up the hornets nest, we don't know. Why did your real father help him out? We can only surmise, but like I said, we don't know. What we do know, is that there was and continues to be a very real connection between your families."

Boyd paused for breath. Although Kerr was sure that Suzanne had switched off soon after being told that Andrew King was her real father. You could see her internal cogs get to work. Her hands were now unclasped and her feet rapidly tapped.

"Anxious thoughts, Suzanne?" Kerr asked her. "Because driving around the block, over and over, faster and faster, my American Grandfather used to tell me was pointless. Sandra, he would say - Stop! Let your thoughts be as a fine car on a good road, taking in both the hills and valleys just the same. Then head off into the far horizon that your passions call you toward."

She tried again to speak to Suzy. "Are you listening to me?"

The homeowner simply stared off into the distance.

"I know that you don't want to right now, Suzy. But if you are really listening. You owe it to yourself to take control of the wheel. If nothing else right now, you need to take control."

Kerr immediately grabbed her by the shoulder and gave her a strong, reassuring hug. Deliberately hovering outside the door, PC Cloy magically timed it nicely with a tray of refreshments for everyone. The conversation continued. Reflective, tearful and in some way possibly even cathartic for Suzanne Cannon, or was it Suzanne King?

Twenty Five

"Would you know my name if I saw you in heaven? Would it be the same if I saw you in heaven? I must be strong and carry on, 'cause I know I don't belong here in heaven."

- Eric Clapton

"I confirmed everything with your brother earlier this morning when we met."

"I knew he was always holding something back from us," Kerr replied.

"Billy knew? All these years, he knew and he never said?" Suzanne questioned.

"What was there to say?" Sandy asked. "He was looking out for you. Like he has always done, as far as I can tell. I mean who brought you up these past three decades?"

"With hindsight, Miss Cannon. Seeing you here with your auburn hair and looking at the red-haired youngster on your father's school photographs, you can clearly spot the resemblance."

Allan Boyd had made the comment, forgetting Billy had said that Suzy was none the wiser about who that man was in his childhood pictures. At that, a single emotional tear appeared in the corner of Suzanne's right eye.

"All those visits to the house. The amount of times I held those frames and rubbed my finger over them pointing out my father to various people. When in actual fact, my true father was sitting right by his side all this time."

"I don't wish to interrupt," PC Cloy said. "But in the cool light of day, I'm not sure he was your 'real' father. I was raised by a step-father from the age of two, and there is no doubt in my mind that he was and will forever be my 'real' dad!"

"I hear you," Suzanne said. "Thank you for the reminder."

Kerr held out a picture on her phone. "Do you recognise this

person, Suzy?"

With only the slightest hint of a smile, Suzanne responded immediately. "Of course I do, don't you?"

"We think we do, Ma'am," Allan Boyd stated. "But we need to hear it from you."

"Oh right, well, sure. It's myself," she said rather proudly. "Dad told me it was the first time that he'd ever had any pictures taken professionally. You know, at a proper photographer's studio. I would have been about five when it was taken, I believe."

Boyd and Kerr glanced at each other. Alexandra Cloy being out of the loop, recognised the look though and began to gather up the dishes.

Suzanne had taken hold of the phone by this point. "At the start of the week my daughter was my life, Sergeant. All that I really lived for. I sacrificed to make sure that she never went without. However, my father was always right there if I needed him. Stacey and I both loved him dearly."

The picture suddenly disappeared from the screen and as she returned the mobile phone, her eyes glimmered with watery tears and she felt as if her whole world had literally crumbled apart. She dropped down on her knees and screamed with all her might. Kerr and Boyd half-dragged, half-lifted her over to the edge of her settee. Cloy had reappeared on hearing the wail of a banshee, but Sandy immediately extended the palm of her hand to signal - 'we've got this.'

Suzanne continued to sob and tears seemed to flood the room like a gushing waterfall. She only stopped to fill her lungs with fresh air, enabling her to desperately finish her emotional rant.

"A few days later they are both gone, brutally and callously murdered. My daughter left to suffocate and starve to death!" More tears and upset understandably accompanied that last remark. "Then in the space of a few seconds, I'm told that Jack Cannon isn't even my biological father and that that particular honour went to an ex- sheriff called Andrew King. A man I never met and never will. Because this very same week, he had also fallen victim to a gruesome unlawful death. One that was no doubt perpetrated by the same ruthless, cold-blooded individual that murdered both my father and my daughter!"

She deliberately slipped down off the settee and sat with her back against its leather frame. As she slid her legs up to her chin, she forcibly ran her nervous fingers through her battle weary, unwashed hair. Her appearance had not been high up on her list of priorities over the last few days and now she still had plenty of angst left to get rid of. She shook her head in total disbelief...

"Get your lucky white heather here," she cried aloud.

Not for the first time in the last few days, Sandra Kerr once again took her by the hand and tried to lend emotional support. To be that crutch that police officers are so often taught not to be in the modern world of policing. She could feel a disapproving look waft across the room from PC Cloy. A disapproving stare that her superior chose to disregard on this occasion.

"Ma'am, Suzanne," Allan Boyd interrupted. "That was our Chief Inspector, Barbra Furlong, that sent us that photograph. It was actually kept inside a silver locket, which was found in Andrew King's safe."

Hearing that news, Cannon's face leapt up and offered a bewildered glare toward DC Boyd.

"And what, what are you saying? I don't understand."

"Just that it was found alongside a letter. Although it was very brief, so maybe a note would be a better, more accurate description. Considering everything that has happened, our Chief Inspector was happy for us to share it's contents with you. If you would like to hear them?"

DS Kerr could feel her fingers being gripped tighter and tighter. Again, she rested her spare hand on top. A reassuring gesture that allowed Suzanne to relax her grip slightly. With her stomach churning and her chest on fire, the woman nodded.

"I need to hear it. I don't necessarily want to hear it, but let's get everything out there for me to deal with at once. Go on, share it with me," she said. Before wiping the edge of her sleeve across both eyes.

This time it was Sandra Kerr's turn to nod, desirous for Boyd to continue. Knowing full well that their DCI had given no such permission to share the details. She nodded and he began...

"The envelope was unmarked Suzanne, but the note read: 'I apologise Andy... to you both.' It was signed... Anne Cannon. That would have been your mother, correct?"

Suzy gave a succession of nods. Sending out her positive response via morse code.

"She was apologising," Sandy offered in a whisper to the woman. "We don't know if that was an apology to Andrew King and your father, or to King and yourself. We are aware that she suffered from postnatal depression, Suzanne, and committed suicide, shortly thereafter."

Boyd recommenced with...

"From bank records between your father and Andrew King, we can gather that King paid your dad what we can only assume was financial assistance every month from when you were born. Then a week after the Fatal Accident Inquiry, a lump sum of twenty thousand pounds was withdrawn by Sheriff King and transferred electronically into your father's account. No future payments were ever made and no further contact seemed to ever take place between the two men."

"For what it's worth," Sandy offered. "I personally believe that he saved your father's business. Yes, maybe out of blind loyalty for a schoolboy friendship, but I suspect it was more to safeguard the future of his daughter. And although it's only conjecture on my part, I would be very surprised given the timing, if that photography session was not part of the deal and a recent picture handed over for a future keepsake, was the official parting of the ways. He may have made a mistake and been respon-

206

sible for not highlighting your father's failings in a business sense. But Andrew King's overall legacy seems to have been only one of good. He was well liked and our officers never uncovered any further evidence of wrongdoings, misdeeds or questionable signs of corruption. All of the legal people our team spoke with, only had positive things to say. However, our very own Constable Hanlon, did tell us that the one question that cropped up continually, time after time was... Why had he not married? He was a rugged, good looking man. He had wealth and a healthy position in society." Kerr then stopped suddenly.

Which made Suzy again look up. This time their eyes met and they both held the gaze.

"I think he had found and lost the love of his life... and with your mother gone, the good man that he was, did not want to take you away from a family that would cherish and raise you well. And that is exactly what Jack Cannon and your older brother did."

Suzanne stood up proudly, she then openly and naturally lifted her arms and proceeded to hug and squeeze the living daylights out of Sandra Kerr. DC Boyd was about to try and escape the octopus's tentacles, when an embrace of gratitude reached the male officer also. It was the ex-military man who then shed a tear, before releasing himself.

"Thank you. Thank you," she cried out. PC Cloy was not forgotten and Suzanne Cannon gift-wrapped her also.

Jack Cannon had certainly survived his fair share of upset and trials in his life and he'd plainly been far from perfect, Allan Boyd thought. But possibly not deserving of the misfortune he'd gone through. A sturdy baton of heartache, that had now sadly been passed on to HIS lonely grieving daughter.

Mitchell Linn's statement was nearly as brief as his 'correlation' with Dr Poll the night before. Curt, courteous and lacking in any real dynamism. So actually, exactly like the night before.

"On behalf of Police Scotland," he began. "We want to firstly reassure the general public that there is nothing to be afraid of. That these were not random attacks on complete strangers. That the perpetrator or perpetrators, had chosen his or her unfortunate victims for a specific purpose. At the moment, ladies and gentlemen, we do not feel it would be wise or prudent for us to go into that particular reason."

Off air, Sgt. Linn then took a further five or ten minutes worth of questions. It was here later on, once journalists and assistants had edited, cut and spliced images and responses together, that your everyday competent police officer was duly made out to be a manipulative, deceitful and incompetent oaf!

"Was that it?" Suzy baulked, confused.

In some respects she was happy that nothing was mentioned about Stacey. Yet on the other hand she does want to be in the loop and fully up to speed. She looked at Cloy, who with her experience could tell exactly what she was thinking.

"I know, I know, that is what I have you for!"

"Suzanne, honestly, as soon as I get any breaking news or updates, it'll be passed right on to you. And that'll be well before any radio, TV or newspaper journalist gets a hold of it."

"Remember, they said that they had a further piece coming up from Alice Jones after the Police statement," Kerr commented. No sooner had the Sergeant spoken and the TV news anchor announced:

"This live report comes from our Crime Correspondent, Alice Jones..."

"Thank you, John. From the warmth of the studio you join us not outside the High Court in Edinburgh as normal. No, today you join us on the damp, dreich, cobbled esplanade outside Edinburgh Castle. For inside this popular tourist attraction is something that residents and tourists alike are familiar with here in the city... Mons Meg! Yes indeed, Mons Meg, better known around these parts and to millions around the globe as the famous, 'One O'Clock Gun. The medieval cannon that is stored here on the Castle's ramparts and is sounded at 1pm every single day."

"Oh, is that why they nicknamed it, the One O'Clock Gun?" Boyd shouted out sarcastically.

Jones then increased her speed and moved up an octave. "And you see that is where the link to all these killings began. The first murder case has since been dubbed 'Humpty Dumpty.' Not only because the victim's name was Cannon, but the fact that a cannon during the English Civil War was called the 'Humpty Dumpty.' Oh, and did I forget to mention..." the reporter instantly changed her speech to slow and mysterious. "... that various evidence had been left at the scene of each attack, to identify it to a specific nursery rhyme?"

With her mint green, branded rain jacket, cosy polo-neck jersey and dangling earrings, she certainly oozed girl-next-door cuteness and charm. It was simply that her journalistic content always seemed to lack somewhat, especially from a policeman's perspective.

"Other victims," she continued. "Apart from retired builder Jack Cannon, have included: Ex-Sheriff, Andrew King and a local Edinburgh GP, Doctor Jeremy Crossland."

She paused before continuing. The reason being it appeared was for nothing more than dramatic effect. Wow! She was some woman our Miss Jones, Allan Boyd carefully considered. Before this time biting his tongue.

They turned up the volume, only to hear... "Plus two more bodies are thought to have been discovered in the early hours of this morning. No further details have been released to us yet by the ever helpful Police Scotland. However, one of which is believed to be the teenage granddaughter of the first victim, Jack Cannon. Even the charred and burnt out remains of the Edinburgh street worker from nearly two weeks ago, have now been urgently identified and credited to our nursery rhyme killer."

"How did she know that about Stacey?" Kerr rose from her seat and screamed. "There is no way that should be out in the public domain yet," she yelled in protestation.

Boyd tried to appease her as best he could. PC Cloy wrapped her arms around Suzanne's weary shoulders to keep her seated and Alice Jones continued her damaging and caustic report...

"So how do you know that you have not been chosen folks? Are you named Jack or Jill? Maybe that was Mr Cannon's unfortunate undoing. He had a double whammy. He was not only a Jack, but also a Cannon. However, let me ask you this at home. Do any of you stay at Banbury Cross? If so, watch out. Is your name Mary? And do you have a little lamb? What if you are a Mary that is very, very contrary. And if so, how does your garden grow? To members of the general public at large, do you even want to be out in your garden at this time of year? Thankfully not. But remember everyone, he could be your brother, your sister, your mum or your... POP." With a sly wink toward the camera, Jones then added. "Goes the Weasel! Stay vigilant everyone. Stay safe at home and out of the clutches of Scotland's nursery rhyme killer."

And just in case you were uncertain as to who you had been listening to. She finished off as normal with the station's traditional ending...

"Alice Jones, reporting live for BBC Scotland, from the ramparts of Edinburgh Castle."

Both Kerr and Boyd were up and ready to leave Suzanne Cannon in the capable hands of Alexandra Cloy.

"We need to be going, Suzanne." Sergeant Kerr stated boldly. Still angry and frustrated by the words of that unpopular reporter. "We need to be back out on the street, locating this mad man and getting Stacey's killer behind bars as soon as possible."

As they made their way toward the door, Suzanne Cannon was composed enough to share one last thought or was it a message with them?

"Officers," she said peacefully. "I only ever memorised one piece of poetry from High School. As I think of its words today, I feel that they may have real relevance at this time. Would you mind if I share them with you before you go? It's only short, I promise."

Before his Sergeant could even think to blink.

"Of course not, Ma'am," Boyd had replied.

So Suzy did...

"It is my tears that keep my soul alive in the furnace of this hurt. They cannot extinguish what has been, yet only carry me forward until a time comes when that searing pain is distant enough to forget more than remember, and maybe one day erase itself fully from my brain. So perhaps it may be an oddity to thank my tears and be proud to cry, yet if that's what saves me from becoming a monster, a person indifferent to suffering and sorrow, then crying is the smartest thing that I can do."

Twenty Six

"Every gambler knows that the secret to surviving, is knowing what to throw away and knowing what to keep. 'Cause every hand's a winner and every hand's a loser and the best that you can hope for is to die in your sleep."

- Kenny Rogers

"She's a law unto herself that one." Steven Murray voiced, as he turned off the car radio and opened its door. Curry himself, was similarly disappointed in the reporter's remarks.

"Always likes to have a dig at ourselves, sir, I notice. Always looking to apportion blame, cast doubt and plant seeds of corruption and cover-up."

"I couldn't have put it better myself, Detective Constable Curry. Well said."

They were parked kerbside, immediately outside the noticeably rundown upper floor tenement flat. Assorted weeds on the pavement had grown higher than the soles on the policemen's shoes and there was a framework for a waist-high gate, but the actual barrier itself was well gone. It was located three storeys up and after a bold knock, the graffiti covered door creaked opened. A steady reassuring tone was soon offered up...

"Ma'am. We're sorry to bother you. I'm Inspector Steven Murray and this is my colleague Detective Constable Curry."

Being referred to officially as Steven Murray's colleague, made the young man smile. However, quickly remembering the reason for the visit, the 'Kid' instantly dialled it back a notch.

"I believe officers already called around earlier today with the sad news in relation to your husband's death.

The woman nodded and quietly added, "Yes."

"Thank you for agreeing to see us Mrs Cadogan. I know it can't be an easy time for you at the moment," Ma'am."

Her look and furrowed brow said that was pretty much an understatement to say the least. DC Andrew Curry, feeling privileged once again at being assigned with his boss, gently closed over the front door. Moira Cadogan, closely followed by Steven Murray led the way down the bare, narrow and musty smelling corridor. 'Kid' Curry had recognised that his detective skills had come on leaps and bounds over the last few days. Being paired with the DI had helped him immensely. Or was it just the placebo effect of being with the boss kicking in? No matter, he watched both of the others carefully and took on-board their different styles and mannerisms as they traversed the brief distance to the living room, sitting room, the front room, lounge or whatever terminology was used in this part of town. Similar to *bathroom, loo, bog or toilet,* it wholly depended on your city centre location!

Moira Cadogan was walking unusually slowly, almost robotically. Suddenly she dropped something. An envelope, card or similar fell toward her feet. Murray gestured and knelt down quickly to retrieve it. Carefully avoiding damaging his hand on her trendy ankle boots. The two-inch studs on her footwear were more akin to a caveman's club than a designer catwalk. The mousy haired woman gazed at him blankly, before uttering...

"Thank you, Inspector. That is my only saving grace these days. My lifeline to the outside world."

The Inspector recognised the symbol on the card, but didn't instantly recall it. For a second, her brain appeared to be struggling to function. Unable to tell each foot to take the next step. It was as if she were in a stupor. Like someone under hypnosis in a Scooby-Doo cartoon. Like someone 'Kid' Curry assumed, who had just been informed that her husband was dead. Murray on the other hand, glided like a waiter in a five star restaurant and his footfall made no sound at all. He oozed confidence in his role. Fully conscious of having just monitored them both,

Curry frowned as he took note of himself walking as if his shoes were too tight. Taking short little strutting steps like a constipated clockwork soldier. At that, they all squeezed into the front room.

With damaged railings outside, flaking roughcast on the exterior wall and at least three junkie needles interspersed throughout the worn down gravel on the unpaved driveway - this was no fancy, upmarket, salubrious dwelling. It was a basic, two-bedroomed, council flat in a poor run down neglected area of Edinburgh. Pilton was a suburb that never quite managed to appear in or on any of the glossy magazines, brochures or websites promoting all that Scotland's capital city had to offer. Although it did manage to finish top in the Anti-social Behaviour League for the past three years running. Only just edging out Niddrie for that coveted number one spot.

In all of the ten carefully choreographed steps it took DI Murray to find a place on the woman's settee, the Inspector found he had travelled back twenty years in time. Not just in the squalid living conditions that he had entered into, but somewhere from the dark recesses of his mind had sprung: Trainspotting, the movie. He could clearly see the lead character, Renton, with his opening monologue: *Choose life; Choose a job; Choose a career; Choose a family.* Today, Steven Murray anxiously studied the black and blue bruises temporarily taking refuge on his host's arms and legs and thought about how an updated, 2016 festive edition might play out: *Choose Facebook, Choose Twitter or Instagram and hope that someone cares; Choose a zero-hours contract and the same for your kids, only worse; And choose to smother the pain with an unknown dose of an unknown drug, made in somebody's nearby clatty kitchen!*

However, he quickly decided on keeping things a little bit more upbeat and productive...

"Delivering leaflets?" He asked. Pointing at a four-inch high stack, sitting on the bare floorboards.

The female occupant ignored his question and instead asked...

"Why am I deserving of a second visit from the police, and an Inspector, no less?" She enquired with natural reservation and sheer curiosity.

Murray and his sidekick were both taken aback. It was direct, to the point and spoken with great conviction, and although Moira Cadogan sat rubbing at her thighs and patting her upper arms in a nervous, timid manner. That one assertive opening line, said that there was so much more to this woman. What was her back story? Where had she ventured and returned from? Murray was thinking more mentally, than physically. In great part, that was exactly why they were there and DI Murray was equally comfortable in being as forthright and honest in return.

"First and foremost, my Sergeant, Ma'am. Sergeant Sandra Kerr?" "Yes,"

"Well, she was initially scheduled to meet with you. But being somewhat mindful of your background and current circumstances, she felt that you would benefit more by speaking to someone that had maybe experienced something similar to what you have previously gone through."

"Mindful of my background and current circumstances?" The gaunt woman repeated. Although her tone was much more cynical, than appreciative and asked coldly as a question.

"Exactly," the Inspector said, without batting an eyelid. "So it's not about my rank, Mrs Cadogan. It is one hundred percent about my experience of life, about its twists and turns. Its occasional ups and its landslide of down, down, downs. If you get my drift." On that note, Murray's voice went deeper and deeper. His mind rocked to the sound of: *'I fell into a burning ring of fire. I went down, down, down and the flames went higher.'*

A faint glimmer of a smile came to the woman's face. Murray nodded. DC Curry took that as a number 8 out of Murray's famous ring-bound compilation of helpful nods - *I hear you!* Murray reckoned it was a number 26 - *Ye right, I don't think so!*

"I have a problem, Inspector," she threw out there. "Don't we all, Ma'am?"

"I'm a gambler!" She announced. And suddenly there was poker-faced silence.

It was an honest admission, yes! But even more than that Steven Murray guessed. It appeared to be a declaration. She was clearly marking her territory.

"And I have been for most of my adult life," she continued. "Those are Gamble Aware leaflets," she added, pointing at the nearby pile. "I distribute those to homes every weekend. I try to play my part. I only hope that on some small scale they might help someone, somewhere. You just never know, do you?"

The look exchanged between her and the experienced Inspector, said that they both knew full well - They didn't help! Maybe one person in every ten thousand, Murray suspected, and even that might be an over exaggeration.

"It started over two decades ago when I first left school," she continued. "I was seventeen and I got a trainee supervisor position in an office and one of the other staff was a big horse racing fan. It was with him by my side, that I first entered through the doors of a bookmakers. And although things were changing quickly, it was still back in the day when no one on the outside ever really knew what went on behind their closed doors."

Curry looked suspiciously at his boss. He had the innocence of age on his side.

"She means the windows were all covered over with their name and other promotional advertising, 'Drew. You couldn't see in. It was for over 18's only Constable and they weren't exactly allowed to entice you inside back then."

A grimace and a short shrug of his shoulders said he understood. "It was a Ladbrokes store in Paisley town centre..."

"Oh, Paisley, sir," Drew Curry quickly interrupted. "That is your..."

"Carry on Ma'am," Murray encouraged. Giving 'The Kid,' short shrift, an unhappy scowl and a painful kick in the ankle.

"The mistake, Inspector, was that I won my first ever race and at good odds as well. So I was hooked. I earned a paltry wage at the time and suddenly I thought that I could supplement it with this new found skill."

Steven Murray could feel his chest close at the woman's remarks. Furlong had warned him about meeting with her. 'Sandy' knew full well that he could help, but again, only if it was not going to be too painful or require time in isolation with his 'black dog' afterward. As his Inspector's heart rate increased, even Andrew Curry's less experienced senses were telling him that his DI simply had an overwhelming urge to flee - a desire to simply bolt and run as fast and as far away as possible from that which he feared, rather than face the fear head on.

Moira Cadogan had also clearly spotted Murray's discomfort. "Bringing back memories, Inspector?"

He gnawed and bit on his lips.

"Uncomfortable ones it would appear, I guess?"

"The Inspector here, is also a Paisley man, Mrs Cadogan," Curry interjected. Trying swiftly to diffuse their current stand-off and happy to take another kick for the team!

"Initially, the majority of my bets went on horses and sport," she said.

Both men listened again intently. Yet the look exchanged between them definitely said... What about her dead husband? Why no concern? How long had they been separated? Because there should still be something. Maybe this was part of her internal grieving process?

With Moira wearing only a short skirt and a flimsy t-shirt, the Inspector's attentive eye fell upon her slight figure. She was certainly clever enough, Murray had already ascertained. So he guessed that her image must haunt her dreams and that her troubled thoughts must always tell her not to eat, not to be who she was supposed to be, not to develop her mind, but instead be a hollow reflection of vanity and her obsession with gambling certainly wouldn't help. The grumpy Scottish Detective

Inspector could testify to that. For once the soul is so thin, the body follows. Instead of a growing sense of self-love and self-worth, there isn't the strength to climb upwards to health. And so it becomes hard to eat more, even when it is a simple bite at a time. And it becomes impossibly hard to listen to the part of one's self that wants to stay alive and be loved.

Mrs Cadogan had been oblivious to his meandering thoughts and was in full flow...

"There was an element of skill involved in it. Studying form and deciding what horse was going to come first, or that Liverpool's odds were a bargain for an easy away win that evening. You could do your research and become good at it, and I was good at it, Inspector. Exceptionally good."

In their body language you could instantly feel both the officer's wonder and ask - How good? In her very next sentence, Moira Cadogan aimed to accurately answer that silent thought.

"I soon dropped all the other sports and concentrated solely on horse racing. I won about two hundred and fifty thousand pounds in less than twenty years."

The men in blue both turned pale. They needed DCI Furlong blasting out an odd expletive or forty at this point. Mouthing - 'Holy Moly,' like young 'Drew' Curry did, just didn't quite seem appropriate or adequate.

The woman smiled.

"On average, it was an extra two to three hundred per week. Ten to fifteen thousand pounds a year! Did you experience that, Inspector?" She asked smugly.

"I think it's fair to say that I never had that experience, Ma'am." He then looked suspiciously around his current surroundings and felt prompted to add. "However, I suspect it's the next part of your story that I am more able to relate to Mrs Cadogan. Although, I hope to be proved wrong."

A brief pause in proceedings for all concerned to get a breath, was deemed appropriate. For such a slight woman, her voice was rugged and powerful.

"It was located in Ratho," she continued.

Murray brought his trimmed eyebrows together. Combined they spelled out...... What was?

"Back then, we had managed to secure a mortgage for a five-bedroom property there. It's now worth half a million pounds and it would have been mortgage-free in two months time, Inspector."

Her body, face and demeanour all looked tired, emotional and totally drained. Bloodshot eyes, unkempt hair and a raw sense of loss made up her remaining character traits. She had appeared to have been holding up fairly well up until then. Both officers gestured that they were aware of the area that she spoke about. In fact, Andrew Curry probably knew the actual home. Mainly because there was a limited number to choose from and he was still a regular attendee at the international climbing centre nearby.

"I was passionate about the facts and figures," she said. "I loved percentages, statistics and educating myself with regards to the form."

Murray could relate to that first part. People didn't always realise how much being brought up in a household that played card games and darts on a regular basis, made you extremely adept with arithmetic and numbers.

"Playing with fine margins, learning about trainers, breeding livestock and a horse's pedigree enthralled me," she went on. "I even joined two horse racing syndicates and regularly visited studs in and around Newmarket and Ireland."

Then, putting on a faint Irish lilt and sounding like a poor relation to 'The T'inker,' Doc Patterson, she added...

"Sure, I never bet on the jumps. National Hunt racing was for eejits. T'ank goodness I stayed well clear of t'at."

"Sensible move," Murray offered with the hint of a smile. "I can understand that," he added.

Curry, meanwhile, couldn't believe that she was joking and making wisecracks. Her husband had just killed himself. Living apart or not, there must surely be some emotional connection still in place, he thought.

"You would think so," she said. Not in response to Curry's private thoughts, but to the Inspector's comment regarding not betting on the National Hunt season. "And in the early years it was never a problem. I had gotten married by then and we would go on sunny, exotic foreign holidays during a good part of the winter months anyway."

Both officers soon grew alarmed at how she self-consciously pulled at the hem of her skirt, and kept touching the bruising on the side of her cheek when she spoke about her marital status. It was then that she first noticed young DC Curry squirm.

"I'm sorry," she said. Appearing to soften slightly. Her tone became reflective and light as she continued. "It's just that, this afternoon my skin ruptured above the growing purple blooms and every single movement hurts."

"Don't worry, Ma'am." Steven Murray said. "But are you sure you're up to this today?"

A tentative nod was offered up and followed by...

"In the past, Inspector. I have healed from sheer stubborn wilfulness, a determination to survive come what may. This time, however, especially based on the news that your colleagues broke to me earlier, you would think I could stretch forward and attempt to imagine a fresh future. But there is nothing there. I have no reserve left to call upon."

Andrew Curry was saddened to hear her words. Maybe now he was gradually beginning to understand why there was no longer that 'emotional connection.'

"When the soul is shattered, can there even be a cure?" She asked her visitors. "I am battered on the inside worse than any broken bone, and yet, no doctor could even detect the damage?"

Murray related to that last part especially. He briefly wondered what breed of 'black dog' Moira Cadogan owned? She'd digressed, but was determined and soon returned to topic.

"Even over all that time, it had been soft, recreational gambling, Inspector. Our marriage was fine." Again instinctively she tugged, stroked and petted herself. "The winter holidays continued and life was good." At that point she rested the palms of her hands onto her bare thighs and her head fell forward.

"You've done brilliantly bringing us up to speed, Mrs Cadogan." Steven Murray offered. "But like I said and without meaning to repeat myself, I suspect it's the next part of your story that I can relate to best and hopefully be of some help and support with."

This time those comments greatly intrigued his host. She had immediately thought that the man was probably being nice and a bit patronising earlier, when he had said that he could relate to her. She thought maybe he'd simply lost his wife or blown a few hundred pounds on the Grand National or on Derby Day. Possibly even all three! Yet here he was, after everything that she had revealed to him, still sticking to his guns with it being relatable. So now it was her turn to wonder. What exactly had this man gone through? What trials and challenges had he battled with in his own chequered past? What life changing events could a highly respected and highly decorated Police Scotland Detective Inspector have encountered? Especially ones that had allowed him to empathise with an abused wife like herself?

The woman regained her composure and slowly lifted her head. He knew fine where she was going with this, she thought. But I bet he has no idea what course of action took me there. She turned her attention to the condensation running steadily down the inside of her forty-five year old window frames, to the gnarled peeling wallpaper in the tiny cramped sitting-room. She gestured with a cough toward the black patches of dampness on her ceiling. Then she lifted her hands heavenward and let out a low, controlled, hysterical scream.

"Sure, you couldn't make it up," she bellowed. Having kept a little touch of the Emerald Isle lilt as a keepsake.

There was no box, cabinet, booth or stall for that matter, in which the couple could sit. No curtain, no latticed opening to speak through, nor a step on which to kneel. However, sitting to the side of them both, 'Kid' Curry felt like a stalker at a confessional. The Priest, Father Murray, had only just clasped his hands and replaced them calmly on his cosy lap. He then sat and patiently waited for his latest penitent sinner to reveal all. And unbelievably, thirty seconds later, she did.

"It was three years ago," she began. "It was winter. The National Hunt season was only half way through completion. But it was no longer safe at home. Our marriage was steadily going downhill." At that point she suddenly shuddered. "He would only hit me occasionally, about once a week or so, if that."

"Can I just confirm, Ma'am. You are talking about your late husband, Barry, when you say HE at this point?"

"Correct, Constable..." She hesitated.

"Curry," he reminded her.

The priest then gave his 'choir boy' another unhappy glower.

"So at this point, Inspector and Constable Curry, it was much better for me to be out of our home in the evening. I told him I was going to do more serious research into the jump side of racing. These days bookmakers are open all hours, certainly up to about 10.00pm. And if truth be told, I think he was just delighted to see the back of me. Things at work hadn't been going well for him. He had started to bring those frustrations home with him also, and unfortunately I was the one getting the brunt of those feelings. If you know what I mean?"

They both nodded in unison and once again the poor woman felt compelled to smooth her skirt, brush at her hair and remove one hand from Murray's grip in a further attempt to cover up another bruise.

"It was then that I made, with the exception of marrying Barry, the worst single decision of my life. That night I walked into a betting shop for only the second time in my whole life!"

All three went quiet.

Twenty Seven

"Well tomorrow is a stone's throw away. I am lost but I can make it up to you. Well this hasn't been my day, but I know I feel okay. On this evening soaked in whiskey, under skies of black and blue.

- Black Water County

"Excuse me, Ma'am." 'Drew Curry said sheepishly. "But I don't get it. It had worked well for you up to that point and it sounds like, as well as being safe for you personally, you were carefully and cautiously preparing to learn all about the pitfalls involved in the world of steeple-chasing and hurdling."

Murray was taken by surprise at his young colleague's familiarity with racing terminology. The Inspector had certainly never taken him for a fan of the so-called, 'Sport of Kings.'

"I don't think I've mentioned it so far, officers. So I can understand your confusion, DC Curry. All my betting in recent years was done over the phone. Until that evening, I had never set foot in a bookmaker's since my first visit all those years ago. Back then, although I won on my very first bet, I never enjoyed the busy, smokey, male dominated environment. It was nothing more than an all day 'Social Club' for wasters and unemployed men of all ages. No, the place itself, certainly wasn't for me. I would give my chosen horses, two or three at the most, to my friend each morning at work. Lunch-time arrived and he would pop round and place our respective bets. He was generous that way. Thing is, like your knowledgeable Inspector mentioned earlier, betting shops are virtually unrecognisable these days. So that night, a few short years back, I was literally blown away by the new interior. They had newspapers, hot and cold beverages and various snacks. There were comfortable proper seating areas and fancy banks of screens and monitors offering you everything you wanted to bet on, from anywhere around the world. It was scary and exhilarating all at once."

Murray nodded in understanding. "And I'm guessing that you were so successful Mrs Cadogan because you stuck to your rule of placing your bet or bets on specifically chosen races and nothing else?"

"Absolutely correct, Inspector. And there I suspect, speaks a man of experience."

'Kid' Curry gave him the eyes.

"It's a mug's game, 'Drew, to sit and bet on every race, at every meeting taking place. Those individual punters were a dream come true for William Hill, Paddy Power and Mr Coral."

Now Moira Cadogan had joined forces with DI Murray, and while the Inspector gave 'Kid' Curry the pitied parental look, she in turn offered some advice from a kindly Aunt...

"That's the truth young man. You'd do well to remember it."

"So you broke your own rule and started to lose playing all the National Hunt races? But surely you could have just placed small stakes or accumulator bets and kept losses to a minimum?" Curry asked with genuine curiosity.

The air went silent. Moira again turned to the Detective Inspector. She was gaining more respect for him with every passing minute. She recognised his astuteness and added...

"Do you think you can..."

"Fill in the blanks, Mrs Cadogan?" Murray offered. "Sadly, I think I can take an educated guess at them."

"Go for it. Knock yourself out, Inspector," she said.

"Yes, please do, sir. Put me out of my misery at least." Curry added.

"I'm confident from what you have previously told us, Ma'am, that you don't bet on foreign races. I'd guess further that you didn't have a flutter on any overseas sporting events, including football, never mind gambling on two Taiwanese tortoises competing over ten inches?" He smiled.

"Correct." She replied. Amused at Murray's example.

"So the British jump season was off the table. Because the races had already finished for the best part, by that time of night. I know we have the occasional early evening meet, but there was no way you'd be putting all that behind the scenes effort into the odd once a week race card. And it was the jumps! So your love of statistics would be up in smoke based on the unpredictability of its outcomes. Horses being pulled up, falls at a variety of challenging fences and the old... 'unseated rider at the last!'

As live commentary on his theory continued, there was silence from the other two figures in the room. Ironically Curry had no idea where he was going and yet Moira Cadogan, given her years of experience in backing winners, was possibly considering placing a hefty wager on the Inspector nailing this. She could see that he was good at his job and up to the task in hand. Unfortunately though, she also now appeared to be stone broke, so no wager or stake would be forthcoming! She would just have to be content with the personal satisfaction, if this DI, the reformed ex-gambler, proved to be correct.

And so Steven Murray continued. "There was one item that you omitted to mention from those futuristic money gathering tax collectors, known these days as... licensed bookmakers!"

"I would have won my bet," she said.

"He's not said what it is yet," Curry exclaimed. "You never know, he might be..."

"Wrong!" Moira dared to interrupt. "Tell me, Constable. How often is your Detective Inspector here - Wrong?" She left that question hanging, whilst pointing at the man still speaking. Her face was drained of all colour. "He doesn't look like a man who gets things wrong."

"The slots, Ma'am?" Murray asked initially as a question, confident he knew the answer.

She offered a sardonic grin before responding...

"They looked just like the sort of machines you would find in any local arcade or at a seaside beachfront. On first inspection they looked fun and innocent enough and for the first evening, I was just happy to be out of the family home and have somewhere safe to go for refuge. In the early days, when they were first introduced into High Street bookmakers and casinos, the machines had a limit of five or ten pounds, and they cost around twenty pence per spin. It would take around ten minutes for a player to spend or lose ten pounds. The equivalent to one pound per minute."

Both DC Curry and his experienced Inspector were more concerned as to where this was heading. It should have been about here that Murray escaped with a parachute from the precipice of this burning building. She had called his bluff. He could no longer compete with what was to come. Sure his wife had died tragically and her husband was now dead, and during his gambling days the Inspector had blown five figures and had in part remortgaged his family home to do so. But what was to come here, whatever it was, he didn't really feel ready for it. But he could lead by example and learn something from her honest words, her grieving heart and her feisty spirit at this time. At least that was what he told himself, as he forced himself to stay.

"Apologies, Ma'am. Mrs Cadogan, Moira. Please finish your story..."

"Over the next few years and in their perceived wisdom and logic. Ruling bodies were allowed to increase the stakes and the rewards." Her head shook at the very thought of it. "Did you know, Inspector, that fixed-odds betting terminals currently allowed people in the UK to bet one hundred pounds every twenty seconds. ONE HUNDRED POUNDS! - It's obscene."

The two Police Scotland officers were genuinely stunned and in awe at that fact.

"Effectively, the punter can lose three hundred pounds in a single minute. Even if you were winning, you could easily lose several thousand pounds in an hour."

Her visitors sat like statues. Shocked and stilled at what they were hearing. Murray had never felt the urge or desire to play the machines. He knew that they were compulsive, but had no idea at the ferocity and speed at which they struck. Moira Cadogan looked at each man in turn.

"I was well and truly hooked, Mr Murray." She then altered her gaze. "Within three months, Constable, I was addicted."

Murray considered himself lucky. In all his years he never GOT slot machines. He had no idea how they worked or what the appeal was. In fairness, that was back in the day when the most you could win was a tenner. Maybe if he'd had the larger jackpot on offer these days to tempt him, he might have reacted differently. The fact that it was all over so soon was another no-brainer for him. For he enjoyed the build up, checking out the racing form, monitoring the betting, etc. Just like Mrs Cadogan, he felt that there was definitely an element of skill and deduction involved. There was also a good thirty minutes between races before you lost your stake. Not twenty flippin' seconds!

There was definitely something wrong with our society and the people passing those laws thinking that they were beneficial. Just exactly who did they benefit? Murray asked himself. Just how much did the Government receive in betting tax these days? It certainly would not be inconsequential, he thought.

"Gamblers desperately need help to beat the problem," Mrs Cadogan stated passionately. "The adrenaline with the machines was completely different, because it was all happening live in front of you. I recognise now that I'd grown bored gambling on the horses and I sought a fresh buzz."

Both men began to try and keep their emotions in check. A tear or two managed to filter down, however.

"The problem is you leave yourself at the behest of a random number generator, and I soon realised that I was losing between one thousand and five thousand pounds per week! One week I lost fourteen thousand pounds of profit. It left me stunned, shocked and ashamed of myself for blowing all my money in one afternoon in a betting shop."

Andrew Curry felt physically sick.

"In recent months, my husband has regularly battered me black and blue. Which actually had nothing whatsoever to do with the gambling. It had just gotten to a stage where he enjoyed it. It had become his favourite pastime. And are you ready for this?" She asked dismissively and then paused.

Both the Inspector and DC Curry winced with uncertainty and pulled their upper bodies away slightly and raised their heads.

Speaking slowly, the agitated woman announced... "I lost about, four - hundred - thousand - pounds in total."

They were gobsmacked. That was way out of Murray's league. Neither man spoke. In her final summation, she added...

"The bank and credit card companies got it all back in full." The puzzled look between both men soon got a response.

"They repossessed the house and managed a speedy sale at a generous 20% discount. That was three months ago. After being in Stenhouse for the first half of that time, I've been hosting friends and honoured guests such as yourselves, in this trendy pad ever since. What do you think?" She let out a huge sigh, before one final offering. "Sincere apologies, Inspector. Rant over." She immediately turned to his companion and added. "And also of course to yourself, Constable Curry."

As those words left her lips, both officers stared into what they imagined had once been bright blue eyes. Yet today, presently, they were painfully tortured. Eyes that still burned with intense anger and guilt. That had endured rejection and hurt in recent times. Other tender flag bearers that sought to send distress signals from her eyelids, included those close bedfellows - regret and personal disappointment. It was the emotionally tortured woman herself, that then once again broke the silence.

"Nothing to say? No follow-up? No sympathetic bereavement counselling? I've just poured my heart and soul out to you and shared my private thoughts and darkest secrets. At least one of you, have the courtesy to tell me what you are thinking!"

Less than tactfully Inspector Steven Murray declared, "What I was thinking Ma'am was, could I please use your bathroom?"

Twenty Eight

"I look handsome, I look smart. I am a walking work of art. Such a dazzling coat of many colours. How I love my coat of many colours. It was red and yellow and green and brown. And scarlet and black and ochre and peach."

- From the musical, Joseph

Whilst the conversation at Moira Cadogan's continued. Classical music rang out vibrantly from a recently converted room deep in the basement of Police Scotland's Queen Charlotte Street premises. To those in the know, it was Beethoven's Sonata No.14 in C-Sharp. The unconventional, newly established location had been aptly named: The Vault! It was now the regular domain for one particular member of the team. The very latest official recruit in fact.

Where does one start? From that flawless, innocent, rosy cheeked and dark haired, 8lb 2oz infant that was born on the 6th of June 1991. She now looked kinda' different. Lizzie, at 5' 6' and with the body of an athletic triple jumper, was born in Dunfermline, Fife. Today she was sporting braided pigtails with a centre parting. The upper half was dark brunette, whereas down below, including the pigtails, it turned into a soft blonde. When asked, Lizzie's take on this cut and colour scheme was...

"My blonde and brunette sisters aren't here to compete, but to compliment and to add to the wonderful variation of life."

Wow! She's most certainly quirky. However, those distinctive pigments would only be for this week. The colours changed at least monthly, often weekly and occasionally from day-to-day. Tomorrow? Who knows? She goes through more tantalising shades than Jacob's colourful son!

One small, single intricate and delicate tear was tattooed below her right eye. Elongated mascara and heavy eye shadow, highlighted her piercing blue eyes. A range of further tattoos adorned her back, forearms and upper legs. Today she wore a black figure hugging dress. It was met halfway down with black, thigh-high casual socks, complete with three white stripes above the knee. A light rose lipstick and bright scarlet nails rounded off today's outlandish, yet stylish look.

DI Murray was confident that it took her longer to get ready and remove everything each day, than the actual time she spent at work. He's not even convinced that was an exaggeration. Without doubt, her attitude matched her looks. Mysterious, loveable, intelligent and sassy. She kept her private life private. But that did not stop her from being continually flirtatious, and that was with both the boys and the girls!

It was just over a year ago, in late 2015, when Steven Murray first met a young woman named Radical Lizzie. His friend Sarah C, who was an ethical hacker, had introduced them. Social media, networking and fake news had been her initial area of expertise. That was her world, her specialist subject and her first love. As part of Sarah C's close sisterhood in the ethical hacking community, when it came to I.T there was not much that Lizzie didn't know. In the intervening months, she had been called upon on a case by case basis to help and assist with cases. As a self-employed consultant, she impressed. In Steven Murray she had a strong ally and number one fan. With himself being highly incompetent and totally backward, when it came to modern technology. The Inspector was won over instantly with the skills that this particular individual possessed. He knew that moving forward, a large percentage of police officers are going to be required to sit, monitor, track, identify and nail the bad guy. The others then go out and get them. On a daily basis, it was already becoming more and more like that.

After several successful outings together, it wasn't long before Murray had gently persuaded DCI Furlong to push her bosses to bring this girl onboard full-time. That is, if they could win her over from her generally unconventional lifestyle. If they could entice her to embrace a more run of the mill, five days a week, holiday and sick pay, plus a regular monthly income job. What say ye? She said yes, a new partnership was formed and a further team member gained. Her pay slip had her Christian name as 'Radical' and her surname as 'Lizzie.' No one questioned that slight irregularity and she's been known as Lizzie ever since!

It was all good and well that the Scottish Crime Campus had 'Doc' Patterson and his team of pathologists, now all working out of brand new laboratories housed at DNA 24 in Gartcosh, Lanarkshire. But I.T support was required in-house and for Murray and his team based in their near two hundred year old building, which in fact used to be the old Leith Town Hall. How fortunate was it that down next to the 'new' toilets in the basement they managed to find three old supply cupboards that they could knock into one suitable room. Most people would not necessarily have taken to it. But then Lizzie was not most people. She loved it, owned it, and had created her very own Bat-cave. It was a bespoke dungeon filled with the very latest in technological gadgetry and wizardry. Having just viewed some footage from a street cam, a quick call to DI Murray was required. On this occasion it went straight to voicemail as he was still busy with a 'grieving widow!'

"Personal demons, Ma'am. I get it," the Inspector mustered. "I've been there, Mrs Cadogan," he further added.

Andrew Curry recoiled at that revelation. There had been talk a while back, rumours as such, but The 'Kid,' had paid them no heed. Not Inspector Murray, he was certain of that. He had always confidently dismissed them as idle locker room gossip.

"A gambler then?" Cadogan boldly asked. "You?"

"I was Ma'am, and to a degree always will be. As you know, we're always just another bet away. It was serious and it was a long time coming to a head. Unfortunately, just like yourself, I was successfully introduced to it when I was young and easily influenced."

Curry was reluctantly enjoying his education. What a riveting series this was turning out to be and totally unavailable on either Amazon Prime or Netflix. He pursed his lips as Mrs Cadogan went to retake the reins.

"I have always taken responsibility for my actions, Inspector. But my addiction was overwhelming. I had suffered bereavements over the last few years and when my depression and anxiety got worse, I would simply head into a betting shop. It became a crutch, but also a burden." She looked around her current, cluttered and uninspiring surroundings. "As you can see, I lost my 'fancy' house. I've lied constantly to friends and family, I've stolen from those that I loved. People that cared for me, that trusted me, that were trying to support and help me. To this day I'm still twenty thousand pounds in debt. I moved into this council house accommodation, slash dump! Otherwise, I would have been homeless. For good measure and by way of a PS. I am due to be declared bankrupt officially, in the coming fortnight."

All the Inspector's heart strings were being mightily stretched by the minute. He had decided to let this poor woman get it all out of her system. Dealing with the death of her husband was not even high up on her list of priorities, that is how distant or broken that relationship had become. Murray's brief was to - Listen and briefly react. Listen and briefly comment. Listen and respond with a gesture or two. Listen, listen, listen. 'Kid' Curry knew the score and what his boss was trying to do and it all helped with his, 'up close and personal' on the job training.

"I can't beat them," the woman said, becoming emotional.

Not that she hadn't already been emotional. But rather than highly nervous, passionate angst. This was the tearful, bog-standard, raw emotion. The one that involved tearful bubbling and verging on hysterical. Murray gave 'Kid' Curry the eye. Basically if this all kicks off and goes south, then it's all down to you was the look. The young Constable had no option but to embrace it. He had suddenly started to think about the increased funding to support online services and helplines, and how it had noticeably failed to stem the tide of violence and ultimately domestic abuse deaths.

"It won't make any difference," she said. "Even a recent government committee, openly said, that they will be dealing with the serious consequences and fallout of this abuse for a generation to come."

Thankfully, Moira Cadogan regained her composure relatively quickly and began what was to be her concluding remarks.

"The low point was a suicide attempt four weeks ago," she offered with a modicum of regret in her voice.

The two officers were not sure if the regret they could hear was for attempting it, or the fact that she had failed.

"I bet you haven't tried that yet, Inspector?"

A question she immediately wished she could retract, based on the contorted look of DI Murray's face. So that gossip looked to have had some substance also, Curry concluded. This video would get great viewing figures, especially if it premiered in the works canteen, he quietly thought to himself. But geez, suicide. This was some serious stuff. He wondered how many, if any, of the others knew this about Murray's undisclosed past. Kerr? Hanlon? Doc Patterson? Some, if not all he figured. But for now, back to the end of season one...

"I was in the hospital for seven days and still the pain of this cruel addiction seeks you out and hits you from the moment you wake up." This time she addressed DC Curry. "And right now, for all he was abusive to me, with Barry gone - I've got nothing left to live for. Not even his impressive insurance policy."

Both officers' eyes lit up at that statement.

'Kid' Curry reacted first. "An impressive policy, Ma'am? As in, worth plenty?"

He soon realised why his experienced Inspector had allowed him to jump in first like a headless, unthinking chicken. Because what Murray heard was different from Andrew Curry. What he heard was...

"So with suicide, your 'impressive' policy would be null and void Mrs Cadogan?"

"Absolutely correct, Inspector. Thanks for that Barry. He just had to deliver and inflict one more painful blow on me, didn't he?"

No amount of words seemed appropriate at this time, but Murray continued on regardless...

"I've been there also, Ma'am," the Inspector stated. Going back to her previous comments. "Gambling and my actions were a major contributor to the loss of a dear loved one."

He's talking about his wife, Curry quickly surmised. He never spoke publicly about that matter. Everyone in his team knew that it was out of bounds, off limits and that it was NEVER up for discussion. Yet here he was, willing to disclose it at a moment's notice if it contributed positively to the outcome of this meeting. If it helped this lady regain a perspective on life and all that it had to offer her in the future.

"The fact that it's all available on the High Street these days is a nightmare for any addict," she added. "I would never go to a casino because of the effort involved in getting dressed up and having to reach a specific venue. Contrast that with the fact that there are at least seven major bookmakers all within a ten minute walk from here. Every one of which contained row after row of addictive FOBT machines."

Puzzled looks were exchanged between both men.

"They are called Fixed Odds Betting Terminals for a reason, gents."

"That the odds are fixed in favour of the bookmaker, meaning they have more chance of winning than you do," Andrew Curry concluded.

"I would go weeks without food and neglect my health."

The Inspector and his TV addicted sidekick for the day had certainly noticed her wafer thin figure. Given the area and locale they were visiting, Curry had immediately jumped to the wrong conclusion. Now it had been confirmed for him - it wasn't drugs after all.

"I haven't left the house for ten days and I have tried to force myself to go cold turkey. I am even scared of going grocery shopping, Inspector Murray, in case I end up in a nearby betting shop. Unsurprisingly, I am getting no help or therapy for my condition. I believe now that I will always have what others may see as an irrational compulsion to go into betting shops."

Nods and facial gestures were once again expressed. You could tell that she was now on the home straight, which was possibly very apt for a gambling addict. Especially one that started with horse racing.

"My body has grown used to sixty pound spins. I couldn't go back to laying a five pound bet. I'd always be thinking - Why? Why didn't I bet more? The limit on winnings was also a problem. As a gambler there's an irresistible impulse to win your money back. But you need to win twice to win back 10 spins. The Gamble Aware charity has a motto." She paused.

"Which is?" Murray obliged.

"When the fun stops. Stop! But gambling is not fun," she continued. "You obviously get that or got that Inspector. It looks like you managed to pull-up part way round the course."

The finishing post, for her, was now only metres away. But her stamina knew no bounds.

"When you're gambling your wages, your benefits and your life savings - it cannot possibly be fun. However, in recent years, the moment that credit was in the machine in front of me, I relaxed. When it was gone, I was just thinking about where my next stake would come from. No different from a junkie."

Murray wondered as she crossed the line, where the money did come from and if she had ever thought about what position she had eventually finished in the race? In his book, she had not only trailed in last, but having lost her overweight, cumbersome jockey. She was about to be put down and out of her misery.

Moira Cadogan was never going to be a course and distance winner ever again.

"I used to think that I was an intelligent person, officers," she said softly. "But this evil obsession has ruined my life."

"Ma'am, we have taken up enough of your time and we are sincerely sorry for the set of circumstances that you currently find yourself in," the Inspector offered up. "However, we just have two or three more questions and one more piece of vital information to pass on to you at this point before we go, if that's okay?"

With a tired nod offered by the woman, Murray began to speedily wrap things up.

"Where did Barry stay Mrs Cadogan?"

"He or we at the time, had been temporarily housed in Stenhouse, at 15a Bamber Street. Having no children or dependents, we had to take what housing was given to us or have no roof over our heads whatsoever. It was a one bedroom hovel and we were not allowed to sublet. Yet funnily enough, no one seemed to mind us sharing it with dry rot, rising damp, condensation and bug infestation."

After scratching at his head and rubbing down his body, Curry asked: "How long since you moved out?"

"Like I said earlier, about a month to six weeks ago," she recalled. "Do you still have a key?" Murray asked.

"Somewhere," she replied nonchalantly.

"It would appear that he was as obsessed with his real life fantasy role play gaming, as you were with your gambling. Would that be true?"

Without the slightest hesitation. "Absolutely, Inspector. In fact, I think that is where much of his brutish behaviour was born. It was only after he started with those consoles, that a fetish for whips, handcuffs and masochistic tendencies seemed to emerge."

"I can understand that," Curry said. Instantly realising how bad that must have sounded. "I meant..."

"We know what you meant, DC Curry. His Inspector assured him with a raised eyebrow or two. "I would stop if I were you, while you're still only just slightly ahead."

Alas, this time 'Kid' Curry was determined to have his say. "It's just that it has been proven and openly exposed, that amongst regular gamers the boundaries between their fantasy escapades and real-life, have become seriously blurred."

"We got that 'Drew." Murray then turned once again to Moira Cadogan and asked with suspicion. "Ma'am, did the officers that called previously, tell you anything else in relation to the death of your husband? Anything at all?"

She shook her head and returned the suspicious look. Then warily offered...

"Just that he had committed suicide and had been found dead in the city centre in the early hours, and that they couldn't say any more at present. That senior officers would be coming to visit with me. I never cried though, I remember that. Maybe that shocked them into retreat. What do you think, Inspector? Why do you ask?"

"Ma'am, when I mentioned about the newspapers and press converging on your home. That was because that in the Cowgate area of Edinburgh this morning at around 4am, they found your husband Barry hanging from the South Bridge."

Mrs Cadogan nodded slowly, several times. "I thought we covered this," she said dryly. No emotion showing whatsoever.

"Yes, possibly. But based on numerous notes recovered from his body, Ma'am. He owned up to being...... 'The Nursery Rhyme Killer! You may have heard that term in the news?"

Curry was taken aback that he had used that terminology.

"What! The man I was just hearing about on the radio. No seriously? My Barry, I can't believe that. Taking his own life is one thing. But murder, surely not? Although..." She hesitated and both detectives focused on her next words. "He had become more and more violent in recent times like I said. So I suppose, I could see it. But I don't think so."

Inspector Steven Murray said nothing. But inwardly, his conscience said, 'Me neither!'

"Did you know Andrew or Stacey Cannon?" Curry asked.

"The ones from the news? No, of course I didn't. Or any of the other Fairy Tale people," she said. Rather disrespectfully, the 'Kid' thought.

Curry corrected her and his Inspector was delighted to see him react when riled.

"Strictly speaking, Ma'am. A fairy tale is a folk legend. Generally with mythical content and it hardly ever involves fairies. Nursery rhymes on the other hand," he continued curtly. "Are poems, sometimes with musical settings. They are often meant to demonstrate basic verse concepts, as well as moral precepts to young children."

Moira Cadogan looked severely underwhelmed, Curry felt much better for it and Inspector Murray was deeply troubled and concerned that we ever taught some, if not all of those wholly inappropriate lyrics to children in the first place.

When the Police Scotland duo eventually left her humble abode, a full sixty minutes after arrival. 'Kid' Curry had learned a lot by listening and monitoring Murray's style and persona. Ultimately, he was still puzzling over a question or two, as they exited the litter- strewn pathway. One he vocally expressed...

"She hadn't worked in six months, she'd said. So how did she earn money to still gamble?"

Considering that, Murray simply pursed his lips and shrugged.

"And although he no longer lived with her, sir. Given the condition he continually left her in, if you were her, wouldn't you want the nasty, no-good abuser, dead too?"

Murray once again pursed his lips in a familiar pose before speaking...

"I think I would 'Drew. Except it was clearly suicide."

After eventually checking his voice messages, he added.

"And it appears Lizzie has tracked down some mobile and CCTV footage to back that up."

Twenty Nine

"The first cut is the deepest. Baby, I know the first cut is the deepest. When it comes to being lucky, she's cursed. When it comes to loving me, she's the worst."

- Rod Stewart

Murray replied firstly, by text to Lizzie. Letting her know that he and the 'Kid' would arrive in shortly to view the Barry Cadogan footage. After that he glanced at his impressive, blue-faced Skagen watch, reckoned he had time and made the other call.

"Why, DI Murray, it is only two hours since you last called me expecting a favour."

"That would be one hour and forty-two minutes to be precise, Ma'am. Any joy?"

It was 1.45pm and Barbra Furlong was preparing for a 2.00pm Friday afternoon Press Conference. One where she was keen to put everyone's mind at rest. Where she could announce to the nation and especially the residents of Edinburgh, that the so-called 'Nursery Rhyme Murderer,' was no more of a threat. That they had recovered a man's body and that alongside it was a detailed suicide note. 'Detailed' was usually, police speak for - he or she had owned up to everything.

"Do you think I'm a miracle worker, Steven? He's a newspaper columnist for Pete's sake, and has pretty high celebrity status in and around central Scotland. The man is..."

"That'll be a yes then, you managed it. Well done, Barbra. What time do we see him at?"

"How did you... I only just... I can't believe... Aaagh!... Nine o'clock tonight," she shrieked. "He only gets home around eight- thirty."

There was a quiet pause in the conversation. Furlong held the phone away from her ear to check that there was still a connection. The seconds continued to count... 46, 47, 48, 49...

"Hello, DI Mu..."

"So how about you and I get a drink beforehand," he interrupted. "I did actually ask you last night, but you chose to blank me."

"In public? Tonight? Steven, I thought we agreed..."

"We are going to be out on police business, DCI Furlong. It will be a little like going undercover, Chief Inspector."

"Actually, it won't! But a light refreshment before we speak to someone that could assist us in our enquiries, sounds okay to me," she said. "So pick me up at seven-thirty. You can choose the pub."

"Oh, I already have one in mind."

"Funnily enough, I thought that you might have. Lemonade and lime for me, Inspector. You can have your usual, a pint... of milk!" Indeed since his schooldays, that had always been his favourite tipple. Murray initially began to laugh, then stopped short. "Ma'am," he said in a serious tone. "I know you know what you are doing and that you're extremely experienced in these situations, but there is just something..."

"In your gut, Inspector?"

"Please, don't make light of it, Barbra. All I'm asking is that you proceed with caution at this Press Conference. It just doesn't feel..."

"Have you seen Lizzie's video of Cadogan's death yet?" She interrupted.

"No, not yet," he responded. "Okay, sure, I understand. Good luck. I'll see you later tonight."

No sooner had the Inspector hung up, than his phone sprang back into life. For a brief second he thought that maybe DCI Furlong had reckoned that she'd been a bit nippy with him, so a quick apology was on the cards. The fact that D. Poll flagged up on his car's multimedia screen, quickly shot that particular notion down in flames.

Andrew Curry bravely took the initiative. His DI liked that.

"Hello Doctor Poll. It's DC Curry here. Our beloved Inspector is driving and listening on speaker," he informed her.

"Hi Danni. What's up?" Murray asked. "Anything we can help you with? Or have you got something new for us?"

"It's the latter, Steven. Now I know we were asked to rush this through and we still have plenty of other tests and procedures to carry out on Mister Barry Cadogan, but what can you tell me about him?"

"Why? What's he been up to?" Murray joked.

The silence on the other end of the line, got that she wasn't amused. "He's in office work, mainly sales I believe, Doc. Although he also loves to get his kicks with fantasy role-playing games by all accounts. Plus speaking of kicks, when things don't seem to be going his way, either at work or at play. His frustrations seem to be taken out on his poor wife."

"He beats her?" Poll enquired.

"It would certainly appear that way," Murray confirmed. "How, what's wrong?"

"Well, nothing wrong as such. But that is interesting."

"What is?" 'Drew piped up. Keen once again to be involved in the conversation.

"Well, DC Curry, it's just that his body is covered in multiple injuries, involving the rupturing of numerous small blood vessels and discolouration without a break in the overlying skin tissue."

'Kid' Curry was dumbstruck. He looked at his Inspector to save him. Which he did. But not before a brief chuckle to himself.

"Ha Ha Ha," he laughed. "He's covered in bruises in other words, you clown."

Curry frowned.

"Doctor Poll please stop picking on my medically challenged officer. I have a hard enough time with him, as it is."

'Sorry,' Curry mouthed. Slinking back into the quiet of the passenger seat.

"So our so-called Nursery Rhyme Killer is himself covered in bruising and that didn't come from hanging himself? Banging against the bridge as he jumped? Or possibly whilst swinging?"

"Not a chance," she asserted. "In fact, Steven. Barry Cadogan's body was not just covered in bruises. In recent weeks, possibly months, he had suffered numerous hairline fractures, broken bones, cuts and injuries. The most recent assault would appear to be the deep scarring to his forehead, cheeks and neck. It was as if a mini garden rake had been drawn several times across those affected areas."

Murray had heard enough.

"I need to go Doc. It's urgent. Thank you so much for that, and hopefully I'm just in time." He hung up and had DC Curry call Barbra Furlong immediately. Her number just rang out.

"Text her," his Inspector encouraged. A text was then sent within seconds. The three words that the 'Kid' was to send were clear and concise... DON'T NAME HIM.

The clock on the dashboard read: 1.58pm. His Chief Inspector hadn't answered because she would have been seated in front of the hoards of cameras and journalists waiting to do her thing.

"Fingers crossed, she at least looks at it before they begin," Murray offered.

"I suspect she will," his Constable said. Crossing both sets of his precious and nimble digits in the car.

The Inspector smiled at the young man's optimism and added, "Let's hope so."

From your humble police officer chapping doors, making phone calls and following up leads. To specialist analysts and blood spatter experts. Even through to your family liaison officers and I.T. support, forensics and beyond. There would be easily 60 or more professionals involved in this case and that was continually rising by the day.

The long-serving and distinguished Barbra Furlong was about to be the high profile figurehead or ceremonial scapegoat. It all depended on her overall performance, her answers, her believability and her persuasive display with the reporters that would ultimately decide her fate. For they're the ones who will cut, splice and edit depending on the public's need for a sacrificial lamb to the slaughter.

There had been no requirement to give a press conference. Certainly not this quickly. Her superiors had not been hounding her to do so. But in the aftermath of current events, she felt it was in everyone's best interest and sooner rather than later. Because otherwise, her thinking was, the fair minded men and women of the media would go out and start looking for their own answers, and that never ended well.

It was nearly time, and as DI Murray's latest Volvo headed at pace toward the station building in Leith, down deep in the somewhat claustrophobic 'Vault,' Lizzie prepared to tune in.

Their DCI began safely and confidently. She named each of the victims. Up to and including Stacey Cannon. She spoke about the harrowing ordeal that their family, friends and loved ones have gone through these past few days and about their need for privacy at this time. Without going into specific details, she gave a general overview about the heinous murders committed and the challenges that they as a Force faced. She was understanding, sympathetic and engaging. She tried for 15 to 20 minutes to answer questions openly and honestly. She relayed certain leads and lines of inquiry that they were pursuing. There was obviously one or two that she couldn't comment on due to their sensitivity in the case. That was fair enough and the press boys (and girls) were understanding of that. She once again informed everyone that these were highly personal and targeted attacks, not random. She then reiterated and assured the community as a whole that she did not believe that there was any ongoing risk to the general public. She had focused mainly on giving the reporters lots of sound bites and takeaways. Plenty of tidbits to follow up on, to research and flesh out. They liked and appreciated that. Although Murray could feel her being gently and carefully reeled in. Like Furlong herself, she could sense that the bigger, larger question was still to come and about to follow...

"DCI Furlong, we are led to believe that you have someone in custody for these crimes. Is that right? Do you currently have the Nursery Rhyme Killer behind bars?"

The mood in the room changed. Like catching up with friends and acquaintances at work, the initial pleasantries had been hastily dispensed with and now it was time to get down to business. The Chief Inspector prudently scanned the seated faces. Had she done enough? Had she worked the room well enough up until that point? Had she read Murray's message? A slow refreshing mouthful of the bottled water in front of her would allow a few more precious seconds to pass. After carefully screwing the lid back on and placing it back on the table. She sat back and reckoned she'd done enough.

'Kid' Curry and his Inspector were now sitting in silence in the police car park with the vehicle's engine still turning over to keep them warm. Lizzie, momentarily found her fingers paused delicately above her keyboard and no doubt various other members of the team were all in position, anticipating their DCI's big announcement. One that said they had captured the bad guy and that a well deserved round of hearty congratulations and celebrations could begin.

It never came.

Thirty

"I know you tried to show me the light, but I feed on the darkness. I've lost control, I'm down in a hole. I'm broken and helpless and the noose is getting tight.

- Theory of a Deadman

Lizzie's petty glower toward DI Murray, as he and Andrew Curry entered 'The Vault' seemed to say it all. But her experienced Detective Inspector was not about to make it easy for her.

"What? What is it young lady?" He asked innocently. Curry casually looked at the floor to avoid eye contact with either of them.

"Weren't you two listening?" Her voice was irked and full of frustration.

Murray maintained the charade. "To what?" Thus allowing Lizzie free reign to rant...

"The bold Barbara's media statement. Her question and answer session. For Pete's sake, what were you two doing? How could you miss it? It was supposed to be a great start to the weekend. Where she tells everyone that we got him! That within days, we not only nailed the Nursery Rhyme Killer, but that we have him lying on a slab in the city morgue! Whoopee Doo!!!"

"But she never said that," Curry jumped in.

"I knew it! You were listening. And I know DC Curry - Exactly! That's my point."

Her blues eyes were now fiercely penetrating the back of Steven Murray's head. Willing him to turn and face her. Which surprisingly, he happily did. But as he calmly turned around, his face was sombre and serious, the camaraderie long gone. Lizzie guessed it would be for the better, if she'd just let it go for now. Which is exactly what she chose to do.

"The footage," her DI said.

"Sure, sir. But probably his mobile would be the quickest and easiest to tell you about firstly."

Lizzie then chewed on a pigtail and ran a scarlet nail or two down an A4 printout, before beginning to read aloud.

"Corresponding with those killed, Inspector. Here's where Barry's phone was at that time: Two weeks ago, Grace Adam - it was in Niddrie from around 10pm onwards. Jack Cannon - it was in the Balerno area from around 9pm onwards. Andrew King - located to Port Seton district at 8pm. Jeremy Crossland that same night at 10pm, it was traced to Morningside, and then finally to Edinburgh city centre, where it was discovered on his body. He did also have another so-called burner phone on him. No doubt to help correlate some of his dodgy dealings," Lizzie opined.

"Four out of the five crime scenes, on the night before each body was discovered. That is pretty damning," Curry concluded. "What are the chances of that? Although maybe just a coincidence!" He then teased DI Murray further, by adding. "Good luck later with DCI Furlong, sir!"

The Inspector's head dropped despondently forward.

"The CCTV footage," he said, frustratedly. Hoping to salvage something of his precariously balanced career.

Investigating analyst and technician, Radical Lizzie, flicked a few switches, turned some twiddly knobs and eventually rubbed two fingers together on a screen the size of a large coffee table. Voilà!

"This is Stramash," she declared. As a pub flashed on screen.

Murray, with his love of music, was already familiar with the place. But he let Lizzie continue uninterrupted.

"It's a 900 capacity, live music venue, sir. It was one of their late night, early morning revellers leaving the premises, that first spotted something. That something turned out to be the body of Barry Cadogan hanging from South Bridge in the heart of the Old Town. He alerted the police and we've now gotten to here." Lizzie, unable to stop herself, then felt the need to add.

"Why DCI Furlong never announced we had the bad guy, I'll never know!"

Before speaking, their Inspector stood upright, maximising his full, six foot one stature. It wasn't something that he often felt the need to do. But when he did so, he did it for a reason. Today, as he surveyed his immediate surroundings and especially the features and face of Radical Lizzie, he wore a disheveled suit and a desperately, disappointed frown.

"What do we have that is so convincing then?" The Inspector said in a rather reserved and slightly understated manner.

The largest screen on Lizzie's wall of impressive and somewhat scary electronic appliances, burst fully into life. Taken at street level, the grainy footage was still a good thirty to forty yards away from the overhead bridge itself. At the very top of the recording you could only just make out the bottom half of Cadogan's body. Although you clearly saw his face when he knelt at the stonework, to attach the rope around it. On what had been a wet night, rain continued to fall lazily from the charcoal-coloured clouds above. This certainly did not help with the clarity of their footage. After making his way up onto the two foot wide ledge. The standard, heavy duty rope was then lifted up and presumably placed around his neck. By this point, all that the camera could pick up was Barry Cadogan's tummy and legs draped precariously over the side. After a further ten second viewing his body shot dramatically out from the edge. It swung briefly with legs flailing and both his head and shoulders flickering faithfully. Nearby Christmas street decorations lit up his contorted face and body.

All three remained silent, even after viewing the twenty second clip for the third time. Murray, having already asked twice to see it again.

"And one more time, Lizzie, please."

Frustration was beginning to resurface on her face. There is thorough and there is taking things to extremes. However, she took a sharp intake of breath, clicked a key and obliged yet again.

"Okay," this time Murray said. "Is it just me, or does someone appear behind him before he goes over?"

"What!" They both shout out in unison

"Are you being serious, sir?" Lizzie spoke bluntly.

"Go on, play it again." This time the fifth review was at DC Curry's request.

"Slow it down and enhance it even more if you can?" The Inspector asked.

Lizzie followed her Inspector's instructions to the letter.

"Now, two things," Murray said. "Watch as he goes over. He has easily been able to get ten to fifteen inches of daylight between himself and the wall."

"But that's not too unusual, sir," 'Kid' Curry mumbled.

"No you're right, DC Curry," Lizzie agreed.

Curry went to rest on his laurels, just as she continued...

"But it is, especially if you don't use your feet or hands to push off with! Watch, again," she added.

So one more time the trio, frame by frame and inch by inch watched as Barry Cadogan tied the knot. Firstly around the masonry and then the noose for himself. He then sat on top, not a care in the world. No drink or drugs were found in his system. Placed as if positioned in view for a reason. Like he was posing for a picture.

"Doing as he was instructed," Murray cautiously put out there. "Implying that he wasn't the one in charge," he then suggested.

Lizzie began to offer up her own commentary, unable to keep quiet any longer.

"He didn't seem to be under any pressure, sir. Giving no indication that he wanted to back out or change his mind."

Curry nodded. From what he could see the female analyst was correct. Cadogan's feet were hanging loose, unable to push off from the side, and his hands were both sat on his lap. Again, there was no way that he was getting any momentum positioned like that. He most certainly wasn't poised to jump.

"He had no intention of jumping off that bridge," Curry confidently proffered.

"If he had leaned forward positioned like that," Lizzie stated. "He would literally slide straight down and his clothing would have had plenty of trace scuff marks and stone residue. Especially with it being wet, and there was none whatsoever."

"Okay. Now that we're all agreed on that," Murray smiled. "Both of you watch carefully and you'll see why your very astute DCI never gave Barry Cadogan's name out to the gathered media thirty minutes ago."

The feisty, female with the multi-coloured hair was about to give Steven Murray the evil eye, before being hurriedly checked back into line by Andrew Curry's disapproving look. She was still fiercely independent and struggled when reproved or chastised openly.

"Here it is," Murray said. "Look out for a shadow and then watch for the..."

"No way!" Lizzie exclaimed.

"Was that a hand?" Curry cried out. "Someone's fingers? He wasn't alone, sir! It wasn't him! He isn't our Nursery Rhyme Killer! But the evidence?"

Lizzie looked at Murray with a mixture of apology and shame.

"I missed it. It was my fault, sir. I was to blame."

"I wouldn't go that far, Lizzie. DCI Furlong did pressure you for a quick result. You saw an initial finding that supported the evidence and ran with it. I think your first comment is the more suitable one. You missed it, and fortunately no harm has been done. Plus Barbra Furlong chose for whatever reason, not to disclose our current findings to the world and that has worked in our favour."

Curry said nothing. But he would be informing Lizzie privately, at just how lucky she had been, and who was really behind the DCI's last minute change of heart. Although, had Danielle Poll notified them 10 minutes later about Cadogan's own torturous abuse, things would have been very different, very different indeed. Would they have even bothered to look so closely either, or just taken his jump at face value because it suited the evidence?

Steven Murray asked Lizzie, if she would kindly update the Chief Inspector. She couldn't quite believe that she was being given the opportunity to atone and break the news to her. DCI Furlong would still inevitably be disappointed that they don't have a culprit in custody. Although as DI Murray had mentioned thirty seconds ago to Curry, after his bluster of comments. Given the phone evidence, putting him at each of those locations and his note confessing to the crimes, Barry Cadogan may very well still be our man. He just wasn't in it alone and his partner was currently in the midst of taking care of any loose ends it would appear.

"I've some personal errands to run and it looks like we'll all be in tomorrow now, as I suspect this news will cancel all weekend leave. So Andrew if you want to see what else Lizzie can do to make a man of you today? Be my guest. I'll see you both in the morning."

As he departed 'The Vault,' his laughter could be heard echoing all throughout the historic basement. Lizzie frantically jumped on to her phone and pretended to be communicating via text with Furlong. Whilst Andrew Curry just stood beaming as bright as a beetroot, imagining what 'Radical' Lizzie could do to him anytime, never mind today.

Steven Murray drove home to hide behind his mask. The one that portrayed him as an 'unflappable and stoic' individual. For although that may be many people's perception of him. It in no way reflected the true man. Today, for some strange reason he was feeling exceptionally emotional and missing his pal, 'Ally' Coulter. He was feeling as deflated and as disappointed as all the other officers would be. He was gutted for the family and friends of the deceased, but he was also confident that they were taking large strides towards catching the culprit. Or, having just watched that footage, culprits plural. They all knew that the first few days in these cases were vital. When evidence was still fresh and people's memories best, although still never fully reliable. Definite links with Cannon and King had been established, which included 14 year-old Stacey. So three out of six. Halfway there. Murray's musings continued with the fact that they had not even begun looking at Barry Cadogan in-depth yet, so plenty to be going on with there. Plus Grace Adam and a local GP to continue investigating. The Inspector was confident that they would turn up something. That Lizzie would feel the need to double down and produce more than ever, after her slip up. An error that although spotted, she had instantly said she was to blame for, that it was her fault. The sad, sorry, society that he was currently a part of, encouraged this nonsense. The 'blame culture's' need for a head on the block! As he thought about his own specific theory in the years ahead, Steven felt his 'black dog' prowl relentlessly for any available spare scraps or morsels. Exhausted, the Inspector lay down on his leather settee and began to ponder on both Mitchell Linn and Barbra Furlong's media experiences today. Those thoughts then became a reflection on his own personal madcap ideology. Murray's theory and starting question for 2030, when it would be too late, was simply...

Who would have suspected that the news media and the advertisers were in on it together. I don't know how we could have missed it. It was pretty obvious. Every news report would ramp up our fear, our anxiety and our tension levels. Then it would end with some nonsense story about a Chihuahua being best friends with an African Parrot. Bang! - The adverts come on, telling us how to make ourselves 'feel happy.' We could eat our way to happiness, or buy fancy clothes. We could feel great in a new car or more secure in an executive home. They knew we'd never buy all their products, bankrupting ourselves into the bargain, unless we felt totally miserable and worthless inside. So the obesity epidemic grew and everyone was too busy being scared to notice what was happening right in front of their very eyes.

Murray's crazy half-farcical, half-sensible futuristic theory continued...

We were the sheep and the media their well trained shepherd dog. The teeth were bared and we ran, herded to the nearest shopping centre, supermarket or fast food store. Then we felt bad for getting fat and living in luxury, whilst most of the world starved and worked in conditions we wouldn't subject our worst enemy to. And how did we afford these products that humans have somehow done without for millennia? Well, we did soulless jobs we hated, we farmed our children into daycare and ended up divorcing the very love of our lives. We lived in misery and forgot what genuinely made us happy, and felt confused about what love really was.

Their products continued to destroy our society and our Earth. Polluting and endlessly filling the emotional void where tenderness and appreciation should have been. So while we sipped on overpriced coffee in fancy cafes, vulnerable children died of starvation and lack of basic sanitation abroad. In our heightened fear, we could no longer feel love. Our noble and courageous natures were suppressed, keeping us in a primal state of survival that did not belong in our so-called golden age. Everyone I knew back then, the Inspector reflected, was good. But to hear the media tell it -We were surrounded by savages, disease and danger.

By this point Steven Murray was grateful to have drifted off to sleep for an hour or so. When he awoke, he was back in this decade and went to meet up with Barbra Furlong for a well advertised, fancy overpriced drink or two!

Thirty One

"Slow down, we've got time left to be lazy. All the kids have bloomed from babies into flowers in our eyes. We've got fifty good years left to spend out in the garden and I don't care to beg your pardon, we should live until we die."

- Fun

The matter of Barry Cadogan hadn't been mentioned. The subject not yet touched upon. It would be at some point in the evening, but currently, it was never broached. They had an official bonafide meeting with an eccentric theatre critic later. So Barbra had opted for something midway between office wear and classic evening attire. It was a deep walnut, double breasted blazer and trouser suit. Finished off with a silky cinnamon blouse and matching heels. Very Rebecca Loggenberg, Murray thought. But the only actual words he allowed himself to say publicly were...

"Impressive. Very impressive indeed, DCI Furlong." And relax he thought to himself.

"I see you made the effort, Inspector," was offered up sarcastically. "It looks like you went to sleep in that thing?"

He thought it best not to dwell on his 2030 theory. Or the surreal sleeping session that accompanied it.

"Remember we are going to some slightly less salubrious surroundings initially, before we pay the author a visit."

"Wait. When did, 'less salubrious surroundings' come into play, Inspector?"

"When you told me to choose the public house, Chief Inspector."

"I don't think I'm going to be too impressed here somehow. Am I?" She offered up discouragingly.

"I personally wouldn't like to say." He then winked and smiled.

When they pulled up kerbside, thirty minutes later, a few locals eyed them suspiciously. Knowing full well, who and what they were. Radical Lizzie had worked her magic for them yet again. Only an hour after leaving DC Curry and her together, the couple had unearthed a local address for Grace Adam through a local medical practise. She had obviously been treated or given prescriptions for things previously. Why this never flagged up on their missing persons database, summed up everything that was wrong with the system, and the inability of the good guys to keep up with the bad. In this case, maybe the bad guy was a doctor. Murray had asked Lizzie to let him know if 'Hickory Dickory Dock,' Jeremy Crossland, had ever practised at that surgery? She had texted him back almost instantly with an emphatic NO! She had already checked. Of course she had, Murray chided himself.

Undercover of darkness, the two senior officers were certainly discreetly parked outside the Blue Lagoon Public House, but so too were several gangs of aging teenagers and adults. On the outskirts of Niddrie, the location was chosen specifically on the basis that it was literally only 200 yards from the address that he had been given for Grace Adam. DI Murray encouraged his senior ranking officer to stay put in the car for ten minutes. He also suggested that if he wasn't back out in fifteen, that she should probably drive straight to the morgue and bring a vehicle back with her to pick him up!

As DCI Furlong monitored the premises, she quickly reckoned that the words 'less salubrious,' were being generous, very generous indeed.

The Blue Lagoon was no fancy bespoke micro-brewery establishment. It was a throwback to a classic 1970's, no-frills, working-class local. Although, how the word class got to be involved in its description in any way, defies logic. It was a rough'n ready, hard as nails dive. Most windows were now permanently boarded up. It was the cheaper option, as opposed to regularly replacing them after every weekend brawl.

"Awright, Mr Murray," a couple of shouts went out. As he strode toward the entrance.

"Lads," he responded in kind, with a friendly, insincere wave.

He then threw some notes from his wallet into the world weary bonnet that a local 'jakey' had at his feet. From the warmth and comfort of the car, Barbra Furlong simply smiled at that selfless gesture. It pretty much summed up the character of that tortured, troubled soul. A man that she apparently seemed to be falling in love with. The recipient of his donation lay still on the ground. His only movement came from continued bouts of constant coughing. He wore several layers of heavy jackets and a pair of sole-less boots. Down low, he sheltered away from the cold wind. His body was huddled up outside the closed down grocery store next door to the pub entrance. Murray, now at the said entrance, pulled open the door and disappeared into an alternative, parallel universe. Furlong began the countdown.

For Steven Murray, it instantly brought back memories of 'The Doctors.' The illicit licensed premises, owned by a certain Mr James Baxter Reid. The location where Tasmin Taylor was brutally slaughtered to death, two years previous. These particular drinking dens were like protected institutions. Every one a law unto itself. Dodgy deals in every corner and a place where morals were seen as a weakness. Where the local gangster's moll, beneath her mask of decadence and delight was actually planning the death and disposal of her husband's latest mistress. The task would be carried out in the same manner most people reserved for a list of household chores.

Again in Murray's 2030 theory, his humane solution to this problem, would not be to force the violent or predatory disordered on the rest of society and expect them to 'deal with it.' No, tongue most definitely not in cheek, Murray was all for their removal from society! And by whichever means necessary. Again he thought it best possibly not to share that opinion with the others in his current company. Certainly not just yet.

He saw and met up with a few familiar faces and got chatting. Ex- cons or not, most recognised DI Murray was a solid guy and that he wasn't out to get you just for the sake of it. That was the reputation he had built up. And tonight he was there to put behind bars some sick perverted, twisted, psycho who in a weak, cowardly fashion, would stone a young defenceless girl to death and then set her body ablaze. An indefensible act. Yet someone will seek to defend them! But not there, not in a place with such working class, criminal morals.

"She was jist a wee lassie, Mr Murray."

"Naebiddy deserved tae die like that!"

"We wid aw string him up and let him swing, man."

Those were just a few of the more acceptable comments and feelings Murray was offered whilst doing his rounds and buying some into the bargain. The last one being possibly closer to the truth, than the scarred faced, pockmarked youth that said it knew. Many of the drinkers, including 'Gus' the manager, informed him that Grace Adam had been a poor soul about these parts for the last few years. Mostly always high on something.

"We all knew her as Lucy," Mr Murray. "She had been 'gainfully employed' by just about everyone in the pub," he continued. "And that included several of the females and a handful of the younger under-age lads outside. You know, one minute riding their bike and the next..."

"I get the picture," Murray told him.

A picture that the Inspector was determined never to share with her parents. There was no need. It wouldn't help them any and it certainly no longer aligned with the memories they kept of her at home. That was of another time and place entirely.

Sad as it may have been, Murray had been told by a number of the regulars, that their busy entrepreneurial daughter had her phone number plastered all over various shops in the area. For example, he was made aware that every takeaway owner and fast-food boss would know her. Because that's how she ate. Other stores offering different services were also included. Launderette, vaping and grocery outlets also made it onto the 'quid pro quo' list!

This poor child, for that was what she was. Had survived like that for six years. What a life, he thought. What a sad, lonely and desperate life. He thanked the strange, assorted cast of drinkers and left. As the heavy door slammed solidly behind him, Furlong's watch hadn't even reached the thirteen minute mark. As he pulled up the edge of his jacket collar and went to return to the car, he suddenly heard a couple of cackling coughs followed by a faint cry.

"Steven, Steven Murray... Is that you?" A low, frail voice seemed to whisper. Gradually the sound grew stronger and more certain. Still sat on the ground, the homeless man from earlier held up Murray's two crisp ten pound notes tightly in his hand. "You've not changed one bit, son. Still as generous as I remember." Each sentence was broken up by a phlegm induced rattle of his lungs.

Furlong watched this strange exchange from the luxury of her passenger seat. She'd already witnessed several other *illegal* exchanges over the past ten minutes between the feral group of youth trading their stocks and shares. Each time a deal was done, they'd focused on her vehicle and dared her to act. Once or twice, several of them even cycled menacingly around the car. Again marking their territory and audaciously challenging her. When Murray reappeared though, their intimidating behaviour ceased immediately and Furlong relaxed, before carefully putting her pepper-spray back into her bag.

The respectful, Inspector, had knelt by the man's side. Much to Furlong's surprise and frustration it must be said. His natural instinct however, had told the detective that a cold night such as this gives us even more reason to draw closer to one another, to feel the natural warmth we are born to give. He was now rubbing this man's shoulder and trying desperately to place him. A previous offender? Someone he'd interviewed in the past? Or most probably a homeless man that he has helped out before on his travels? He was getting there, Murray took great pride in remembering people and in recalling their...

"MACCA," he suddenly yelped. "Is that you? No, surely not. Davie!"

"Aye, ye've still got it, young Murray. Word on the street is that yer an Inspector noo. Wid that be right?"

As Murray welled up with tears. A scraggy greying beard climbed the poor man's chin like raggedy vines after a severe winter. The lines on his dirt-ingrained face etched the story of a once happy life. His crow's feet spoke of significant laughter and the deep creases in his cheeks told of a man who gave away smiles like they were wishes.

The man's name was Davie McIntyre. 'Macca' to his mates. This poor soul in front of him, had been one of Steven Murray's role models in the Force when he had first moved over to the Lothians. Nothing was ever too much of a problem for him. Good-natured banter and kindness were always in great supply if you were ever in Macca's company for long. Yet tonight, a more sorrowful face Inspector Murray had never seen. A film of water made the man's dark eyes, glossy and his face appeared fallen, having submitted to gravity. His trademark silver hair, normally neatly combed. Bore all the tell tale signs that his mottled, gnarled hands had been run through it once too often in distress. It was the face of a man who had lost what he knew he must lose, yet the knowing had not softened the desolation.

Vividly and heartbreakingly, it all came back to the Inspector. He hadn't seen David McIntyre for easily ten or twelve years by this point. He remembered that he had been working out in the sticks. Either Haddington or Dunbar, somewhere in East Lothian. It was then that fate dealt him an awful blow. He had been away on a training course in England for a few days. Then in the early hours of his first morning, he was given the news to travel back up the road immediately. The previous night, his all female family had perished tragically in a deadly house fire. Trapped in the 'supposed' safety of their own home. Each one, his wife and three daughters all were overcome by smoke and fumes. Ann, 35. Eva, 12. Lilly, 7 and Abigail who would have been 4 on that very weekend. The McIntyre family ceased to be that evening. Already harrowing and soul destroying as that was, Davie McIntyre was to be further punished. Several days after the fatal fire, and with investigations fully under way, he was informed that his wife Ann had been ten weeks pregnant.

Recalling in seconds, all of those desperately hurtful memories from this man's past, allowed the disillusioned detective to shed even more tears and to be overcome with grief. He just sat by this poor man's side and hugged and hugged and hugged him. Steven Murray generally hated this life and more specifically his own life. But walking in another man's shoes every now and then, certainly helped put an awful lot of things in perspective.

"I'm working, Macca," he told the man. "The poor girl that was torched nearby here, a few weeks ago."

It dawned on Murray that he had spoken stupidly and without thinking. As if this man in his current state was even aware of what day it was. Never mind news or topical events over the past fortnight.

"Sorry Davie, I really need to get going. It's just that a certain unforgiving DCI is waiting for me in the car. You can relate to that still, right?"

Macca nodded, scraped up yet another drum roll with his vocal chords and offered Steven Murray a thankful wave with his tenner's.

With a heavy heart the DI left it at that and dragged himself up from the cold ground. You can't follow that up by saying - 'It was great to see you, or let's catch up soon.' He fought back more tears, waved and walked away. It was the run up to Christmas after all and Steven Murray realised that he'd just had 'A Wonderful Life,' moment. Because, unless he seriously looked to address and change a few things in his normal schedule, that could very easily be him in the near future. He could no longer kid himself. He'd had a fright.

As he walked back toward the car, he recalled how he had taken in Davie's features for as long as he dared look. The man was skeletal really. No-one's cheekbones should stick out that far. His face had no trace of life other than not being blue. Murray swallowed at that grim thought. It was like the man was breathing without really being alive.

Davie McIntyre had unfortunately turned to drink. He'd wanted no help and lost everything. The once warm, loving and generous man had shut out his extended family of brothers and sisters and closed down all relationships. Hurting and grieving as he most obviously was, he literally went off the grid and no one knew how to reach out to him anymore, or indeed what had become of him.

Murray was churning up. Appropriate seasonal echoes of, A Christmas Carol and Ebenezer Scrooge ran through his tormented mind, and certainly thoughts of Grace Adam and her squalid existence didn't help matters.

"A friend?" DCI Furlong innocently joked with him, when he returned to the warmth of the car.

He started the engine and gave one long, last reflective look toward the isolated and shadowed figure, lying motionless on the frozen ground.

"Absolutely," he said, with a genuine smile. "An extremely good friend. Although, I doubt he could say the same of me!"

Furlong could feel his pain. They drove off in muted silence.

Thirty Two

"And just because you're gay I won't turn you away. If you stick around I'm sure that we can find some common ground. Sexuality - Strong and warm and wild and free. Sexuality - Your laws do not apply to me."

- Billy Bragg

It was Sandra Kerr during their first round of brainstorming that had actually spotted his book and pointed it out to DI Murray. She was aware of the man from TV and radio appearances, but had no idea that he was originally from Edinburgh and still stayed there. Given his polite English public schoolboy tone, you would never have guessed that he was from Scotland's capital city. Although, on the other hand...

Johnston Webster lived in an affluent Georgian apartment, bang in the middle of Moray Place in Edinburgh's New Town. They eventually got to his impressive premises at ten minutes after nine. Furlong would happily state that as... nine, ten. Murray, as a lesser mortal, would say... ten past nine! And with that in mind, the Inspector got the impression that if they bothered to ask this particular homeowner, the response may well be... 'Twenty-One Ten!" Ahh, Education/Education/Education, he thought.

Barbra grinned at him. "Did you know, Inspector, that this area was part of the extension to the original New Town?"

"Funnily enough, I didn't know that, Chief Inspector. But why am I not in the least surprised that you know that? Plus may I repeat, you look absolutely stunning. That's merely a casual observation, mind," he smiled. It felt nice to smile, he reminded himself.

As they stood on the front steps, both ranks appeared amused and content with that exchange. Murray then pushed a bell the size of three golf balls and waited for lift-off. Unfortunately all that he heard was an old-fashioned... DING-DONG. However when the heavy white door finally opened, a good sixty seconds later. There was no discreetly dressed butler or attractive housemaid from the Philippines, which seemed to have been a recent pre-requisite for all wealthy Edinburgh socialites. Last week the Inspector was even told of a Buy One, Get One Free deal on offer at Costco! That last thought may have been made up and over the top. Which was also an expression or tag that could have been labelled on the individual who actually did answer the door. He was kitted out in salmon coloured trousers with a tan belt. His pink and blue checked shirt was partially hidden by the rich Egyptian blue blazer with gold trim and buttons. Shoes in the same blue shade, adorned his sock-less feet. To be fair, Steven Murray thought, in his grubby, grey two-piece suit. Neither him nor his host was wearing a tie. Now that was a result. Cool or what?

"Ah, Chief Inspector Furlong." Webster exclaimed, excitedly shaking Murray's hand. "And Inspector Murray, welcome." He added, clasping the smooth hand of DCI Furlong.

The bold Barbra bit her lips and said nothing. Maybe this would benefit them somehow, keeping the mix-up quiet for the time being.

"Sorry, for the delay in getting to the front door. I was up on the second level, officers."

He made it sound like he was on a fancy Caribbean Cruise Liner or the Starship Enterprise. Especially with his colourful clothing and gregarious voice. The happy, go-lucky attitude was not too dissimilar to a certain occupant in a Greenock Hotel that he knew. The only difference, apart from their living conditions, would be that one is a well respected TV, radio and media personality. Whilst the other - Is not!

Murray was blown away by the man's beautiful crisp cut, blue blazer and its neat trim.

"That is one stunning jacket, sir. Workmanship of the highest quality," he gushed. As he immediately took hold of its cuff and admired it fully. "And just the perfect length on you."

"Thank you, my good man. Thank you for saying so. One tries one's best." He paused slightly. Mainly to soak in the adoration. Another second or so should just about do it - and relax. "When your secretary or public relation's person called earlier today, Chief Inspector," he continued to address Murray. "She told me all about some case that you were currently investigating and how my recent book may help offer you a different perspective or something like that. I'm not sure she was very clear in her communication that she knew exactly how I could help, and I must say, neither am I."

"Yes," Murray added poshly. "She does rather like the sound of her own voice, somewhat!"

Furlong's eyes suddenly gave off a glare that froze the Inspector's bones. Like being nude in the middle of a hailstorm, where every chunk of ice was a frosted dagger cutting into his skin. Maybe it was time to come clean about who was who? And although panicked by Furlong's murderous wanderlust, he decided to hold fire on any potential reveal to Mr Webster at present.

"I have a rather quaint, little writing study through here detectives. Shall we retreat there and continue our chat?"

The pretentious sounding Paisley man continued to, at least he thought, mess with Johnston Webster. But Barbara's understated smirk grew into a monstrous beaming smile. Because under the experienced eye of Chief Inspector Furlong, Steven Murray was most definitely, although unintentionally, flirting with the celebrated author!

"A writing study. How charming!" Murray continued, stretching forth his arm and indicating for Furlong to swiftly follow their genial host.

As they entered the room Webster picked up a copy of his new book, signed it and thrust it confidently into Murray's hands.

"Enjoy!" The tall, thin, upright figure said softly.

Momentarily clasping Steven Murray's nail-bitten hands in the brief exchange. The Inspector had bitten his fingernails for as long as he could remember. A bad habit that had followed him from at least his earliest schooldays.

"Oh, Mr Webster," Murray piped up. "Forgive me for just thirty seconds, I have to let our colleagues know where to reach us. We forgot to inform them earlier."

Their host raised his arms in a gesture of solidarity and understanding. Barbra Furlong just wondered what her crafty DI was up to. As well as quietly questioning to herself, her host's definition of a 'quaint little room.' The rectangular location they had just entered into was easily six feet wide and twenty feet long. In fact, it was nearly as big as her whole 'quaint little cottage.'

Murray had ended his call.

"So how can I help officers?" The man asked with a bewildered grin and arms gesticulating wildly, as all three tried to take a seat around his normal sized writing desk.

Furlong updated him on several of the scenes of crime. All details that he could have read or seen on TV. She also informed him about visiting with Scotland's leading authority on Nursery Rhymes and on Maurice Orr's particular take on events so far.

Murray produced his signed copy and placed: 'Being Inside: Thespians, Lesbians and Plays,' on the desk in front of them.

"Nice to have some visual context," he added.

"Yes, yes, I agree, Chief Inspector. Very stimulating," the man said. Sitting cross-legged and swaying his right ankle clockwise.

Murray looked across at his DCI. The ice daggers had melted and been replaced by a jovial wink. The three plain speaking people had some interesting discussion over the next twenty or thirty minutes. Could the murderer be gay or not? Whoever it was, they enjoyed being the centre of attention. Theatrical no doubt, Webster agreed. Possibly an ex-prisoner, based on his familiarity with the system. Or simply someone with a grudge against a group of people for whatever reason!

"You know I have a chapter in my book all about the sexuality of many of these nursery rhyme characters?"

Murray held up both hands and winked in Furlong's direction. His actions clearly indicating - I'll take this...

"Like we said at the start Mr Webster, one of our colleagues pointed that out to us. Several of us were fascinated, myself in particular by your interesting, unusual and bizarre take on those childhood favourites. So much so, that I felt encouraged to ask," Murray paused and gestured toward his female companion. He then finished with, "Actually, I felt encouraged to ask my esteemed colleague Detective Chief Inspector Barbra Furlong to phone and speak to yourself in person, and she did just that. Wasn't that charming of her?"

Webster instantly changed his gaze from one to the other and back again. His tingling cheeks were kindling up nicely. Moving gradually from two glasses of light rosé, to raspberry ripple ice creams, and then on to fully fledged, bright beaming candy apples! And although mortified, frozen to the spot and slightly traumatised. He took it all in good spirit and responded well by going straight over the top and into high-pitched presenter mode.

"I can't believe I made that horrible assumption. Oh, how my head is spinning. I'll never live this down as long as I live. You both know that, right? People. Yourselves, will be reminding me of this as I eat my fruit and jelly in the care home. There is nothing for it, I'll just have to leave town, cast off my identity and start off again somewhere new."

The well-dressed brunette in the heels laughed heartily. Impressed that the man was grounded enough in reality to laugh at himself. Furlong had met many celebrities at various events or on the job over the years and sadly that was not the case with the vast majority of them. Normally they were so full of their own self- importance. His humility was refreshingly charming.

This at least meant that her less than impressively dressed partner, the one with the 'distinguished' hair colouring, would be glad to no longer have the extra responsibility as ranking officer. He threw his head back and laughed with the others. They then continued to speak about various backgrounds, foundations, suspicions and origins again in relation to many of the ancient fairy tales and nursery rhymes.

"Tracy Adam, you said. That was your Lucy murder?" Webster sought clarification.

"Grace or Gracie Adam," Murray corrected.

It was a rather obscure nursery rhyme. It was certainly one of the shortest. Which made it super easy for Johnston Webster to recite from memory. Incorporating several short animated action sequences and a slight American lilt, the popular reviewer continued in style to great aplomb...

"Lucy Locket lost her pocket, Kitty Fisher found it. Not a penny was there in it, only ribbon round it."

As he took his exaggerated bow. Both officers joined in with a round of silent applause.

"Like many of those songs, ditties, fairy tales and legends of their day. There can be many variations on their beginning, their birthplace or origin, DCI Furlong," he said. This time staring at the only female in the room.

"Oh, I know all about origins," Barbra Furlong grinned.

"Well in my version, Lucy was a homeless beggar, a lost soul. It was over two hundred years ago and here was a story, a song at least, that spoke about a gay prostitute."

The way it was told to them by one of Scotland's top theatre critics, especially in the comfort and luxury of his Edinburgh home, made it sound exciting. With a touch of illicit, irreverent scandal and intrigue thrown into the mix.

"It was to be a famous spat between two highly charged 18th century bi-sexual prostitutes," he said.

"Can you shed any further light on it for us, Mr Webster? I know we are clutching at straws, but right now, every little helps," Furlong pleaded.

Webster snorted a little with derision. "Well of course, Chief Inspector. I can tell you that with the right amount of bad language and gratuitous sex thrown in, Netflix could string it out for over three seasons!"

"Very good," Murray laughed. "My colleague here, is currently trying desperately to give up one of those bad habits."

Furlong was mortified and Johnston Webster was once again highly embarrassed, because he had never heard her swear, so he assumed...

And DI Steven Murray was certainly no role model for Radical Lizzie when it came to the old adage of: Always remembering to put your brain into gear, before engaging your mouth. With the awkward impasse over. Webster did a quieter, more acoustic take, whilst sitting comfortably.

"Lucy Locket lost her pocket, Kitty Fisher found it. Not a penny was there in it, only ribbon round it. Historically," he announced in a rather dramatic fashion. "The term 'pocket' referred to a pouch worn around the waist by women in the 17th to 19th centuries."

"Fascinating. I never knew that," the Inspector said.

Furlong simply nodded. She was well aware of that fact. Of course she was, Steven Murray reckoned. She loved her historical origins and back stories and as if to prove her credentials, right on cue she offered up...

"Would I not be right in thinking, Mr Webster, that skirts and dresses at that time had a slit at the waistline to allow access to the pocket that you refer to?"

Mr. Webster was about to respond, when Barbra added...

"Because normally it hung around a woman's waist by a ribbon or something similar."

"Spot on, Chief Inspector. You really didn't have any need for me, after all."

Trying desperately to keep Barbra Furlong's feet firmly on solid ground. Her senior, yet junior officer, put a reassuring hand on the shoulder of the man's figure hugging blazer and stated confidently...

"Oh, don't you dare go underestimating your years of experience and knowledge Johnston. What an unusual name by the way, may I call you that? I'm sure there is much more that you can tell us and we would be ever so grateful."

This made Detective Chief Inspector Barbra Furlong smile like a repentant rabbit. Mainly because she was certain that DI Murray in his haste to rain on her parade, had no idea that he was once again openly flirting with one of Edinburgh's most eligible and in her book, blatantly handsome homosexuals!

The thing is, gossip columns, magazines or reality TV, no matter - Steven Murray didn't do Celebrity! He would have no idea who this man was or his mini iconic status within a certain high profile community in Scotland. However, at this rate if he wasn't careful, an invitation to an up and coming red carpet event would unquestionably be on the cards.

As the night progressed Webster and Murray continued to build a rapport with one another. Steven Murray loved his musicals, including plays. So he was grateful to discuss their relevance to society back in that era. About how they came to be and how they were financed by the political satirists of the day.

"It was a huge, huge hit when it first appeared in 1728, Inspector and has been extensively revived and imitated ever since."

By this point, the subject of their attention was John Gay's, The Beggar's Opera, which Webster had wrote about at some length in his recent work. It was ranked as one of the biggest successes of 18th-century theatre. Both Furlong and Murray had been fascinated by the outline of the story, especially the way Webster described it to them. No wonder he was a highly successful commentator and reviewer. His dialogue was compelling, his ability to initially enthral his audience and then engage with them, simply a joy to be a part of. With the poise of a regal Prince, the man was now pacing frantically up and down his 'quaint little study.' Like an intrepid adventurer he was seeking to pull Furlong and Murray head first into the tantalising vortex that he'd created. Here was an emotional hurricane in full force. For as quickly as he took flight, he then allowed his tall, impressive body to relax and his voice to ebb and flow in calmer waters. He carried on with a further engaging narrative...

"Set partly in Newgate Prison and populated with a back-stabbing cast of con artists, highwaymen, corrupt jailers and prostitutes, the piece is an audacious blend of lowlife farce and high art, comedy and cruelty. It was one of the first so-called 'ballad operas,' employing pre-existing popular songs. These days we would call it a jukebox musical, like Mamma Mia or We Will Rock You."

"Or, Our House by Madness," Murray offered up excitedly.

And although the man said, "Quite so."

Webster's curled up eyebrows and pained expression was more akin to a Marks and Spencer shopper, mistakenly entering into Lidl. Captivated by the man, even Barbra Furlong was won over by his pulsating energy levels and love for his subject matter. As he concluded, he finished off his descriptive narrative with yet another few informative lines...

"It mocks the conventions of fashionable, baroque Italian opera. It also takes aim at the grim realities of early 18th-century London and at its political corruption in particular. Its author's epitaph in Westminster Abbey, records how Gay's 'native humour' and 'virtuous rage' enabled him to 'lash the age.' As its continued popularity around the world demonstrates, The Beggar's Opera has resonated in many other ages and countries too."

At that, he lit himself a cigar and sat back briefly to contemplate. He then politely addressed each of them correctly, and enquired if they were done with him for the evening.

"It's just that I've had a long day. I also have an article required for midnight tonight, which is due for publication on Sunday. So I suppose I had better make a start on it."

The officers understood and began to gather together their jackets and belongings. They got their exercise in by walking steadily back down the lengthy staircase of the affluent townhouse. Approaching the front door they both expressed their gratitude to the man.

"Thank you so much, sir," they offered up in unison.

"You are most welcome. I thoroughly enjoyed myself also. Oh, and don't forget your book Chief Inspector Murray," Webster reminded him. "And congratulations and best wishes with the promotion," the charismatic man added.

To which they all laughed, as he gently closed the door behind them.

Thirty Three

"You can shine your shoes and wear a suit. You can comb your hair and look quite cute. You can hide your face behind a smile. But one thing you can't hide is when you're crippled inside."

- John Lennon

Driving back to Furlong's cottage in Dirleton the atmosphere was playful, but reflective. Both officers were keen to ponder and discuss some key moments of the evening. In the passenger seat, Barbra, like most people, never fully understood exactly what was involved in being a theatre critic or reviewer. The strict deadlines that they adhered to, to contribute articles to print media, such as newspapers, magazines or books. Johnston Webster did all three, and he certainly seemed to be highly regarded. Occasionally with his popular profile, he would also write for online sources or share new production opinions through radio and television. He had told his visitors that several theatre critics, especially those trying to build a name for themselves, work primarily as freelance writers. Who ultimately sell their work to a wide variety of commercial outlets. Thankfully he had already served his time and built such an impressive reputation, that he now regularly worked as a columnist and weekly contributor to several successful magazines, as well as to one specific top-selling Sunday newspaper. Having listened and interacted with the man himself, Barbra also much better appreciated how in addition to providing literary interpretation, the writings and musings of a top critic can help create and raise general awareness about the overall 'theatre experience' amongst a new generation of readers. Thus increasing overall circulation numbers.

Like herself and her Inspector and all the unseen tasks that they had to undertake on a daily basis, DCI Furlong now had a newfound respect for all writers, reviewers and critics and for their ability to continually meet those deadlines, both visually and vocally, as well as juggle multiple award-winning writing projects all at once. Detective Inspector Steven Murray on the other hand, had different priorities. He had reflected solely on how he could help a man he once considered a good friend: 'Macca!'

Parking in East Lothian, made you fully appreciate that winter had definitely arrived and was determined to settle down and make camp for another couple of months. On the street itself, it was the type of coldness that reached deep within your bones and the only thing to do was keep moving. To keep heading toward the front door and the steady warmth of the hearth. The sky was a rolling blanket of clouds, each one the colour of wet ash. Every step along the path became more hurried by the second. Oh boy, it was chilly. Which was similar to the reception Murray was about to receive. That was until she spotted the beautiful basket of dried flowers that had been delivered and were sitting on her doorstep. Although quickly witnessing the surprised look on DI Murray's, Barbra returned him swiftly to the draughty doghouse. The floral arrangement appeared to be the third anonymous gift in recent days that Furlong had received. She had not mentioned the previous two to any of her colleagues, including Detective Inspector Murray.

Once inside Barbra Furlong made herself a lovely warm mug of hot chocolate and escorted her scruffy lodger through to the guest bedroom for the second consecutive evening. DI Murray was usually quite perceptive about these things and with his memory still in good shape, he smiled and readily recalled the bad language and gratuitous sex jibe from earlier. He knew it would come back and bite him for sure. He just hadn't expected justice or retribution to have been meted out quite so soon. With an apologetic and accepting look, he waved her good-night and yelled.

"You still look stunning by the way!"

His host's door gently began to close over without response.

However, before shutting fully, the bedroom mirror caught Furlong offering up the briefest of amused looks. There had been no malice or petty tit-for-tat revenge planned. There had been no fallout or mean words exchanged. Except in the car when his companion for the evening had expressed just how exhausted and drained she'd really felt. That was when Steven volunteered for day two in the hospitality suite. It had been a long day for his Chief Inspector. Another murder, alongside TV and press conferences took up most of her morning and afternoon duties. Before late night evening inquiries, including seeking assistance from a national celebrity had kept her busy. All of that and she still hadn't actually gotten the drink he'd invited her out for. On second thoughts, Murray reckoned he'd got off lightly.

Barbra Furlong, unsurprisingly, was an avid reader. She had a collection of books in every room in her idyllic cottage. In the guest bedroom it seemed to consist mainly of crime fiction and autobiographical works. As Murray scoured the two lengthy shelves of hardback editions. He was about to opt for either the life story of Bruce Springsteen or Willie Nelson, when another book from a different genre entirely, suddenly caught his eye. Still a biography, but this one was about playing on a field, rather than a stage. A football field. It was: *Gary Speed: Unspoken, In Her Home,* which had aroused a strange curiosity in the man. Because Barbra Furlong's brother had committed suicide, it made Murray doubly intrigued as to why his DCI would feel impressed to have a copy of this particular book in her collection. The Inspector took it back over to the bed for a little bit of cheerful nighttime reading and began with the foreword...

'Football star Gary Speed's suicide, whilst manager of the Welsh national team left millions devastated, but no-one was more broken than the woman who cut his body down and had to carry on without him. His wife kept hearing how the football world was struggling to come to terms with the

shocking loss of an apparently happy-go-lucky, 42-year-old icon who was not long into his dream job of managing his country, Wales.'

Louise Speed lost the soul-mate she'd been with since she was 13 and the father to their two teenage boys. At 41, she had to pick up the pieces of a world torn apart by, in her words, *"sadness, heartache, a sense of abandonment and anger."*

Mystified about why he'd taken his own life, unsurprisingly Louise became extremely depressed in the aftermath of Gary's suicide in 2011 to the point where she couldn't get out of bed. Murray continued to read...

"I did start to drink an awful lot. I didn't need a drink as soon as I woke up, but I did drink virtually every evening for the first two years. It was always wine and I felt it helped numb the pain that I was suffering. For a few hours it helped make me forget the terrible event," she says. "I was at the lowest point I could possibly reach. I couldn't function. But I could never have done what Gary did. I could never have given up on my two sons. Which makes me think Gary must have been so ill to do what he did."

What kept her going was focussing on her boys, Ed now 20, and Tommy, 19.

"Hearing them laugh again, having their friends around, helped so much. I'm very proud of them and how they have coped with everything. Their take on life is to take every opportunity you have and go for it," she says. "We talk about their dad and the things we did together, the great times we had. We don't talk about why. I wish he was here now to see how well they've done. He would be very proud of them. He has missed out on so much of their lives. We've missed out on him and gone through so much pain," she says.

"It's something Gary obviously didn't think of at the time. The rippling effects of what he did have devastated so many people. But you have to move on. You can't stay trapped in the barbed wire. You have to box it away to move forward, although you never truly do. For it's always there. A big scar inside you that will never disappear. It's tough. We had a lovely life. After Gary's death, I woke up thinking I don't want to be me today. I don't want to carry on. But I've got myself to a place of stability. I've got to find my niche now. I've got another good 10-20 years or more in me, hopefully,

and I look to the future with optimism. One of Gary's great sayings was, 'You can't move forward, while you're looking back'. I still use it now. Because there is no going back."

Murray had enjoyed the women's honesty and frankness. So much so, that by the end of those telling paragraphs and coupled with witnessing first hand at what had become of an old friend earlier. A certain deeply troubled, serving police officer had gone online and booked some long, well overdue, therapy sessions for the new year. After which, he poignantly placed the book and his iPad on the bedside cabinet and openly cried himself to sleep.

Thirty Four

"Cowboys ain't easy to love and they're harder to hold. They'd rather give you a song than diamonds or gold. Lone-star belt buckles and old faded Levi's and each night begins a new day. If you don't understand him and he don't die young. He'll probably just ride away."

- Willie Nelson

Saturday 17th December

All the team had been prepared to work around the clock. No coaxing nor encouragement would have been required. No promise of overtime or extra pay or holidays in lieu. Each was simply keen to see justice done and as quickly as possible. With Barry Cadogan's dead body and literary confession, they thought they had managed that. Several had been about to take some much earned time off. It was an opportunity to catch up with family, recharge batteries and breathe a huge sigh of relief. Only the paperwork remained to be clarified, underlined and signed off on.

So it had very much been a morning that many of the team had been expecting to have a long lie in from. Recovering from the celebratory drinks festival the night before. Continually patting themselves on the back for catching the 'Nursery Rhyme Killer,' as all the tabloids had dubbed him. A time to have enjoyed a long overdue meet and greet with family and friends. However, DCI Furlong in her perceived wisdom or rather, through the gentle encouragement of DI Murray, as Andrew 'Kid' Curry informed the others, chose not to make the anticipated announcement. And so, the reality this Saturday morning looked different. Very different indeed.

It was a bold statement and one that took everybody by surprise. None more so than his DCI. He had never mentioned anything to her over breakfast. They travelled in on separate cars, but had no radio exchange of views or phone call discussions. This was the first that she'd heard of it and there was no going back. Was he going to regret his words?

"Be prepared everyone. By Tuesday, our so-called 'Nursery Rhyme Killer' will be safely locked up behind bars. Of that I guarantee!"

They were all there and the glances began immediately. Hayes squinted at Curry. Lizzie swivelled to view Furlong's reaction. Linn eyeballed Joe Hanlon, who in turn glimpsed Allan Boyd's scepticism. Whilst Sergeant Sandra Kerr simply shook her head in disbelief and stared at Murray's sheer bloody-minded bravado. And here she thought he had stopped gambling. This roll of the dice was only just the beginning, as he continued on...

"Each of you is about to be involved in the busiest, craziest and most jam-packed 72 hours of your police careers," he lectured them. "Most of you know me well enough, I don't just act on blind faith. I have one or two hopeful theories that need supporting, that means evidence. So I don't just want you metaphorically rolling up your sleeves and getting stuck in these next three days. We need fast, effective investigative work done. Interact regularly with each other, because I know that on satellite images a devastating storm can often look beautiful, like a perfect swirl of white no more threatening than cream stirred into coffee. But trust me when I tell you that the truth of this is going to come at you so fast and from so many varied directions, that it will be hard for you to fathom. This house of cards is about to come crashing down, and it'll take no prisoners."

The silence stretched thinner and thinner, like a balloon being blown big, until the temptation to rupture it was honestly too great to resist and Radical Lizzie did just that.

"So what do you require of us all, sir?"

She then physically rolled up the sleeves of her white 'Be More Kind' hoodie and added.

"The notable fact that a great grandfather who died in a wall collapse in 1986 would have celebrated his 100th birthday this year. May well have been an indirect catalyst for some other form of dramatic action to mark his death? Just a thought," she added.

"And not an unreasonable one at that," Murray declared. "Brilliant. Do we have a name Lizzie?"

Her playful facial expression simply said - 'Oh, please, sir. Really?'

"Listen up everyone," the Inspector announced. "We can't afford to be out of the loop on any information this weekend. That's how this will all come together. We'll pick up and recognise clues that have been sitting right in front of us." He then paused before announcing... "Fire away, Lizzie."

She responded immediately.

"The mystery man we have been trying desperately to track down, sir. Was neither a Liam, or an Iain Frost. Born on the outskirts of Cheltenham, in a small charming village called Churchdown, his name was Ian Foster. At the time of his death he had resided in Edinburgh for nearly forty-years. Thirty-five of them as a research Doctor at Napier Technical College and latterly when it became a University."

"Another medical connection," Sgt Linn stated mindfully..

"Exactly, Mitch. I'd like you and 'Sherlock' to go back to Jeremy Crossland's and check if there was anything we missed. Revisit his surgery as well and stir things up. Then both of you see if there is any, or was any crossover with Napier University and or Ian Foster." "In relation to his family," Lizzie interrupted. "I told you previously, sir, all the Fatal Accident Inquiry paperwork from back then had disappeared and nothing entered electronically. However, I have my ways and I thought I had found out the name of the young 6 year old great-grandchild."

"Fantastic Lizzie. Another gold star and another piece of the puzzle solved."

"Not quite, sir. Two years later, at age 8, most of his family were wiped out in a car accident. The grandfather, who was already widowed and the child's parents, all died instantly."

"You said, most of his family, Lizzie. So who else survived?" Allan Boyd asked.

"Miraculously the boy and his younger sister survived. When they awoke in the hospital, they had already been entered into our wonderfully sympathetic and caring foster system. In the months that followed they were adopted and their name officially changed, including their Christian names, which was rather unusual. However I am close and working my way through the red tape! But tracking them down through Ian Foster's family tree, they were Bruce and Becky Foster at the time of the fatal incident.

Murray's eyes gave off a potential glimpse of a 'Eureka' moment. "Lizzie, double-check the electronic record at Greenock Prison for me, please. And let me know if Barry Cadogan was ever one of Maurice Orr's visitors. Possibly check his phone calls as well."

He could feel the weight of mass expectation on his shoulders. "Seriously everyone, let's get working. I'm not there yet, but with each of you helping me clarify and confirm a couple of potential thoughts and leads, we can still all have a great weekend. Anything else from the 'Vault' Lizzie, before we hit the streets running?"

"Two things I think might be worth everyone hearing, sir."

"Go ahead, enlighten us."

"Well I checked and double checked Barry Cadogan's game console," she said. Showing some large pixelated slides on her fancy large screen monitor. "It had hardly been played, sir. Not only the buttons on the controller, but his keypad to interact and play with others. One of the last scenes or re-enactments that he played out was attempting to save himself from being hung at dawn. He didn't win that game. But he had also created a list of scenarios for other role playing games. They included one where a large house collapsed and killed people. One where a King was poisoned whilst eating at a banquet and another where a pile of furniture came hurtling down a stairway at speed and you had to try your best to avoid it or die."

"And a sick scenario for Stacey Cannon's death?" Sandra Kerr asked emotionally.

"Nothing." Lizzie shook her head. "Which I did think was strange."

"He probably just hadn't got around to it," Hayes contributed.

"Possibly," Lizzie said, as other heads nodded or shook and were generally undecided as to why.

"The others all tie in nicely with everything, Lizzie. So thanks for that." Murray grinned.

Taking the lead from his cheesy smile, she began to laugh.

"What's so funny?" Her Inspector asked.

"What's so funny! Really? Really?" She repeated in front of all the others.

"If I had said that the machine doesn't seem to have been played much, that's a coincidence. You would have immediately jumped in with, 'There is no such thing!' But today you opt for... 'that ties in nicely.' Again I say, Really?"

Barbra Furlong had remained quiet throughout all this over-hyped excitement. She knew that Steven Murray was just trying his best to rally the troops, as it were. However that seemed a very fair rebuke for a senior officer that should've known better. Especially from a raw, fairly inexperienced, twenty-five year old. But that was what the Inspector loved about her. He may have been twice her age, but she most certainly always fired him up and made him feel unbeatable and eighteen again. It was her vitality and enthusiasm for life that was simply a joy to be around and the older, wiser Inspector knew just that. Plus strictly speaking, he wasn't her boss. She was an independent information technology specialist, currently employed on a rolling contract with Police Scotland.

"So what are you actually saying, young lady?"

Murray often addressed females in that manner. It was meant as a compliment. It was reminiscent of how his late father spoke.

"What I am saying, aged, sir."

Murray immediately raised a delicate eyebrow. An eyebrow that whispered, 'line crossing - be careful.'

"What I am saying is that I think this is a brand new machine. One that has been set up and programmed with certain scenarios and role playing commitments and stages specifically to match up with his killings and supposed movements. Barry Cadogan was most certainly not on it for hours at a time. I doubt several minutes even of every day. In fact, considering I never retrieved one single print to match Barry's. I would guess that Mr Cadogan didn't even know that he owned one of these machines. I suspect that it was placed in his home some time after his death. At least, that is my own humble, little theory."

Murray aggressively clapped his hands and fiercely pumped his fists into the air.

"And we love you for it!" He shouted. "So myself and the 'Kid' are heading straight back to see the abused wife."

Andrew Curry smiled eagerly. Back in the saddle... he really had to come up with a suitable cowboy name for his Inspector, he thought.

"Wait, you said two things Lizzie. What was the other?" DCI Furlong asked.

Lizzie only had two moods. Just two. Today her dial was set to 'good.' That means nothing can go wrong, everyone is lovely and only the most optimistic of forecasts (on any topic) will do. It is irritating, but her alternative mood is so bad and never up for discussion on a 'good' day.

"Wow, how appropriate that it is you that asked, Ma'am. Because I share this with you in mind, Chief Inspector."

Barbra Furlong always had less time for her playful manner. For her cheeky put-downs and sarcasm, and looked at her accordingly.

"It's just a little something I learned from making inquiries into Barry Cadogan's death, Ma'am. Did you know that when the South Bridge was finally completed in 1788, it was deemed to be an appropriate and fitting honour that the Bridge's eldest resident, a well known and respected Judges' wife, should be first person to cross the fine architectural structure?"

The others looked around in bewilderment.

"Unfortunately, several days before the grand opening, the lady in question passed away. But promises had been made, hands shaken and the city fathers felt obliged to honour their original agreement. And so it was, that the first 'body' to cross the South Bridge crossed it in a coffin. Amazing! Isn't it? I thought you'd like that Ma'am. With origins and everything."

"Thanks for that." Furlong expressed. "That was much appreciated. A little hidden gem about a lively and often congested part of Edinburgh city centre these days."

DI Murray spoke up once again. "I've one more task for you Lizzie, before we head off. I'd like you to revisit the footage. I suspect if you check his burner phone, it will only go back two weeks. Because that's when he lost his proper mobile. I'll wager it will have made no calls in the last fortnight. But if you track it, it will have been to all those areas. Of course it had. Because the real killer had taken it with him. And also, although we can't see it clearly enough, my educated guess would be that not only is that mystery hand helping him over the edge, it has also just returned his original phone back into his pocket. That is why he had two phones on him. It was meant to help frame him."

"So Barry Cadogan is still our man for all the other murders." Hayes issued as a statement, rather than a question, and it was their DCI that took to the floor to respond to that one.

"That would certainly be what someone would like us to believe. It's certainly the easiest and cheapest option for us as a unit to follow."

Everyone in the 'Vault' got her unspoken message. They each had their various tasks assigned and headed out the door.

Thirty Five

"Here's tae the bonnie lads who ride in Edin's name. Here's tae the lassies who welcome us back hame. I'll be dancin' till the morning wae the Belle o' Liberton, if they're ridin' the Marches o' Edinburgh."

- Ted Christopher

Whilst accompanying his Detective Inspector over the past few days, 'Kid' Curry had grown in confidence and was much more relaxed about airing viewpoints and contributing constructively to discussions or not! And that was the point. The Inspector was happy for you to chip in, no matter how silly, meaningless or foolish some theory or idea may have seemed. He had also learned a few tricks of the trade as he watched Murray's body language and had slowly begun to understand why his often unconventional DI did and didn't do certain things.

"So Barry Cadogan, boss. Do we think... "Sir.""

"Sorry! I don't...""

"Sir, Inspector, or nothing at all even, 'Drew. I thought you would have known by now not to call me, 'Boss.'"

Curry never apologised. He was proud of himself for that. Instead he just straightened his shoulders and began again. Steven Murray's slightest of lip movements also registered a level of satisfaction in his young Constable's wise decision. Good for him it implied.

"So, Inspector, do we still reckon Barry Cadogan is a deranged wife- beating murderer? One with fantasy role-playing addictions?"

As if listening in to her colleagues' conversation, an opportune phone call from Lizzie was about to play a big part in answering both of those questions.

"Haven't we just left your lovely underground domain?" Murray teased.

"What? Sure! Yes, well that's the thing, sir. I was so keen to get one up on the DCI, that I forgot to tell you what else I did and have since discovered on that computer."

"This all sounds rather juicy, so just mind your language as I have a young, innocent DC hanging on every word you utter."

"Suspenders," she deliberately rasped huskily down the line.

Curry's eyes played table tennis with each other. His fingers formed fists and a throbbing tongue had no emergency escape plan in mind.

The seductive playful voice of the girl continued with, "I don't wear..."

"Behave yourself," Murray laughed. "You take things too far."

"I think you'll find that you start it, sir. Or at the very least, encourage it."

He could see the 'Kid' nod from the side of his eye. Ignoring the poor lad, he asked...

"Okay, Lizzie, what did you forget?"

"A host of things. At least three, maybe four." She replied, slightly embarrassed. "Firstly, one I didn't forget. I followed up regarding Barry Cadogan's phone like you asked, and you were right about all of that, sir."

"Yes," Curry added. "We reckon they just hadn't checked that he'd a replacement phone on him. Which defeated the purpose of trying to set the poor man up for all the murders in the first place."

Murray continued. "They defeated themselves, by killing him too soon after the other deaths. Although let's remember, he could still well be the killer. It's just that he definitely has an accomplice or accomplices, plural. I mean even if they had left it 24 hours longer, we may have started to suspect him more naturally. It was all done too soon and it's been far too convenient. DNA at all the scenes. Really?" he questioned. "A man that has been so precise and organised in his staging and planning in all other aspects of the crime. Yet is so slipshod when it comes to leaving trace evidence behind. I don't think so! Sorry, I got on my soapbox there, Lizzie. You were saying..."

"It gets better. I discovered that it was his wife who enjoyed the role playing fantasies, sir. Not necessarily poisoning or beheading people as such, but real life sexual meet and greets. She has her own user name and promotes an erotic escort website online. It's called The Belles of Liberton."

"Which you have obviously checked out." DC Curry cheekily interrupted.

"I wouldn't open that door, young Andrew," the female voice flirtatiously proffered.

Curry swallowed and decided to once again remain silent.

"Best option, 'Kid', Murray whispered.

"I heard that," Lizzie countered and continued. "So all the while we are busy confirming he is or was our killer and his back-stabbing partner takes no chances and silences him forever. We then complete the necessary paperwork, yet all the blame is still heaped upon Barry Cadogan."

Quarter of an hour gone and their car was now only five or six minutes away from Moira Cadogan's new trendy abode.

"Why? Why? Why? Why?" Murray shouted at the top of his voice, whilst parked stationary at traffic lights. "What? What are you looking at?" He then screamed at an older, genteel lady in the car next to his. He accompanied it with an apologetic wave. Unhesitatingly, the thin featured woman with the purple rinse, smiled serenely back at Steven Murray and accompanied her grin with a nonchalant, yet sinister, two-fingered salute!

Although taken aback somewhat, Murray continued his rant in a quieter, calmer tone. "Killing King and Cannon and even Cannon's granddaughter, I get that," Murray extolled. "That is all about the 'Wall.' Possible retribution and revenge for what happened there with the death of Ian Foster all those years ago. Out of curiosity Lizzie, although you are still searching for their names, did you ever find out just how serious the great-grandson's injuries ultimately were? I'm guessing he was unable to walk again. Am I close?"

'Kid' Curry stared at his Inspector. Who in turn gauged from the icy silence that he was correct.

"No way!" Lizzie eventually succumbed.

"So don't waste any more time tracing their surname, I have that figured out young lady. But where did Grace Adam and Doc Crossland fit into things? And why was Barry Cadogan mixed up in any of this in the first place?"

This time, both the voices of Lizzie and 'Kid' Curry were conspicuous by their notable absence.

Eventually Andrew Curry offered, "There would appear to be too many links, clues and pieces of evidence pointing directly at Barry Cadogan, for it not to be him, sir. However, like you said, surely that is just too convenient and easy. Logic does seem to suggest that he killed them and was then in turn silenced. But by whom?"

"Well I don't know if this helps any in regards to that," Lizzie ventured. "But I have another couple of interesting results for you, sir. Firstly, someone else that we are familiar with was also a member of that fantasy playing erotic chat room. Lizzie then proceeded to name the individual.

"I know, right!" Lizzie shouted out excitedly to the two silenced officers. "A clear link."

"And now before you tell us Moira Cadogan's username? I'm guessing it is..."

Murray put forward his answer just as they pulled up outside her rundown flat.

"How did you do that?" Lizzie mumbled, gutted and amazed. "Oh, never mind," she added. Before confirming that he was correct and had stolen her thunder - As always.

It was all starting to come together. The pieces were still scattered wide and far, but they were at least all beginning to surface. He had been quite literally blown away by Lizzie's twin newsflash and a multitude of sudden thoughts went racing through the Inspector's confused mind. The first was all about his initial meeting and interaction with a man who was to become his favourite English teacher in High School. Not unlike Robin Williams' character, Mr Keating in Dead Poets Society, Mr McKillop's opening Q & A session to his first year students was an inspiring oratory masterclass.

It went as follows: '*What is a thought? But a screenplay in invisible space. Is it a safe place to experiment with ideas before we speak? For sure it is a ballroom for unseen dances, a race track for cars that speed without worry for the next turn. It is freedom to roam without the fear of getting lost. For all it takes is the bark of a dog to bring us home.*'

Or in Steven Murray's case, the sound of his mobile phone.

The screen registered as identity unknown. No caller I.D was most unusual these days. So his official professional voice was called into play.

"Hello, Detective Inspector Steven Murray speaking. How can I help you?" He was already exhausted with that mouthful of an introduction.

"Mr Murray," the secretive sounding whisperer stated. "It's Gus. Gus Gillies here from The Blue Lagoon.

"Aah, yes, Gus. How can I help you?" Murray asked politely. Surprised to be hearing back at all from the unscrupulous man.

They were on speakerphone and 'Drew Curry had no idea who this person was. But to Steven Murray the quiet, nervous tone made sense now. The man couldn't possibly have one of his regulars overhear him speaking to a member of the thin blue line. Even though Police Scotland wore black these days, and that Murray was a plain clothes officer.

"Gus, Mr Gillies. It's been awhile," he joked. "What can I help you with?"

"I think I may have something to help you, Inspector."

"You think?"

"Aye, well actually it's a message from your old buddy, 'Macca.' He dragged himself into the bar after you left last night. He was feeling a bit flush and bought himself a few pints."

Murray sat upright and began to feel guilty. The DI didn't know it was Davie McIntyre when he gave him the money, but should that have made a difference? Are we saying that it's alright to gift cash to a random stranger, a possible alcoholic or recovering alcoholic, but not to a friend? The Inspector was confused and undecided, as he listened further.

"At the end of the night," Gus went on. "He was out of it. Rambling nonsense and speaking gibberish. However, earlier when he first came in, he had asked me for a pen and paper. He mentioned he knew you and had a message for you. I think he recognised, Mr Murray, that he would be in no fit state later on to write, talk or do anything. And by the way, he was quite right. There's no sign of him outside, today. He'll be in some obscure corner of the city sleeping it off."

Steven Murray had no desire to dwell on that particular thought and already had a Christmas gift in mind for his old friend. One which he would deliver personally in a few days time, after he confirmed a certain something. He had become noticeably distracted and quickly responded with...

"A message?" Murray quizzed the bar manager. "What kind of message? What did it say?"

"Well, that's the thing, Mr Murray. It's a bit obscure. It doesn't really make sense to me. Kind of krypton, do you know what I mean?"

The DI smirked and Curry's contorted face went blank.

"Cryptic," Murray whispered, and Drew's head and hand gesture said... 'Oh, of course!'

Sounding like a slithery skinned lizard when described in this way, *the monster from The Blue Lagoon* continued. "The crumbled note says - Tell Inspector Murray that Lucy was attacked by a leaping feline. I've every confidence in him!"

"Go on," Murray encouraged.

"No, that's it, Inspector. That's what I mean by krypton."

With a larger than life grin, DI Murray simply nodded at his end of the line, thanked the man for his call and hung up. So

'Macca' had not only heard him last night, but was fully aware of the event and obviously of Grace Adam, aka 'Lucy.' A leaping feline? What did or could he mean by that though? 'Macca,' would no doubt tell him when he saw him next. However, he had chosen to allow Murray to figure it out for himself. Which is why he used the line that he remembered a young Steven Murray beginning to use with many of the new recruits and probationers. Murray still used it to this day. Only now it was offered generously in support and praise of many officers during interaction with them. 'I've every confidence in you,' he would say to them and then leave it up to that individual to prove him right. So that's what he must do, prove 'Macca' right, before reporting back to him.

"A giant cat roaming around Niddrie, certainly might survive the chaos and bedlam on its streets at night better than most of its residents," Murray declared. But it made no sense.

Drew Curry shook his head, also none the wiser.

"Before we go back in to revisit this lying toe-rag. Call Lizzie back for me 'Drew. Ask her to take another quick look at Grace Adams' case and especially at the fire itself. Get her to check if there was any clue or connection that stuck out as being in tow with any leaping cat or feline as such. Thanks."

It was Saturday, mid-morning, and they had gave no notification to the woman that they might be stopping by. As 'Kid' Curry called Lizzie, Murray stood outside the car looking up and down the street. For a working class district, something was missing and it soon dawned on him exactly what it was...... Children! There were no kids out playing. It was cold certainly, but it was a Saturday. He knew in the past, there would have been no keeping him indoors at the weekend. It was a completely different generation and mind set. Black dogs never got a look-in back then. They were probably too scared to hang about with that crop of school kids, because they were wild, but in a good way. Now as DCI Furlong saw first hand on Friday evening for herself. The 10, 12 and 14 year olds are still wild, but in a distinctly different way altogether. They now roam the streets looking for prey, like undomesticated savage animals. Possibly ferocious cats? Murray questioned briefly, before thinking how games dominated his childhood. Chinese ropes for the girls, football for the boys, plus hide and seek played altogether. There were so many variations of each game and each one kept you running about all day long, he vividly recalled. We would climb trees, race plastic bottles down streams in woodland forests and catch tadpoles in our local reservoir or dam. There were games with rhymes, ball's and skipping once again for the girls. Whilst the rugged male of the species would climb roofs, play Red Rover and give each other the occasional doing! We were always busy and getting up to no good somewhere, he remembered. We were always with friends, together we learned how to get along. Isn't that what it's all about? The police officer pondered on those words, as he headed off to tear a strip or two from a certain female. A woman who played decidedly more adult games. Several of which were more dangerous and possibly even murderous, the Inspector suspected.

"Let's go 'Drew," he shouted. "I need someone to accompany me here. It's all part of the training," he smiled.

Curry was soon to learn what that actually meant. Beginning the short climb up the stairs to her flat, Murray's commonplace song link-up went straight to...

"If I had a million dollars..."

He looked at 'Kid' Curry, who instantly responded with... *"If I had a million dollars..."*

His Detective Inspector was most impressed. Not everyone was aware of the Barenaked Ladies. But in fairness, he suspected based on their group name, Andrew Curry would be!

Thirty Six

"It's only 8 o'clock but you're already bored, you don't know what it is but there's got to be more. You'd better find a way out, hey kick down the door. It's a rat rap... and you've been caught."

- The Boomtown Rats

The man outside Moira Cadogan's front door had heard singing voices approach. Inside locks and chains were beginning to be undone faster than a politician's lies. Today this poor man's fantasy would have to wait, he scurried back down the stairs barging through the middle of the two officers.

Murray's song changed instantly to, *"Like a bat out of hell I'll be gone when the morning comes."*

"Sir, should I..."

"No, let him go, Constable. I've seen that look on plenty of married men's faces over the years. He was just in the wrong place at the wrong time. But hey, he already chapped and it's just about to open, so all's good."

The look on Moira Cadogan's face was, as they say - a picture! The wild eyes and scowl displayed both anger and surprise simultaneously.

"I believe your scheduled appointment has just run home to his obviously boring, humdrum wife and family, Mrs C. Or," DI Murray announced quickly. "Should I refer to you as Six-geese-a-laying? Nice touch that by the way, using the first horse you ever bet on, as your username. Well, except for one thing."

With a look of repugnant loathing, she uttered. "What's that?"

"Racehorses can only have names up to 18 spaces long. Plus we checked, and there was no such horse ever registered with the name: Six-geese-a-laying. Sadly, you should have chosen differently Moira. So it would appear that you lied to us and backed the losing horse on both accounts - and not for the first time!"

Then rather cheekily, he added. "And why are you keeping us waiting out here?"

Undeterred, Steven Murray was in no mood for pleasantries. He immediately strode straight past the woman and up the narrow undecorated corridor.

"Detectives!" She stuttered. Slamming the door firmly behind them and pulling desperately at her skirt once again. Only this time it wouldn't pull down any lower. It was a tiny little red micro, worn only with the skimpiest of scarlet briefs and stockings. A matching basque covered her top half, yet the most notable of things on display... was the absence of any bruising.

"I see you decided today not to apply the 'war paint' that I found in the bathroom on our last visit, Ma'am. More lies and deceit."

Cadogan's face colour now matched that of her near nonexistent outfit.

I should have known that there would have been a good reason for him nipping off to the toilet during our previous chat, Curry thought to himself. Although the sly old devil never once shared his find.

Mrs Cadogan had now joined them. She sat herself nervously down on the settee next to 'Kid' Curry. This time it was the turn of his burning cheeks to act as camouflage cover for her meagre display of clothing. Her red fishnet clad leg rubbed teasingly up alongside Drew's thigh. The home of this particular 'Belle' was certainly not overly warm, yet the perspiration on the poor Constable's face would have you believe that he was in a sauna. His Detective Inspector wanted to be forceful and blunt from the beginning, so refrained from offering up the laughter that currently paused for respite on his smirking lips.

"As I said, it would appear that you've lied to us already on more than one occasion. Then again it is fairly apparent that deceit and deception are your forte, Ma'am. You should list them as likes on your naughty profile page. Never mind GFE,

Erotic Massage and BDSM. You could add dishonesty, spousal abuse and murder!"

"Murder!" She exclaimed. "Murder? What are you talking about?"

Interesting that she did not object to 'spousal abuse," Murray considered. Even Curry was taken aback by this turn of events. For the first time in a while, he was about to witness the maverick detective at work. The eureka moment, the hunch. The good old gut feeling, but I have no proof scenario. This front row 'Edinburgh Fringe' production was about to play out in front of his very eyes.

The adrenalin pumped Inspector encouraged both to remain seated, whilst he took to the floor. The 'Kid' edged cautiously away from the woman's naked thigh tops, as Steven Murray's accusatory tongue switched to rapid-fire mode.

"You are in a home provided to you through a Women's Refuge, Mrs Cadogan. Yet you dare to support your addiction, your compulsive gambling habit. You escort in broad daylight from the premises, using your 'Belle of Liberton' affiliation and the user name - 'Six-geese-a-laying?' The name supposedly chosen after the racehorse that started it all for you. Yet we now know that is a lie."

"Inspector," the woman said with a quizzical look upon her face. "Six-geese-a-laying does only have 18 letters. It would have fitted perfectly well within the Jockey Club terms for naming a horse."

"You are quite right, Ma'am. It absolutely would have done the job. But you never corrected me when I challenged you about it not being the name, thus confirming the suspicions I had about it being your username instead. Which was earlier confirmed for me by another member of our team just before we met, and they actually proceeded to delve further into your online profile and discovered the real seedy story behind your chosen working name."

Normal blushing would have been no problem. But what Moira Cadogan did, was go as red as a beetroot and radiate heat like a hot frying pan. You could have easily cooked a three-course meal on her face. All she wanted was the earth to open up and swallow her whole. Andrew Curry glanced at them both. Hoping for either an explanation or a revelation. But neither was forthcoming.

"That supposed winning bet that you made that day, the one that got you hooked, that was made at the Paisley bookmakers with your fellow new start. That would be your downfall. For that man gave you a nickname. Believe it or not, he called you 'Ra.' As in 'Moi-Ra! He then simply shortened it to 'R.' Unfortunately for you, he kept an online journal of all of this. An account of your time back then, two decades ago. And then in more recent times when you bumped into him and he was now a successful professional working here in Edinburgh, he once again scorned your advances. Sadly for the man in question that had been enough to tip you over the edge and you cried rape! An allegation that went no further, because there had been no merit to it. It was simply yet another one of your lies. Am I beginning to sense a pattern here R?"

The woman glowered at him.

"He was the man that you supposedly blamed for introducing you to the sport of kings. The same man that years later you would accuse of attempted rape. So when you decided that you wanted out of your decade old, loveless marriage, he was always going to be on your retribution hit list when the time came. Dr Jeremy Crossland never stood a chance. Did you even tell Barry that you had known the man previously? Or was that it? You told him that he was the man that raped you and that by killing three or four people the real target would be hidden amongst all the other deaths. Even more lies and deceit, young lady."

"Well that's our Doctor accounted for, sir. But what about the others? Collateral damage?" Curry asked, whilst fascinated and intrigued by what Murray had disclosed so far.

"Behave yourself Drew," Murray responded with dismay. "Like we have always suspected," he continued at pace. "This game of smoke and mirrors starring Jack Cannon and Andrew King was the whole reason this murderous charade had taken place."

Concern was written all over Moira Cadogan's freshly un-bruised face. Whereas 'Kid' Curry was poised on the edge of the sofa waiting for the next thrilling instalment. The experienced Inspector had already bluffed a couple of times today, including knowing that she was the 'R' in Crossland's online journal. But the timings and the Paisley connection, made it seem worthy of an educated guess. His next bluff though, would be make or break. Ultimately, if he was wrong, there would be no harm done. Mrs Cadogan would be slightly miffed in the short term, but he could live with that. However that particular piece of subterfuge would have to wait a while longer.

Now desperately trying to cover herself up with a cosy throw from the settee, Moira Cadogan stood abruptly and rounded on Steven Murray, or at least attempted to. But it was time for the west coast council house boy to make an unruly appearance.

"Sit down, Ma'am," he yelled coarsely. "You'll get your chance to speak up soon enough. And trust me, a court of law would be my SECOND option, if I had my way." He then pointed aggressively at her spiked boots. The very ones that he scratched himself on last time. "You can take them off for a start," he demanded.

"What!" The woman began to remonstrate. "Murder! Court! A Doctor Crossland! Have you gone mad?" She screamed.

"You heard me. DC Curry please remove those from Mrs Cadogan's feet, bag them up and keep them safe. Because I would happily take a bet that we'll find some trace evidence on them. Proof that they inflicted the recent horrendous scarring found upon her dead husband's face. I have no doubt, that HE was the one being abused in your relationship, Moira, not you. We even discovered through Barry's work colleagues that he had been off work regularly throughout this year. He claimed to have been physically assaulted on numerous occasions."

Her eyes met briefly with Steven Murray's. "His bosses told us."

Her shoulders visually fell.

"But no one was ever held to account. 'He had been left crippled with fear,' his manager said. So I'm pretty confident that it was indeed he that left you, Moira."

This time, Cadogan's whole body slumped. Her mouth fell open and forward, yet no sound was uttered. For Steven Murray on the other hand, he reflected on that manager's words. There was a delicious moment where initially his own countenance washed blank with confusion, like his brain cogs couldn't quite turn fast enough to take in the information conveyed from a sudden realisation. Every muscle of the Inspector's body simply froze, before a grin of understanding crept onto his face. An expression that soon stretched from one side to the other, showing every single tooth, crown and filling. More of the puzzle had just slipped into place and DI Murray was about to ramp things up quite considerably with the occasional gamble of his own.

"We both think that you killed your husband, Ma'am."

We do? Drew Curry silently questioned to himself.

"You had him kill for you, didn't you? But then what? Did you ask him to pretend that he was in a snuff film? Because I've been told you have a few of them also on your website. Barry thought he was in 'acting mode,' that night, didn't he? It would certainly explain why he looked so relaxed only seconds before his death," Murray asserted.

Slightly questioning that train of thought, Curry offered up...

"Which would then possibly imply a third person, sir. Because that would have to have been filmed separately. Our footage was from the bar's CCTV, remember?"

Before the Inspector could rebuke Andrew Curry or ponder that specific point, two bare arms leapt up in defence, revealing the woman's semi-naked torso.

"But he hung himself!" She announced in animated fashion, with both arms swinging and flailing. Her long, slender fingers conducting an imaginary orchestra. "From a bridge at Cowgate, that was what you, yourself, told me, Inspector."

The alarm in her voice continued to escalate, remembering all of his other accusations.

"On much closer inspection, Mrs Cadogan, we were wrong. He was most definitely helped on his way. But then again, we suspect that you already knew that. Didn't you?"

'Kid' Curry was beginning to like this 'we' business. And growing in confidence, added some thoughts of his own.

"That was probably why a glimpse of hand was shown. You had already done your surveillance and knew that it would hopefully be captured on CCTV and that if it was, then it could no longer be considered a suicide, but ruled a murder. That being the case, someone would then be entitled to a very, very healthy insurance payout."

"Unless that particular someone also happened to be his killer!" Steven Murray proffered, impressed by Drew's on the spot synopsis.

As DC Curry hastily, yet timidly, removed her lethal footwear. 'Six- geese-a-laying' had nothing further to say.

"Was it meeting up with Grace Adam, a.k.a. 'Lucy Locket' that gave you the idea to theme the deaths as Nursery Rhyme characters? Or was it just that the poor unfortunate girl was vulnerable and easy prey to try out and test your ability to murder? Mind you, myself and young Curry here, still have a hunch that you had Barry actually carry out the killings. Under the pretext of some fantasy, role-playing scenario. He had no idea that you were planning such a big send-off for him."

"You are not making any sense, Inspector. Are you allowed to just throw around wild accusations about me like that? Is he?" She asked, staring intensely at 'Kid' Curry.

Wisely, he chose not to reply.

"Am I like the perfect scapegoat here or what? The sacrificial lamb to the slaughter? Unlikely to be taken seriously, until it's too late. Maybe I'll get hit by a bus or catch a bullet in a few years time or some other deadly fate. But right now, I think you had both better go. I'm confident that you have nothing whatsoever to substantiate or back up any of those crazy notions and theories do you? Do you?" She repeated louder and more aggressively than before.

There was silence from her accuser and major disappointment from Curry. He'd naturally assumed that his Inspector had something concrete or would never have spoken up.

"No, I didn't think so," she continued. "So you'll both be leaving now, thank you very much." Her words angry and terse. "Get going, the pair of you, and close the door properly on your way out."

These past few days the 'Kid' had learned to follow his Inspector's lead in these situations. Thus far, DI Murray had remained unfazed and unmoved.

"Are you both deaf?"

Still none of the officers stirred. Although with the woman now standing, DI Murray decided to step forward and lean inward, down toward her face. Only inches separated them. She would feel his rustic breath with every spoken word.

"The need for revenge must've been like a rat gnawing at your soul," Murray began. He continued slowly. "It would have been relentless and unceasing. It could only be stopped by the cold steel of a rat- trap. A deadly contraption that you could have devised simply by yourself. But the reality was, you allowed others to help assist you. He would have celebrated his 100th birthday earlier this year, isn't that correct? I even questioned a few days ago, if that had maybe been the catalyst for all the chaos on offer this past week."

"Once again, I have no idea what you are..." "Ian Foster," the Inspector broke in.

Immediately, he could feel the icy breeze sweep past him. Pushing against her like an incredible invisible gale. Alarm, suddenly locked up the stomach muscles of this lying fantasist. Closed shut, nothing was getting in or out. Dread had set upon her face like rigour mortis, as her teeth clenched tight together. So unless she could replay the previous week, drag the sun from the sky and inject amnesia into the mind of Inspector Steven Murray, her time had come and his words would continue to chill her to the bone. She was speechless. His monologue on the other hand was unhurried, deliberate and he now believed, wholly accurate. Slowly but surely, they were getting closer. Much, much closer.

"Your need for retribution was determined," the Inspector cried. "It was like an abscess on the skin of your soul. One that I guess could only have been cured by the cruel, sharp, steel point of revenge. It had festered with you all these years, Moira. Like a septic wound, with the only effective antibiotic being a suitably fitting reprisal."

"Savage. Spiteful. A dish best served cold," added Andrew Curry, desirous to play a part. Although having no idea what retaliation or redress Murray was actually referring to.

"As requested, Mrs C, we'll let ourselves out." Murray said coldly. "You'll be pleased to know that we're off to finish gathering proof over the weekend for those crazy notions and theories, as you call them. With that said, be mindful not to travel too far from home. Because next time when we come back we'll probably be using handcuffs. Which means those fluffy ones that you have sitting over there on the coffee table, could probably go straight back in the drawer!"

Thirty Seven

'When the winter yields to summertime. The whip-poor-will she sings. My heart is in the puppet box and Satan pulls the strings. My heart is in the puppet box and Satan pulls the strings.

- The Avett Brothers

Before setting off back to their Leith headquarters, Steven Murray made a phone call to a nearby specialist bookstore.

"You do. Great. It's a Mr Murray here. I'll have someone pick it up in the next twenty minutes. Thank you."

That someone, Andrew Curry recognised as being himself, and sure enough sixteen minutes later, they'd arrived.

"Drew, I'm sorry not to be taking you back to Greenock on this occasion. But you've done a great job at my side these past few days and I thank you for that."

Curry's cheeks gently blushed. Though he was grateful once again for his Inspector's honest words of support and encouragement. Seeing as he was already feeling flushed, he thought it best to ask a question that had been bothering him from The House of 'R.'

"Sir, back at Mrs Cadogan's you mentioned that her online name had in actual fact nothing to do with racing."

"That's right Drew, for whilst you were on the phone to Lizzie about any possible links with a leaping feline. I had a quick look at the 'Belles of Liberton' website. In particular the specialities of certain females." He then paused at that.

"And?" Andrew Curry asked in suspense.

"Well, I'm only telling you so that you don't have to go and find this out for yourself mind."

"Of course, of course, absolutely. I understand, sir."

"Well, I believe sadly, this was how she and Grace Adam met. They both had the same specialty. Which was not a twosome, but in fact... three men at once. They would do joint meets for that special service - Thus: Six-geese-a-laying."

Andrew Curry's face was now brighter than ever, and he was delighted to go on an errand and pick up Murray's classic paperback after that. Five short minutes later and he had returned. Meanwhile driving on to Leith, the Inspector began to explain his rationale to 'Kid' Curry.

"I was going to take Sergeant Kerr down to meet back up once again with Maurice Orr. The theory behind that was to exorcise a few demons, Drew, and possibly confirm a few things for me. However there is no need now. I've already had the one major thing that I was curious about, confirmed for me earlier. And whilst you were picking up the book set aside for me, I texted Sandy to change that plan also. No, this time, I need DCI Furlong to accompany me when we revisit. There is something I would like her to witness firsthand."

Swiftly changing the subject, Andrew Curry piped up with...

"I got it gift-wrapped, sir. I hope that's okay. I wasn't sure who it was for?"

"Brilliant. Thank you for that," his DI said excitedly. "It's intended for a certain inmate at Greenock Prison. I hope he likes it." Murray smiled, offering up a rather contorted, twisted, devilish expression.

Barbra Furlong was standing outside at the front steps of the station when Steven Murray drove up. Pleasantries were exchanged briefly, as DC Curry exited the vehicle to check out a couple of things for his Inspector and his DCI jumped in.

"Cheerio, sir. Thanks again," was Drew's parting shot. Simple nods were exchanged between both his two superior officers.

"No advance warning on this occasion for the Governor, I take it?" Furlong checked.

"Oh, I've already called her to let her know that we are on our way. I said hopefully we'll be there for about two o'clock, give or take. She was fine with that."

"It's just I thought on the phone you'd said that you wanted to surprise her?"

"I did and we will Chief Inspector, don't you worry about that."

Before they had reached the By-Pass, 'Kid' Curry had rang.

"Just checked on those phone calls to the prison, sir. Like you asked."

"Any joy, Drew?"

His excitement was hard to contain. He felt that in this particular case, he had been at the coal face more than any other in recent months.

"Absolutely," Curry responded. Barry Cadogan on numerous occasions, each one during normal scheduled phone call times. But in the last hour he had an emergency call put through to him."

Murray nodded his head in a knowing manner. "Those calls are all recorded aren't they?"

"They are indeed, sir, and I've already requested that they have copies ready for you when you arrive. I asked for the last three weeks worth. Hope that is enough?"

"Perfect. Speak soon." And he was gone.

With weekend traffic light on all the major bottle-neck sections of the M8, the two officers arrived around 1.45pm. As they drove into the car park, Steven Murray was surprised to hear a slightly croaky and off-key voice serenade him...

"There's no Michelin stars, no beer only bars. The paint's peeling in the rooms..."

"Enough already. But well remembered. Give me the gift-wrapped present from out of the glove compartment, please, Chief Inspector."

Murray hadn't wanted to criticise her singing. So by way of distraction had asked for that small favour instead. Once received, both made their way across to the Prison entrance to proceed with all the standard security checks and formalities. Beyond the front door, Rebecca Loggenberg stood waiting for them. How did she manage that? A questioning look between the two work colleagues was exchanged. Murray screwed up his eyes and Furlong first bit and then pouted her lips. It was all the confirmation needed for the Inspector to make a phone call.

"Excuse me just a second," he said. Leaving the two old friends to discuss old times for sixty seconds while DI Murray got through to 'Kid' Curry.

"Drew, no need to ask any questions. I need you and DC Hayes to get over right away to Moira Cadogan's and bring her in. She is all yours Constable. Arrest her in connection with these murders and myself and DCI Furlong will be back around six o'clock to start interviewing her."

An enthusiastic, positive response from Curry was offered, as his Inspector hung up.

The prison Governor once again led the way. With lengthy strides she strode assertively down the lengthy corridors. Today, she was to be found dressed in a dark green Georgette trouser suit. It had a very mixed ethnic look to it. The hem and yoke were beautifully embroidered with gold sequins and finished off with a Chinese collar. The santoon trouser came well below the knee and the dupatta scarf draped around her slender shoulders had an intricately designed lace border. Each garment was once again finished off to the highest quality.

When they eventually arrived at the familiar location. It was as if Steven Murray for the first time, actually recognised the room as a fully functioning library. On all of his previous visits, he had merely saw it solely, as a meeting room. An area that had been set aside for them to meet in privately. A quiet spot away from the prying eyes of other inmates. Lessening the ability for them to draw incorrect conclusions. But again, idle prison gossip would always abound. Today, Detective Inspector Murray was able to witness row after row of neatly lined books, each with their spine facing outward. Colour coded with dots, a fiction section arranged in alphabetical order, floor cushions, comfortable leather arm chairs, tables for hushed study and a librarian

(Orr) at the help desk. There were computers for doing book searches and computers for surfing the web also. Overall an impressive centre for inmates that were keen to expand their horizons. Individuals that wanted to learn, grow and develop themselves.

The blonde locks and smarmy grin sat ready for them behind the table. This time his progressive pyramid of cards sat at five rows high. Impressive! Only the last two cards were required to complete it. A non-threatening prison guard sat just off to the right-hand side, with Murray, Furlong and Loggenberg sat directly opposite in that corresponding order. The Chief Inspector flanked either side.

"Do I have permission to sit in for this one DCI Furlong?" One tumbling panda asked.

"Oh, I'm merely an observer today also. This is all DI Murray's baby." The other replied.

Rebecca gazed across at the Inspector thinking he would instantly reply. But he didn't.

"Inspector?" She reluctantly quizzed.

"Of course you can Governor. I wouldn't want you to miss any of this today."

His smile broadened as he turned to face Maurice Orr head on.

"Inspector," Orr said. "You'll be excited to..."

"To keep interrupting you at every turn unless it's helpful to us, sir. And I don't remember asking you anything, so keep quiet."

No courtesy or respect was shown and Orr hated being interrupted. In fact it was stronger than that. It was a definite anxiety and anger management issue that kicked off, if he was repeatedly cut off.

"So just a little bit of housekeeping before we begin today," the Inspector announced. "I only have a couple of brief questions for you today, Maurice. Everybody okay with that?"

He was really only speaking to inmate number 2764. So when the affirmative nod came from across the table, Murray began.

"Firstly, do you know of any nursery rhymes, Mr Orr that are all about strings?"

It was a library, even in prison it was normally quiet. But no one
moved. Part intrigue, part puzzlement. What is he up to? Was he having a laugh? Orr pondered. Eventually the man spoke up...

"What kind of question is that?" he replied rather timidly.

"Well I asked it Mr Orr, simply because I think you've been pulling ours right from the start."

Puzzled looks came his way from both females in the room.

"Because you were never assisting us after the fact. Indeed, I believe it was quite the opposite. You were pointing us in a certain direction each time we visited. Cajoling, guiding, throwing us bait and reeling us in. Then all you had to do was check up on us and reconfirm that everything was going to plan."

Maurice Orr said nothing. Murray briskly nodded to DCI Furlong and she happily took the gift-wrapped book out of its brown paper bag and slid it slowly across the table.

"For you, sir." Murray offered. "One to add to the vast collection that surrounds you."

Orr looked warily at the package. His suspicions heightened further.

"Detective Sergeant Kerr sends her love by the way."

That unsettled the man even more, as he tentatively began to unwrap what even he knew to be a book of some sort. Furlong and Murray had both noticed a palpable difference in him. His previously ego driven arrogance, swagger and confident manner seemed to have disappeared overnight. Each of those smug character traits had been posted missing. Someone or something had gotten to him. On all the previous occasions he also knew that they were coming to visit him, but they had been on his terms. This time he was worried because the tables had been turned and he was unaware of what to expect. As Maurice Orr revealed the novel. The orange and black cover announced it as part of the well loved Penguin Classic Series.

"I suppose sooner or later in the life of everyone comes a moment of trial."

As Steven Murray eloquently spoke the words, Furlong remembered that was the line that she had previously recognised, but couldn't quite place on their first visit to Maurice Orr. A visit that he himself had orchestrated, by implying that he could help with the case.

Barbra Furlong turned to her left. Murray could feel her staring. She simply wanted to admire him for a second. Do not ever underestimate this shrewd, perceptive man, she thought to herself. Before eventually blurting out...

"I knew, I knew that line when I heard it last time."

"Yes, but it wasn't for our benefit back then DCI Furlong," Murray stated firmly. "Oh, no. It was just after his Governor here, had threatened to replace him."

On hearing that, the shimmering lime green sparkly fingernails of Loggenberg began to beat either nervously or aggressively on the table top. For whatever reason she was agitated and equally rattled.

"I don't remember that Inspector," she declared. "Look at the name of the publication, Governor."

"REBECCA," DCI Furlong proudly announced. Raising her voice slightly, recognising that she was the umpire in the middle, and knowing Steven Murray, that was also a deliberate ploy.

"Exactly. Rebecca by Daphne Du Maurier," the Inspector continued. "It wasn't just a meaningless throwaway line as it may have appeared. Oh no, it was a deliberate rebuke to someone in the room that day. A clear message, a reminder even, for that particular individual to rein themselves in and take a step back. In other words it was an admonition. *I suppose sooner or later in the life of everyone comes a moment of trial.* It was a warning to you Miss Loggenberg, Rebecca."

Orr sat still, his face far from impressed. Barbra Furlong on the other hand, was both highly impressed and mightily intrigued.

Whilst her friendly gift-giver by her side, had initially slowed down dramatically with the finger strumming. After hearing her name called, it was now a regular, steady two-handed demonstration on display. Steven Murray meanwhile, still had a second question to ask.

"I believe that this was the book that you delivered to your murder victim, Maurice. Was it not?"

Orr hated almost everything about this man. He recognised that he was respectful and devious. Plus he was possibly the most thorough detective that he had ever came across. He must spend countless hours on his preparation, Orr reckoned. Every angle would be covered, every detail examined and re-examined. His colleagues would love him and so would the families of victims. He oozed an effortless charm whenever he spoke and he would own the proceedings, by way of holding everyone's attention. It was impossible not to admire him, but that didn't mean that you had to like him and Maurice Orr, for one - certainly didn't!

"I'm waiting," Murray said.

A nod from Orr was followed up with, "You know it was. I don't even think..."

"A simple yes would have sufficed," came the interruption.

Murray stood up to walk away, so Furlong and Loggenberg began to follow. He then glanced over at the librarian's face, which by this time was smouldering nicely underneath his stony expression. His internal rage seemed to be exactly the response this particular Detective Inspector was aiming for.

"Goodbye Maurice. We will speak very very soon. Of that I can promise."

The three figures exited the library and embarked on the lengthy sponsored walk up the corridor once again. However, after twenty seconds, Steven Murray decided to play his Lieutenant Columbo card. Always a great admirer of Peter Falk's portrayal of this bumbling TV figure. He loved how that particular character would always have just one more thing to be asked and as if right on cue he then offered up...

"Oh, I've one more thing I'd like to ask him, Miss Loggenberg. There is something that has been bothering me." Murray said forgetfully.

Immediately, the Governor, dressed in her exquisite green Mandarin apparel, turned on her no doubt highly expensive heels to start back down the corridor.

"I'll just go and ensure the guard is still in place and check that Mr Orr is okay to continue.

Barbra Furlong took a step to her right and immediately blocked Rebecca Loggenberg's stride.

"You'll do no such thing, Ma'am. Let me tell you how this is going to work. Inspector Murray will quietly walk back toward the library by himself and we will then follow at least ten paces behind. Do we understand each other Miss Loggenberg?"

The woman's eyes were like a knife to Barbara's ribs, the sharp point digging deep. Where there had once been undying love, her pupils were presently displaying an emptiness. However, uncomfortable with the void, the prison Governor filled it with an emotion DCI Furlong suspected she was much more at ease with these days - A raw, visceral anger. The unmoving gaze was accompanied by deliberate slow breathing. Like she was fighting something back, but losing. DI Murray meanwhile had reached the door.

Thirty Eight

"If I could turn the page, in time then I'd rearrange just a day or two. Close my, close my, close my eyes. But I couldn't find a way, so I'll settle for one day to believe in you. Tell me, tell me, tell me lies. Tell me lies, tell me sweet little lies."

- Fleetwood Mac

"Tell me Maurice, do you need any help getting back into that... wheelchair?"

Orr, caught by surprise, looked toward the doorway and froze. As the prison guard held it in place, the librarian was caught in the desperate act of stepping back from the table and into his personal carrier. His breathing instantly turned rapid and shallow. His mode of transport was obviously regularly hidden behind the neat row of computer desks that were generally obscured from full view. The man's pulse began pounding in his temples. It was a relief for him simply to get seated in his robust, charcoal grey chair. With his heels and legs beginning to shake and tremble, his true vulnerability was on open display to all and sundry. In those intervening seconds, the continued look of disgust, anger and outrage on the man's face shot way over Steven Murray's shoulder and landed directly at the feet of his now less than favourite Prison Governor.

"Mr Orr was always entitled to his privacy," Rebecca stated defensively. "And he was uncomfortable when others saw his disability. So he had simply sought that we put discretionary measures in place when you visited and I was happy to oblige."

"Which means that both you and inmate 2764 here, deliberately hindered us from our inquiries," Murray confirmed. "And for a change Miss Loggenberg, I would like you to visit me at Queen Charlotte Street police office tomorrow morning at 9am sharp. That's in Leith by the way. A place where the sun always shines," he mocked. "You might have to leave at four in the morning to beat that M8 traffic though. So good luck with that," he smiled, before adding thoughtfully. "Oh, but it'll be Sunday, so you should manage another couple of hours in bed before setting off."

"Me? Leith! What cock'n bull stories have you been listening to, Inspector?" Rebecca announced. "I don't think so."

At this point Orr's rage was vexing strong. It was twisted and distorted. It burned so bad, like a fire lacing his veins and creeping up his damaged spine. The devious officer could feel the man's grievance; his determined desire to hate. Taken by surprise, this inflamed puppet master was intoxicated with emotion. The acidity of his disdain was residing in his stomach waiting to be spat out in foul and vulgar words. That was DCI Furlong's terrain and she could relate totally with that overwhelming urge. Maurice Orr would be stared at for saying them, except he wasn't going to say them. Instead, he was going to screech them out with every last ounce of breath that dwelled deep down from within his lungs. And off he went...

It was a full five minutes after the ceremonial tongue lashing, before DI Steven Murray began...

"Sandra Kerr would have assumed that we knew that you were crippled. That we had met with you normally whilst you were in your wheelchair. So she had no reason to make special mention of it. But it was a schoolboy error on our part. Because we never managed to ascertain the full extent of the great grandson's injury from back then quick enough. What do you remember of that day Maurice? I mean it was over three decades ago, but you've obviously wanted payback all this time."

2764 sat emotionally drained. His previous vocal exertions had clearly taken their toll on his body and spirit. Though from the distant recesses of his mind he vividly recalled how, for as long as he could remember, he had been unforgiving when it came to his great- grandfather's death. He swore that he would bear a grudge until he died or took revenge, whichever came first.

He was determined to settle the score and he knew that he wanted it to be brutal, callous, satisfying and mean spirited. Whatever that all looked like, it appealed to the twisted and dark sense of humour that he had acquired throughout the intervening years.

"History would likely record," the Inspector continued. "That thirty years ago, when a young six-year old Bruce Foster was badly injured - no one took any notice."

Orr flinched abruptly at the mention of his childhood name and knew then, that it was all over. That this was the beginning of the end.

"That would certainly have been any young lad's mindset growing up," Murray stated honestly. "No one had ever been brought to court and prosecuted for the death of your great-grandfather. There had been no justice in your eyes. No one held to account. Until now of course - Vigilante style. We know that in recent years your sister, Moira Cadogan..."

He kept that quiet also, thought a mightily surprised DCI on hearing all this news for the first time. He was quite the lone wolf when he wanted to be, she thought. A trait that he had to forego moving forward. But one that she knew would be exceptionally difficult to change or alter. Steven Murray meanwhile, continued unabated...

"We know that she regularly reported physical abuse," he went on. "Although with no real proof. But to the outside world and yourself, it would have appeared yet again that no one took any notice. That under pressure and with individuals simply too busy to cope, the system was broken. That for victims like your sister - no one was ever held to account."

Maurice Orr cried out... "Someone, somewhere, took notice this time!"

In recent weeks that had most definitely been his anonymous rally call. Secretly planned, prepared and operated from behind his desk, which acted as his safety blanket. But unmistakably, he was no lone wolf. Although given his recent interactions with him, Inspector Murray was convinced of one thing. Which was that Maurice Orr was a coward. A sociopathic coward, but a coward nonetheless. Throughout his childhood years and with his mobility and zest for life gone, Murray could see that he had opted to go down the victim route and take no further responsibility for his decisions and ultimate actions, and one of those decisions was to hate those who tried to understand him. So over the years, Maurice Orr became emotionless, heartless and manipulative. On his pauper's gravestone, Murray believed that this man's legacy, his poisoned creed would read as:

'Too many accept so little - when they could have so much more.'

"Aren't we all liar's?" The Inspector heard him quietly ask Barbra Furlong. "Like little children, desperately biting our tongues to keep the truth intact."

"Well it's funny you should say and question that Mr Orr. Because your sister Moira or Becky as she was christened, certainly is. She has lied to you about nearly everything, and I suspect you had no idea. Because you only heard what you wanted to hear. Whatever fitted with your murderous ideals and makeshift plans. Interestingly, I actually visited with her this morning," Steven Murray informed him.

The librarian's eyes met and interlocked with the Inspector's.

"But sorry, of course you knew that already, didn't you? Because she called you immediately after we left I believe, didn't she? At least according to the phone log here at the prison that was when you got your last call."

Loggenberg's jolted body, declared clearly to the officers that she was oblivious to the fact that they had obtained this valuable information. Especially as she had left clear instructions to be made aware of any such requests. Then again - Radical Lizzie having been an 'ethical hacker' in her previous life, was both dogged and tenacious. Also, being extremely good at her job, some basic prison security software was never going to stop her. Unofficially, at least.

"Some sort of family emergency, I believe," Murray put forward. "No worries, we'll listen to it later. Before your guardian angel here, mistakenly has it erased."

That last remark was directly aimed at the now surprisingly quiet as a mouse, Governor.

"Whatever do you mean by..."

"I don't quite know your full involvement yet, Miss Loggenberg. But the fact that you were waiting for us behind that door when we arrived here today, was certainly enough to convince me. And on reflection, the fact that inmate 2764 was always seated in advance and that his wheelchair was deliberately hidden out of sight and not merely by his side, has persuaded me even more. Plus again, the early warning quotation from 'Rebecca' to Rebecca was also no coincidence. DCI Furlong can attest to that."

"He doesn't believe in coincidences, folks." She said. "So I guess you might want to bring a good lawyer with you tomorrow Governor Loggenberg."

That last instruction had been delivered in a remote, yet totally professional tone. The words had been difficult to say to an old friend and University flatmate, but the Detective Chief Inspector felt comfortable in all that she had heard so far, and knew that Steven Murray was only just getting started.

"As for you Mr Orr," she added. "I doubt you'll see the outside of a prison wall ever again."

Murray began to hum *'Seasons in the Sun.'* Maurice Orr smiled and played the game with him by opting for an obscure verse to return fire with...

"Goodbye Papa, it's hard to die, when all the birds are singing in the sky. Now that spring is in the air, little children everywhere and when you see them, I'll be there. Everyone called him Papa, Mr Murray. That song became his party piece."

The Inspector was once again happy to take the jibe regarding his name. Knowing full well that Maurice Orr or Bruce Foster would only be picking up the odd consolation goal from here on in. The competitive element to the match was well and truly over.

"He was an avid bookworm, Mr Murray. He loved fiction and would always sit me upon his lap when we visited and then read to me endless tales of action and adventure. He would take me on fascinating childhood journeys. Sometimes to the centre of the earth, but more often back in time."

Murray witnessed first-hand, just how much this man had meant to Orr. He nodded in understanding, whilst the two females sat very much nonplussed.

"Now you may think, what was the point? That I was too young to remember, Inspector. But amazingly two books always stuck with me."

Murray wasn't surprised and he allowed his intrigued eyes to ask the question for him.

"Gulliver's Travels and The Three Musketeers. Tales of little people and a world of dashing sword fights. What more could a six-year old boy ask for?"

His audience remained respectfully quiet and still. Each one, no doubt touched by a piece of overly sentimental yearning.

Maurice Orr continued with, "I always remembered those visits and I soon fell in love with reading and the opportunity to escape briefly from the real world. He began shortly afterwards to take me on a regular basis to the library. That soon became my highlight of the week."

"And the rest as they say, is history..." Murray echoed.

"Pretty much," the man confirmed.

"And the novelty of the nursery rhyme themed deaths. Did that all stem from murdering Angela McMinn?" Barbra Furlong dared to ask, after having sat quiet for far too long.

Orr hesitated. "Well, not really," he said. "It actually goes much further back than that, Chief Inspector.

"But we don't have any suspicious or unaccounted deaths before that," she exclaimed.

"The fact that you are both here and have tracked down Bruce and Becky, then I would be surprised and slightly disappointed, if your colleague has not already figured it out."

"Yep. Sure. Of course. Why didn't I think of that Mr Orr?" Barbra promptly turned to her left. "It's just another nugget that MR MURRAY has discovered and chosen to keep to himself!"

That deliberately caustic remark nearly made Orr and Loggenberg smile. While her so-called pal, Steven, was smirking from ear to ear.

"That was all down to Papa himself, DCI Furlong," Murray enlightened her. "He was to be the catalyst, driving force and ultimately the divine inspiration behind that particular murderous theme," he then reliably informed her.

Still Furlong didn't get it. The shaking of her head was a clear indication as such. Rebecca Loggenberg, although supposedly involved in some way and under the microscope herself, also drew a blank on any reasoning behind his words.

"That was how I first got wind that you were involved Maurice. So you have no need to be disappointed. I did figure it out," Murray confirmed.

Orr rubbed gently at his forehead. It was a brow-beaten look that said - I knew you had.

"When I found out that your great grandfather Ian was originally from a small place on the outskirts of Cheltenham. An area I know well, having visited it several times with an old work colleague. Three times in fact my friend, Ally Coulter, and I travelled down their for the Cheltenham Festival race meeting during mid-March."

"Of course you did," Furlong whispered. No matter how low she spoke, everybody heard. It was a library after all.

"I also have friends in that neck of the woods, literally next door at Gloucester in fact. And like my Chief Inspector told you earlier, I really don't do coincidences. So can you imagine how I felt whilst investigating deaths involving nursery rhymes and I heard that the man killed all those years ago was a Doctor Foster from Gloucester? That was just too good to be true."

"I have nothing to fear officers," Orr butted in. "I love being a librarian, I love my job, I love to exercise my mind and to pit my wits against others. Although on this occasion the better man won. Well done, MISTER Murray," he added indignantly yet again. "I expect I'll be here a little while longer if this house of cards is about to come tumbling down around me."

He finally added an Ace of Spades and a Queen of Diamonds to his ascending column. It completed the look and finished it off.

"More than a little while longer," Furlong smugly suggested. "In the words of the film, I would suggest you are looking at - From Here to Eternity!"

Maurice Orr wrinkled his nose at that prediction and offered up a resigned shrug of indifference.

"Did you know, Mr Orr..." Barbra began. "That the term 'House of Cards' was an exceptionally old expression that dated back to the 1640's. It meant a structure or argument built on a shaky foundation or one that would collapse, if a necessary but possibly overlooked or unappreciated element was removed."

"I think you'll find that your sister Moira is that *'unappreciated and overlooked element,'* isn't that right, Maurice?" Murray asked.

"Both the member House of Representatives and House of Commons," DCI Furlong further informed them. "Change their stances based on cards dealt to them. So, the House members change their position on issues. Hence - House of Cards is most apt."

Murray thought initially that he and his team had simply out-witted Maurice Orr. Mainly through good thorough police work. Now given the man's deference to him, he was having second thoughts. For whatever reason, he now felt that the knowledgeable historian on all things nursery rhyme related was actually holding back on yet another secret.

"If you give me until Monday morning, Mr Murray, I will happily reveal all. What do you say?"

The Inspector and DCI Furlong observed the man carefully. After several seconds Orr added...

"By way of a sweetener, what I can tell you is that the schoolgirl, Stacey, was never on any agreed list between myself and Barry Cadogan. Even my sister denies having anything to do with her. However, my own personal thoughts are that Moira crossed the line and is simply in denial or lying."

"In denial?" Furlong gasped, staring testily at Orr. "She killed her own husband!"

Inmate 2764, grimaced at that thought.

The Inspector's choice would have been lying. Because with the exception of her gambling habit, she had failed to tell the truth with regard to anything else! No matter, Murray knew Maurice Orr was desperately stalling for time. Certainly they were about to arrest his sister, Moira Cadogan, in the next hour anyway. Which would mean they would be busy tomorrow interviewing her and also chatting with Rebecca Loggenberg to uncover her full involvement. With all that in mind, he glanced at his DCI. After a considered pause, a slow blink of her eyelids was all the confirmation Steven Murray needed to move forward a stage.

"Monday morning, bright and early it is, Mr Orr. I look forward to seeing you then."

As the two officers went to take their leave, Murray remembered to acknowledge the frustrated Governor.

"And tomorrow morning, bright and early for you, Ma'am," he reminded her. Following those words up with a broad, satisfactory grin.

As all three proceeded to head out, this time it was the turn of Detective Chief Inspector Furlong to stop in her tracks and turn back. She tugged firmly twice at her black Police Scotland tunic and calmly strolled back toward Maurice Orr. Five paces in all took her to the edge of the desk. She leaned forward and inmate 2764 flinched slightly. In a low, threatening voice, she spoke softly.

"There is no need to be afraid, Mr Orr. Well certainly not in a physical sense. No, I just wanted to confirm to you, that your house of cards is not just falling down gently around you. It is about to be completely blown to smithereens!"

With that and from only six inches away, the DCI proceeded to blow Maurice Orr a farewell kiss.

"No," he yelled out in despair.

Furlong's sweeping breeze took out the whole fourth row of his playing cards. From there an overall implosion was inevitable. In the aftermath of the destruction and turmoil, Queens, Kings and Jokers lay scattered all around. How appropriate DI Murray thought. Because that same trio appeared to be key participants in this unraveling case also. Actually based on Mr Cannon, we could include a Jack in the quartet of characters also, he surmised.

On approach to their car a mobile began sounding. Both officers began instantly patting their pockets. It belonged to Steven Murray and was immediately answered.

"Drew. How did you get on? Yes, we're just leaving Greenock. Is everything in hand?"

The detective suddenly stopped abruptly in his tracks.

"I see," he said. "Okay, and that was about forty-five minutes ago, you say? Fine, go back one more time in about an hour and let me know if anything changes. Thanks. See you soon."

On their drive down, it had been dull and overcast all the way. Now DCI Furlong eyed the sky nervously. The clouds that had been wispy and white earlier that morning, were now darker and more dense. The Chief Inspector quickened her pace, not desirous to be caught in a localised downpour. The alarm beeped, lights flashed and the door locks on the Volvo popped open. Once inside and behind the steering wheel, Steven Murray spoke passionately to Barbra.

"Two things," he said excitedly, as he started up the engine and began to drive off. "No, three in fact. Firstly, the way that you brought that house of cards down was eccentric, erratic and totally erotic all rolled into one."

Furlong nodded and blushed. She would gratefully accept that praise from her supposedly junior officer. It was after all, just a bit of fun and oneupmanship.

"Secondly, we are going to park here for a couple of minutes, Barbra." He couldn't quite believe just how comfortable he had become using her Christian name. "I want to check something out," he enlightened her.

Murray had pulled in between a couple of parked cars on a busy stretch of road only two to three hundreds metres outside the prison gates.

"And thirdly?" She asked nervously, having seen the colour drain slightly from her Inspector's face, seconds earlier, when he himself had just heard from 'The Kid.'

"Thirdly, is what DC Curry told me just now and I will reveal that after our brief stakeout," he said slowly and smiled.

"Oh, that's what this is, is it?" She shook her head.

It was getting dark when Murray saw the next set of car head-lights drive out from the prison gates. He had positioned him-self carefully, so that he could still see anyone entering or exiting the *'Greenock Hotel.'* Again DCI Furlong was impressed. Write this man off at your peril, she thought to herself. Before actually vocalising something else entirely.

"What is it we are actually..."

"That," Murray interrupted. Pointing at the car approaching them from behind. "See if you can spot who is driving it," the Inspector encouraged.

It was a powerful beast of a motor. It swept past them smooth-ly and quietly, careful to maintain the speed limit. The impres-sive executive vehicle came complete with tinted windows and sunroof, as well as the standard marque badge on the front.

"Damn!" Murray exclaimed. "I was hoping for a bit more, but I got something at least."

"What did you get?" Furlong asked with an overly smug look.

"Why the big grin?" He said. Knowing full well she was about to raise the stakes and outplay him. Or was she? He then offered a rather confident smart-Alec grin of his own. "I got the make and model of the car," he offered rather sheepishly.

"Well I think I win this one," his DCI announced. "I know who was driving," Furlong's face beamed as she went to announce...

"Rebecca Loggenberg!" Murray threw out there. "I obviously knew that," he added dismissively. "Why else do you think I pulled over?"

"Surely not just to get the make of car. Please tell me it wasn't as simple as that?"

She could see from Murray's extraordinarily quiet response, that, that was exactly why he had pulled over.

"Not purely that," he then confirmed. "I wanted to see if she was in a rush to contact someone. If she had a need to get away as soon as possible? The fact that she high-tailed it straight after us, settled that argument for me, and the fact that she drives a Jaguar, the one car that I would suggest is as close to..."

"A 'leaping feline' as we are going to get!" Furlong concluded.

They both gave each other a knowing look.

"And thirdly?" The Chief Inspector reminded him.

"Well, I wonder now who she is racing off to meet, Ma'am? Because by all accounts - Moira Cadogan is missing!"

Thirty Nine

"Man there's an opera out on the turnpike. There's a ballet being fought out in the alley. The hungry and the hunted explode into rock'n roll bands. That face off against each other out in the street, down in Jungleland."

- Bruce Springsteen

Saturday evening...

Returning back to the station at approximately 6.15pm, Murray met up with his cowboy team of 'Hanna'bal Hayes and 'Kid' Curry in their closed-up canteen.

"So Mister Maurice Orr was the injured six-year old." Hayes announced.

"And he's owned up to masterminding this whole thing from behind bars. Impressive, sir" Andrew Curry expressed. Bringing looks of concern from the other two.

"You know what I mean," he responded. "Do you want us to babysit Moira Cadogan's place all night then?"

"No. I wouldn't worry about it. Leave it this evening. Who knows where she might be heading. Wherever it is, I don't believe she is a threat to the general public. Tomorrow just pop by at regular intervals. If she still hasn't turned up, then we can begin to worry. In the meantime, 'Hanna,' I've done enough driving for the day. How would you like to drop me off somewhere?"

"Homeward bound, sir?" Hayes asked with a cheeky glint in her eye. Thinking that he was heading back east, toward DCI Furlong's place.

"Not quite," he replied. "But give me five minutes to make sure the people I need to meet up with are both free."

Elsewhere, someone else received an unexpected visitor. In the split second it took for their features to be illuminated by the flickering street light. The person answering the door's face went from elated surprise to horror, and then back again to a controlled visage of concern.

"What are you doing here?"

Without answering, the body burst past and came inside. Their jacket collar high up, hiding their face. Louder this time, the voice again asked.

"Why are you here? I thought we agreed..."

The visitor's head simply shook.

"All agreements are null and void. I am now officially your worst nightmare." The voice was a jarring, petulant whine. "Those two police officers were back again today and this time, the name of Ian Foster was mentioned."

The homeowner stood perfectly still and listened, without any real worry or trepidation.

"I listened to your worst fears," the voice said. "I even understood what made you tick. Then after a while, I controlled you like a remote control toy. I started you out with small tasks that you may have found distasteful, until I gradually worked you up to things that you never dreamed you were capable of."

Up until now there'd been no disagreement, no dissenting voice. It all sounded truthful.

"So why did you do all that for me?" The trespasser continued. "Was it because I dangled the illusion of love before you and let you get close enough to almost attain it. If that is the case, then maybe I'll just ask you for one more little thing to prove your true devotion. However, I believe that you've now become the person that your old self would have loathed beyond all others. Thus it has come time for me to disappear. For that, I need documentation and cash. Do I even hear you ask - Why?"

No other sound was forthcoming.

"Well let me tell you, it's because this is the end of my adventurous fantasy. I helped you and you helped me. But you never truly meant anything to me and now it's... game over!"

From a nearby cabinet, the expected envelope of money with a private dossier of any incriminating evidence or fresh new I.D and passport never materialised. No, the large drawer in the expensive looking desk slid open and a near twenty-year old object was retrieved. There was no mistaking its distinctive shape, as the householder began to respond.

"That was a worthy monologue. Bold and unrehearsed, I gathered. Yet sincere and heartfelt," the host said strongly.

The unwelcome visitor on the other hand was now suddenly feeling rather anxious and afraid. From their earlier confident and articulate assertions, there was now no doubting the trepidation, hesitation and fear in their voice.

"What are you intending to do with that?"

"I'm surely allowed to respond with a discourse of my own. Am I not? Although my preference would be for a soliloquy."

The evil dark, not the noble dark, will come at you through your primitive urge and drive. Any hunter will go for the weak spot of an animal and that is yours, my love. First there will be a trigger to open up the primitive drive, to activate it as fully as possible. Then will come the impulse to cause harm, one that hurts both others and yourself. Your only protection is to love fully. Love yourself. Love others. Be present in the moment. Question your own actions - own them fully, for regardless of the evil force, except in the case of true insanity, they are yours. And long after we have forgiven you, you will struggle to forgive yourself. If an action feels as if it comes from your survival drive, with a feeling of malice, hate or fear - Stop. If an action feels as if it comes from your higher thinking mind and with a feeling of love, kindness and compassion - Proceed.

Inspired by those choice words, the potent blade of the machete struck instantly and with one slash their opponent's abdomen opened up. Intestines spewed onto the floor in pinkish brown coils. All eyes focused downward in disbelief, as the air took the aroma of a butcher's shop. Up, down, forward and back. The thrashing was relentless. As if clearing a path in a densely populated jungle. Within a minute, where once there had been smooth unblemished skin, there now sat torn muscle and blood. It was as raw as any slaughtered carcass. The body lay still, its shade so pale as to make the oozing blood from the heinous wounds appear more red.

The savage victor felt sweat drench their skin. Their eyes throbbed as terrifying screams, although gone, continued to vibrate and ring relentlessly in their ears. Their chest rose and fell as the rapid thumping of their heart took its toll. By this point with the weapon discarded, their fingers were curled into fists and nails dug deeply into their palms. The killer could no longer hear their own erratic breathing. However, they could feel the crashing tide of oxygen flood in and out of their lungs. Reluctantly, they eventually forced themselves to view the dead corpse.

Trembling, suddenly they were overcome with fear. It was an interesting sensation, because this fear tortured their gut and churned at their stomach with intense cramp. It engulfed their very conscience, knocking all other thoughts aside. This immediate fear overwhelmed their body, making it drastically exhausted. But greater than all of that, this particular fear calmed the individual immediately and that overwhelming sense of peace is what scared them most of all. That night they slept like a child. Although it would be a further 48 hours before they could comfortably put in place travel arrangements, then safely transfer and withdraw funds without any troublesome questions being asked.

Sixty minutes later, Detective Constable Hayes pulled up and parked immediately outside Jack Cannon's home. A house that only 24 hours earlier, had still been officially cordoned off by a Police Scotland forensics team. With normally some form of method in his madness, Suzanne and Billy Cannon had agreed to meet Steven Murray there. He had felt prompted to share something with the brother and sister pairing. The choice of venue was central for everyone, but he had wanted the deaths of their father and teenager Stacey to be uppermost in their thoughts still. The Inspector had asked Susan Hayes to wait on him, as he literally only expected to be a few minutes.

True to his word seven minutes later, he re-emerged and had Hayes take him back to the station. It had been a long, taxing, yet worthwhile day and it wasn't over yet. Initially, he had planned on heading over to Barbra Furlong's to talk about some 'tumbling panda's' from her past and her recent spate of gifts from her anonymous benefactor. Each one, unsurprisingly postmarked from Greenock. Earlier in the day, while they were driving down the coastal road to chat with Maurice Orr, yet another postal delivery had been made to the station addressed to DCI Barbra Furlong. Now that Loggenberg was scheduled to come in and visit with them in the morning, he had decided to hold off on his discussions until later on Sunday evening.

As DC Hayes drove back to Leith, Murray reflected on his visit to Jack Cannon's home. He had only one question to ask the brother and sister. It was clear and straightforward.

He'd asked, "How would you feel, if I told you that we had got someone in custody for every death?"

At that, he watched as the siblings shared a huge personal hug with each other. Relief written all over their body language. Smiles surfaced and broadened upon their faces. Unfortunately it was at that point that DI Murray felt the need to add...

"With the exception of Stacey."

The siblings, arms fell back to their sides. Their vibrant smiles replaced with shock, awe and amazement.

"What do you mean?" They'd asked him in utter amazement. "Why would they admit to killing all the rest and not Stacey?"

That was when all eyes shifted onto the rugged, unshaven Detective Inspector. Why would he invite them here to meet with him, only to deliver a blow like that? They liked the man. From their brief interactions with him and his team, they knew he was a dedicated officer and inspired those around him to be equally committed. Again they thought to themselves. What was he about to bring to the table?

DC Hayes had witnessed all the animated gestures first hand, from her position in the front seat of her official Police Scotland vehicle.

"Hypothetically speaking," he told them. "This individual is going to get off Scot-free. With all the others, we appear to have strong, solid evidence, alongside clues and DNA. By Monday I even expect an actual confession as well. But for here, we have none of that. For your daughter's brutal and callous murder, we have nothing." He informed them.

Suzanne Cannon burst into tears at that news.

"As a last roll of the dice," Murray continued. "I wondered if any of you could identify this person?" The DI then handed each of them a postcard sized image.

William Cannon immediately locked eyes with Steven Murray. Was this police officer doing what he thought he was doing?

"From everything I have heard, I believe you to be a man of principle Mr Cannon."

Suzy went on to question, "Is this who killed my..."

"Shh," her brother instructed her. "You can't be asking that of the Inspector, Sis."

"I'll leave them with you. Just in case something jogs your memory," the experienced officer had then told them.

'Hanna' had witnessed all of this without the sound. But she was aware that her DI had put two small photocopied pictures of a suspect into an envelope before they set off!

After his seven minute visit, Suzanne and Billy Cannon were left checking out the features of an individual that they assumed to be Stacey's killer. They stared at each other in disbelief. Their twin expressions questioning if that extremely surreal moment had just actually happened. It was the same individual Murray had asked each of them to identify. Only, on the back of one picture there was a name and address. On the reverse of the other, nothing.

DC Hayes pulled into the car park and drew up smoothly alongside Murray's S40. Wary and suspicious, she offered her Inspector a rather cautious and less than convincing,

"Good-night, Sir."

"Good-night," the Inspector, replied cheerily. As the butter began to slowly melt in his mouth!

Forty

"I know that we won't need much. You and me, the house and the dog. Our best years are yet to come. Thanks for choosing me. Do you know how lucky we are?"

- Lucy Spraggan

Barbra Furlong had just returned home from walking '3 miles,' when DI Murray, complete with music blaring from his car stereo turned into the seriously tranquil East Lothian street. The Dropkick Murphys were immediately switched off for fear of him being arrested. In some areas in Scotland it was still against the law to be seen enjoying yourself! On spotting Barbra with her pooch in tow, a question fleetingly ran through the Inspector's mind. What clever or playful name would he give to a dog? A canine that he actually owned, as opposed to the 'black dog' that currently shadowed him everywhere, if and when it liked. Using his Chief Inspector's clever strategy, plus being a bit of a Cher fan, he quickly opted for one of her top tunes. It would be great fun to continually tell people that he was busy walking 'In Memphis!'

No longer in their teenage years. Semi-clad, fun frolics and fumbles on the settee had been suitably replaced with oversized cardigans, chocolate digestives and a blazing hot coal fire.

"It all seems to be coming together," Furlong said. In a very understated manner. "Don't you think?" She added. Spotting Murray's hesitant reluctance to agree.

"Something's not right, Barbra."

"Do you really think Rebecca is involved? I mean, what could she possibly know?"

"I do! Is the short answer to question one. And, plenty! Works well for your second inquiry."

Murray, knowing that these two females had a history of sorts, seemed unwilling to elaborate further. Although the masculine, partner driven curiosity in him, couldn't help but ask...

"What is it with all the recent gifts?"

It was now Furlong's turn to be less than forthcoming...

"I don't really know how we came to be, Steven," she said quietly. Cuddling in and laying her hand upon his. She then asked, "Do you know how lucky we are to have each other?"

"I think I do, actually," the man said. "Why? What is it? Did '3 miles' eat my toothbrush?" He laughed, squeezing her tight and pulling her close.

Her fingers slipped effortlessly behind the patterned cushion at his back. Finally the slimline envelope was delivered into the palm of his warm, empty hands.

"What's this?" The man asked in genuine surprise.

Leaning forward, the woman of the house flicked at his nose and kissed his cheek. Before a gentle rub, erased her 'Pillow Talk' lipstick from his burning face.

"I know it's a week early, but Merry Christmas," she exclaimed. Steven Murray was taken aback and extremely humbled. Although he recognised fully, that it instantly allowed Barbra Furlong a 'Get Out of Jail Free Card,' regarding speaking further about her so far undisclosed relationship with a certain prison Governor. It was a card mind you, one that DI Murray was confident the lady in question would soon be requiring. The Inspector chose to open the envelope by ripping off one end, whilst running his finger up the inside, singing... *"Oh, I wish it could be Christmas everyday."*

"Behave yourself and get a move on," Furlong suggested.

"When the kids start singing and the band begins to play."

A light-hearted punch to his shoulder seemed to concentrate his efforts somewhat. Building up the excitement the Inspector reached in slowly with the tip of his fingers and delicately slid out one very special return ticket. Another 'Pillow Talk' kiss and rub was given and a moist tear from Murray's eye began to glide onto the remaining remnants of lipstick. *Undeserving* was the word that first sprung to mind, as the recipient continued to read the fine print.

"This Saturday, Barbra? That surely won't be possible," he said, before adding. "Will it?"

"Absolutely," she said adamantly. "Look, you told us that you would have this case all wrapped up by Tuesday and I believed you. So a few clicks on-line before we left for Greenock this afternoon and hey presto. With the help of modern technology and print-at-home options, here you are with the end result. Some people reckoned it would have been better if I had just gotten you a one way ticket. To those individuals I said... Rampant Rugged Sausages!"

They both laughed.

The early morning Saturday flight to Oregon, USA, was timed perfectly to allow him Christmas Eve with his daughter, Hannah, and her family. What a very special festive season this could now turn out to be. With all that had transpired, the Inspector was now more than happy to forego discussions about a certain Miss Loggenberg. Pulling Barbra Furlong even closer, Steven Murray passionately kissed his Detective Chief Inspector fully on the lips, and oh boy did that 'Pillow Talk' taste great.

Next morning...

Once again the sound of a Sunday newspaper dropping through the letterbox, brought a welcome smile to DI Murray's face. It was a most welcome distraction from the sound of Scotland's tried and tested roads and pavements taking a battering from the early morning downpour. The poor paper boy or girl must have been absolutely drenched out there. Whilst indoors, in the warmth, Barbra Furlong was busy boiling a kettle and buttering some toast, as Steven Murray rose to retrieve his sodden copy of the nation's best-selling Sunday read.

"What time do you think your favourite prison Governor will arrive at?" She asked, with a playful expression of mischief.

"George Smith is the Desk Sergeant on duty and I've already spoken with him. So he knows what to do."

"Which is, Inspector?" Knowing full well that he had deliberately blanked answering her.

"Well, we were both supposed to have had some time off to recharge our batteries today."

"Still you've avoided the question."

Two slices of toast were abruptly dumped in front of him.

"I told George to call me directly, as soon as she arrives at the station."

"You mean you are not even going in, in advance of her getting there?"

"Correct," he smirked. "I thought that she could have a taste of her own medicine for once. She always keeps us waiting in her office. Plus I'll get there within half an hour of her arrival. So I reckon we are all good and ready to go regarding, 'Becca' Loggenberg."

Furlong shook her head, dismissed his remarks and poured herself a black coffee. Five minutes later, Murray's mobile vibrated.

"That'll be him now," the Inspector exclaimed.

He was already salivating and relishing the opportunity for a frank exchange with the 'power dressing' fraud. At least that was certainly how Steven Murray saw her, and on many levels. So a chat with her on home turf, stirred his loins. Although, that piece of information he would be careful not to reveal to the female prison Governor.

"Hello, George. Is that her arrived?" He uttered quickly. "Oops, sorry. Apologies," he then added. "I was expecting another call."

Furlong looked across the table as Murray planted both elbows forcefully upon it for support.

"Yes, I hear you," he said quietly.

Barbra was experienced enough to recognise 'bad news.' Both when it was being broken and received. This call captured those two sides perfectly.

"Thank you for the call, Gus. I owe you one."

DI Murray then finished the conversation with what had become one of his stock in trade sayings over the years. His default setting perhaps.

"Much appreciated."

His tone was low and emotional. His Chief Inspector could clearly see he'd been left hurting.

"I have always been a giver." Murray managed to blurt out. One hand rubbing his brow.

Furlong nodded in genuine agreement. But said nothing.

"Even as a child, I sought to make others happy."

As his black dog entered the room. Furlong reached across the table to take a firm hold of his trembling hand.

"Yet again, I feel like I've been ambushed and left hollow inside." *A dark, bushy tail began to wag.*

Barbra knew that he'd had more than his fair share of heartache and tragedy in recent times. Several police colleagues and of course his youngest son, David. A young man gunned down in Glasgow, on the very day he was being released from prison. Steven Murray pursed his lips, shrugged and tried to pull himself together and shake off the downcast emotions.

"Any grieving for this would have to be put on hold for 48 hours," he announced boldly.

Although nervous to ask, she did so. "Grieving for what or whom?" Furlong enquired quietly.

DI Murray turned to look at the top of the freezer and at the impressive Christmas hamper that sat there patiently waiting for delivery. Wednesday had been the agreed date to take a couple of his colleagues along to The Blue Lagoon and introduce them to a friend of his. Both 'Hanna' Hayes and 'Kid' Curry had been looking forward to the educational visit.

"Macca died last night, Barbra. That was Gus Gillies, the bar manager. He found him frozen to death earlier this morning at the doorway to the pub."

On hearing that news, even the Detective Inspector's black dog fell to the ground and whimpered.

By ten minutes past ten, no further calls had been received. Murray had taken another shower and composed himself well. He made a point of reading through most of the newspaper headlines and any articles that he may have missed throughout the week on his phone or BBCiplayer. He then called Andrew Curry for an update regarding the hopeful, imminent arrest of Moira Cadogan.

"Me and Hannah are outside her place now, sir. No answer. We're not sure if she arrived home last night or not. We looked through the letterbox, but no apparent sign of any movement or activity and no radio, tv or music playing. We are due back between 2pm and 3pm this afternoon. What do you reckon?"

"I reckon," their DI stated with frustration. "That it's not dragging on any longer than that. If she's not there or you get no answer later, kick the door in. Concerned for the resident's health and well-being will suffice," Murray informed them. "If she's not there then things will be put in place to increase it to a proper missing persons manhunt."

Having washed, shaved and dressed ready to be called in at any moment. Murray was now feeling troubled. The heavy rain had stopped as quickly as it had appeared. With the time approaching 11.00am, his DCI prepared to walk '3 miles,' while the dark rain clouds had gone for a short tea-break.

"What's up?" Furlong asked.

Sitting in the front room, the fireplace was like a tiny sun as it cast long shadows over the rug. The flames curled and swayed, twisting this way and that, crackling as they burned the dry wood. Murray was hypnotised, his features illuminated by the flickering light. As he sat cosy in front of the orange glow, he held out his hands and rubbed them vigorously. In part to get a little more of the gentle heat running through his body, but mainly with nervous, anxious energy and concern. The air definitely wasn't smokey, but you could smell the pine as it burned. It offered a faint fragrance. One strong enough to reassure the senses that there would be comfort in the long bitter winter ahead, and that reassurance was what Inspector Steven Murray needed more than anything right now.

"I think I've seriously messed up, Barbra. Something's not right. Cadogan's still unaccounted for, possibly taking no chances and making a run for it and Rebecca Loggenberg has failed to show."

"She still might, it's not even noon yet."

"Yes, but when you are asked to be in at the station bright and early, I would have expected to see her between nine and ten, and even that would be late in most people's book."

"You really think that she is involved in some way?"

In true Jack Reacher form - Murray said nothing.

"Possibly for allowing Maurice Orr too much freedom and autonomy from behind bars?" She persisted.

Again her Inspector was reluctant to say anything.

"Worse than that?" She quizzed.

The best Murray could offer her was... "Let's just wait and see. Best not to speculate on these matters."

During the next couple of hours or so, Furlong had walked '3 miles' two miles, and bright blues winter skies broke out. Making the most of the time, Steven Murray spoke with each of his team individually. He was soliciting updates and any strange notions or gut feelings that they thought may be worthy of consideration. So far, to no success. Although Lizzie, who like Murray, appeared to have no social life outside work and was busy analysing events in her personalised 'Vault,' said that she would get back to him. His phone calls even included a voice message left on Governor Loggenberg's mobile. 'Rebecca I hope you are safe and well. It's Inspector Murray here. Both myself and DCI Furlong are concerned that you didn't show this morning.

Please can you contact me just to let me know you are un-harmed. We can always re-arrange our chat.'

He had been courteous and polite, but was slightly alarmed that subconsciously he had used the word 'unharmed.' Suggesting in his mind that there was now a definite fear for her safety.

Rampant Rugged Sausages, Murray thought to himself. Re-membering accurately Barbara's latest original offbeat outburst in a bid to clear the crazy thoughts that were beginning once again to clog up vital parts of his head. He was currently dwelling on all the deaths - Lucy Locket; Humpty Dumpty; Sing a Song of Sixpence; Hickory Dickory Dock and Old Mother Hubbard. That last one being the rhyme posted in connection to poor Stacey Cannon. Maurice Orr blamed his sister for that particular unplanned death. And as inmate 2764 continued to dominate Murray's impressions, it was interesting to note that Moira herself, had always been posted missing throughout Orr's life also. Her brother had always been the major focus of atten-tion. Ever since the death of their great- grandfather all those years ago, everyone had forgotten that there was actually a baby sister. Throughout the passing decades it was all about little Maurice or Mo as he was known. Mo this. Mo that. Mo the flamin' grass, Murray abruptly laughed to himself. He was a cripple. There would be a special sit-on lawn mower assigned for him, no doubt. Whatever had transpired between them over the years, somewhere along the line Moira Cadogan had cracked. Steven Murray was convinced that she had become even more deranged than her seriously challenged brother. At present, that had been a grave error on his part. A pivotal mis-take. She should've been taken into custody twenty-four hours ago.

His mind was now taking him on an epic surreal adventure. Coupled with little sleep the previous night, DI Murray instantly imagined Furlong's fireplace in a host of different styles. He visualised a marble surround, a ceramic surround, a wide mantle decorated with porcelain figurines and family photos. He pictured assorted vases of colourful flowers and an impressive panoramic mirror hanging high above the hearth. Next up in his thought process, the solid oak fireplace had been transformed into a specially commissioned, multi- coloured tile mosaic. No matter, the common denominator that all of the displays had, was a familiar 'black dog' positioned in front of each one of them. The Inspector's unwanted canine buddy was presently wagging his tail, displaying how immensely happy he was to be back in the fold and in his thoughts. As the uncommon sound of Barbra Furlong's BT landline sounded, Steven Murray heard a 'black dog' bark loudly and his head dejectedly slumped forward into his large, but slender hands. After thirty seconds of Barbra listening intently, Murray heard...

"Okay, thank you for letting me know so quickly, Sergeant."

Furlong then carefully replaced the sturdy handset into its receiver and wearing dark denim jeans and a casual, decorative floral top on her day off, duly announced...

"I'm going to get changed and travel into the station with you, Steven."

Murray was both alarmed and alerted by this news.

"About time," he screamed. "She should have come in bright and early as she was asked to do and we wouldn't have had any of this anxiety nonsense. We need to talk about her later by the way. Check the doorstep, 'cause she's probably sent you yet another little weekend gift!"

Furlong knew he had been feeling down and troubled, that he was just letting off steam and ranting aimlessly. But nonetheless she felt slightly hurt at the personal dig he was having at her friendship with Loggenberg. But she also knew that could be put on the back-burner until later.

"Steven. It's not Rebecca. It's Moira Cadogan," Furlong announced, before going silent.

Murray stared despairingly at his DCI. This wasn't good. Her features were small and perfectly related; her nose deliciously interrogative at the tip. Her brows and lashes, drawn in a darker hue, gave her individual touches of character and distinction. Slender and erect, her mouth was desirous to share once again. As she looked around, she remained strangely poised and calm. Possibly relieved that it wasn't news regarding Loggenberg.

"Mrs Cadogan was shot and killed a short while ago," she declared coldly. No emotion was contained in her voice or portrayed facially as she further revealed...

"She was gunned down this afternoon by the one o'clock gun. Poetic justice or what?" She questioned.

Murray, visibly shaken, spoke aloud. "Billy or Suzanne?"

His Chief Inspector shrugged slowly. "Why would you think that? How did you get that from *gunned down*?"

Thinking on his feet, he quickly responded.

"It happened at one o'clock, Ma'am. Edinburgh Castle, Mons Meg CANNON and poetic justice. Plus, am I not a DI into the bargain? Do you really want someone on the payroll that has to wait five minutes to try and figure that all out before googling it and repeating it back to you in some bog standard antiquated fashion?"

Barbra Furlong now had no idea what he was going on about. Which would have been Steven Murray's plan all along. If in doubt, opt for crazy. Either Mel Gibson, Lethal Weapon 'kooky' crazy, or Jack Nicholson, One Flew Over the Cuckoo's Nest 'insane' crazy. From experience, Murray found they both normally did the trick. The trick being - Distraction!

"Do they want us there straightaway, Ma'am? Barbra."

"That appeared to be the point of the call, Inspector. Steven."

Furlong hastily changed and the awkwardness between them continued all the way out to the car or cars, and which one to take? Their first destination was going to be the home of 'Six-geese-a- laying.' A goose that had now been well and truly cooked, although Murray chose to keep that particularly insensitive thought to himself. As a couple, they wisely decided to travel separately and took both cars. Arriving approximately six minutes apart.

Forty One

Sunday afternoon - 3pm...

SOCO, forensics experts and detectives were still actively involved at the Moira Cadogan murder scene. When a well dressed female walked though the swing doors at QCS police office in Leith and asked for Sergeant Sandra Kerr. After being shown through to an interview room, the lady in question was joined less than five minutes later, by both DS Kerr and Detective Constable Allan Boyd.

Suzanne Cannon seemed relaxed and contented when she casually announced to Sandy that she had shot and killed 'that woman,' in revenge for the callous, cold-hearted murder of her teenage daughter. So far the interview had been informal and off the record. Kerr, taken aback, had encouraged her carefully to think about what she was saying and doing. Boyd and his Sergeant exchanged glances. The look from both said - 'no way she did it.' By all accounts it was an execution. Two successive bullets at short range to the forehead. This was someone who'd had previous experience of handling guns. However, when the desperately grieving mother proceeded to produce a small handgun from her leather handbag, there was no going back.

"It belonged to my father," she said. He had been in the T.A and had acquired it many years ago. So possibly we got some retribution for him also," Suzanne stated.

"We?" Boyd asked, inquisitively. Latching on to her error.

"Simply a figure of speech, Constable," the woman replied confidently.

"Just answer one thing honestly right now, Suzanne. Will you do that for me?"

Suzy Cannon was reluctant to agree. However she recognised how much Sandra Kerr had invested in her over the past week. How this female police officer had tried her best to support her and give her strength and hope when she needed it most.

"One thing," she said firmly.

The mother of twin girls, looked forlornly at this grieving heartbroken female and asked...

"William. Your older brother Suzanne. Was he also a member of the Territorial Army?"

Cannon never spoke. Her eyes were bloodshot, yet fully attentive and aware. Wasting no further time, the woman looked directly between both officers and nodded gently.

Kerr shook her head and had DC Boyd officially caution and charge the woman. Leaving her with George Smith to be booked in and given a 'non-refundable' room for the evening, Allan Boyd then turned to chat with his friend, Sandra Kerr.

"Are you okay, Sarge?" He asked softly.

"Mitigating circumstances, surely? A heartbroken mother seeking justice on the woman that she believed brutally took the life of her teenage daughter."

"You would like to think so, Sandy. But what kind of justice did she deal out? Because being an ex-soldier, I recognise vigilante justice when I see it. It was nothing more, nothing less. She had already decided that Moira Cadogan was guilty and dispensed out her punishment in accordance with the crime, proof or no proof. I suspect the court will not be able to turn a blind eye to that."

"Really!" Kerr pleaded with him for some moral support. "The fact that she has never been in trouble with the police in her life. That both her father and daughter have just been murdered in the past week. Surely no jury in the land will come down hard on her?"

"I reckon that you are right on that score, Sarge. They may not come down hard on her. In fact, many, if not all the members of the jury would probably fully sympathise with her. But there is no way that they can be seen to be condoning her behaviour."

"Initially, Allan, I was thinking and hoping that she might not even serve time."

"I think the major problem though, Sandy, is that there is no clear evidence against Moira Cadogan. In fact, at this moment in time, Suzanne Cannon targeted a totally innocent party. That is, if she even fired the gun in the first place."

Both Boyd and Sgt. Kerr left the room, confident that it was her brother, William, who had actually carried out the killing and that was where their inquiries would begin. Of course, that was after giving Furlong and Murray a current update.

Coming back to the station directly from Cadogan's flat, Furlong headed straight to her room, whilst Inspector Murray literally went deep underground and opted for 'The Vault.' Neither chose to get involved with the accused at this stage. Intriguingly, 'Hannah' Hayes actually stopped Steven Murray when he'd arrived inside from the car park. She'd wanted to ensure that her Inspector knew that Suzanne Cannon was in custody, and currently charged with Moira Cadogan's murder. DI Murray acknowledged that he did and thanked her for her concern. Although as he descended the stairs to chat with the proprietor, he began to question why Susan Hayes felt the need to check that he knew. What was she trying to say or imply? He soon shrugged off those negative thoughts as soon as he saw the brightly attired, 'Radical in the Basement.' With no pigtails in sight, today her hair was fully blonde. Its extensions dropped as far down her back as the extra-long, oversized Chelsea FC top that she wore like a draped night-shirt. Bright arctic white tights were worn underneath and were impressive branches emanating from her royal blue Converse baseball boots.

Wow! Murray thought, as he began singing a song that was a hit several decades before she was even born...

"Blue is the colour, football is the game. We're all together and winning is our aim. So cheer us on through the sun and rain, 'Cause Chelsea, Chelsea is our name."

Pointing both her hands inwardly toward her chest and in particular to the adorning Chelsea FC crest and emblem, Lizzie offered him a cheerful, radiant smile. He questioned if she even knew that they were yet again dealing with another gruesome, callous murder? Especially as her chosen soundtrack playing in the background was a reggae tune belting out... *When in Rome, do as the Romans do. Far from home, all I got is you. Everyday we got a song to sing. All you need to live as a true new king.*

Which tied in rather nicely, (but was certainly not a coincidence, Murray smiled to himself) with why he was visiting this colourful, charismatic individual on a Sunday afternoon. Knowing also, that her dress sense had just instantly inspired him further.

"Two things, Lizzie," Murray announced. "Firstly, I mentioned it before, but I need you to double check everything to do with the jacket left in the kitchen at Andrew King's home. Size, make, model, stitching, length, etc, etc. You get the gist of what I'm saying. Because your outlandish fashion sense has just given me an idea."

"Glad I could be of help, sir," she proffered. "And 'thing' number two," she then chirped merrily.

Murray was delighted that Lizzie was in 'happy' mode currently. Because he hoped the switch wouldn't be flicked when he told her...

"Put some shorts on please, Lizzie. I need you to come with me on a trip."

Lizzie's smile grew and grew. She loved the banter with Murray. The cultural divide of old and young, the different mind-sets, coupled with how her cheeky flirtatious manner cheered him up no end. As an added bonus they would always laugh continuously in each other's company. With all that said, like an open necked businessman required to put on a tie - a desk drawer was instantly unlocked and out came a pair of matching blue silk football shorts. Swiftly they were teasingly pulled on over her tights and under her shirt and she was ready to go. Bouncy from one foot to the other, like a professional athlete involved in a warm up. As her Inspector edged closer to the exit, he added...

"So I'll meet you in the car park in ten minutes," Murray confirmed. "And ensure you bring all your magic gadgets and gizmos," he reminded her.

"Absolutely," she said. Appearing delighted at the prospect.

"Oh, and by the way," he added. "Keeping us both company, will be ...... DCI Furlong."

At that, Murray proceeded to take the stairs two at a time and found himself out of earshot before a barrage of expletives chased him up from 'The Vault' at one hundred miles per hour.

"You're a dirty #**!!$ §@#?? &**\!"

Murray, Furlong and 'Radical' Lizzie who was wearing a long ex-army style trench coat, had only reached the outskirts of West Lothian when the DCI's mobile phone sprung into life. Murray lowered his singing voice, whilst Lizzie pretended to be busy on her laptop. Both soon realised that the caller was Desk Sergeant George Smith. It appeared that in the intervening twenty minutes since they'd left the station, a large special delivery had been received there. It was specifically addressed to Detective Chief Inspector Barbra Furlong.

"I wasn't sure what your plans were, Ma'am," Smith informed her. "So before I finished my shift, I thought I'd let you know that it was here at least. You can now decide whether you want to pick it up on your way home or not. I'll leave that with you, Ma'am."

"Thanks for that George. Yes I think I'll probably swing by and get it later on this evening."

Murray raised his eyes at that comment. There was no probably about it. Of course she would pop by and pick it up, he thought to himself. Her 'missing' tumbling panda, still had her wrapped around her little finger. But with every passing minute that the elusive Governor failed to get in contact, she was slipping deeper and deeper into the mire. What had gotten to the woman on their last visit? She was obviously running scared. So why not speak to her old friend, and if Murray's suspicions were correct, sleeping partner? Barbra would have been understanding and calm about everything. So again, he questioned, why not seek her help? Her non-appearance worried the DI and he began to wonder if in fact the gifts and mementos that she had previously sent Furlong, were possibly potential clues and not simple keepsakes, as he had first thought? Now that was something to definitely be aware of later on when they got back to retrieve her most recent delivery. Although sending it to the station seemed unusual, given that all the other drop-offs were made directly to Barbra's East Lothian cottage.

"Now Lizzie," Murray spoke up. "I don't think you've had the pleasure of hearing this little ditty yet. Has she, Chief Inspector?" He grinned mischievously toward DCI Furlong and added. "Would you like to start it off for us, Ma'am?"

Her synchronised shrug and sigh said it all. Lizzie loved that this man deliberately wound her up, even and especially in the presence of others. Because as lovely as Barbra Furlong could be. Privately, Lizzie always thought of her as a stuck up snob. Although snob wasn't usually the word foremost in her mind. So just to continue riling her, Lizzie was on board straightaway.

"What song is it, sir?" She asked enthusiastically. "Although, no matter what it is, I'd love to hear it."

Murray, already on her wavelength, knew exactly what she was up to and he was happy to play along for a minute or two...

"So many house rules, but no swimming pools and its lights out every....."

"So are we off to a Greenock Hotel, Ma'am?" she asked. Deliberately flashing Furlong, an eyeful of white thigh from below her dark Army coat.

"Lizzie, what in the name of the Bunny Boiling Burritos are you wearing, or not, under that coat?"

Her Inspector nearly choked at the wheel as the 'radical minx' in her came to the fore.

"Ma'am, it's Christmas time and Inspector Murray always said that he liked me in this particular outfit!!!!"

Forty Two

"Oh, he can see us, hear what we say. But he was resting on that seventh day. She met a serpent that afternoon. He smiled at her and she broke the rule. Come on, we're leaving, no time to waste. The Garden of Eden's no longer safe."

- Bob Seger

They hadn't visited in the early evening before. Tonight they were met by the Assistant Governor. A white haired, middle-aged man, with a George Clooney-esque look to him. Late forties would have been Murray's guess. Barbra Furlong opted for early fifties. Unsurprisingly, the DCI never even asked for Lizzie's thoughts. Although, the prison's radical visitor did think that the good looking individual that went by the name of Hay, Cameron Hay. Reminded her of the distinguished gent that she snogged for over two hours last weekend whilst out celebrating a friends Hen Night!

Asst. Governor Hay spoke with a clipped accent. More likely from the land of the First Minister's Bute House, Edinburgh - than the derelict, run down streets of Easterhouse, Glasgow.

"Evening everyone. No word yet on Miss Loggenberg?" He asked immediately. Genuine concern and worry on his face.

"Not so far, Mr Hay. But she might well just be taking a little ME time," Murray expanded.

Unlikely, Barbra Furlong thought. Becky Loggenberg simply didn't do self-pity and introspection.

Lizzie remained in the background and stayed quiet at this point. She wasn't overly convinced that Cameron Hay wasn't the man that she had met up with recently. It was dark after all. So she was more than happy presently, to skulk around in the background. DCI Furlong then allowed Steven Murray to lay out his plan of attack.

"We would like to visit the Governor's office first please. Whilst we are doing that, if you would be so kind to once again set up a meeting with Maurice Orr in the library that would be appreciated. Thank you, Mr Hay."

"No problem. I'll get that sorted for you."

"Inspector Murray did tell you why we want to see Maurice Orr again," Furlong checked.

"He did indeed, Chief Inspector. Sorry state of affairs altogether," the man said mildly. He hesitated before adding, "And Rebecca? Governor Loggenberg. How does she factor into all this?"

"Not entirely sure ourselves at this stage, Mr Hay," Murray interjected. "But if you can let our Lizzie here, work her technical magic for a few minutes in her office, then that could be a massive help in tracking her down."

Cameron Hay initially baulked at that idea. Personal privacy, reprimands and things coming back to bite him on the backside all ran briefly through his mind. But the *'massive help in tracking her down,'* comment, seemed to win the day.

"When we get there. You just do what you have to do," Hay announced to the 'radical' Chelsea FC supporter. "Let's sign you all in and get you straight to her office." He then radioed ahead for Maurice Orr to be brought along to his favourite reading room.

On arrival at the Governor's private domain, Lizzie's eyes were fully focused on her office door, with the half-eaten fruit and droplets of blood dripping down from her nameplate. On spotting the apple with the bite taken out, the talented hacker instantly got the whole Adam and Eve thing. The symbolic comparison between the daily temptation in the Garden of Eden and the confines of a working prison. The arousing, erotic artwork on her desk was the second item to catch Lizzie's eye. She had already started to fondle it, but it was the first item on Murray's hit list.

"Bag that artistic display up for a start," he asked her, pointing at the pieces of stone.

Furlong pondered. "Even as the Senior ranking officer, I think it would be better if I got that for you, Inspector. Shall I?"

"Sorry, Ma'am, I've gotten so used to Hanlon or Curry being at my side. Apologies Lizzie," he added. Realising that although on contract to Police Scotland, the young talented female was a specialist freelancer and NOT a police officer. But she was an invaluable member of the team nonetheless. The very point that he had highlighted to DCI Furlong just last week at her special house party - come - second brainstorming session.

Left to her own devices, Lizzie bade them farewell. Asst. Governor Cameron Hay then walked at the head of the trio as they made their way to the familiar block containing the library. It was a seemingly throwaway comment from Hay, but one that aroused Murray's instant curiosity.

"Rebecca normally always met with Maurice Orr and his visitors in her office. That was why I was rather surprised that when she'd met you previously it had been arranged for the library. But I suppose she had her reasons."

Furlong looked awkwardly at her Inspector. Murray had simply initially thought to himself - That yes, she didn't want us to know that he was in fact a cripple in a wheelchair! Although he then dwelt slightly on the man's phrasing and as DCI Furlong went to take a seat directly opposite a currently vacant chair, Murray took Hay to the side and quietly whispered to him.

"Cameron," he prefaced his remarks. Making this brief covert discussion very personal and intimate. Intimidating actually for a tender soul with a Bute House upbringing.

"When you say Maurice and his visitors. Who exactly would you be talking about? How would you describe them?"

"Well, it was only one really in recent months, Inspector. I believe it was in the name of research and fact gathering. But sure, I can describe them."

Now supplied with that further knowledge, a nodding and exceedingly grateful Steven Murray quickly took his seat as the door reopened and the man himself, Scotland's self-proclaimed nursery rhyme expert, was wheeled in directly across from them.

Tonight, the seat opposite was carefully removed and Maurice Orr manoeuvred his wheelchair suitably below the table. No longer any need or desire to hide his disability. Like previously they were positioned as if they were on an interview panel, although on this occasion they were a body down in Rebecca Loggenberg. There was also no need to bombard this so-called 'black sheep' with a barrage of quick-fire questions. They had already gone through all those cat and mouse shenanigans on earlier visits. DI Murray had discovered what lay below the veneer of this man's persona back then. And during those previous discussions the Inspector would have been monitoring thoroughly his every micro-expression, but not this time. For apparently, Cameron Hays' information had now convinced him, that he now had all that he required.

"Officers, really! So soon? Who's dead this time?" He mocked them. Realising that as soon as he said it, and based on their solemn expressions... someone was!

"They say a man who lives fully is not afraid of death, Maurice." It was Steven Murray that spoke first. "Yet, I have not lived fully, Mr Orr, but for some strange reason I'm not scared of death. In fact, I find death intriguing, filled with limitless questions. Where will I go? Will I be a ghost? Or will I sleep forever? Will I go to Heaven or Hell? Valhalla? Reincarnation? Do I become one with the stars, even?"

"I get the gist, MISTER Murray. Who is it?" Orr impatiently inquired. Slamming both hands flat upon the table.

The Inspector ignored him and continued with his remarks. Intentionally making inmate 2764 even more agitated. Furlong smiled inwardly. Her outward expression, remained unaltered.

"I don't know what I will face when I meet death, and that should scare me," Murray declared. However, it doesn't, because it's a mystery, and I love mysteries. Many then would ask if I suffer from depression?"

Furlong winced slightly at that remark.

"Sometimes it's just hard to find people who get what I mean, Maurice."

Orr's agitation previously, had now scaled up a notch. As if he'd momentarily swallowed that anger in the form of a tiny fire-seed. Having forgotten to drink something cool to quench and smoulder it, it grew in his belly. Simmering and bubbling under the surface, it was now desirous to exit fully and it would come out as hot as any dragon had ever flamed.

Murray had witnessed it clearly in the man's eyes. This fire would burn the Inspector to ash. At that point, he had thought of stopping. However, unless this putrid man had the wings of a dragon to accompany its belly. Enabling him to fly over the four foot wide table, then Murray reckoned he was still safe.

"Who is it?" He roared. "Which one of them?"

Orr again thrashed and banged at the table. This time his hands had become solid 'hammers' resembling clenched fists.

"Death is a painful truth. That's what some say," the DI continued. "I think death is a foggy road and we must get through that fog called life, to finally see the clearing. It's yet another path to walk and who is to say it will be our last?"

The flames of anger had begun to recede from the inmate's demeanour. For he, like Barbra Furlong, no longer had any idea what path, clearing or walkway Detective Inspector Steven Murray was on, or on about!

"I mean, life may well be the beginning. But who is to say death is our last path? What if death is the middle of the story, and you have to read through that to get to a place beyond death. Is there a place beyond death? If we go onto the next path after death, will it be our last path, or are we fated to keep walking?"

The Asst. Governor standing to the side, was equally as baffled as to what was going on.

Murray finally divulged, "Maybe your sister could now answer some of those questions for us, Mr Orr. Because she was found dead this afternoon. It would appear that someone had put a hit out on her."

That was the first time DCI Furlong had heard that particular theory put forward. Although she understood fully the premise behind it.

"Assassinated on her doorstep at precisely one o'clock," Murray confirmed. "Bullet to the forehead."

The brother sat surprisingly silent and pale. Possibly not the news or the name he had been expecting. At least that was what both Furlong and Murray gleaned from his stilled reaction. In that precise moment of loss, the Inspector witnessed Orr's utopian world fully implode. Where there had remained remnants of light and hope. Those select chambers had instantly became darkened shadows of despair. The lapping pain came and went like waves on frigid sand. The collapse was all but complete. Rather harshly and on behalf of Sandra Kerr, the Detective Inspector delivered a final blow way below the belt.

"So what do you think, Maurice, Heaven or Hell? What path would 'Becky Foster,' currently be on?

Orr flinched.

Murray concluded. "Is there a place beyond death?"

With Heaven and Hell presently being discussed elsewhere in the prison. Lizzie, as fate would have it, was actively wading her way through several disturbing aspects of Rebecca Loggenberg's daily online diaries. Including the fact that it looked increasingly likely that this University educated woman, was in fact the individual that originally worked under the pseudonym of: Six-geese-a-laying! Various dates, times and locations could be clarified throughout the coming week, but links and profile photos on the 'Belles of Liberton' website, showed plenty of images of a scantily clad female behind a range of masks, capes and gowns. The mystery temptress held only a riding crop or whip in most of the black and white stills, leaving nothing to the imagination. In other revealing shots, Cadogan's well- toned and seemingly well-oiled naked partner, displayed only her feet, earlobes and an emotionally challenged 'tumbling panda!'

Other fascinating details emerged that made the colourful I.T specialist wonder if someone else had downloaded specific details, making it look like Loggenberg was trying to frame Maurice Orr. Was she infatuated by him? Trying to keep him from getting parole? Was she intent on extending his time at her humble hotel for a good while longer? Lizzie quickly decided that each of those questions were way above her pay grade and immediately sent off a text.

A whole nano-second later, Steven Murray, not DCI Furlong received confirmation that the missing Governor was a *working* associate of Moira's. It now became apparently obvious to DI Murray, why Maurice Orr appeared to have been given special privileges and treated with kid gloves in recent months by Rebecca Loggenberg.

Having just read Lizzie's text and thinking about the Governor's leniency toward Orr, Murray recalled how DCI Furlong would occasionally refer to her friend from Uni days, as 'Becky.' Was that why inmate 2764 initially flinched? For a brief second, had Maurice Orr been expecting to hear that it had been 'Becky' Loggenberg that lay dead? Was that their latest pact? With everything going pear- shaped, was little sister supposed to tie up some loose ends? Which then beckoned the question in Murray's mind - Had Moira Cadogan actually managed to do so, before her own untimely demise?

Forty Three

"On your feet my friend. Run they're closing in. Follow me for protection. Keeping you safe from destruction. I am the one who's sent to save you. I can help replenish what they've taken from you."

- Sick Individuals

The words were delivered with a hushed cadence and rhythm.

"Last night I dreamt I went to Manderley again. It seemed to me I stood by the iron gate leading to the drive, and for a while I could not enter, for the way was barred to me."

Murray's countenance portrayed only a glimmer of content-ment. It was coupled with an understated, dry smile. Barbra and her origins had surfaced once again, he thought wryly to him-self. On this occasion though, it was very clever. On a literary level, quite possibly brilliant in fact. She was most definitely on to something, the Inspector reckoned, as he sat back and watched his Chief Inspector in action. After quoting the open-ing line from the novel, 'Rebecca.' It's author, Daphne du Mau-rier, would have been exceptionally pleased with the officer's intonation and speech pattern. Which was just as well, as Barbra Furlong still had one more rather pertinent question to ask of Mr Orr.

"The first sentence of any piece of writing is arguably the most important - both in terms of hooking the reader in and of doing justice to the body of work that it is introducing. Wouldn't you say so, Maurice?"

Orr's usual robustly ruddy complexion was gaunt. His shoul-ders curled in, towards his chest. His body drilled down with a sense of being completely exposed and on display. Each of his fingers were intertwined with one another. He was literally holding himself together amidst prevailing fragility. Both Police Scotland Inspectors could see a chink in his armour and some light at the end of this particular tunnel.

"It really only requires DI Murray to type up his report when we head back to the station, sir," Furlong announced. "In theory it's all over. The Nursery Rhyme killings have come and gone. We have the majority of the pieces already in place. Whatever way you look at it... **The End** has already been positioned and printed in bold font. However, like Rebecca, Mr Orr, maybe the story would be better told retrospectively, with yourself filling in the blanks. What do you think? After all, accuracy as you well know as a librarian, is everything to the story-teller."

Murray looked at the books beyond the man and reflected on how each one had to wait patiently to speak their words. How they each had the ability to invite a conversation with the reader's thoughts. And how one can always walk away from a book if one chooses, and then return when ready. In a way, they were the legacy of their author's thoughts. Preserving ideas that would otherwise be as fleeting as the song of a bird. Surely the opportunity to leave such a lasting legacy would be too much for this man, and so it proved to be...

"*And the ashes blew towards us with the salt wind from the sea.*" Orr stated.

He directed the sentence specifically toward DCI Furlong. The very woman that he never even gave the time of day to on their previous meeting. Although Detective Inspector Murray was well versed enough with the popular novel to know that Maurice Orr had responded - with its very last line.

"I'll take that as a yes then, shall I?" Furlong nodded gratefully.

A disenchanted whisper from the wheelchair asked, "Why does the world fear those who lead the path of society, Mr Murray?"

Both the Inspector and his DCI had no idea what the murderous sociopath was on about, but they both nodded and shrugged nonetheless. Maurice Orr then gestured, as if opening a book and announced in low staggered tones...

"Once upon a time, many many years ago, thirty years ago in fact. A young, innocent six year-old boy witnessed his great-grandfather die in front of his very eyes. A brick wall suddenly collapsed rendering the 70 year-old man unconscious. So yes, on the anniversary year of his 100th birthday, it seemed a suitable time had emerged to seek satisfactory retribution. That coupled with my sister needing rid of a useless, down and out husband and wife beater."

The Inspector raised his head at that last comment in a questioning fashion.

"That was certainly how she'd described him over the past twelve months, MISTER Murray."

Murderer or not, Orr's eyes glistened with moisture as he recalled the events of that day. Steven Murray witnessed pain in those heavily bloodshot eyes. An agonising torment that had obviously festered within Maurice Orr for all these years and had lain dormant for over three decades.

"There is so much of your life that is hell for your soul, Mr Murray," the man said. "But, I suspect you already know that."

This time DI Murray glowered at the man. Even though being addressed as Mister, no longer bothered him. So what did inmate 2764 think he had on this heavily distinguished officer?

"And you stay there from strength rather than weakness, and I know," Maurice Orr continued. "If only I could walk, Inspector. Maybe I would join you in eradicating that pain. Taking each step alongside you, feeling the same torture that I know you bare."

Trying to help out her colleague, Furlong interjected with a few comments of her own...

"So let me get your synopsis just right, Maurice," Barbra cried. "This is in fact a misguided tale of vengeance, retribution and justice. So do you think the aged centurion at the centre of this whole thing would have seen it like that? Your great-grandfather, was that his moral compass also? Because I would doubt it very much."

Before Orr could dismiss or rebuff her honest question, Steven Murray had his own thoughts regarding the origin of the nursery rhyme killer or killers for that matter.

"You had kept this basic idea alive for long enough, hadn't you? Knowing that your father's, father had been referred to throughout his whole working life as Doctor Foster, and although he had originally moved away from, rather than toward Gloucester, the scene was already fixed and set in your mind for a theatrical staging."

"You couldn't make it up, Inspector." The inmate grinned from ear to ear.

Was that a slip of the tongue from Orr? Or was he actually warming to Murray, willing now to call him by rank again.

"I was sitting reflecting on my great-grandfather one day, when I began reciting that particular rhyme over and over again. Outside, the traditional Scottish downpour was unrelenting, and I fully imagined stepping into 'a puddle right up to my middle' and beyond in fact. I instantly pictured in my mind's eye, the builder of the wall, Jack Cannon, drowning in it! Being sucked under, with every cell of his body screaming for oxygen. He kept fighting desperately for a breath, right up until the end. Unfortunately it didn't seem to hurt like I required it to. So I came up with my own, better form of retribution."

Unfazed by his candid honesty, both Furlong and Murray pursed their lips and shrugged.

"From that particular nursery rhyme I became fascinated and addicted to them, and the dark and deadly secrets contained within their disturbing lyrics. It wasn't long before Jack Cannon became an obsession also, and with a few tweaks and adjustments along the way, I had his ending planned out well in advance."

"And all the others?" Furlong questioned.

The prisoner initially ignored her query. He continued to twist and turn his neck muscles. The Chief Inspector recoiled as she heard the numerous cracks and pops as he did so.

"Feeling uptight and tense?" Murray inquired.

Orr drew a slow, deliberate hand through his greying blonde locks.

"It was firstly meant to be all about getting rid of Barry," he said matter-of-factly. "The man was a waste of space and Jack Cannon was just going to be an added bonus. My sister had told me that her husband had been abusing her for the last eighteen months or more."

"She lied." DI Murray informed him. Simply shaking his head. "Not an ounce of truth in it," he added curtly. "Your sister was a deeply troubled soul. She was addicted to gambling and had lost everything. Did you know that?"

Murderer or not, Maurice Orr was a reader. A clever self-educated man. He wouldn't normally suffer fools gladly, Murray surmised. With the one rare exception, possibly being that of his little sister. Ultimately though, the Inspector reckoned that on this occasion, he knew full well that he'd been played and had allowed his emotions and family ties to interfere and get in the way.

"Having to fund her gambling habit by offering personal services. I'm guessing that it was because they were both on the same adult escort agency that Moira came across 'Lucy Locket' for you. Would that be correct?"

At this point, Maurice Orr went silent again and his demeanour cold. You could literally feel the chill from his blood. The six year-old damaged child in him had obviously gone through many, many painful, tortured sleeps. Where night after night and without anaesthesia, he'd endured false hope.

"This is my winter, officers. I now wait for spring and the chattering of the birds." He spoke it so eloquently. A quote from one of his favourite authors, Murray assumed.

"Never mind the birds," DCI Furlong encouraged. "What about Lucy Locket?"

"Lucy, Lucy, Lucy. Yes, dear young innocent Lucy," he responded. His voice fulsome in its disregard for her. "A life on the game, on the streets. What a waste. Moira had seen her name on the site and was fully aware of my murderous nursery rhyme idea. So she thought having a 'Lucy Locket' onboard would be a good starting point, and sought out an introduction through the original user of Six-geese-a-laying. Enter, Miss Rebecca Loggenberg."

DCI Furlong flinched on confirmation of that fact. Murray knew it was coming, so was nonplussed. There was a further brief pause before Maurice Orr resumed...

"Did she really lose everything to gambling, Mr Murray?"

Calling him Inspector never lasted very long then.

"Afraid so," DCI Furlong contributed. "But surely the fact that she was prostituting herself to fund her addiction, just like Grace Adam, must have told you that?" Barbra threw back at him.

"When Jack Cannon's granddaughter was found murdered, I realised then that she had lost the plot."

"What do you mean?" Furlong persisted.

That was when Orr once again strenuously denied to the Police Scotland officers any involvement in that particular crime whatsoever.

"Loggenberg and myself, never orchestrated Stacey Cannon's death, I can assure you of that," the man said. "Only one other person could have. Me and Rebecca simply figured that Moira had obviously lost it for a bit. That she had allowed some red mist to descend and went way off base. We got around it by happily allowing Barry Cadogan to take the blame for that murder, as well as all the others. Lucy, Cannon, King and that Jeremy Crossland. He was the one that got her hooked on gambling in the first place, wasn't he?"

"What is it that you are struggling to grasp, Maurice, when I tell you that your sister lied about everything?"

"You mean, Crossland never attempted to rape her?"

"Tosh!" Murray exclaimed. "Lies, lies and..."

"More lies," the librarian finished off for him. Shaking his head in disappointment. "How could she lie about it all?"

Orr had always thought that the killing of Stacey Cannon had been carried out by his sister. He had deliberately dropped a trail of breadcrumbs that in his belief of wanting it to be true, Steven Murray had followed blindly. Was there fresh doubt as to Cadogan's guilt? Especially now that the full scope of Rebecca Loggenberg's involvement was out there. Could it be that the Governor saw the schoolgirl as some sort of loose end? A full minute of silence entered the equation. Eye contact between Orr and Steven Murray was held throughout. Inmate 2764 was first to hold court further...

"Personally, I have to wonder how on earth a single mother, who had just lost her aging father and teenage daughter in the same week, had the contacts, knowledge and wherewithal to locate and kill my sister? A woman living way below her means and well off the radar and hidden away in a location provided by a refuge shelter. Even you have only just made the link in recent days. So how come this angry grieving mother was even aware of a Mrs Moira Cadogan?"

You could see that question register at least with the DCI. Murray on the other hand, said nothing.

"Any ideas, secretive Paisley man?"

Orr had always maintained that they never once spoke about Stacey Cannon and now worryingly, the Inspector believed him. As things stood, the lying manipulative and extremely dead sister of inmate 2764 had killed nobody. Leaving unanswered questions for Murray. Like who had in fact murdered 14 year-old Stacey Cannon? My oh my, what had he done? An instant defence mechanism had kicked in as he spoke up.

"The gambling was real, Maurice. Very real indeed," Murray whispered, as if confiding in the man. "Like any addiction, it screwed badly with her mind and her actions. Now you will never see the light of day and all for a series of lies."

"Not really, Mister Murray," Orr sneered.

Forty Four

"He can feel the night, the last sunset is in his eyes. They will carry him away, take his beauty for their prize. But hunger would have come when the bamboo forest died. Oh Panda Bear, you can't seem to win, no matter how hard you try."

- Jefferson Airplane

Heading back to Edinburgh, the trio sat reflective and quiet. Queen Charlotte Street would be achieved minutes before 11pm. It had been a tiring day and it was a long drive back, but DI Murray felt good inside. It's unfortunate that the outward expression had failed to materialise. Furlong was equally satisfied, keen to take delivery of her latest package and excited to re-examine the others. Having spoken with Murray and agreeing that it was much more likely that Rebecca Loggenberg had reached out to her through a series of clues. The fact that her old University friend seemed to be on the run however, still concerned the Chief Inspector. The youngest member of the 'travelling circus' was full of energy and busy organising her social life and meet-ups for later, via text from the back seat. A change of clothing at the station, where she kept plenty of spare outlandish outfits and then out on the town for midnight, was her plan of attack to unwind. The roads and motorways were relatively quiet. They hit a little bit of extra traffic and slight congestion heading off the Kingston Bridge into Glasgow city centre, as restaurants, theatres and nightclubs anticipated one of their busiest and best nights of the year, with Christmas only a week away. During the peaceful, silent journey, DI Murray began mulling over and recycling plenty of thoughts of his own...

They had been prepared to kill several innocent people, just to bump off Barry Cadogan and even that was to be done on a premise of lies. They would set him up for the series of nursery rhyme deaths and then have him

359

murdered. Barry thought he was role playing as part of an online game. That was why he had never looked concerned on the bridge. Because he was supposedly only posing for pictures to add to the fantasy website. He had no intention of hanging himself and certainly had no idea he was about to be pushed. And as Murray reflected, he realised that a figure had to be seen pushing him, not only to get his original phone back in his pocket, but for exactly the reason DC Curry had questioned - suicide! If Barry had taken his own life, Moira Cadogan would have gotten nothing and that couldn't happen, because it had always been about the money for her. Nothing more, nothing less. She couldn't even remember her great- grandparent. There was no photographic memorabilia in her flat whatsoever the Inspector recalled. She lived from day to day, and the cruel harsh world of gambling dictated her routine. So possibly pictures from a happier time in her life, simply added to her current angst and her new found aversion to images. Her brother on the other hand was more than happy to assist her. It allowed him the chance to avenge at long last, the untimely and needless death of his great-grandfather, thirty years previous. If all had gone to plan, she would have escaped prosecution, received a sizeable sum of cash and Maurice would have added to his nursery rhyme legend status, with the ghostly tale of Doctor Foster returning back from the dead to carry out satisfactory reprisals.

As they drove on the outskirts of West Lothian, a series of flashbacks played throughout Murray's internal projector. Unbridled, off they went - raging and excessive!

Orr wanted payback and became a librarian. A historian on all things nursery rhyme related. The Tracie tag on the wall and magnifying glass were done at different times. So plans may have changed, but it was prearranged and planned. No one took notice when he was crippled. No one found to be responsible. No one held to account. When his sister was (allegedly) raped, no one took notice/found to be responsible or held to account. The same for his great-grandfather. But NOW people sat up and took notice! From his prison cell he'd killed another innocent individual. Yet he denied actually killing anyone. They'd no way to punish him. He loved his library/his prison/his life. He was living the dream. But on the day Moira discovered: Six-geese-a-laying! All their lives changed forever.

Inverclyde, Renfrewshire, Glasgow and West Lothian had all been left behind. The historic streets and houses of Leith were within touching distance. Home to hip, creative types and long-time locals. The Royal Yacht Britannia, a former ocean-going royal residence, was a whole five minute drive away from QCS police station. Into whose very car park DI Murray was smoothly entering, just as a certain worn-out 'Radical' Lizzie awoke from a brief, but obviously much needed 'forty-winks.'

As a young, spritely, ethical hacker bounced down the steep steps to 'The Vault' two at a time, DCI Furlong felt the need to vent her thoughts as she awaited delivery of her package. She and DI Murray chose to wait in the public seating area opposite the front desk. They both knew that if they buzzed in, a multitude of bodies seeking help or assistance would instantly appear and they'd be there all night. It was currently 10.55pm.

"Maurice hadn't actually killed anyone this time," she offered conspiratorially. Whispering the words and moving her head from side to side, in case someone overheard her.

Murray pursed his lips, but remained silent.

"Moira Cadogan has also killed no one!" She announced quietly. This time the Inspector spoke up.

"Using that logic then, you are putting your secret admirer, your gift-giver in the frame for Barry Cadogan's death. Plus, based on Orr's earlier contribution, he still widely favours his sister for lashing out at the Cannon family and for the demise of a fourteen year-old schoolgirl."

"And if that is the case, she certainly got her comeuppance, Steven. Killed on her own doorstep by one of Jack Cannon's children. They may have both been grown ups, but they were still his kids."

And although Suzanne Cannon had held her hands up to the crime. Both Furlong and Murray wondered just how true that may have been. With her ex-territorial army brother, William, being the much more likely candidate of the two.

"How did they know where she lived, Inspector? Barbra Furlong asked in a serious concerned manner.

"Good question, Ma'am. Very good question. I'll get someone to check that out," her Inspector confirmed.

"Would you like me to get on to that, sir?"

The voice belonged to DC 'Hanna' Hayes. The Constable had been standing directly behind the Inspector during the whole of the exchange. Her eyes then gave a knowing look to his, as he swivelled around on the balls of his feet.

"What are you still doing here at this time of night?" Her Chief Inspector asked.

'Hanna,' ignored her superior officer and again addressed Murray. "It would be no trouble. No trouble at all, sir."

The Inspector was surprisingly silenced. He opted for a deep reassuring nod of his head.

"You're most welcome," 'Hanna' announced, before returning the nod and swaggering off. Although not before remembering to answer her DCI's lingering question...

"Back-shift and paperwork, Ma'am. And plenty of it!"

Furlong smiled initially. Then suddenly her features resembled that of 'Little Bo Peep' witnessing a male streaker strutting his stuff amongst her lost sheep and their desperately wagging tails! She immediately grimaced in disbelief at the size of package being brought out to her. Barbra had been expecting flowers, or something similar in size to a book, a CD, a shoebox or a small bottle of perfume perhaps. With this particular special delivery, even Steven Murray's jaw dropped substantially and hung wide open. The departing Hayes held open both doors as the female civilian clerical officer wheeled out a humongous crate!

It was a galvanised steel storage container. It had carrying handles at both ends and was about four foot long and two foot deep. A definite sturdier alternative to plastic storage bins, as well as being heat and oil resistant. This was a sealed unit more suited to factory, warehouse or heavy industrial use.

The size of it had Steven Murray deeply concerned. However, only after it was opened would his worst fears be confirmed. Several stickers on the outside stated clearly - 'This Way Up.' It had been important for the sender to ensure maximum shockability and as far as Barbra Furlong was concerned, it certainly worked. When the solid metal lid was pulled back, Murray's first thoughts immediately went back a week to when Hanlon had told them the story about Andrew and Abby Borden. The two parents that had been hacked to death in the late 1800's by their churchgoing daughter. It took 19 blows to crush Abby's skull, Murray recalled. This individual's skull however, was perfectly intact. Unfortunately, it had been severed from the body and was currently under a leg, two arms and a blood drenched torso! Furlong instantly threw up, projecting instinctively to the side of the crate. She was promptly followed by the young civilian worker, although DI Murray had to drag her quickly away to avoid her from vomiting fully into the corpse filled container. 'Hanna,' having spotted all the commotion was back supporting DCI Furlong who had collapsed to her knees. A panic button on the counter was struck forcefully by Murray and within minutes the place was overrun with men and women of all shapes, sizes and ranks.

Barbra Furlong turned away from the crate, no longer able to look inside. She had witnessed the exact same imbrued body parts as Murray. Each one slashed open and sliced apart. Hands sat on knees. Whilst feet and thigh bones were connected to nothing else. An arm and shoulder blade, as far as Murray was concerned had been deliberately squeezed in on top. DC Hayes simply stood there and shook her head in disbelief. The victim had been mutilated beyond all recognition. That is, unless of course, you'd already met up previously, with the owner of a distinctive 'tumbling panda' tattoo!

Evil had rubbed his hands together that evening in the classic offensive way that villains do. He wasn't about to pretend to be anything other than what he was. A corrupt reprobate, destructive and depraved. He enjoyed it, to him taking more power and having the upper hand was only a game. He had made his heinous move and now sat back for his opponent to offer their response. Knowing full well what it would be, and asking himself seriously, where was the challenge in that? However, it was certainly more fun than not playing at all.

Loggenberg hadn't been seen since Murray and Furlong last saw her speed off from the prison gates. Cadogan was dead and Maurice Orr was safely behind bars. His sister meanwhile had gone missing for a good period of time on the Saturday, before being gunned down the next day. Had she really been busy tying up loose ends like the Inspector had previously suspected? Was it in fact Moira Cadogan that Loggenberg had rushed out to see after they visited with her? The gambler was a nervous wreck when Murray visited her last, alongside 'Kid' Curry. Did she really have it in her to do this? If so, how did she get the body delivered to the office by midday on Sunday, then find herself gunned down an hour later? Nothing made any sense right now, except getting Barbra Furlong home and settled.

A lone pigtailed female, dressed for a festive night out on the town, stood in the shadows at the exit and watched the two officers leave together. Fully aware of many vehicle makes and models due to the nature of her work, Lizzie remembered that earlier in the year with a host of innovative and advanced features in their cars. Murray's 'old man' Volvo, was once again awarded the title of... 'Safest Car Manufacturer in the World.' 'Let's hope so, for their sake,' she whispered. Before quirkily blowing a kiss off into the distance.

Forty Five

"It's a long road out to recovery from here, a long way back to the light. A long road out to recovery from here, a long way to makin' it right."

- Frank Turner

Once back in East Lothian and with a heavy heart, DCI Furlong slowly made her way across to a small bookcase that sat at the end of her hallway. She removed a well-thumbed notebook and turned to a familiar page.

"Would you mind?" She said.

"To read something to you?" Murray checked.

"It's a book of poetry that Rebecca wrote during our years at University. It was one of the gifts that she sent me last week."

Murray, although aware of the gifts, had never asked about them. He reckoned when the time was right, Barbra would tell him. Although he never quite envisaged that it would be under these particular circumstances.

"There was always one that stood out for me. I would read it and read it, over and over again. I could most likely quote it to you verbatim."

She managed the briefest of smiles at that simple reflection.

"No, no, I'll happily read it for you," Murray offered.

"It's on page 17. It was one of her earliest attempts and it's called The Ocean."

They cuddled up together on the settee. It was nearly 2am. Exhaustion and heartache were etched firmly across the DCI's pale complexion. Her head rested comfortably on Murray's chest, as he began to try and do justice to Barbra's favourite poem and to Rebecca Loggenberg's poignant, moving words...

"I wonder if now the world is but one ocean, the waves moving freely, gathering pace. Perhaps that's what happens when you are adrift, you fear that the perfect circle of blue is all that exists. It feels as if the wind comes to bring some sensation of touch, a soft hello from nature. And I have learned, in

this desert of company, that it's better to let the brain be as empty as that horizon, rather than to suffer loss of hope and the tide of emotions that it brings."

Murray once again repeated the words. Emotions were raw and tender, both sets of tears very real indeed.

They were operating solely on adrenalin now. Although even those levels were running exceptionally low. Murray had been 99% certain before the discovery of the Governor's butchered body, about how everything had come together. The reality had simply been confirmed when Furlong held back the lid. After reading the poem together for a final third time. The Detective Inspector offered up another narrative. He shared his thoughts and conclusions regarding poor Dr Foster's endearing legacy, or not, as the case may be. Barbra snuggled in tight to listen to one of the infamous Murray monologues. This one by comparison, was shorter than normal and revolved mainly around the most recently 'dearly departed' of the nursery rhyme syndicate. As always he told it as he saw it, and some of the highlights included

How giving Murray contact details for the specialist tailor had been a poor error in judgment on the Greenock Governor's part. The fact that she had mistakenly written Steven Murray off as a bumbling, nervous and possibly clueless detective, also didn't do her much credit. Certainly his manner and actions whilst in the woman's presence had helped confirm those character traits to her. But that also firmly established for him, what he had always suspected. Like so many people in responsible jobs in society, she inevitably talked a good game. Yes, sure she was visually stunning, a very impressive and confident sounding female. But good looks and a University degree or not, Murray had already decided that underneath the surface not only was she ruthless with people, she simply wasn't very bright! She may well have been articulate and media savvy, with curves in all the right places and sparkling nails. But having had her checked out, the Inspector soon discovered that the same independent, bespoke tailor that she used regularly, whilst only earning local government wages, had premises in Greenock and Edinburgh. Really?

Murray had smiled two days ago when he first received this news from Lizzie. Closing in on his prey like a Golden Eagle, his talons were poised, ready to strike when they visited with her on Saturday. Because, once again, he was no believer in co-incidences. During the meeting he had changed his mind. She wasn't going anywhere at that point, he had figured. After all the highlights, he sat up and had DCI Furlong prepared to interact with him.

"She liked to be up close to the action, Barbra," he said. "She mixed all day with bad people and enjoyed being their temptress? Who knows how many inmates she has actually been extra close with?"

Furlong, although disappointed and disheartened to hear those words. Couldn't disagree.

"She was happy to continually egg people on," Murray insisted. "But she would never normally be the baddie herself. Until Barry Cadogan came her way and crossed her path."

"What do you mean? I thought we assumed that was Moira, his wife, with him up on the bridge. Wasn't it?"

"I don't believe so," the Inspector informed her. "Lizzie told me on Saturday morning about a new digital analysing program she had started using."

"And?" Furlong pushed him.

"And that very morning she showed me the enhanced footage once again."

"But even last time all we could see was the fingertips, Steven."

"And that was all we needed, Ma'am." He said officially.

Furlong didn't follow.

"Even you would have recognised her shimmering, scarlet red nail varnish, Barbra."

It had been a while, but Murray knew it was long overdue...

"Pheasant Plucking Beccy! Stupid, stupid, stupid woman."

"She undoubtedly loved the thrill of the chase. You've more or less admitted as much to me in the past. To chase or be chased. Either one seemed to work well for Rebecca Loggenberg."

The DI was keen to continue. He stared at his commanding officer and let fly with a few other notable observations.

"The woman liked to be in charge. Her clothing. Her Hair. Her walk. Her tempting fruit and flirtatious manner - they all made her feel in control. Her tattoo - your tattoo," he went on. "That was her branding you, Barbra. You knew that though, right?"

Furlong paused, reluctant to badmouth or acknowledge Loggenberg's bullying ways.

"You still belonged to her, Barbra. There was no denying that as far as she was concerned. She authorised Orr to be the librarian. She learned of Maurice's sickening story. She read up on him and was impressed. Impressed at his dominant and forceful manner and at his ability to manage and bridle his emotions."

The Chief Inspector frowned and grew concerned at those intimate revelations.

"It resulted in death and suicide for the poor McMinn family. He never bridled any urges or emotions that day," Murray reminded her. "But it no doubt added a fresh adrenalin rush for our Rebecca. Someone," Murray stated, "Let her in on the devious plan, because she was most definitely not the mastermind. That would have been our librarian friend; Inmate 2764. Remember, this had been a long time in the planning."

Murray stood up and offered some encouraging words...

"Anyway, let's get some sleep DCI Furlong and seek to avenge your friend's death first thing in the morning. I have a crafty, somewhat devious plan all of my very own," he winked.

"So in about 4 hours time," Furlong replied.

Her words had been followed up with the faintest and weakest of smiles. DI Murray recognised that as a start. However, he also knew it was going to be a long, long road to recovery from here. For both of them.

Forty Six

"Faithful departed, look at what you've started. An underdog's wounds aren't so easy to mend. Faithful departed, there's no broken hearted and no more tristesse in your world without end,"

- Christy Moore

Monday 19th December...

They had squeezed in nearly five hours sleep, some washing facilities and warm croissants before they set off. There had been someone that had helped both senior officers immensely in wrapping all this up and was fully deserving of an early morning thank you visit. They travelled once again in Murray's white, second-hand Volvo S40. A model that, safe as it may well be, was no longer in production. One that he'd previously had blue, black, silver and orange versions of over the past 16 years or so.

As their journey passed, the December sunlight aroused more colours from their sleepy monochrome and though the road still had the black look of night, the sky was already more bluish than charcoal. Under the fumes of the morning traffic a tincture of the dawn lingered, like dew on leaves, a gift of freshness bequeathed anew each day.

Once outside the residential property and with the wintry mist, cold upon their skin. Both the Inspector and DCI Furlong realised that in front of them was an impressive door. A barrier made to keep out the worst of the weather, rather than intruders or uninvited guests such as the two early morning hawkers currently standing on its steps. It had been beautifully handcrafted and varnished, highlighting its striking arctic white finish. Soon after the bell rang, the police officer's jointly watched it open. For a brief second it creaked eerily and the sound brought a modest chill to Inspector Murray's spine. It was rem-

iniscent of some dying animal crying out in pain and relinquish-
ing its last breath. How ironic, he thought to himself.

"Officer's!" the man gasped. His voice, high-pitched and nervous. A cough was offered before he continued. "You've caught
me at a really bad time," he said. "I was actually just about to
leave."

"Yes, we guessed that you might be," Furlong smirked. Having
discarded any lingering remnants of emotion from the previous
night.

"Sorry! What do you mean by that?"

"Just that you are such a busy individual, sir." Murray chirped
in.

"Oh, and I see that you have a case or two with you. Let me
assist you with those."

Red faced by this point, the tall figure felt obligated to explain.

"A few days away to work on a specific piece, Inspector."

"Well that being the case, I insist on helping you out to your
vehicle at the very least."

The Detective Inspector stepped forward and lifted both the
medium and large, olive green pieces of luggage. One in each
hand. Their frayed and worn out straps indicated they'd been
well used over the years.

"Seems an awful lot just for a few days, sir?" Barbra Furlong
quipped.

"From experience I've learned, better safe than sorry, Detective
Chief Inspector."

"Yes, quite," she simmered quietly. Her eyes burned deep, un-
masking his every thought.

The well dressed man then hurriedly threw his brown leather
satchel over his shoulder and prepared to exit the premises.

"We just wanted to let you know, sir, that we got him," Murray
said. "The so-called, 'Nursery Rhyme' killer. He's getting arrested as we speak."

"Fantastic news," the man replied, whilst closing his front
door. "I'm just parked along here to the right, Inspector." He

then turned sharply to address both officers. Slowly he began to proffer up...

"Wait! A him? A he? I thought you already had the late Barry Cadogan and some female Prison Governor? Who herself was killed by Cadogan's wife? Is that not the case? I just can't seem to keep up."

"Neither could we for a while," Furlong smiled. "But it all became clear after checking out a couple of library books," she added.

"Wow! The plot thickens," he said. "This is my car here, right here, Inspector. And thank you so much for your help with those."

Murray duly sat down both pieces of luggage at the side of the vehicle. Their olive shade contrasted nicely with the car's fern green exterior.

"It's thirty-years old, Inspector."

Both himself and Barbra Furlong duly nodded in appreciation.

Steven Murray then walked slowly and deliberately to the front of the 1987 XJS V12 COUPE. The Inspector's grin grew broader and broader with each step. He carefully stretched out a hand to gently stroke the brand's legendary symbol. A leaping cat upon its bonnet.

"You appear to own a Jaguar, Mr Webster. That's one mighty impressive beast," Murray confirmed.

Getting back on track, Furlong added. "What a complex parade of shady mysterious characters we had involved in all of those deaths."

"What! Oh yes, absolutely," the man's voice announced. Slightly taken aback by everything. "Well done though on eventually getting the true culprit. Congratulations to you both."

"Thank you, sir. Although, like DCI Furlong said, believe it or not, it all came down to the help and assistance of a couple of pieces of inspired literature."

The Inspector immediately delved into his coat pocket and placed one of those very books on top of the man's large suitcase. There it was, 'The Beggar's Opera,' published by Penguin as part of their all-time classics series. Furlong then hastily leaned forward and placed the second book on top of that. It was DI Murray's copy of 'Being Inside: Thespians, Lesbians and Plays!'

"The opera as you told us so eloquently recently, sir, was a fascinating political satire. And just like our case, it involved thieves, informers, prostitutes and poisoners. But rather than thronging the slums and prisons of the corrupt London underworld and successfully exposing the sleazy dark side of its crooked, jaded society. It was set in and around the cosy, warm, eco-friendly suburbs of Edinburgh, with a little bit of the west coast flung in for good measure."

Sirens sounded, as a van and two further Police Scotland motor vehicles made their way around the crescent and over to the gathered trio.

"Chief Inspector. Inspector. I don't understand, what is all this? You just told me you were arresting the man as we ......"

"Yes, exactly, sir. And is it not a bit disrespectful to refer to Rebecca Loggenberg as 'some Prison Governor.' When in fact you have visited her on a regular basis for months whilst researching your book and then blank her in your acknowledgments section with a, 'you know who you are.' She must have subconsciously rubbed off on you though, because you used the phrase, 'Cock'n Bull' several times in your book."

"And?" Webster questioned.

"And in recent years, sir. I have never heard anyone use that term as regularly, as I've heard it used in the last week by the poor, faithfully departed and desperately misguided Becca!"

Barbra stared at him incredulously for using that description.

"So your visit here this morning is to do what exactly?"

"This morning?" Murray replied. "Oh, it's a courtesy visit Mr Webster to allow you to confess to the murders of Grace Adam, Jack Cannon, Andrew King, Stacey Cannon, Jeremy Crossland and Barry Cadogan."

The man's immediate response of...

"Are you both insane?"

Was followed up with a high cold cackle, which indelicately pierced the wispy air around the quiet Georgian streets and buildings.

"Now we can keep it simple, sir. Where you say, 'Alright I confess, I did it.' Or we can explain it all to you, give you the chance to remember and then you say, 'Alright I confess, I did it!' Which one would you prefer?"

"We very nearly gave you a five-star write-up as well, Mo," Furlong stated smugly.

Webster's face fell dramatically on being referred to by that name. His energy, sparkle and colour all vanished in an instant.

"You'll just have to wait for the critics reviews tomorrow now."

Murray shrugged, as he placed the man's hands behind his back, and put on the plastic restraints in one smooth easy movement.

"Explain it all to you at the station it is, then," Furlong said. "Maybe we should have called you first?"

She began dialling, and few seconds later, a well known ringtone surfaced from within yet another uniquely bespoke tailored jacket. This morning's choice was an expressive plum colour with an obligatory lime green pin-stripe.

"So I'm carrying my phone on me. Is that a crime these days also, Detectives?"

"No, not normally, Mr Webster," Murray informed him. "But my Chief Inspector didn't actually call you, sir. She called one of the Belles of Liberton."

The man's face fell several levels.

"So if it's not a coincidence, which I don't believe in. We've just located the missing phone belonging to poor defenceless Grace Adam. Unless that is, you also have *Lucy in the sky with diamonds,'* as your ringtone, Mr Webster?"

Barbra, in her well pleased and jovial mood, felt further inclined to share the good news with Johnston Webster...

"That will probably have your number stored in it, sir. From when you called to initially arrange a meet with the desperate teenager. How fortunate is that?"

"Oh and by the way, sir," Murray added. "I searched high and low for your article that you had to get written last weekend. The one with the upcoming deadline that encouraged you to show us the door. Sadly, it appears that you didn't have one. You only write a monthly column these days and it's not due for another week yet. So what did you need that time for instead? Did you happen to have a late night telephone conversation with a Prison Governor perchance? We'll check your records and hers for that also."

Webster struggled to maintain eye contact any longer. Again, he had underestimated the DI.

"Were you keen to find out exactly what she knew about us? And any suspicions that we had?" Murray continued. "When in reality, we had genuinely only stumbled across your book by..." The Inspector hesitated. "Good fortune," he finally added. He couldn't quite bring himself to say that it was a 'coincidence.'

He wasn't fully finished however.

"Perhaps you were concerned that Rebecca would spill the beans? Possibly based on the fact that she once had a close, intimate relationship with DCI Furlong here."

Barbra flinched and immediately soared crimson. Part embarrassment, part anger. Steven Murray had known all along. But since when she wondered. However, based on the fact that nothing normally got past him. Could she really be surprised? Certainly on reviewing Johnston Webster's bemused and startled countenance, he plainly was!

Forty Seven

"Make lots of noise and kiss lots of boys, or kiss lots of girls if that's something that you're into. When the straight and narrow gets a little too straight, roll up the joint or don't. Just follow your arrow wherever it points. Follow your arrow wherever it points."

- Kacey Musgraves

The officers soon discovered that the man had throat cancer. During their evening visit, they had witnessed first-hand, his continual bouts of coughing and shortness of breath, but thought nothing of it. Death was on the horizon. Months rather than years. Had that been the catalyst for this farewell tour? Ultimately, the failed drama student that turned judge and critic for a living, had been the star performer and in the limelight throughout this devastating major production. Joseph Hanlon feared that we could make 'the killer' out to be some sort of 'Iconic' personality. However, they were too late. That was exactly what Johnston Webster was attracted to. It was the infamous adoration, the plaudits and the sheer showbiz factor. He was fed up writing about others. It was to be his turn in the spotlight. A rather surreal and at times horrific mini-series. A kind of 'Nursery Rhymes of the Unexpected.'

Becca Loggenberg on the other hand, was only cast in a supporting role. She was the curious professional, the star-struck audience member with a deviant predilection. The mystery voyeur who was thrilled and excited on many levels to simply be invited along. She was the temperamental diva that turned up for the red carpet treatment and Gala nights, but didn't necessarily stay afterwards to mingle with the crowds. With her preference to remain in the shadows, she may not have been in her front row seat for all the performances. But most importantly for Murray and Furlong, she was definitely at the dress rehearsal for that first evening with 'Lucy Locket.' Her mistake however, was to take home some 'rock solid' mementos of the fiery occasion and have them turned into artwork. Killers and their trophies, it always proved to be their downfall.

They continued interviewing the flamboyant individual late into the afternoon...

"My old work colleague and friend, 'Macca,' left what turned out to be an invaluable clue," Murray informed Webster. "He told us that he saw 'a leaping feline' the night Grace Adam was stoned to death. Sadly, he had no idea that he would pass away before putting me out of my misery, and telling me face to face that what he'd actually seen that night, was an animal nearby. At first glance it meant nothing to me. It was too... Krypton!" Murray offered.

Webster's confused look and open mouth, worked a treat for the playful Inspector.

"Later I discovered that Miss Loggenberg drove a modern Jaguar, that seemed to tie in perfectly with the 'cryptic' clue. Except that it didn't. According to her GPS, she never visited any of the other Edinburgh addresses, including the scene of Grace Adams' funeral pyre."

The man of letters and academia sat silent and still. That was until Barbra Furlong spoke. In a resigned, rather disheartened manner, she offered...

"She was my friend once, Mr Webster."

His head turned to stare up at the politely spoken DCI. The very same demure female that only days previously on their first meeting, the celebrity critic had mistaken for some 'rookie' policewoman. He then turned to her junior officer.

"Oh, I may have appeared surprised earlier, Inspector Murray. But that was more to do with your willingness to openly share that rather confidential and personal information."

Swivelling back toward Furlong, he added.

"Than about the close relationship we ALL KNEW that you had enjoyed with her, Chief Inspector Furlong."

Murray watched helplessly as Barbra tried to remain calm and composed. However, it was not only her smooth flawless cheeks that had turned red on this occasion, but her whole face and neck. And although her ears were cleverly hidden away behind the bouncing curls of her dark hair. It was obvious that they too, were equally rosy.

Just then, a small beep immediately followed by another, alerted DI Murray to the fact that he had two new text messages. At the same time, he questioned. What were the chances of that? Tapping and scrolling on his phone, he saw one was from Lizzie down in "The Vault.' The other from Danni Poll. Both would be relevant. The first read:

Footage of Cadogan filmed in a bookmakers during the time that Stacey Cannon had gone missing. It has also been confirmed that she never owned a driving license and travelled everywhere on public transport. Lizzie.

The second was even shorter, but equally helpful:

Blood match confirmed on stones to Grace Adam. Also prints belonging to Becca, Webster and ...

Murray instantly remembered Moira's remark about her 'one saving grace.' Which had turned out to be her bus pass! Great, he thought. Blood and DNA back for the sexy 'Stonehenge!'

"A penny for them," Webster teased. As he continued to talk freely about Governor Loggenberg. His appetite and enthusiasm for life having seemingly returned.

Murray, meanwhile, groaned inwardly. Not the kind of news he was looking for.

"In our private moments alone," Webster smirked. "Even during the 'Six-geese-a-laying' group meets, our Rebecca was keen to regularly talk and share her experiences about her time with her police colleague. She never mentioned you by name or rank of course. But referred to you often as her personal WPC. Her open-minded and adventurous 'tumbling panda.' Which we all took as a throwback reference to the good old nostalgic days when the police rode only 'Panda' cars!"

With regard to that last comment, Detective Inspector Steven Murray knew that in recent months, Johnston Webster had obviously learned differently about the tattoo.

"I digress though, Inspector. Apologies. What were you saying before DCI Furlong so aptly jogged my memory."

"Rebecca Loggenberg's GPS only had one Edinburgh address used regularly on it, sir. Unsurprisingly, Mr Webster, it was conveniently located only a seven minute walk away from your luxury home. So doubtless, she would drive there and travel with you to the next location. Your phone on the other hand, sir. It matched Barry Cadogan's mobile identically, even including NOT being at Stacey Cannon's location EVER! And by the way," Murray added, whilst throwing his hands into the air in a 'who knew' expression. "You do know you'll never get those deeply ingrained red stains out of your beautiful cream, Axminster carpet, right?"

Thank you, Steven. Barbra Furlong sighed inwardly. She desperately needed her DI to quickly throw Webster off balance and regain the upper hand. The theatre critic had begun to cross over into cocky, assertive and over confident mode. A peg or two strategically removed was exactly what was called for.

The Inspector's mind began to wonder. He had thought it unlikely when he had Furlong first bag them. What are the chances, he reckoned. He just considered that if she was present during the savage attack on Grace Adam, then like many deranged killers and their willing sidekicks, she may well want some form of memorabilia. A so-called trophy or keepsake? Absolutely, it was a long shot. But the misshapen stone testicles or so-called erotica inappropriately placed on her desk, seemed the most probable and daring culprits. It allowed her outlandish hedonistic influences and bravado to be highlighted fully and brought to the fore. Broadcasting it right there in front of everyone, flaunting it openly because she could. An action that again seemed to run in perfect tandem with the very extroverted and 'cocky' nature of the individual.

The Inspector knew that it was always going to be difficult to get DNA from such surfaces. Although it was much more awkward and challenging, it was still very doable. Fortunately in Danielle Poll, he had a top notch scientist. One that excelled in her job and had managed to confirm that the blood belonged to 'Lucy Locket.' But equally as important they had gotten that DNA match to the prison Governor and also thankfully, a second match to Johnston Webster. Which was pleasing and satisfactory for all involved. In fact, the text also confirmed a third possible match - Radical Lizzie!

The artwork had obviously caught her attention before they had gotten around to bagging it up on their DI's instructions. Her gregarious nature and natural curiosity had apparently gotten the better of her. Steven Murray would have words with her later.

Barbra Furlong decided that enough was enough and that anyone who entitled their latest work: *Life Inside: Thespians, Lesbians and Plays,* was duty bound to have the proverbial book thrown at them and ultimately charged for every murder. She rose to leave and Murray happily followed suit.

"Wait, wait, before you go," Webster cried out in a high-pitched frenzy. With his arms, wrists and hands conducting their very own symphony with the Royal Philharmonic. "You both realise that I didn't carry out all of these killings by myself, don't you? Surely you had figured that out by now."

In a no-messing, no-frills voice, DCI Barbra Furlong asked -

"Do you require us to sit back down Mr Webster, while you fill in the blanks?"

With his fifteen minutes of fame guaranteed. One arrogant nod of his head was offered. Webster then gave them all the finer details involving the deaths of Jack Cannon, Andrew King, Doctor Jeremy Crossland and Rebecca Loggenberg.

Steven Murray had in turn briefed him also...

"After noticing how Crossland's body, like that of Grace Adam and Andrew King had been carefully put into place and positioned like props on a stage, in a very particular and theatrical manner. It was then, that I had a good idea that our main culprit had to be a bit of a showman himself. Thankfully you didn't disappoint Mr Webster."

The Governor had known too much, but more importantly, she had simply made him jealous. She had flirted too openly, and too often with Maurice Orr, and the author, radio and TV personality couldn't handle it. That specific admission to the officer's, reminded Murray of the personal acknowledgement that he had read in Webster's book. *Thank you to my friend at Greenock Prison,* it said. *You know who you are.* And that was the beauty of his hidden message. Rebecca Loggenberg thought it was aimed at her. When in fact it was for Maurice Orr!

"She had certainly been present and witnessed each of the killings," Webster confirmed. "Although South Bridge was never planned. She just took it upon herself to step forward and help nudge Barry Cadogan over the edge. But for that, it would have been declared a suicide and we would have been in the clear," the man claimed.

Neither Murray nor Furlong had the energy, strength or desire to argue his point.

"Her extreme lust for death and taking things to extremes, possibly began on our very first venture out together," Webster reflected.

Knowing plenty of her previous salacious antics. The DCI suspected not. Although, she fully understood why, when Rebecca delivered the fatal blow that cracked Grace Adams' skull wide open, Johnston Webster would have thought as much. Both on the bridge and at Niddrie, the reckless 'Tumbling Panda' had become Judge, Jury and Executioner. That was the role model a younger Barbra Furlong remembered.

Thirty minutes later in the open-plan area directly outside DCI Furlong's office, Steven Murray addressed a wide range of officers who had all worked on the case.

"No real satisfactory outcome," the Inspector began.

Some somewhat surprised faces stared back at him.

"But it's been solved, sir." An anonymous voice shouted from the back of the group. Murray bit on his bottom lip and shrugged disappointedly.

"Yes, but from the initial five willing, unwilling or unknowing conspirators and that includes Barry Cadogan. No one will really be held to account. No justice is going to be served."

Again he looked out at a sea of bewildered faces.

"Three of them are now dead. Orr will remain in prison for life and the ostentatious animated features of our five-star theatre reviewer will be lifeless soon enough. Eight to ten weeks at best the medics reckon."

There was a brief pause at that news, before Murray further informed his colleagues...

"Inmate number 2764 had manipulated Johnston Webster." The wordsmith liked to have some of his more specific fetishes taken care of by a 'Bill' of Liberton, as opposed to a 'Belle!' So as a member of that escort agency, Moira Cadogan became better acquainted with the man and his predilections. Passing on this information to her devious brother. Maurice Orr liked what he heard, saw an opportunity and began to correspond with him from prison."

Nods of the head and positive murmurings could be forgiven. Enthusiasm was key.

"So it was all pre-planned, sir?" DC Boyd piped up.

"Without a doubt, Allan. Revenge for his great-grandparent had been in the works on and off for a while. Years in fact." Murray carried on with. "He gradually played on Webster's overinflated ego. He praised him continually and lauded his reviews. He complimented the man on his integrity and admired his sartorial elegance from afar. Soon the 'bad boy,' the convicted murderer, became the forbidden fruit that the beloved theatre critic just had to taste."

Heads shook in disgust, others in sheer suspense - hanging on every word.

"In the summer, he eventually visited Maurice Orr in jail. He dressed down, was less flamboyant and no one ever noticed him, or so he thought. For even although he wore plain suits and dark, wide rimmed glasses, Cameron Hay recognised him. Yes, I knew Mr Webster, the Asst. Governor told me. He visited regularly whilst researching his book. He desperately tried to keep a low profile and used an alias when he signed in, the man later informed me. Which he sadly didn't question at the time, as he reckoned the media celebrity was just seeking a little bit of privacy and discretion. But he recognised him easily enough from TV, magazines and the like. Hay also confided in me, that Rebecca Loggenberg had begun to allow Maurice Orr and Mr Webster private use of her office. Her very own Garden of Eden."

Heads straightened at that announcement. Lots of nudging winks and raised eyebrows.

DI Murray continued by adding to his last reveal... "She would sit in on their sessions. That was the only way she would give them permission. He also mentioned how the regular visitor was far from discreet. He began to dress more and more like a Mafioso lawyer or an accountant from The Sopranos, Mr Hay was keen to tell me. But the man in the disguise was oblivious to the fact. For Johnston Webster, it was a job well done. An outstanding performance. Sadly however, one that on this occasion, he would not be able to write or leave a stimulating review of. It was also to be his final swan-song and ultimate downfall."

"Out of curiosity," Sergeant Linn asked. "How did he sign in, sir? What alias did he use? Did we not spot it when we went looking?"

"On each scheduled visit Mitch he would sign in as normal. Next to the column asking who you were visiting, he would write: Maurice Orr. So, so far so good. Then in the column requiring the visitor's name, he would enter: MO. Initially when we got the Cadogan connection, we assumed that it stood for his sister, Moira."

'Baldy' and the others nodded their understanding in that straightforward logic.

"In fact though, it was Webster's pet name from Orr. And once Lizzie accessed the prison's footage covering the visitor's area. It soon became apparent that MO was a man. 'Old Firm' aficionados, Celtic and Rangers fans would figure it straight away. From hero to villain. Transferring from Celtic Park to Ibrox Park. A real nursery rhyme character if there ever was one. The ex-footballer's name bonded both men. Maurice Johnston. Mo to his friends, family and teammates."

Allan Boyd couldn't resist a short blast of... *"Hail, Hail the Celts are here!"*

"Calm yourselves," Furlong interjected. Hoping to eliminate any more lightheartedness. "Listen carefully to Inspector Murray and then let's make sure we have all our bases covered. I don't want any slip ups. Double check all your paperwork before it's submitted."

Her Detective Inspector offered a grateful nod of understanding. He knew well enough what she was trying to do and the gentle hush that fell over the small crowd, said - Success. Taking back the baton Murray continued. His voice, even more assertive, having increased in pace and delivery...

"At the prison, it was Loggenberg that Webster was actually interviewing. Because she was gay, her articulate way of describing life inside the prison as a bi-sexual person was fascinating - although she deliberately told it from an inmates perspective. Thus, Webster's reason for the ongoing pretence of meeting up with Orr and getting his take on things. However, once meeting in person with the charismatic Webster, Maurice Orr knew that this might have been the ideal opportunity that he and Moira had been waiting for. Webster soon became besotted by the prisoner. He was his beautiful, muscular Adonis, worthy of praise and worship. So along with his troubled sister Moira, Orr casually used Webster to help set up Barry Cadogan for the early series of murders. Supposedly in revenge for his ill treatment of his lying sister. That was with the one exception, unsurprisingly, being that of Stacey Cannon."

Again the denial of that particular crime brought a host of sighs and groans back to the surface. Murray simply raised his voice an octave or two...

"Varying from the original script folks and improvising and ad-libbing, Johnston Webster had brought the curtain down on his ruthless productions by killing Rebecca Loggenberg. After her meaningless death, he was always going to get caught. His health had doubtless played a part and he had dramatically failed his final audition. The applause, the encore, the standing ovation could no longer be merited. His performance had been for a limited run only and the show cancelled."

Joseph Hanlon had been quietly impressed at how his friend, the Inspector, had constructed his words around the theatre critic's very own world. A fitting critique, 'Sherlock' thought. Hardly pausing for breath, Steven Murray continued to arouse admiration and enthuse his fellow colleagues in the 'stalls.'

"With bodies positioned carefully and staged. Every death was portrayed as a separate act. Each dramatic and very deliberate. Purposeful and reasoned. Every murder scene was a monologue in itself. Put on display for the approval of the audience. To get a reaction. To soak up the adoration. Invite a round of applause. To receive a standing ovation. The need for an encore."

Hanlon and one or two others now began to smile and appreciate that they had all become part of this interactive 'Synopsis in the Round.' Although the room dimensions were cube shaped!

"Right from the start everything was extremely theatrical," Murray declared. "Now I may be taking liberties with a few words here, but fundamentally; 'Those that can - Do! And those that can't... talk about it!' Or in Johnston Webster's case, write and talk about it. The man reviewed, he reported, he analysed and studied others. He critiqued and he created a host of stars over the years. Eventually that wasn't enough for him. In conclusion, he himself ultimately sought to be a part of that revered galaxy also!"

"Well, I don't know about a star," Barbra Furlong voiced. "But he is certainly going to be infamous for the next few weeks, maybe even a month or so."

"If he lasts that long?" Her DI chirped in.

"Regardless," Barbra announced. "He is certainly going to have plenty of column inches dedicated to himself now. Every newspaper, every blogger in the land will want to tell his story. Even Maurice Orr will have to be happy and content with the Best Supporting Actor, on this particular occasion."

Hanlon smiled at her willingness to play along with the Inspector's whole 'performing arts' analogy.

"Well said," Murray began.

He looked briefly toward his DCI. It was a fleeting glance that she acknowledged with a slow curious tilt of the head. It accompanied raised eyes on Furlong's part.

"On that evening we first visited him, Ma'am. I knew as soon as I saw his fancy blazer and inspected its buttoned cuff that he was involved somehow."

"Your thirty second phone call?" Furlong questioned.

The others watched in awe.

"Exactly, Ma'am. That was to 'Sherlock.' I knew he'd still be at the station doing some late night research."

Hanlon blushed slightly, whilst the others all offered up a unified smile that said - 'Of course he would be.'

"I had quickly figured that our Mr Celebrity was part of it. Now whether he was a stage hand, had a minor role or was the leading star at that point, I had no idea. But I knew that I needed confirmation and quick. That jacket we recovered at Port Seton was far too small to be Andrew King's. It had to have been left behind in error by his killer. You see all of those 'Walls' props - the toy car, the wrapper and postcard. They all should've been deposited alongside Jack Cannon previously.

However, it worked in our favour, giving us an instant link between both men."

"Like the Inspector said," Joe Hanlon spoke up. "The jacket would have been lucky to have gotten three-quarters of the way around King's body and its arms were far too long," he added. "I texted him back within the hour, Ma'am."

"From a female perspective," Furlong offered. "I examined it at the time and I should have noticed those anomaly's. That was a major discrepancy and slip up on my part." Their senior office owned up to willingly in front of the others.

"Not sure many of us would have caught that, Ma'am." Sandra Kerr insisted.

"Especially us guys," Allan Boyd yelled out. "We would have thought it normal. Trying to kid ourselves that we could still fit into gear two or three sizes smaller. It shrunk in the wash scenario," he smiled.

They all laughed. A light-hearted moment that this time, had been much needed.

"Although," DCI Barbra Furlong further added. "I did spot something unusual."

"And what would that have been, Ma'am?" Her semi-regular house guest asked.

"That the smart, impressive garment had no labelling on it. No inside branding, no washing instructions. Nothing whatsoever."

"And that in itself was the brand, Chief Inspector. Welcome to the world of: *The Invisible Touch*," he said. Whilst holding up the card that a rather photogenic, although now sadly deceased, prison governor once gave to him.

It was now 'Kid' Curry's turn to speak.

"So that was why you were so keen for me to take close-up photos of her clothes?"

Once again listening to those words that he'd just uttered publicly. The poor detective could feel his cheeks warming up nicely. Although that might also have had something to do with the suggestive, nudging elbow to the ribs that Radical Lizzie had just inflicted upon him.

"I made inquiries, Ma'am," Murray proffered. "The Invisible Touch bespoke brand, is all about exclusivity. No one knows who creates the garment for you. But you firstly have to be in the position financially to afford their custom made, highly tailored apparel. Their signature is in their finish. Every product is produced with fine triple-crossed stitching. It passed me by on my first visit to Greenock. It was only when I later examined the abandoned jacket at King's, that I was intrigued by its finish. Then when visiting Maurice Orr next time, I made a point of getting up close and personal with Rebecca Loggenberg and sure enough, there it was - 'Fancy stitching and no inside labelling.' That in itself seemed a very appropriate tagline for many of Orr's fellow inmates in Greenock Prison."

"And because you famously don't believe in them, I guess your intimate dalliance with Mr Webster at his home that evening and your love of his outfit was... no coincidence?"

"That would be one hundred percent correct, Ma'am. Surprise, surprise, his impressive blazer was triple stitched and nameless too!"

Their official attendance seemed to have increased in number, box office sales had soared as other colleagues were equally intrigued and impressed at the wonderful 'live' double-act taking place that afternoon. Tickets were becoming scarce, even with the fact that audience participation was mandatory!

Forty Eight

"When you go, will you send back a letter from America? Take a look up the rail track from Miami to Canada. I've looked at the ocean and tried hard to imagine the way you felt the day you sailed from Wester Ross to Nova Scotia."

- The Proclaimers

Late afternoon...

After deliberating and sharing his thoughts privately with Barbra Furlong for twenty minutes. Steven Murray messaged all the relevant parties and invited them back to meet with him urgently at 4.30pm in Interview Room Three. The largest of their current interview rooms. The time had just gone 3.45pm. Within forty minutes, most of the others, many of whom were still in the station had gathered and been rounded up, even Danielle Poll who was on call at an incident at The Meadows on the outskirts of the city centre, was in attendance. The full roster that squeezed snugly into the room consisted of: Three seated individuals - Poll, Furlong and Murray. Constables Curry, Hayes, Boyd and Hanlon. Sergeant's Sandra Kerr and Mitchell Linn then took up two of the remaining three spaces. Leaving just enough room in the corner for a pink haired, ponytailed female in a blue denim boiler-suit. Lizzie certainly always made an impression.

 Chit-chat, gossip and waffle potentially filled the air, then at 4.32pm Detective Inspector Murray stood up and the 'intimate sauna' fell silent. Before he began his remarks, he scanned the faces in the room. Each one he knew to be a dedicated officer, scientist or civilian worker. He nodded to express his appreciation and gratitude...

"As each of you are well aware, just less than two hours ago myself and DCI Furlong finished an extensive interview next door with Johnston Webster."

A slight murmur surfaced within the group.

From her seat, Furlong contributed. "Again you know that in his normal courteous and amiable manner, he helped us fill in the blanks to a few outstanding bits and pieces in relation to our Nursery Rhyme killings."

A few 'Whoops of delight' and the occasional 'Yes,' could be heard. But it remained relatively subdued. Many had guessed an almighty 'But' was waiting for them just around the corner.

DI Steven Murray took up the baton once again...

"Some people are scared of clowns, some afraid of heights or falling. Mr Webster was not anxious or frightened by any of that - not spiders, not snakes or the dark," Murray informed everyone. "What petrified him more than anything, and I'm sure several of you may have already guessed this - was being forgotten. He was quite literally fearful and scared to death that when he died that time itself, would forget him. That he had lived an unimportant life, yet was surrounded by people who would go down as 'greats' in the history books. Afraid that despite all his good works and dedication to the arts, he'd still be a no-one."

The room remained silent. Part in bewilderment, part in not understanding fully what DI Murray was trying to convey.

"The recap and review are always helpful," Murray maintained. "And although we covered all the deaths and disclosed and revealed plenty of sub-plots earlier on today. The one outstanding reason I asked everyone to gather here again for, was to remind each of us that Stacey Cannon was never targeted and certainly not murdered by any of the key players in our nursery rhyme production."

Eyes met across the room. Micro gestures signalled out like radio waves. Privately several of his colleagues had suspected this to be the case, but had been waiting on official clarification.

"Webster will admit to eliminating our prison governor, Rebecca Loggenberg," Murray confirmed to them. "But as for the death of the young teenager, he, like Orr, remain adamant that they did not touch her. In fact he went as far as to say, he had no idea what she even looked like. Actually our beloved theatre critic assumed, wrongly, as it turned out. That Stacey was Jack's daughter. The media had never put her name out, never mind her age. It was only when he saw Suzanne Cannon had been arrested for Moira's murder, that on spotting her age, he then figured out that the other dead female must have been HER daughter and that was why, Suzanne, understandably had gone after Mrs Cadogan. Because even Webster and her own brother, Maurice Orr, had presumed Moira was guilty."

Why did their DI currently feel the need to draw attention back to that fact? Attentive eyes continued to peer at each other in curiosity. Until eventually all attention returned and rested upon the six foot plus, straight talking Murray. Unsurprisingly the Inspector decided not to sugar coat it...

"Why the murderer struck, I don't know. But having worked so hard at eradicating corruption within the force in recent years, sadly it is my solid belief that the depraved individual that kidnapped poor Stacey Cannon and then left her to die, was a serving police officer and is today, presently standing among us!"

DI Murray immediately cut all eye contact with everyone, raised his voice and offered...

"Dismissed."

He immediately freed himself from the claustrophobic room, by exiting left down the lengthy aged corridor. All of the others with the exception of one, stayed put. Some to have a brief chinwag about what they'd just heard. Others in the main, to give themselves a safe distance from their sour faced Inspector. Joseph Hanlon was the exception to the rule. 'Sherlock' had followed him out faithfully. The Constable had been specifically challenged with passing on some vital information to DI Murray before his Inspector headed home.

DCI Furlong had handed the human trafficking case, the one regarding the shipping container of illegals over to Detective Inspector Tom Collier. He had been given all of the relevant documentation, case files and history, the very same day that Furlong and Murray came back from their first visit to Greenock Prison. Furlong knew then, that she wanted Steven Murray's full attention to be concentrated on unravelling new leads and developments and on what Orr had to offer up.

She literally only needed Collier to dot the i's, cross the t's and join up all the other squiggly writing in between! All of which he did splendidly. He was simply a safe pair of hands. Someone who could be relied upon. An Inspector who caused no fuss, stuck to protocol and stayed well within policy guidelines. He was now approaching retirement age and had been in and around things for thirty years. He was a no excitement, no drama, no wife, no life, kind of a guy. Today he could be found currently walking toward Steven Murray, as the Inspector hurried away from his group meeting, with his friend Joseph Hanlon in close pursuit.

"Afternoon, Steven."

"Inspector." Murray replied. They'd never been close friends. But got on well enough with each other. So there was no animosity or ill feeling between them. No hidden agendas.

"I just wanted to give you a heads up on this personally."

"Grateful, I'm sure, Tom. But a heads up on what?"

"Your container truck of Vietnamese women, Steven."

Murray's widened eye contact signalled - continue. Joseph Hanlon had reached him and now stood by his side.

"With the exception of the one that you detained. The video evidence on the night showed 27 females. Poor souls if truth be told, traipsing wearily out of the box, Inspector."

"That sounds about right, Tom. So what seems to be the problem? What's happened?"

"We are one short, Steven. That's the problem. Thankfully, we know who it is that's gone missing."

Both Hanlon and his boss were incredulous. They shook their heads in total disbelief. With 'Sherlock' instantly thinking back to Murray's remarks of a minute or so ago - *With someone on the take, as well as being a murderer.*'

"But how could that happen, Tom? Are you talking about going missing between the yard and getting them back to the holding cells at the station? Seriously? I thought we had put an end to all of that."

Murray was now having to talk openly about the police corruption that had been uncovered and supposedly dealt with in the last couple of years. He made no mention of his most recent suspicions. But he did add...

"So how did she manage to slip through the net?"

"Like most of these sleaze-ball, opportunist thieves and dealers, they have exceptionally deep pockets. A year's wages, sent instantly, electronically, is hard to turn down!"

Murray's face briefly questioned his counterpart's own personal integrity. Although, even Murray knew better than to offer up an opinion on that in public.

"Too much to lose, Steven." The man had read his thoughts to a tee. "Inquiries are currently ongoing, Inspector. That's why I wanted to speak to you privately about it. But mainly because the missing person is a man!"

At that intriguing revelation. Even Joseph Hanlon cocked his head and became drawn into the conversation.

"A man you say? So in fact, he had nothing to do with our raid that night at all?"

"Oh no, he absolutely came out of your shipping container, alright. But your Inspector here, never even noticed him!"

Steven Murray was happy to take the flak and a bit of a ribbing, or whatever else was about to come his way officially. He knew better than to mention that Constables Curry and Coull were also there watching everyone depart the scene that night, and obviously the poor officer behind the camera hadn't spotted it. Nevertheless it was Murray's team and he would take full responsibility for any slip-ups. Although, he didn't count a dirty officer as something that he could have really foreseen, though given their poor recent history...

"He had an accent of some sort," Collier informed them. "Gaelic, possibly Scots or Irish. That information came from others in the container, though there is no breaking the female that you caught, Steven. We haven't found anything to identify her whatsoever and she is not saying a single solitary word."

"So she is scared?" The Inspector asked tentatively.

"Scared? Absolutely petrified out of her mind, would be a far more accurate description I suspect," said his fellow Inspector. "It would appear that he went by the name Sean C or Shaughnessy. Something like that. But that's all we have."

"Show, do you shink we will shuckshessfully find Mister She?" Sherlock's, Sean Connery *'shpeech pattern'* was actually pretty good.

"DC Hanlon, I've told you before on numerous occasions that there is a time and a place for humour in the workplace."

DI Collier was impressed at the Inspector's high standard of expected professionalism. It was inspiring. Then his face went a seething shade of red as he instantly had to withdraw all previous salutations of respect. The reason being? Steven Murray had continued to offer counsel to DC Hanlon...

"Show, shink yourshelf lucky shunny boy. Just shit over there and keep yourshelf to yourshelf."

Both men struggled to contain their laughter and went into convulsions. DI Collier was most offended and *shertainly shocked, that was for shure!*

"Shorry Tom," was Murray's desperate plea to regain his composure.

"Apologies, Inshpector," DC Hanlon added also. "As shoon as I heard Sean C, the bold Mr Connery immediately popped into my mind, sir. Shorry."

"Quite," was all the sombre-faced officer could dredge up. "To be fair, it took US three attempts sitting in front of a screen watching the video before we even spotted him. He had soaked his lengthy dark hair with water and swept it backward, so he immediately looked more feminine. Add in the fact that he wore flip flops, had a floral shirt on which he had dirtied up and wore loose fitting trousers. All in all he was a very believable female."

Collier slowed his speech dramatically as he stood directly in front of Murray's face. Joe became apprehensive at what appeared to be transpiring into something physical. A potential showdown. The visiting DI spoke quietly this time, it was an elongated whisper...

"Right up to and including the moment - *he showed you his shooper shexy shmile,* DI Murray."

Tom Collier winked cutely, turned on his heels and began the long walk back up the lengthy linoleum clad corridor.

Murray nodded. Sherlock laughed heartily, mainly with relief. Then as Collier continued at pace toward the building's exit, Joe Hanlon found the most appropriate of acknowledgements. His shrill voice resonated up, down and around the office fairway as he cried out in bold Sean Connery tones...

"Touché, Inshspector Collier. Touché!"

As an afterthought, he then turned to Steven Murray and added. "Oh and by the way, Inspector. DCI Furlong wanted me to let you know that this Friday is fine!"

"Sure. Great." Murray replied instinctively. Before adding curiously, "Fine for what?"

"She has a treat lined up for you, sir. You leave to visit your daughter and her family in the States on Saturday morning, isn't that right?"

"Absolutely correct in every detail, Joe." Murray smiled in anticipation. "So Friday is?"

"Oh, that's your one remaining 'Training Day,' sir. You've to enjoy it thoroughly, she said!"

Epilogue

"Remember when the music came from wooden boxes strung with silver wire. And as we sang the words, it would set our minds on fire, for we believed in things and so we'd sing."

- Harry Chapin

Murray had caught a taxi from his home in nearby Barnton to Edinburgh's International Airport. It was just after 4am and the whole journey took less than twelve minutes. Departures were possibly slightly busier than the Inspector anticipated. Scots weren't overly keen in getting ripped off with sky high, overly inflated prices for the Festive holidays. However, obviously enough of them had relented or been given a seasonal gift like his. He smiled in anticipation as he passed through security, bought some bottled water and headed straight to his departure gate. Once there he rested his head and dozed soundly for about an hour. At 5.25am he decided to make his early morning alarm call. It was answered after one ring. Someone had obviously been anxiously waiting.

"Steven," the voice said. Sounding alert and ready for the day.

"Are you up, Barbra? Have you walked '3 miles' already?"

He could feel her smile.

"I couldn't sleep," she said. "If truth be told, I had the phone under the pillow."

"Sharmy Walloping Legwarmers," Murray voiced loudly.

"What's wrong?" Furlong exclaimed.

As she asked the question, it was her turn to imagine a large grin on Steven Murray's face.

"I was just getting in some practice for when we go to see Carly Connor when I return. She is headlining what should be a good night at St.Luke's in Glasgow. It is literally around the corner from the iconic 'Barrowland Ballroom' in Glasgow's east end."

Barbra enjoys her music, but not to the level of her enthusiastic Detective Inspector. She could already hear in his voice the excitement of the built-up. He'd be listening to her non-stop for the next few days, checking out her Facebook page and watching endless videos of her on YouTube.

"Are you ready to board?"

"Ten minutes," Murray replied.

There was then a brief awkwardness as a quiet lull embraced the conversation. Barbra's silence was somehow comforting and spoke for itself. It was peaceful in a way where you could feel at home and know that no matter what was happening, she was forever there for you. And that reassured him before he spoke again...

"It was over a week ago now and you may have thought that I was asleep and oblivious to all that you said. But that couldn't be further from the truth."

"I believe you, Steven. But I have no idea what you are on about!" She said candidly.

In a low, gentle whispered tone, the America bound Inspector confided in his DCI...

"I just wanted you to know that my favourite drink has begun to taste magical once again. When my music plays, I now sing along and get up and dance. Random strangers are able to make me smile, and the beautiful night sky reached down and touched my soul the very day that you came back into my life. I think your prayers may have been answered, Inspector Furlong. For I have truly fallen in love with being alive again! Thank you, Barbra - Thank you for everything."

In Roseburg, Oregon, it was Christmas morning and some hastily delivered presents from Santa had only just arrived. Steven Murray had sat down and was about to listen to his beautiful two year-old granddaughter. With the patient help of her mother, the talented toddler had learned a Christmas song especially for her Scottish grandfather. As she began, Murray smiled to himself and thought - What were the chances? The Detective Inspector listened carefully as Maisy got into full swing. Her cute voice stopping and starting on every second or third word.

"On the first day - of Christmas - my true love - gave to me..."

At the halfway mark, Murray hummed along and tried desperately to restrain himself from laughing at their choice of tune. It was absolutely appropriate and for most would have conjured up festive images galore. For Steven Murray, not so much. He was about to enjoy an extra special yuletide season with his daughter and her family, as he heard young Maisy belt out...

"Eight maids - a milking; Seven swans - a swimming; Six geese - a laying..."

Her Grandpa grinned at that last one and then unleashed -

"Five... Gold... Rings..."

THE END

In memory of: **Ashie McAulay**.

Who sadly passed away in the Summer of 2020.

She was one of Inspector Murray's
oldest and most dedicated fans.

*"I'm a cat, I'm a cat, I'm a Glasgow cat
and my name is Sam the Skull."*

Printed in Great Britain
by Amazon